"An impeccably researched tapestry [...] and heady feminism...refreshing."

"A complicated mystery turns into a [...] liantly captures the heated tension be[...] ousy as the root of political and personal turmoil." —*Los Angeles Times*

"An enjoyable romp...A warm, promising continuation of the series."
—*Kirkus Reviews* (starred review)

"Set in twelfth-century England, Franklin's mesmerizing second historical delivers on the promise of her first, *Mistress of the Art of Death*. Franklin...brings medieval England to life, from the maze surrounding Rosamund's tower to the royal court's Christmas celebration, with ice skating on the frozen Thames. A colorful cast of characters, both good and evil, enhance a tale that will keep readers on edge until the final page."
—*Publishers Weekly*

Mistress of the Art of Death

Winner of the Ellis Peters Historical Dagger Award and Sue Feder Memorial Historical Mystery Award

"Great fun! Franklin succeeds in vividly bringing the twelfth century to life with this crackling good story. Expertly researched, a brilliant heroine, full of excellent period detail."

—Kate Mosse,
New Times York bestselling author of *Sepulchre*

"[A] vibrant medieval mystery. Outdoes the competition in depicting the perversities of human cruelty. Adelia is a delight, and her spirited efforts to stop the killings...add to our appreciation of her forensic skills. But the lonely figure who truly stands out in Franklin's vibrant tapestry of medieval life is King Henry—an enlightened monarch condemned to live in dark times." —*The New York Times*

"It's hard enough to produce a gripping thriller—harder still to write convincing historical fiction that re-creates a living, breathing past. But this terrific book does both...fascinating details of historical forensic medicine, entertaining notes on women in science (the medical school at

continued...

Salerno is not fictional), and a nice running commentary on science and superstition, as distinct from religious faith...both the mystery and the romance reach satisfactorily unexpected conclusions. It's a historical mystery that succeeds brilliantly as both historical fiction and crime-thriller."

—Diana Gabaldon, *The Washington Post*

"Smart and sophisticated and relies as much on the brilliance of its detectives as it does the existing (or lack of) technology of the time. The charming Adelia is a fascinating creation. Franklin uses her to capture the frustrations of being a brilliant woman in a time and place when women were valued only for their homemaking and breeding. A rollicking microcosm of budding science, medieval culture and edge-of-your-seat suspense."

—*USA Today*

"This is one of the most compelling, suspenseful mysteries I've read in years. Adelia is a wonderful character and I cannot wait for her next adventure."

—Sharon Kay Penman, *New York Times* bestselling author

"The bold, brilliant heroine of *Mistress of the Art of Death* is the medieval answer to Kay Scarpetta and the *CSI* detectives. This is a compelling, unique and vibrant page-turner."

—Karen Harper,
New York Times bestselling author of the Elizabeth I mystery series

"Thanks to Franklin's research and evocative prose, the reader not only enjoys a good whodunit with exceptionally well-formed characters but also learns much about medieval England....Franklin weaves a frightening story of serial killings with a cautionary tale of ethnic and religious hatred."

—*Richmond Times-Dispatch*

"Intriguing historical fiction. A fabulous read...irresistible."

—*New York Daily News*

"Will surely please mystery fans as well as lovers of historical fiction."

—*Library Journal*

"Franklin delivers rich period detail and a bloody good ending reflecting the savagery of the times."

—*Booklist*

Writing as Ariana Franklin

GRAVE GOODS
THE SERPENT'S TALE
MISTRESS OF THE ART OF DEATH
CITY OF SHADOWS

Writing as Diana Norman

THE SPARKS FLY UPWARD
TAKING LIBERTIES
A CATCH OF CONSEQUENCE

DIANA NORMAN

The Sparks Fly Upward

BERKLEY BOOKS, NEW YORK

THE BERKLEY PUBLISHING GROUP
Published by the Penguin Group
Penguin Group (USA) Inc.
375 Hudson Street, New York, New York 10014, USA
Penguin Group (Canada), 90 Eglinton Avenue East, Suite 700, Toronto, Ontario M4P 2Y3, Canada
(a division of Pearson Penguin Canada Inc.)
Penguin Books Ltd., 80 Strand, London WC2R 0RL, England
Penguin Group Ireland, 25 St. Stephen's Green, Dublin 2, Ireland (a division of Penguin Books Ltd.)
Penguin Group (Australia), 250 Camberwell Road, Camberwell, Victoria 3124, Australia
(a division of Pearson Australia Group Pty. Ltd.)
Penguin Books India Pvt. Ltd., 11 Community Centre, Panchsheel Park, New Delhi—110 017, India
Penguin Group (NZ), 67 Apollo Drive, Rosedale, North Shore 0632, New Zealand
(a division of Pearson New Zealand Ltd.)
Penguin Books (South Africa) (Pty.) Ltd., 24 Sturdee Avenue, Rosebank, Johannesburg 2196,
South Africa

Penguin Books Ltd., Registered Offices: 80 Strand, London WC2R 0RL, England

PRINTING HISTORY
Berkley Signature edition / September 2006
Berkley trade paperback edition / October 2009

Library of Congress Cataloging-in-Publication Data

Norman, Diana.
The sparks fly upward / Diana Norman.
p.   cm.
ISBN 0-425-21158-8 (trade pbk.)
1. France—History—Reign of Terror, 1793–1794—Fiction.   I. Title.
PR6064.O73S66   2006
823'.914—dc22   2006049008

PRINTED IN THE UNITED STATES OF AMERICA

10   9   8   7   6   5   4   3   2

Catherine and Alice,
with love from their aunt.

Chapter One

I T had been a mistake to use the alleys rather than the main thoroughfare of Rue Saint Antoine but she'd wanted to avoid the patrols. Since the Charlotte Corday business, the National Guard was as likely to search a woman for an assassin's knife as a man. Not that she was carrying a weapon, but the letter to England up her sleeve was a death sentence in itself.

It was a mistake, though. Instead of losing her pursuer in the traffic, she'd made it easier for the man to follow her; he knew the back ways better than she did and she hadn't been able to throw him off.

On the other hand, it was the quiet of the alleys, out of the wind, that had alerted her to the fact that she was being followed at all. There'd been a persistent and sibilant echo to her own footsteps through the slush.

She kept going, trying to keep her pace, not to give way to the fear that was affecting her legs by transmitting the impression that they had become very short.

Think rationally. Reason precludes panic. Most likely, the man's orders were to discover where Nicolas was hiding and he'd do nothing until he found out where she was going. If she could gain enough distance she'd lose him once she reached the alleys beyond the wallpaper factory.

Keep walking. Reason precludes panic, Nicolas always said. *Stay rational, that's it.* Nicolas would have tried to analyze the phenomenon of one's legs; why, now, she felt she was plowing the snow with her knees when, in the first three years, she and the rest of France had seemed to walk on a cloud, as if the Revolution had literally cut the ground from under everybody's feet and released an entire population into the air.

Terror and joy effect displacements in the mind, Nicolas would say. Joy and terror, both are delirium.

That's where the Revolution went wrong, she thought, it had ventured too far in its joy; it had abolished the familiar. North and south had been spun to different headings, it had shaken the world so that men and women, tumbling weightlessly with nothing to hang on to, had chosen despotism as the only certainty.

Jagged outlines against the moon told her she'd reached the Place de la Bastille. It was empty—people were saving on light and fuel by going to bed early. The great rounded emplacements where cannon had once been trained on the people of Saint Antoine were now reduced to rubble, most of their stones gone for souvenirs. In daytime the stalls that sold the little carved replicas were tricked out in red, white and blue and, despite the weather, still carried on a brisk trade with sightseers up from the country. Tonight they were stacked high under a tarpaulin, one corner of which had come loose and was flipping energetically in the wind with a sound reminiscent of a face being slapped. Terror again. It distorted things so that all noises were alarming and all images ugly.

Suddenly, she couldn't bear it that she was frightened here, of all places. *How dare they.* This was where tyranny had been brought down in one glorious crash so that nobody should be frightened or cold or hungry anymore.

She turned round to face her pursuer. *Do you think I'd lead the likes of you to* him?

There was nobody there. Moonlight shone on empty, snow-furred ruins.

Then she saw a tiny trickle of steam issuing from behind a broken pillar, and knew it was the man's breath as it vaporized in the air. His mouth was open while he hid, perhaps smiling.

Unnerved, she began to hurry. Slush had soaked through the cardboard covering a hole in her left shoe and was numbing her toes so that her stride was lopsided.

If she couldn't throw him off, if he arrested her and she was searched . . . Eliza would be left alone, her baby, in a world where even children went to the guillotine. Before she'd left the apartment she'd agonized for their daughter's sake about whether to set out at all. 'I have to deliver a letter, darling. I won't be long. Be quiet as a mouse.'

A very little mouse. Five years old and left alone.

I can't do this again, not even for him. He'll understand I can't leave her again.

She'd reached the Saint Antoine Faubourg, that vulgar, vibrant highway. She'd loved it; now it menaced her. Only the munitions factory poured out noise and light, giving a glimpse as she passed it of frantic, gleaming bodies outlined against the furnaces, like an advanced vision of hell. Everywhere else was closed. The little man on the corner who used to sell and mend umbrellas had shut his shop for good; afraid, so he'd told her, that umbrellas were suspect—as if a desire to fend off the rain was counter-revolutionary. Across his shutters was scrawled LIBERTY OR DEATH. It was on every door she passed.

On the other side of the road, moonlight shone onto the cold frontage of the Visitandes convent and the steps she'd climbed so often in the glorious years. When its nuns had been evicted, she and the other republican women had used it for their club. They'd cut their hair and worn red phrygian caps and danced the *ça ira*. Wonderful, noisy meetings, shrill with previously undreamed of possibilities.

'Citizenesses of the Revolution, women are entitled to have rights, too.' A right to fight alongside the brave men of Paris against the royalist enemy, a right to education, a right to divorce, a right to equality of inheritance. They'd greeted each one with exhiliration, put it down on paper and sent it with a deputation to be argued before the Assembly.

She remembered the silence when Nicolas had got up to speak and told them they must also have the vote. For a moment they were stunned; even they hadn't considered Utopia. Then the cheering broke out.

Robespierre had closed them down, of course. Well, if nothing else, they'd won the right to divorce and equal inheritance before they were suppressed.

Oh, Christ. She'd been maundering. The factory was coming up, the empty tops of the pillars that had once carried the arch of gilded letters, REVEILLON WALLPAPERS, stood stark against the moon. Beyond them was the bend she'd hoped would allow her to swerve to the left unseen.

She bent to fumble with her bootlaces and risked a peek behind her. A shadow whisked into a doorway. He was too close, she needed to gain ground. Gathering the front of her skirt, she stood up, prayed to the God she didn't believe in—and sprinted.

She took him by surprise; she'd gained fifteen meters by the time she heard the splash of running feet at her back.

Reveillon's gates were coming up. She was tiring; slow starvation had weakened her. The brute behind would be well fed; the Committee of Public Safety kept its agents loyal with extra rations.

Past the gates and into the bend, its side alleys were like rat holes in a river bank. Rat holes with high-sounding names—Impasse de Montmorency, Rue de Venise, Passage Taillepain; holes infested with rats who could read, who'd stood up and torn down the Bastille with their paws.

She was just past the bend now and had to risk it. She flung herself to the left. Instantly, she was in stinking blackness. The alley was so narrow she could touch the wet, leprous walls on each side. When her fingers found a doorway, she pressed into it, pulling her skirt tight against her body.

He went past. She heard the curses as they grew loud then diminished. Even so, going on, she trundled her feet through the snowy sewage rather than stepping in order to make no sound.

Along here somewhere. Please God, let it be along here.

Sweet Jesus. He was coming back, sniffing for the trail. She stopped breathing; he was outlined against the mouth of the alley. 'Come back, you bitch.'

Then he was gone and she heard his shout of 'I'll catch you' echoing down the next passage to the left.

She crept on until her right hand touched nothing. She was at the edge of a courtyard dimly lit by a glow coming from a grating set low in one of its walls and, with it, like fresh breath in a graveyard, she could smell the scent of baking bread.

Taking the letter from her pocket, she went up to the grating and bent down to listen. She could hear Bercy swearing to himself as he beat the next batch of dough. Not a sight for the squeamish, as she'd learned when Nicolas insisted they watch in action 'this most essential and noble of industries.' By the time Bercy had finished punching and stretching the twenty-pound chunks, so much sweat from his face and hair had flicked into the dough that she'd put herself on a breadless diet for days.

A good man, though. An even better friend.

She rattled the grating and the swearing stopped instantly.

She looked around to make sure that all the court's shutters were closed. They were, but who could tell that there weren't ears pressed to them? One word could compromise her and the baker onto the guillotine's steps.

She poked the letter through the bars of the grating and let it sway downwards out of sight into the warm, yeasty interior.

There was a pause and then his voice. 'Yes.'

Done.

Thanking the God she didn't believe in, Sophie de Condorcet made for home.

Chapter Two

O N the curlicued dais of Lord Ffoulkes's London house in Saint James's Square, thirty wigged and liveried musicians played in ravishing three-quarter time to those guests, the French and younger English, who swirled like blown flowers beneath the blaze of a thousand candles burning in ten gigantic chandeliers made of the best Venetian glass.

The rest of the company, those of a certain age and all of them English, clustered about the gilt Louis Quinze tables and chairs around the walls, and stared at them in something like shock.

'It's a what?' asked Makepeace.

'A waltz,' Philippa said. 'Don't start, Ma.'

'I'm not starting. But in my day you did that sort of thing in private.'

The circling dancers were grasping each other *all the time*. White female hands lay on male shoulders and masculine hands pressed intimately into the small of feminine backs.

From the next table, Lady Gladmain called: 'What ye say, Makepeace? A French thing, so they tell me. Popular with Marie Antoinette, wouldn't you know it.'

Philippa winced. Lady Gladmain had a voice that could drill pig-iron, and there were two elderly French marquises at the table beyond hers.

'Small wonder they cut her head off,' Makepeace called back.

'*Ma.*'

'Well.' The severe American Puritanism of Makepeace's youth had been dissipated by an adventurous life and two English husbands but occasionally it pulled itself together and said something. At the sight of supposedly well-brought-up men and women publicly pressing their bodies together, it was positively strident.

The fact was that her Puritanism had been nagging since the ball began. Even in small numbers those French exiled by the Revolution were irritating; en masse, like they were here, the emigrés exasperated the daylights out of her. A decadent load of wasters, in her opinion.

However, as guest of honour, she could hardly walk out.

One of the guests of honour, at any rate. Andrew Ffoulkes was killing a lot of birds with this ball; his one stone was having to ricochet between honoring herself—it was her fiftieth birthday; introducing his young French wife to his English friends; and, to please her, smuggling down from Scotland the Comte d'Artois who was not only the bride's kinsman but, as brother to the late Louis XVI, the highest-ranking Frenchman in Britain.

Andrew had gone to a good deal of trouble, especially with regard to Artois, whose attendance had necessitated a word with the prime minister in order to release him from virtual incarceration in Holyrood Palace, as well as a promise that he would be returned to it immediately afterwards. That the count had to be smuggled out of Holyrood in an unmarked carriage was not so much due to his anomalous diplomatic position as to the bailiffs who hovered around the palace waiting to arrest him for debt.

The man's emergence into the ballroom had occasioned incoherent joy among the other French exiles and an exhibition of bowing and curtseying and hand-kissing which, in Makepeace's view, would have been more called for if the woman on Artois's arm had been his wife and not his mistress.

The music was slowing, the dancers making a last regretful twirl. Judging from the calls for an encore, the next dance was to be yet another waltz.

A thin, pale young man had appeared in front of Jenny. 'If you please to honor me, mademoiselle?'

'And who may you be, young man?' Makepeace felt the pressure of Philippa's foot against her ankle. *Don't start.* But if sixteen-year-old Jenny was to be clasped to a male bosom, her mother wanted to know whose it was.

The boy bowed. 'Jean-Marie, Comte de Latil-Dupeyroux, *à votre service*, madame.'

A long name for a skimpy youth but Jenny, under cover of her fan, was pinching her beseechingly.

'Oh, all right then.' The poor child had sat out most of the previous dances while her official escort, the Reverend Deedes, had been elsewhere in the room talking business.

Watching Jenny's delight as she was swept off, Makepeace thought guiltily what a good little thing she was. This was Jenny's first season in London and she could have expected more from it than the sedate weeks she'd spent uncomplainingly at the house in Chelsea where Makepeace had been unable to rouse herself to do much more than arrange a couple of whist parties and accept tonight's invitation.

She should have done; she knew that. Force of circumstance had meant that others had played a greater part in bringing her three daughters up than she had; she'd been too busy. In the case of Jenny and Sally, the two youngest, they'd been left in the care of their father's Northumbrian sister-in-law while she herself worked on the coal-shipping end of her and her husband's mine.

The mine accident that had caused Andra Hedley's death had imbued Newcastle and its surroundings with insupportable horror for Makepeace and she had moved away, refusing to return. Jenny and Sally still lived there. These last few weeks had been the longest time mother and daughter had spent together since Jenny reached puberty.

And I've done nothing for her.

Even less had been done for an irate Sally, who was too young to come out and had been left behind in the north.

No, she had done nothing for her daughters, except to make them rich.

She nodded her head towards the dancers. 'And if young Frog-me-lad thinks he's getting his hands on a penny of our Jenny's money, he can think some more,' she said out loud.

'Oh, Ma,' said Philippa sadly.

'What? *What?*'

'Listen to yourself.'

I do, she thought. I can hear my own discontent and I can't stop. Time had ameliorated shock and grief but not the way she had accustomed herself to them; misery had become a habit. So had its infliction on others.

When she'd entered her dressing room tonight, she'd seen that Hildy had lain a gray silk gown out for her because 'Ah'm not lettin' ye flap round that theor ballroom like a craa.'

She'd supposed she could not but she'd sworn at her maid for making her put off the deep mourning she'd worn for nearly two years. Not that it made a difference; Hildy was used to being sworn at.

For a long while after Andra was killed she'd not cared what she wore, wandering like a madwoman in a shift and bare feet. Now the customary mourning period was long past, but she still wore black so that she could be a mobile memorial to him, a bitter remonstrance for those who persisted in getting on with their lives, even though, as time went on, her own pain treacherously lodged itself in an attic of her brain where she could begin to live with it.

She would put on black again tomorrow because to wear anything else would mean exerting herself out of her irritable inertia and she had no idea how to do it. Her habit was black, like her temper.

And you look well in it, said Makepeace's conscience. This was a new and guilty realization that made her crosser; black suited her white skin and her red hair which was still only slightly frosted; she'd begun to suspect that vanity was superseding sorrow.

Two tall men took their seat at her table. 'I am surprised Miss Jenny has been permitted to take part in this exhibition,' Reverend

Deedes said. 'Had I been here at the time I should have advised against it.' He addressed the air as if it were a congregation.

'Where were you then?' she snapped. Deedes, cadaverous and forty, was not a young girl's dream as an escort, certainly not Jenny's, but he was Makepeace's neighbor in Chelsea and, due to her reduced social circle, the only bachelor she'd been able to think of. It had been nice for him to be asked; the bugger could at least do his job.

His companion leaned across the table. 'William, we have been so neglectful of the ladies it little behooves us to complain if they desert us.' He put his hand over Makepeace's, smiling. 'But forgive us, missus; William and I have been about the Lord's work.' He inclined his head towards the back of the ballroom. 'I believe we have persuaded Lord Malthrop to vote for the abolition bill at its next appearance.'

As always, when she looked at Stephen Heilbron, Makepeace saw terrifying goodness staring back at her. An admirer had once likened his face to that of Christ at Gethsemane and, while shocked by the blasphemy, she'd never been able to rid herself of the comparison. He was about the same age as crucified Christ and, yes, the face on the cross might have looked like this one, ravaged by his own and others' pain, luminous with love for sinners.

He'd come into their lives through Deedes. At that neighbor's insistence and because she supposed she ought to do *something*, Makepeace had joined the Chelsea branch of the Society for the Abolition of Slavery with her eldest daughter—and nearly been thrown out of it. The other members got on her nerves. It seemed to her they spent too much time prattling in justification of what they were doing as if they needed to cite reasons why negroes qualified as sensate beings.

To Makepeace, born in multicolored Boston and raised by a rescued slave, this was so self-evident that comment on it was not only unnecessary but impudent. Betty had made a motherless childhood supportable and, now that Betty herself was dead, Makepeace's love had been transferred to Betty's American son.

'It don't need saying that black people are people, so why do they keep saying it?' she'd grumbled to Philippa about her fellow members. 'If Betty and Josh don't qualify for the human race, it ain't worth running. Slavery's evil, everybody knows that. Let's just get on and fight it.'

Philippa, typically, had advised patience and diplomacy. But then the consignment of Wedgwood medallions had arrived, ammunition for the Society's battle, depicting a kneeling black man with upraised chained hands encircled by the inscription: 'Am I not a man and a brother?'

The Society had been proud of them. Makepeace, shown one, had looked at it and said, 'Of course he damn well is,' and been ushered out of the door.

But then Stephen Heilbron, already one of the Society's best-known campaigners with Wilberforce and Clarkson, had come out from London to encourage his Chelsea troops and paid her a visit. ''I beg you to come back, Mrs Hedley.'

Philippa must have talked to him and he must have talked to Deedes. He played to what she realized had been her sense of superiority over the other anti-slavers.

'You are advantaged, you see, experienced as we are not . . . So few of us have the privilege of intimacy with the race we are trying to serve. It is not enough for those of us like me who do the work for the love of God, we need those, like you, who will work for the love of the people themselves.'

Seductive stuff from a man who'd risked beatings from the slavers of Bristol and Liverpool to gain evidence for Parliament of their trade's innate barbarism, who toured the country to proclaim it—and looked as if he neither slept nor ate in the process. 'You must forgive the mundane, Mrs Hedley. William Deedes and the others may not be pierced by the sword that pierces you, but they help us roll the stone uphill, and they want you back.'

'They want my money,' she'd said, nastily. She'd given near a thousand pounds to the cause since she'd joined.

Beautifully, he'd smiled. 'So do I. But I want you, too.'

Oh, undoubtedly one of God's anointed. With charm.

'Surely you will not subscribe to this appalling display, Heilbron?' Deedes was asking now.

Stephen Heilbron looked tenderly towards the rippling dance floor. 'I fear I should be no ornament to Vanity Fair. Instead, I shall beg Miss Philippa to accompany me in a turn around the garden.'

Philippa laid her hand on his sleeve. 'With your permission, Mama.'

'Time you had that young woman married, Makepeace,' yelled Lady Gladmain as the couple walked away.

'Ain't found anybody worthy enough yet,' Makepeace told her. *One in the eye for you, you harpy.* Gladmain's son had offered for Philippa and been refused.

'Preserve us from worthy old maids is what I say,' Gladmain slung back.

Makepeace disengaged from the skirmish. No use saying that she did not, thank God, belong to the circle that married its daughters off, willing or unwillling; Lady Gladmain knew she didn't. The *haut monde* had come to accept Makepeace because she was rich and favored by Lord Ffoulkes and now old enough to be considered as an eccentric but she did not belong to it. No use saying, either, that one had as much chance of persuading Philippa into something she didn't want to do as shifting the Rock of Gibraltar.

None of this bothered Makepeace much, but it struck her now that Philippa, at twenty-six, was undoubtedly the oldest unmarried female at the ball. Immersed in her own grief, she had not, until this moment, considered the matter.

She watched her daughter leave the room with Heilbron. As ever, Philippa was dressed to avoid attention rather than attract it but the new simplicity suited her; her gown's low-cut white gauze over silk showed to advantage the fine, almost olive-tinged skin she'd inherited from her father. Nothing could persuade her mousy hair to curl but it had been piled neatly into a smooth and shining top-knot decorated with pearls.

Whether she could be regarded as pretty depended on how well you knew her; first acquaintances tended to think her plain—and, indeed, as a child her face had resembled that of a small and studious camel—but, given time, they could be astonished by a smile, a turn of the head, that took the breath.

When Jenny was returned to her chair, panting and exuberant, Makepeace kept her voice low and asked a question she should have asked before. 'Philippa's happy enough, ain't she?'

Jenny thought about it. 'There's no saying with Pippy, Ma, but I reckon she took a tumble over Lord Ffoulkes's marriage. When we got his note telling us about it, she looked poorly all day.'

'She loves *Andrew*?'

Jenny was wriggling on her seat. 'Don't quiz me, Ma, I don't know, I just wondered. If you remember, it was immediately after Andrew's wedding to poor Miss Tate that Pippy went abroad.'

'So she did.' Makepeace began connecting events. Receiving the news of this most recent marriage, Philippa had shown her usual equanimity but had soon after gone to her room with a headache. And nearly four years ago, when Ffoulkes had married a wispy little twig of the nobility, Philippa had set out on the Grand Tour with friends less than a week after the wedding.

Poor little Lady Ffoulkes had died in childbirth, with the baby, nine months later.

She should've nabbed him then, Makepeace thought irritably, aghast at her own lack of perspicacity. But Philippa wasn't a nabber. She'd stayed on with some people in France, only returning to comfort her mother when Andra was killed.

Pippy, my poor girl. I didn't know. What comfort have I been to you?

I T was bitterly cold outside but Heilbron had fetched her wrap. Together they stood by one of the burning braziers with which Ffoulkes had lined the terraces that tiered his steep garden.

'Did you receive my letter?' Heilbron asked. His voice was usually melodious; she'd heard it move a meeting to tears but at the moment, bless him, it cracked with tension.

'Yes.' Philippa indicated the tiny pocket attached by velvet strings to her left wrist. In fact, it contained three letters, among them the one from Andrew Ffoulkes telling her of his marriage. The other two had arrived that morning.

'And what is to be my answer?'

She could hear the crunch of wheels breaking puddled ice as carriages took playgoers and revelers home along Piccadilly at the top of the hill. *Time's winged chariots hurrying near*, she thought, *and all before us lie deserts of vast eternity.*

Marvell might have been writing for her. *You ain't getting any younger, Philippa Dapifer.*

She had received several proposals in her time; some of the best families in England, even one or two in France, had found her an eligible choice for their sons, being prepared to overlook her mother's lack of breeding in return for her money. Her suitors had proclaimed their love, had sworn to make her happy and compared her to various flowers.

Stephen's letter had told her he loved her but had dwelled more on his passion for God than his passion for her; he had nothing to give her, he said, but the satisfaction of being his comrade-in-arms against the world's evils.

She found it a better offer than any—and from a better man than any of her previous suitors.

'Philippa?'

She looked up at the cold stars and went over the equation again to make sure she had it right; she took comfort in stars and mathematics.

Accept this good, good man and she'd be saved from the humiliating minus of waiting for someone who kept marrying other people. Saved from that most despised of human conditions, elderly spinsterhood. Plus she would have a worthy husband, a *very* worthy husband,

and, most of all, she would have children. The thought of life without children had become intolerable.

Plus, she would be of use. Stephen would gain her person and her fortune in his fight against slavery, the greatest cause any man had ever undertaken.

This would equal a profitable life for them both.

It worked out very well. The only missing factor was love, but there was no point in including that.

'Yes, Stephen, thank you,' she said, 'I shall be happy to marry you.'

He crowed for a moment, laughing, before he bent to kiss her. The smell of the herbs in which his valet kept his clothes enfolded her, some combination that reminded her of incense. She thought of their marriage bed. She had factored it into the equation—how else to have children?—and tried to give it a low quotient. After all, Stephen lusted after Heaven more than the flesh. And he would be away a lot.

Bless him, he was telling her how happy he was; how fortunate in her tranquillity, the sense of peace she inspired in him, her modesty . . .

You don't know me at all, she thought. *Pray God you never will. I am a stricken, turbulent, calculating bitch who would run off with Andrew Ffoulkes this minute if he asked. Which he won't. But you shall have what fraction of my heart is left to you. You will not be shortchanged, dear man. I shall love you.*

She kissed him back with energy. 'We'd better go in and tell Ma,' she said.

T HE voice on Makepeace's left cranked on in the rising and falling cadences parsons learned at preaching school. '. . . were my sister to be seized by a strange man and subjected to his embraces and canterings, indeed I should not. I confess surprise that Lord Ffoulkes should introduce this foreign contagion to our shores . . .'

Shut up, thought Makepeace, *shut* up.

'Indeed, I would say obscene. Were I not a guest, I should be forced . . .'

'Voulez-vous m'accorder cette danse, madame?'

The lifeline was elderly and missing a tooth or two but unhesitatingly Makepeace put out her hand to grasp it. 'Certanmon, monsewer.' Anything, anything.

As they approached the other dancers, she held back, shocked at herself: 'Better not. I don't know how to waltz.'

'Leave it to me, madame.'

A firm hand on her back pressured her into the sway, a cracked, once-elegant shoe gently nudged one of her feet back and to the side, then the other . . . they were off.

Her mind still on her eldest daughter, Makepeace asked dully: 'Have you got children?'

'One son, madame.' The little French face twisted. 'No, two, *two*. For me, always two. But the elder went to the guillotine last year.'

He had her attention now. He was a valiant little bugger; he wouldn't let her grieve for him. He said, 'Now we dance and think only of the dance.'

She smiled and had a second to think, *This will ruin the dancing-master trade; it's so easy*, before the pleasure of movement swooped and carried her away. So long, so *long*, since she'd been held; her skin was grateful for the touch of even this elderly hand. She was young again; there was no guilt, just memories. Under the white blaze of candlelight, Makepeace Hedley danced to the sweetness of past chimes.

She found herself crying. She smiled: 'It's been a long time.'

There were tears on the lifeline's cheeks. 'I, too,' he said, 'At Versailles.'

They waltzed on in perfect understanding.

When they paused, waiting for the next turn, she discovered that he was the Marquis de Barigoule and the least irritating émigré she'd encountered so far. His conversation was less about his wrongs at the hands of the revolutionaries than his gratitude to the English for taking him in. The brocade of the rubbed waistcoat he wore over a shirt of sacking had once been remarkably fine. He still wore his hair powdered; she wondered how he could afford the flour.

'What do you do now?' she asked. It was the most fascinating thing about the émigrés, how they coped with their fall.

'I give dancing classes.'

'Your pupils are fortunate.'

She approved of him; there were too many who couldn't or wouldn't adapt. Makepeace had known poverty as bad as theirs and had no time for the young and fit who took the government's shilling a day and shivered complainingly in their attics. Exiles like this one and the Comtesse de Guéry, who'd discovered an unsuspected talent for making ices and was doing a roaring trade in them, were people who were prepared to roll up their sleeves—these were a breed after her own heart.

He had only one grumble.

'Tiss?' She had trouble with his accent and its occasional whistle.

'Teess.' He grimaced to show the gaps. 'In the haste to get away, they were lost, *quel désastre*. Beautiful tiss *en porcelaine*. Do you know the work of M de Chemant? A dentist of genius.'

If the man made china teeth that fitted, he must be. Such English as were both rich and dentally unfortunate were ever complaining that teeth taken from the dead rotted too quickly. Makepeace smiled again, showing teeth that were her own and very nearly perfect.

The Marquis stood on tiptoe so that his mouth could approach her ear. 'Poor De Chemant, he is still in France,' he whispered through a cloud of bad breath. 'Some of us have asked Lord Ffoulkes to save him.' He stood back.

Makepeace stopped smiling.

De Barigoule said: 'A fine young man, Lord Ffoulkes. He talks of you as a mother.'

'He was my first husband's ward,' Makepeace said, vaguely.

On the way back to her table, Ffoulkes himself came up to claim her for the next dance. 'Fun, ain't it? Never thought to see you waltzing, missus.'

'Me, neither,' she said, shortly. 'Andrew, what are you about letting everybody know what you lads get up to in France?'

'Who said so?'

'That Froggy just now.'

He looked around, 'Oh, de Barigoule? One of last year's deliveries. Can't help that, missus. Packages are bound to know the postman.'

'They don't have to yap about it; Robespierre's got spies everywhere.' She herself only knew of Andrew's and his friends' secret activities—they called themselves The League—because a fishing boat they were using to bring some aristocrats back from Cherbourg had gotten blown off course and landed at Start Point. It was in Makepeace's interest to be informed of the movement of all craft along that stretch of South Devon coast, and she was.

It turned out, somewhat irritatingly, that Philippa had known all along of the existence of The League and what it was up to.

'Andrew. I want you to stop now.'

'Goin' to, missus. League's being wound up. No more adventurin', I fear. Benedick the married man, me. What d'ye think of Félicie, eh? Approve?'

'Very pretty.' Indeed, the little figurine she'd had been introduced to a day or two before was unbelievably lovely. Makepeace, always prejudiced against the French aristocracy, had been overcritical. 'The female made me feel I was baa-ing at her like a damn sheep,' she'd told Philippa afterwards. In the company of her husband and her peers Félicie overdid the pathos; in the company of lesser mortals, like Makepeace herself, she kept an uninterested distance.

'Give her time, Ma. England's new to her and she's just lost everything.'

'She's gained Andrew.' Félicie couldn't be luckier than that.

Makepeace had loved him from the first, a motherless, miserable but brave six-year-old who'd just lost his father. And he'd come to love her—she was always better with boys than girls. Neither had disappointed the other over the years.

Except now, she thought. *Why didn't you marry Philippa?*

She had never entertained the idea until tonight; there had been no indication in the past. Or, if there had been, she supposed she hadn't seen it because, regarding Andrew like a son as she did, a match between the two would have seemed incestuous. In any case, Philippa's admiration of Andrew had always resembled that of a younger sister. Makepeace now wondered if she'd done wrong in asking Andrew, when he was seven years old, to be Philippa's godfather; perhaps it had distorted the relationship for him. Could godfathers marry their goddaughters? Too late to find out now.

He whirled her into the dance with more speed than the Marquis had done, and considerably less expertise. 'Married men have heavy expenses,' he said. 'Any room for me in the smugglin' trade?'

He found her connection with her Devonian smugglers endlessly diverting. Before his last trip to France he'd sent her a note saying: 'Fly, all is discovered' signed 'Brandy Bill,' followed up by a footman dressed in Revenue uniform with orders to search her premises—a stratagem that, oddly enough, had provoked Makepeace sufficiently to give her depression a temporary lift.

'Oh, *hush*. You'll have me in clink.' Others would not be similarly amused. Nearly every English person in the room drank brandy and tea on which no duty had been paid, yet would call himself or herself a law-abiding citizen while at the same time condemning those who illegally imported the stuff as criminal.

'Wish you could've been at the wedding, missus,' he said. 'But this time we were delivering our packages over the Swiss border; had to get her on my passport there and then.' He grinned. 'Her aunt insisted on drawing up the marriage contract as if the wedding was to be at Versailles under the old regime; all the diamonds, carriages she would have had included. And the poor little thing shivering in her one chemise.'

'You made it up to her tonight.' The new Lady Ffoulkes sparkled like one of her husband's chandeliers.

'Hope so.'

She'd better be good to you, Makepeace thought with ferocity. Out loud she said: 'Well, stick to your guns. Don't go risking that head of yours for a damn dentist. I've put plenty of plasters on it in my time, but I can't stick it back on once it's off.'

'Anybody could, you could.'

He led her in to supper, fetched her champagne and went away to see to his other guests.

The supper tables against the gold and white walls looked like someone's bas-relief of a gastronomic mountain range in autumn color. Sugar-capped heights of fruit decorated with ivy leaves towered over silver chafing dishes giving off steam like volcanoes, crags of pastries, parsleyed meats, lemoned fish, appled pork, brown-hilled pies, black pools of caviar, and, here and there, a shining sculpture of ice in the shape of a fleur-de-lis.

Gloved footmen hovered with plates and tongs, ready to help those who wouldn't help themselves.

The emigrés, Makpeace noted, tried to appear casual but couldn't hold out. Her little Marquis was sucking asparagus with the energy of a baby at his mother's breast, but most were going for bulk, attacking the beef and capons and ragouts—sallets could wait.

She saw one old lady in an unfashionably towering headdress—why would one save that from a revolution?—look around craftily before tipping a plateful of *vol-au-vents de quenelles* into a large, battered reticule for later, followed by some meringues.

It was like watching beggars scramble for pennies so she stopped doing it.

A flushed and happy Jenny joined her. 'Aren't you eating, Mama?'

'Andrew's told a footman to get me something.'

'I'll wait for him, then.' She sat down and eased her shoes, squinting at her mother and falling into dialect. 'Wait for Maister Deedes and ah'd be half-deid for want o' battenin'.'

It was kindly meant, a whiff of fresh Northumbrian air in this London hothouse, but the expression of face and voice brought back Andra so sharply that it ran a dagger through Makepeace's ribs. She fought the pain with anger. 'That's the last time he comes anywhere with us. He's supposed to be looking after you. Where *is* the bugger?'

Immediately, Jenny became emollient. 'It's natural he and Mr Heilbron would want to talk abolition with all the important people here. God's work, Ma.'

'God's more of a gentleman, I hope.'

But here was Heilbron leading her eldest daughter towards her. There was something about the two of them . . . Not usually percipient, she knew in an instant what it was.

Charmingly, Heilbron asked for her permission and blessing. She gave them—surprised by her own reluctance. As he turned to receive Jenny's exuberant congratulations, she whispered: 'Are you sure?'

Philippa kissed her. 'He is a fine, good man, Mama. I am both fortunate and content.'

She looked well enough, but in Makepeace's experience you didn't marry a man because you were fortunate or content, you married him because you couldn't wait to rip off your stays and jump into bed with him. She herself hadn't even waited that long; she'd anticipated her wedding night with Philip Dapifer and, later, with Andra Hedley, those two very different, lovely men. And if she'd known that she was to lose them—in Dapifer's case after only a year—she'd have done it even quicker.

He *is* a good man, she assured herself. But is he *too* good? Heilbron was a valiant fighter against slavery, yes, but he subscribed to this new thing, the Society for the Suppression of Vice, with equal vehemence.

They'd argued about it. 'Surely you cannot uphold the state of licentiousness and drunkenness we see all about us, missus?'

'No, I'm agin it. But the trouble with your lot is you want to suppress the pleasures of the poor, which is all they've got, not the vices of the rich.' She was thinking of Reverend Deedes who would reduce the streets to decorous gloom while disregarding the sins of the drawing room.

'*I* don't.'

She had to admit that Heilbron practiced what he preached; he'd resigned from all the drinking and gambling clubs he'd joined in his youth, while still managing to retain the friends he'd made in them and without becoming a prude.

Nevertheless, as a son-in-law he worried her; she was prepared to stake her fortune that Philippa's stays were as yet unripped.

She reminded herself that the young didn't wear stays anymore—the Revolution having freed the female figure at least—but her principle held true.

Well, there was nothing to be done about it; she'd never fully understood Philippa but she knew better than to try and persuade her against something she'd set her mind to. Just as long as it wasn't because she'd been disappointed by Andrew . . .

'Forgive me, Stephen,' Philippa was saying, 'but I must go and tell Lord Ffoulkes the news—he is my godfather, after all.'

'By all means. There are some here tonight I can't resist informing myself. I shall be the most envied man at the ball.'

Perhaps it'll be all right, Makepeace thought, watching her daughter go. *Perhaps Jenny's wrong. She seems happy. He's a kind soul and, undoubtedly, with her money and common sense she's exactly what is needed by a man careering towards greatness.*

She just wished the word 'sacrifice' didn't keep occurring to her.

P HILIPPA thought that if it had done nothing else, the Revolution had caused men to show themselves off to greater advantage than at any time in their history. Gone were the wigs, the over-pocketed coats and ribboned stockings, all the brocaded fuss. Line was in.

Andrew was the shortest man in the group but, like the others around him, had his head held high by his enormous collar and cravat. As with the rest, it was as if silk had been merely painted on his body; not a wrinkle disturbed the run of limbs—except for the lump which made an unabashed ruck in the frontal sweep of the britches from which ladies were supposed to avert their eyes.

Her eyes suitably averted, Philippa said: 'My lord, may I have a word with you in private.'

Lord Ffoulkes put his arm around her shoulders to bring her into the center of the circle. 'William, I don't believe you've met my god-daughter, Philippa Dapifer. Pippy, this is Mr Pitt.' She curtseyed to the prime minister.

He'd always delighted in being her godfather and so close in age. When he was ten years old and she'd accompanied Makepeace on a visit to him at Eton, he'd not been embarrassed to take her by the hand and toddle her around the school, trumpeting their relationship to his friends.

'You've met these other gentlemen, of course.' She acknowledged Henry Hastings, Boy Blanchard, Snuffy Throgmorton, Peter Saint James, Kit Pellew.

These last were The League, to be found at most high entertainments when they were in England as well as in the society papers and scandal sheets, all of them Old Etonians, gamblers, fast livers, redeeming their souls by secret rescue work in France.

Viscount Throgmorton was in financial straits from playing too heavily at White's; she knew because he'd asked her to marry him. He'd been charmingly honest about saving her from being an old maid. 'We get on well, old thing, don't we? I can offer the title and a castle here or there . . . and, d'y'see, it would get me out of a frightful hole.'

'Bless you, Snuffy,' she'd said. 'I'm afraid not, but I can lend you a thousand if you'd like.'

It was a thousand she hadn't seen again but it had kept them on good terms.

The others had married and fathered early, though their wives, poor things, were rarely in their company. Lady Blanchard was never seen; Mesdames Hastings and Saint James were here tonight but abandoned, as usual, to talk to each other.

Eton, Philippa had long decided, was an octopus that never let go; if she and Stephen had a son, he would be kept from its toils.

Andrew took her into his library, her favorite room in the house.

'*Waltzing*,' she said, once they were inside. 'Ma nearly went home.'

'Didn't, though, did she? Bein' whisked 'round like a spoon by some elderly Frog when I found her. And one's got to keep up with the times.' He collapsed into a chair and put his legs on the massive table that served as his desk in order to massage one superb boot. 'Feel I've kept up with a couple of centuries.'

He was up again in a second to light a cigar, to check on a new saddle that lay across a wooden horse at one end of the long room. He was rarely still; among the other members of The League, who adopted fashionable indolence when on show, he resembled an energetic sheepdog keeping a long-legged flock together. But The League had been his idea and his was the busy brain that had enabled it to snatch nearly fifty people from the guillotine.

Philippa crossed to the room's other end and automatically adjusted a Stubbs painting of Andrew's Derby winner. 'I wish you'd get this chain fixed. Poor Corsair's always running either uphill or down.'

'Fussbudget.'

'Slobberguts.'

'What d'you think of her, Pippy?'

'Very lovely.'

'Told her all about you. She's dyin' to be friends.'

She turned round, smiling. 'Then we shall be.'

'Takin' her on a tour of the estates tomorrow, beginnin' with the north. She'd like you to join us at some point.'

He's no idea, Philippa thought. He's not only dragging his bride to a Cumbrian castle in midwinter, he's suggesting that another woman join them on their honeymoon. She'd prefer a stretch on the rack. *So would I.*

'We'll see.'

He went back to the table to light a cigar. 'What's up?'

She sighed and went to stand in front of him, her hands folded. 'First of all, you've got to promise you won't be going back to France.'

He shook his head. 'Feel a bit liver-faced about it, but no. Me wife'—he paused to relish the term—'she won't have it. Made me swear it on our wedding day—got a horror for her own country, which ain't surprising. I need a son or two before I risk the old neck again.' He glanced at her sideways. 'Tell you the truth, Pip, it was gettin' a bit warm over there. Had a narrow shave or two with the National Guard. Seemed to be on the lookout for me. Popped up in Paris once too often, I suppose.'

'A carroty, freckled Saxon among all those Gauls? Surely not.'

Every time he went on one of The League's missions, she'd imagined him, standing out among the Parisians like a Union Jack, every beat of her pulse asking: *What if I lost him?*

'I'll have you know I am a master of disguise.' He squinted at her again. 'You never approved, did you?'

'I approve of saving people.' It had been a treasured moment when he'd discussed The League's formation with her before anybody else. 'I just think if the French peasants had been saved from starvation, there needn't have been a revolution in the first place.'

'I didn't *know* any bloody peasants.'

Typical, she thought. Politics meant nothing to him, only people. He's like Ma in that. If he'd met a family of French destitutes, they'd have been made rich within the minute; he just hadn't met any. There had been no destitutes at Versailles, whence he'd been sent in '88 as an unofficial British ambassador to make trade agreements with Louis XVI's officials. It was to save his acquaintances there that The League had been formed.

'There's talk of rescuing some French dentist,' she said, doubtfully.

He smiled, showing good teeth of which one in front was missing a small diagonal chip, benefit of the Eton Wall Game. 'Ah, that's Boy Blanchard's private enterprise, nothin' to do with me. Boy shouldn't have much trouble gettin' him out, the fella's not in any danger I gather. Even Robespierre don't object to a good tooth-puller. But our Frogs want him rescued and Boy's keen—has a lot of trouble with his toothy-pegs, has Boy.'

She thought that risking one's head was possibly a drastic way of seeking a cure for toothache, but it wasn't her business.

There was a footman at the door. 'Her ladyship's compliments, my lord, and she wants you to begin the toasts.'

'I'll be there in a minute.' He took a puff of his cigar and settled himself on the horse. 'What is it, Pip?'

'Andrew, I want forged papers for a friend of mine. He's hiding somewhere in Paris. If I can send a *certificat de civisme* to his wife she can give it to him and he can travel to the coast.'

'Who is it?'

She said, reluctantly: 'It's Condorcet.'

Cigar smoke streamed from his lips under pressure. 'Phew. Our revolutionary ex-Marquis, eh?'

She prepared to fight. 'He's a great man and a great friend.'

'Don't say he ain't, don't say he ain't.' Lord Ffoulkes's hands went up in mock surrender. 'But you certainly pick 'em, Pip, old thing. He may be in hiding from Robespierre but he'll have to take cover from our noble Froggies if he gets over here. They tend to spit when his name's mentioned.'

'Do I get the *certificat* or don't I?'

''Course you do. Always rather liked him when I met him. Didn't understand a word he said, him bein' an intellectual. But he's a decent enough fella, I thought, despite his damn politics. How'll you get the papers to him? Won't be easy.'

'His wife sent me this letter.' She took Sophie's letter from her pocket, less in confirmation than to show him how stained and battered it was. 'She's got a friend whose brother drives the diligence that goes between Paris and Caen and he took it to Gruchy and they gave it to one of Ma's smugglers to bring over. I can send the *certificat* by the same route. If Nicolas can reach Gruchy, Jan Gurney will carry him back across the Channel on one of his trips.'

'That missus and her smugglers . . .' He shook his head in amused wonderment at Makepeace, then sobered. 'When did Mme Condorcet send the letter?'

'Two and a half weeks ago.'

'Things could have changed, old dear. Can't hide long in Paris nowadays; too many informers. You have to reckon he's been discovered by now.'

She had indeed reckoned it; since the letter had arrived this morning she'd reckoned that every day, every minute of Nicolas's concealment in some Paris cellar, Sophie had worried her husband would be found.

'I have to try.' she said. 'They were so good to me when I stayed with them and Sophie's in great distress for him. She's scraping a living for herself and their little girl in Paris by painting portraits.'

'Her Ladyship is getting restive, my lord.'

'I'm coming, dammit.' Lord Ffoulkes hoisted himself off the wooden horse and crossed to the desk to stub out his cigar in the hands of a bronze Echo. 'Stay here and I'll send Blanchard in—he organizes the forgers. A *certificat* shouldn't take more than a day or two.'

'Thank you, Andrew.'

When he'd gone, she walked across to the desk where the statuette held a still-smouldering cigar in bronze hands stretched beseechingly toward an invisible Narcissus. Philippa picked up the stub, crossed to the fireplace and threw it into the grate before returning to wipe the Echo's blackened palms tenderly with her handkerchief. 'Show some pride, woman,' she told it. 'He's never going to love you.'

Next to Echo was a turnip; he was experimenting with turnip-growing at his estate in the Fens. Papers concerned with his many projects leaned untidily against the model of a new village he was building for his workers in Kent, putting them on higher, healthier ground—a note to himself stuck out of one of the chimneys: 'Mem: Mrs B don't like thatch.'

She made herself sit down in a chair by the fireplace so that she would not be tempted to tidy it all up for him. 'Bedlam's full of ti-diers,' he'd told her once.

The library smelled of him: cigars, his books—of which she'd read more than he had—a tin of liniment left open on a Benares table, two glasses containing dregs of malt whisky on top of his drinks cupboard . . .

She breathed it in. So far, Félicie's scent had not penetrated but it wouldn't be long before her embroideries and sachets would dominate the room.

At the moment, pride of place was still given to his mother, a touching portrait done while she was pregnant; whether he'd meant to or not, Reynolds had caught her frailty, as if he'd known the energetic baby she was expecting would literally take the life out of her.

All the women Andrew had fallen in love with had resembled this portrait of the mother he'd never known; he'd made Philippa his confidante and gone to her with his woes or happiness over this or that wispy blond maiden whose fragility had attracted him. She'd listened without flinching, like the Spartan boy enduring the fox gnawing at his vitals.

His first wife had possessed the same quality as his mother and had come to the same end. Félicie, with her pale skin and hair, her small bones, was yet another in the line, though, Philippa thought, there was an element of steel to the Frenchwoman that the others had lacked.

'God send there is,' she prayed in sudden, desperate contrition. 'Lord save me from the sin of waiting for another of his wives to die. Let there be a baby and let them all live happily ever after. I mean it, Lord.' She did mean it, but because her conscience was as honest as her mother's, she added: 'He wouldn't marry me anyway, I'm too hard and brown.'

It would have surprised even the intimates of the small, collected figure sitting in the large library chair to know that Philippa regarded herself as analogous to a coconut. During her childhood in America, her Aunt Susan had once shown her one that had made its way to Boston and had explained that, when young and green, the things were awash with a liquid like fermenting milk.

Even then Philippa was aware that very few of the people she loved returned her affection with the passion with which she wanted to extend it; Aunt Susan perhaps; Betty, her nurse, certainly, but not her mother.

When Makepeace had given her, then aged seven, the choice of staying in England or sailing to Boston with Aunt Susan, Philippa had seen the offer as betrayal. The child had considered that if her mother loved her with the intensity with which she loved her mother, the idea of their parting—which had extended into years— was a suggestion that could not have been made.

It had always been part of her nature to hide any hurt, either physical or mental, a legacy from the father who had died days before she was born; a father who, in turn, had inherited it from a long line of Dapifers who had cultivated English sangfroid to an almost ludicrous degree.

So it had seemed good to little Philippa to hide pain by inflicting it and telling her mother, with apparent composure, that she chose Aunt Susan and America.

Just as it had seemed good to twenty-six-year-old Philippa to accept Stephen Heilbron as a husband within hours of hearing that Andrew Ffoulkes had taken a wife.

She realized she hadn't told Ffoulkes that she and Heilbron were engaged and wondered if it was because there hadn't been time or if she hadn't wanted to, and if so, why.

Oh, most definitely, she was a coconut. Philippa saw her exterior as brownish, unattractive and impermeable and thanked her God that it gave no indication of the love, the tenderness for creatures as hurt as she was, the horror with which she regarded the world's wrong-headedness, the tears which, if she wasn't Philippa Dapifer, she could even now shed in fellow feeling for a forlorn statuette, the raging jealousy, the bad language, the whole boiling of pitching, shuddering, emotions that seethed through every organ of her interior being.

And she knew that, had she been capable of showing Andrew Ffoulkes all or any of these passions, he might not now be married to that aristocratic bit of French flummery but be wed instead to Philippa Dapifer, who would suit him much better.

A ridiculous fruit, the coconut.

'Lord Ffoulkes said you wished to see me, Miss Dapifer.'

She stood up. Before she'd met Blanchard, and knowing the esteem in which Andrew held him, she'd asked what he was like. 'Imagine a Machiavelli that plays cricket,' Andrew had said, 'and you've got Boy Blanchard.'

The description was just; the Italianate beauty of an Elizabethan courtier, a Raleigh or an Essex, combined oddly with the breeziness of an Old Etonian. In fact, he was Ascendancy Irish on his father's side, though his early childhood had been spent in France with his mother. His spoken French was that of Paris; the others, Francophiles though they were, spoke fluently but with an accent that, fortunately, the critical Parisians put down as belonging to the Languedoc.

For Andrew's sake, Makepeace had often included the young Blanchard as her guest during the boys' holidays but hadn't liked him much; she was always at a loss with subtle minds. 'A schemer,' she'd called him.

Philippa, who'd seen less of him and for whom he was The League member she knew least, had wondered if this was pique on her mother's part, or competitiveness for the ruling place in Andrew's heart, though this was uncharacteristic; Makepeace had always reckoned that love couldn't be rationed and there was enough for everybody.

Anyway, Makepeace had denied it. 'I ain't jealous of him, he's jealous of me. He's jealous of everything Andrew has.' Which had seemed equally unlikely; for there was no denying Blanchard's ease and popularity with his friends. Better-read than they were, with only his baronetcy to set against the others' peerages, with less money and fewer estates, they nevertheless deferred to his cleverness and included him in every venture. Andrew teased him unceasingly and called him 'Reynard.'

'Sir Boy . . .' As always she found the address awkward; to christen one's son 'boy' argued indifferent parents.

He interrupted to beg her to sit down and took a chair opposite hers. She found that she had gained his interest as never before. While she explained that she wanted papers for a friend, she felt him trying to assess her with a care she was unused to from men and very few women.

She was dismayed to see it resulted in a sympathy he might have extended to a stricken warrior—one who'd fought on the other side, though what battle they had previously been engaged in she wasn't sure. He was being kind.

She reminded herself that this man had trouble with his teeth—it was the most reassuring thing she knew about him. His lips stayed over them, even when he smiled.

'Delighted to be of service in plucking another brand from the burning,' he said. 'What's a little forgery among friends?' He got up to seat himself at Andrew's desk, rummaging in its drawer for paper. He dipped a quill into the inkwell, keeping it poised. 'What name shall he travel under?'

'Oh, I don't know,' she said, 'Something middle-aged and respectable.'

'Let us say . . . hmm . . . Auguste Bourrelier. It breathes respectability, not to say bulk. I hope your friend is rotund. But if he has been in hiding these weeks, I suppose that's unlikely. Is one to be vouchsafed his real name?'

She was reluctant to give it. Andrew obviously hadn't mentioned it to him.

Blanchard was watching her. 'It would help to know his identity,' he said, gently. 'Perhaps The League can be of assistance to him.'

'Condorcet,' she mumbled.

Blanchard lowered the pen. 'The *Marquis* de Condorcet?'

She met his eyes. 'He and his wife are good friends of mine.'

He leaned back in the chair. 'And were good friends of the Revolution, I believe.'

Philippa said nothing.

'Which has now turned on them,' he added.

'Nicolas refused to vote for King Louis's execution,' she said in explanation.

'How good of him. Nevertheless, I understand the Marquis previously played a large part in His Majesty's overthrow.'

She was becoming angry, as she always did when she heard the Revolution's founders villified. *Where were you when famine was decimating France? You saw it, you lived there with a nobility that not only didn't care but didn't notice. How many men and women did you rescue from death then?*

She gently reminded him of his place. 'Lord Ffoulkes sees no reason to deny him a *certificat* on that account.'

He was drawing the quill's feather down his long cheek. 'Lord Ffoulkes is an amiable man.' Then he surprised her. 'I shan't, either.'

He scribbled something on the tablet. 'Memo to forger—one *certificat de civisme* in the name of, what did we say, Auguste Bourrelier?'

'I am grateful.' Suddenly she was tired, as if the two of them had been physically fighting.

'*Je vous en prie.*' He folded the paper as he stood up and tucked it in his cuff. 'It may take a little time, of course, but you should have it in a week or two.'

Shocked, she got up. 'There are no weeks to spare. Andrew said it would only take a day or so.'

'Yes, I have yet to inform Lord Ffoulkes of a recent reversal. Our counterfeiter has hurt his forging hand. Naughty man, an injury from beating his wife somewhat too vigorously I understand. He assures me the sprain will be mended within the month.'

Sophie. *Sophie*. She kept her face expressionless. 'Is there nobody else you might use?'

He smiled. 'Contrary to opinion, Miss Dapifer, my acquaintance with the criminal classes is limited.'

Ma was right, she thought; *she never liked you*. She allowed herself a lunge. 'Is that not unfortunate for your French dentist? How will your poor teeth fare now?'

She'd scored a hit; he was less amused than he had been. 'Ah, yes, the Froggy tooth-puller. Luckily, his papers were completed before the forger fell out with his wife. Never mind, I am sure the good Marquis will be attended to before the month is out.' He bowed. 'Miss Dapifer.'

'Sir Boy.'

But it was her blood left on the floor.

Stephen Heilbron found her standing in the middle of it. 'My dear, your mother is asking for you. What is the matter?'

She was in Paris, in a cellar; she could hear the approaching footsteps of National Guardsmen. 'I'm sorry, Stephen?'

He sat her down in the chair by the fireplace and took the one Blanchard had occupied. 'Tell me what's wrong.'

She stared at him; confidences were foreign to her. In the firelight his face was not unlike that opposite hers minutes before, dark and aquiline, both of an age, but whereas Blanchard's had been careless, her fiancé's was careworn, the Devil obviously having more concern for his followers' complexion than God had.

I have to learn to talk to him, she thought. *We must share things.*

What he wanted from her was friendship, comfort, devotion to his cause, absolute loyalty, not least her fortune, all of which she was happy to give him. Her own character would be a casualty, of course; his personality was such that it robbed other people of theirs but, again, that was a gift she could easily render in recompense for not loving him as her mother had loved her father.

Her return would lie in being useful to a man who would one day abolish the greatest evil under the sun. And the knowledge that Andrew Ffoulkes would never know he had wounded her almost to death.

She must not shortchange this wonderful man; theirs could at least be a meeting of minds, in which case she had to open hers to him.

So she told him—she was so unused to explaining her thinking and motives that it took effort.

He was astonished by her, as if he hadn't accounted for her having a life before she met him. Nor had he known there was such a thing as The League; he was both surprised and pleased. 'Christian work,' he said.

'Apparently, Sir Boy imposes limits to its Christianity,' she said. 'He is not prepared to save those who do not agree with him.'

'Condorcet,' he said. 'Condorcet. Where do I know the name from? And you are friends with this man?'

'Yes. I spent four summers in France with him and his wife. Busy as he was, he was good enough to give time to my mathematical studies. In '91, his wife and daughter came to England to stay with Mama and me.'

'Mathematical studies?'

'I am interested in mathematics,' she told him.

'How very unusual.' She watched him turning the pieces of the jigsaw to make them fit. '*Condorcet*. Philippa my dear, are we talking of Condorcet the *Encyclopédiste*?'

'Yes,' she said.

He sat back, his elbows on the arms of the chair, clasping his hands so that his mouth rested on them while he thought.

Philippa waited.

'A revolutionary,' he said, without looking up.

'And a republican. Yes.'

'A member of the National Assembly.'

'Yes.' She went on waiting.

'An atheist.'

There it was. 'But a great humanist, Stephen.'

'A contradiction in terms, my dear. And this is the man you wish to see escape from a predicament that was much of his making. You would see him brought to England.'

'Yes.'

He got up and walked around the room, while she watched him, his hands behind his back

He had never approved of the Revolution in France, even when it was young and fresh and Englishmen and woman less large-hearted than himself had been flocking excitedly across the Channel to witness the most radical experiment in history. He hadn't sought her opinion of it, presumably believing it to be the same as his own.

Blame Makepeace Dapifer Hedley, she thought.

Not that her mother advocated revolution; she had suffered too much from both sides during America's fight for independence, as had Philippa herself. 'Causes kill people,' she'd always said. But during a life that had seesawed between poverty and riches she had discovered both conditions to possess an equal share of saints and sinners, and that class divisions were a nonsense. In Makepeace's book, so was patriotism. People—individuals—mattered, not countries.

Perhaps now was not the moment to mention that, during the war between the United States and England, Makepeace had helped American prisoners of war to escape from England via her smugglers. She had not felt she was betraying her adopted country by doing it; the men were suffering, *ergo* they ought to go home.

It was her mother's love of freedom for the individual that Philippa had inherited. With gratitude.

Stephen, though, only loved God. She thought God frightened him somewhat; he was haunted by the judgment to be passed upon him when he died. It was as if he were one of England's prefects squirming with shame under God's schoolmasterly eye at the antics of a class for which he had responsibility.

The common people's disregard for Sunday worship, any worship, the drunkenness, crime and prostitution of the streets filled him with as much shame as if they were his family's. He didn't see them as the outcome of demeaning poverty, like Makepeace and Philippa did, but thought they could be cured by suppressing licentiousness, 'which is the parent of every species of vice.'

God had told him to free the slaves and that would be done though it killed him. But God had said nothing about dividing property equally between rich and poor—an idea he regarded as born out of madness. Liberty, equality, fraternity would be found in Heaven and not before.

'The Almighty has set before me two great objects,' he'd told her once, 'the suppression of the slave trade and the reformation of morals.' Sometimes she didn't know which he wanted most.

Condorcet, who called God a superstition . . . Condorcet, the advocate of women's rights, of divorce, who'd helped to pull down a king in order to set up a people . . . Condorcet was Stephen Heilbron's nightmare.

A hand came to rest on her shoulder. 'I don't know any forgers, either,' he said. 'I wish I did.'

A sob came up from her chest. *I was right to accept him.*

He sat down opposite her again. 'I shall speak to Blanchard,' he said. 'But if he is telling the truth and no counterfeit papers can be produced immediately, there's little for us to do but leave the fate of your friend in God's hands. Isn't that so?'

'I suppose it is.'

'Philippa?'

She looked up. 'Yes, Stephen?'

He's reassessed me, she thought. His face was as loving as ever but there was disappointment there; he had metaphorically shouldered her—she'd become a burden, more interesting, perhaps, but a burden that he must either bear or lighten.

'Philippa, if eventually we do get those papers and send them off to France and Condorcet comes to England, that must be the end of it. Consorting with an atheist is something I could not endure my wife to do. You see that?'

She nodded. She saw that.

'Then I'll pay for the letter's stamp.' He clasped her hand and pulled her to her feet. 'Shall we go and shout at the bandsmen until they play a minuet for us?'

She walked out of the room with her hand on his arm.

Chapter Three

THE toasts were still in process—the French had taken them over. Glasses had been raised to His Majesty King George III.

To King Louis XVII in whatever darkness and filth the revolutionary *canaille* had cast the poor little boy.

To the remaining Bourbons.

To Andrew and Félicie, with gratitude for their hospitality.

To Makepeace, happy birthday.

To the emigré regiments aimlessly crumbling on the banks of the Rhine as they waited for the rest of the world to take up arms against the Revolution.

To whomsoever, whatsoever would enable them to keep on downing Lord Ffoulkes's champagne in the warmth and reminiscent brilliance of Lord Ffoulkes's house for a bit longer.

'We are *now* on the Empress of Russia,' Makepeace said distinctly as Philippa and Heilbron joined her.

She'd been disappointed in her little Marquis who, maudlin with homesickness and liquor, had got up on a chair to declaim a poem to his dead King:

> *'Son trône est usurpé mais sa vertu lui reste*
> *La mort, O ma patrie, à toi seule est funest . . .'*

There'd been several verses.

A weeping abbé clutched Makepeace's arm for mental and

physical support. 'What did these generous masters do that the French people so cruelly massacre them every day on altars dressed by regicides?'

'They didn't feed 'em,' Makepeace snapped.

Quickly, Heilbron signaled to a footman to fetch their cloaks. 'Philippa, if you'll take your mother into the hall, I'll go and have a word with Blanchard. Where's Deedes?'

Philippa ushered Makepeace and a reluctant Jenny towards the door. 'Are we going home? I'm booked for another waltz,' Jenny said.

'Ma's getting ugly,' Philippa told her.

They stood behind one of the marble pillars to shelter them-selves from the cold admitted by the open front doors. Outside in the square a gathering of local vagrants stood around flaming tar barrels and toasted in ale 'Good old Ffoulksy who don't never forget us.'

The three women acknowledged the bow of a departing young Frenchman who was taking his pregnant wife home. At the steps he shouted for his carriage: 'James, James,' and tutted, 'Where *is* the man?' He helped his wife down to the street and disappeared into the night with her, still shouting.

'That's a naughty coachman,' Jenny said.

'There isn't a coach,' Philippa explained.

'Oh? *Oh*. Poor things. Can't we ask Sanders to take them home? The lady shouldn't have to walk in her condition.'

'Tried that once,' Makepeace said. 'Humiliated 'em. Stiff-necked buggers, all of them.'

Reverend Deedes joined them, still put out by the waltzing. 'And I fear we have lost Lord Malthrop. Lord Admiral Rodney intervened in our discussion and told him that he'd never heard of any negro being ill-treated in the West Indies.'

Philippa found Andrew Ffoulkes beside her. 'You didn't tell me,' he said; he was looking at her oddly.

'Tell you what?'

'Heilbron. I came on him talking to Blanchard—he says you and he are engaged.'

'Yes,' she said.

'You didn't tell me.'

She smiled. 'You've had other matters to concern you.'

'Well, but . . .' He recovered himself. 'As your godfather . . . What about it, missus, isn't she supposed to get her godfather's permission? Anyway, he's a fine fellow.'

Heilbron had come up and Lord Ffoulkes pumped his hand. 'My congratulations, sir. You have plucked the finest rose in England's garden.'

'That's my opinion as well, sir.'

It was awful. The footman was taking an age with their cloaks, the good-byes took another. At the bottom of the steps Heilbron bade her good night and kissed her hand. For a moment, she thought he was going to kiss her on the lips but he leaned close so that he could whisper: 'Blanchard has convinced me he is telling the truth about the forger. I fear there is nothing to do but wait.' She was aware of Andrew standing above them in the doorway. Both men remained where they were while the closed carriage that was to take her, Jenny, Makepeace and Reverend Deedes back to Chelsea circled the square and headed for Piccadilly.

Damn you. Did you imagine I was always going to be an old maid? An elderly spinster aunt to your children?

She just hadn't thought he would be so . . . so disturbed.

On the journey back, the silence of his companions was filled by the Reverend Deedes's opinion of the ball and the intransigence of the great men who had resisted his and Heilbron's arguments against slavery. His hearers were as devoted to abolition as he was but he continued to address them as if they, as well as the noble lords, needed persuasion.

After a while, Makepeace reached into the rack where she kept a loaded pistol—on quiet nights highwaymen sometimes abandoned their usual haunt in Kensington to attack the homegoers of Chelsea. She laid it meaningfully across her knee but it didn't stop him.

The Watch was out in the village. As Sanders brought the carriage to a halt outside Deedes's house, bobbing lanterns came up to it.

'We're after fugitives from Lunnon, Mr Deedes. Evenin' Mrs Hedley, Miss Hedley, young mistress.'

'What fugitives, Pocock?'

'Don't rightly know, ma'am. Two of 'em. Wanted bad, seems. There's the government's own constables here to gee us up.'

Pocock was pushed aside and another lantern was held up at the carriage interior while its owner inspected their faces. Deedes reached for the door handle to let himself out. 'As you can see, fellow, there are no fugitives in here. Are these men dangerous? Will the ladies be safe to go on? Had I not better accompany them home?'

'No need,' Makepeace said quickly.

The government lantern bearer swung his light once more from Mr Deedes and Makepeace and decided the man was more in need of protection. 'They'll be all right. I see their driver's armed. Where d'you live, ma'am?'

'Reach House. Along the river.'

'We'll follow you down, then. Reckon they'll make for the Thames but they ain't violent, not so's I've heard.'

'What have they done?'

'Sedition,' the man said, shortly. He shouted at Sanders: 'Drive on, but go slow.' They heard his saddle creak as he climbed onto his horse.

The carriage turned away and the village smells of horse manure, thatch and the Bun Shop, where Mrs Hand was already mixing her dough, were overwhelmed by that of the Thames, sweeter here than farther down and always better at high tide than any other time. Jenny let down her window and sniffed joyfully at the bitter, misty air. 'Oh, Ma, waltzes and fugitives in one night. This is life.'

Makepeace was reflective. 'Sedition,' she said.

Philippa asked, 'Do you think it's John Beasley, Ma?'

'I do. Where else does he run when he's in trouble?'

Jenny turned. 'Mr Beasley? I remember him. Oh dear, will he bring the law on us?'

'Probably,' Makepeace said, bitterly. 'I'll give him sedition.'

John Beasley, printer, publisher, anarchist and thorn in the flesh of both Tory and Whig governments, had been a frequent visitor to her house and its mine in the days when Makepeace and Andra had lived in the northeast but his friendship with Makepeace went back to the time of her first marriage—a choppy relationship that had nevertheless withstood the years.

'He wanted Sally and me to raise the school against Miss Hardcastle,' Jenny recollected, with awe. 'He said she was teaching us old wives' tales and should be ducked for garbling history.'

'He would,' Makepeace said.

'It may not be him,' said Philippa.

But, more than likely, it was; else why should a fugitive from London make for the Thames at Chelsea when he had all the city's docks to get away in? And Beasley was a publisher of Tom Paine's *The Rights of Man*, which Prime Minister Pitt, alarmed that England might go the way of France, had recently caused to be proclaimed seditious. Already, at Beasley's request, Makepeace had allowed her smugglers to take a group of his friends to France—all of them political offenders escaping imprisonment . . .

And will do again, Philippa thought, watching Makepeace's shape square its shoulders in the darkness. *Does she know how dangerous it is?*

Not only was the law coming down heavily against dissent but the savagery of the Terror had fuelled the ordinary Englishman's old antagonism against France. The very word 'reform' now suggested nasty, violent and, above all, foreign revolution so that, ironically, those who mouthed it were having their homes burned down while magistrates stood by and watched.

Only two nights ago a mob had broken the windows of a house in Cheyne Walk that belonged to a certain Mr Scott, writer of mild pamphlets advocating universal suffrage. Watching from the safety of their gatehouse, the women had listened to the crack of glass and the howls of 'No Popery' from the attackers.

'What's Popery got to do with it?' Jenny had asked, bewildered.

'I think they're unaware the Revolution abolished it,' Philippa told her.

Compared with some riots, that one had been restrained, the rioters having been dispersed by the cold more quickly than by the Watch. The Scott family had been frightened, no more. But if it were known that one of Mr Pitt's despised 'Jacobins' was taking refuge in Makepeace's house . . .

Why does it happen to her? Philippa wondered at a woman who'd been born to trouble as the sparks fly upward. She certainly didn't seek it, merely waded unseeingly into it. Her original problem in Boston, which had led to all the rest, had only occurred because she'd dragged Philippa's father from the harbor whence American rioters had thrown him for being English and, therefore, a representative of their oppressors.

That act of humanity had cost her a home and a country and gained her a husband, none of which had been looked for, as had none of the other predicaments into which she had become entangled and, eventually, triumphed over.

It occurred to Philippa, belatedly, that these things happened because her mother was a victim, not of fate, but of her own character. Another woman might have lacked the courage and capability to fish Sir Philip Dapifer out of Boston Harbor, might not have survived the mental and economic devastation of his later death, might not have had the business acumen to exploit the luck which had subsequently provided her with a piece of ground containing coal. Another woman would not have resorted to using Devonian smugglers to ferry abroad escaping Americans for whom she was sorry, nor would another woman have found those same smugglers so congenial that she joined them in their enterprise.

It's her breadth of friendship, Philippa decided. Makepeace was blind to class and liked or disliked people according to their character. Middle-class ladies were careful to restrict their acquaintances to people of their own status and outlook; they would shun someone as gauche and incendiary as John Beasley, refusing to recognize his innate kindness and loyalty. The fact that, so far, they didn't also shun Makepeace was because she was rich and now accepted by a society above their own, among the headstrong, titled families of England where another eccentric more or less passed unnoticed.

But Ma's not eccentric, Philippa thought, *she's just . . . wider than anyone else.*

And here we go again. It would not occur to her to be cautious, either on her own behalf, or mine, or Jenny's. If the hunted man out there in the cold is John Beasley, she will take him in. She may take him in even if it isn't. What would Stephen say?

There was no censure in any of this; Philippa's own shoulders had become as square as her mother's. Uncle John Beasley's right to publish a democratic opinion not only went without saying, it didn't even need deliberation. But it was a nuisance that it might get them all hanged.

Makepeace reached up and opened the flap in the carriage front that allowed communication with the driver. 'How many horsemen behind us, Sanders?'

'Four.' Sanders was keeping his voice low. 'Missus?'

'Yes?'

'Are they after who I think they're after?'

'Maybe.'

They could hear his hiss of resignation over the noise of the churning carriage wheels; Sanders and Beasley were well acquainted.

It was cold to have the windows down but Philippa and Jenny peered out of the one facing the river while Makepeace kept watch on the landward side. Despite the advance of London, this was still deep country. Once they'd passed Chelsea Hospital and the red brick terrace of Cheyne Walk, they were among reeds, meadows and copses interrupted here and there by the drives to large, aloof houses. 'Plenty of places to hide,' said Jenny.

'He'll keep to the road,' Makepeace said. 'He's no countryman, our Beasley.'

There was a moon, the mist giving its light the texture of gauze so that objects were indistinct except when lit to the front by the carriage lamps and, to the rear, by the horsemen's poled lanterns, both sending a wavering, passing light on the erratic levee, picking out mooring posts, flashing on water and boats upturned like stranded seals on the slipways.

On Makepeace's side a badger that had been trotting along the side of the road turned away from the sudden glare, showing a disgruntled, striped backside as it disappeared into undergrowth.

They began to breathe more easily. Reach House was just ahead. If that was where the fugitives were making for, they were either already there or would turn up when the lawmen had gone.

Makepeace had chosen somewhere to live that was secluded and had no reminders of the past yet would allow Philippa access to London society. She was never happy unless she overlooked water, so she'd picked a house in an area once favored by distinguished men and women who had also valued the river, good air and privacy. Philippa's researches into the history of this part of Chelsea had uncovered both Anne of Cleves and Katherine Parr managing to survive their marriages to Henry VIII nearby. 'Though I fear Sir Thomas More—his house is to our north—was less fortunate,' she'd told her mother.

'What's happened to him, then?' Anything that occurred before the Mayflower set off for the New World fell through Makepeace's grasp of history.

The house was understaffed by the standards of the locality since Makepeace only wanted servants around her that she knew and liked and, in any case, preferred to wait on herself much of the time—a preference that might prove a blessing tonight. Apart from the vegetable garden and frontage, the grounds had none of the manicured neatness of its neighbors and its park was returning to wilderness.

Philippa loved it. It was a kind house; she liked to imagine that Cleves, Parr and More, walking by the riverside, had watched workmen building it for the then Marquis of Berkeley. True, the men hadn't built it very well because its middle had fallen down, leaving only one tower, but its replacement by bowed, Queen Anne rose-colored brick gave the house an architectural irregularity that added an apparent contentment, like a plump wife and tall husband posing together for a portrait.

Joining Makepeace at the right-hand window, she saw the flat, slated roof of their gatehouse a little way off between the trees, a remnant of the old house where Sanders and Hildy now occupied the apartment above its narrow arch.

The carriage jerked suddenly as Sanders pulled the horses from a trot to a walk. Makepeace reached for the flap. 'What is it, Sanders?'

'Spotted 'em, missus. Two figures, just nipped inside our archway.'

There was no outcry from the horsemen behind them; only Sanders had seen what he'd seen. But from the gatehouse to the house lay a carriageway circling a large lawn, all of it open. If the constables followed them in, the fugitives would be caught in their lights as well as those from the front windows of the house.

Philippa met her mother's eyes. 'Block the archway,' she murmured.

Makepeace nodded. 'Stop in the archway, Sanders. Block it.'

'Right y'are, missus.'

There was no time to consult, they were turning in, had stopped. 'Open your door,' Makepeace said, opening hers until its jamb scraped the gatehouse wall. 'You two get out your side, Jenny stand, Pippy get 'em in.' She leaned from the angled window and raised her voice. 'Safe home now, lads, thank you.'

'Reckon us'll see you up to the house,' the leading constable said.

Philippa pushed Jenny out. 'Stay there.' Jenny's skirts would cover the gap between the carriage door and the ground should any of the lawmen dismount and be in a position to look through it. She flattened herself, squeezed past and came out onto the drive.

And there they were; two shapes caught in Sanders's lamps, crouched and blinking in the center of the lawn like a couple of hideous ornaments. She began gesticulating for them to run towards her but they were confused and she had to go to them. 'Get in the carriage and lie down. Quickly.'

She could hear her mother bantering with the men in the road-way, offering them liquid refreshment, which, presumably, was what they'd delayed for in the first place. She teased them. 'But I suppose you ain't allowed to drink on duty.'

By the time the denials occasioned by that remark had died down, Beasley and his companion had wormed their way into the bottom of the carriage. Philippa shut the door on them.

'How's that wheel now, Sanders?' Makepeace called.

'Stay on a bit longer, I reckon.'

'Get on then.'

Philippa took her half sister's arm and together they walked up the drive as if enjoying the night's freezing air, slowing down the cavalcade coming politely behind them.

Hildy had heard their approach and opened the front door on to the steps where Makepeace was already alighting and giving orders. 'Off to the coach house with you, Sanders, and see to that wheel. Ale for four, Hildy. You lads can come into the hall for your drink, but take your damn boots off.'

Nobody paid attention to Philippa and Jenny as they followed the carriage around to the side of the house where an arch in the wall led to the coach and stable yard.

Jenny was patting her heart. 'I nearly swooned. How did you know what to do?'

'Practice. Living with Ma you get used to it.'

'That you do,' Sanders said.

Both exaggerated for old-times' sake—apart from aiding the group of Beasley's friends who'd wanted to escape to France, Make-peace had spent the last five years in law-abiding grief.

Beasley and his companion were too tired and too cold to talk. Stumbling, they followed Jenny and Philippa around to the kitchen yard and in through the back door. The large kitchen was empty and lit only by the glow of the fire banked down for the night. Beside it, a kettle stood on a trivet. A cloth covered half a goose and some ham. The women immediately started preparing food.

The man with Beasley sat down at the table and put his head on it.

Beasley slouched in a corner. 'You've grown a fine pair of bubbies since I saw you last,' he said to Jenny. Jenny blushed.

'Don't you start that,' Philippa told him. He was especially graceless when frightened, but if he'd been scared so had she and Jenny.

Makepeace came in from the hall passage, her fingers entwined through tankard handles. 'They've gone. Hildy's upstairs preparing the beds in the attic.' She looked without warmth at Beasley. 'Well?'

'Didn't know where else to go.'

'To hell would have been a good idea,' she told him. 'What is it this time?'

'Meet Tom Glossop,' Beasley said. 'He's a bookseller.'

Glossop raised his head and nodded, 'Ma'am,' before sprawling once more on the table.

'Bastards caught us in my print shop,' Beasley said. 'The place was stacked with *Rights of Man*. Glossop here was going to distribute them in the morning. Fanny next door heard 'em coming down the street and warned us. We got out through the back window. Been running all night. They raised the hue and cry and I swear they had forty after us down Piccadilly. I thought we'd given 'em the slip in Saint James's Park, but no. Couldn't even stop to piss.'

Reminded, he went outside and they heard the hiss of fluid spattering onto the stones of the yard.

Makepeace put down the tankards, went into the pantry and came out again with a bottle of rum. She found two beakers, half filled each with rum, poured in a dash of hot water, added a spoonful of butter from a crock, stirred in some treacle and put Glossop's unresisting hand round one of them. 'Here.'

'Thank you, ma'am.' He was a mild-looking little man, unshaven and with exhausted eyes, whose long run had left his attire surprisingly neat, apart from his boots and the loss of his hat. 'I don't know what the wife'll say.'

Beasley, when he came back in, looked considerably less healthy than his companion, but he always looked unhealthier than anybody. His face was white and shiny, like fishmeat, his coat wore the droppings of recent meals, his cravat was grubby and carelessly tied. It was Philippa's belief that any new clothes he purchased were immediately and deliberately soiled in some sort of protest against a society he despised; it seemed to give him satisfaction to be dirty, like a child smearing itself with porridge. It sent her mother mad. Yet he had gained and kept the friendship of men like Dr Johnson, Garrick and Joshua Reynolds.

All dead now, Philippa thought. *There's only Ma.*

'Sedition,' Makepeace said flatly.

'Reform,' snarled Beasley. 'Paine ain't out for violence, he just happens to think a system by which a mere eleven thousand people elect a majority in the Commons is so unrepresentative it needs changing. Silly old him. That ain't sedition. *Rights* ain't even anarchy, missus, it's just common sense.'

Makepeace wasn't arguing against it, she agreed with it, as did every person in the room; she merely resented having to cope with its consequences at three o'clock in the morning. 'So it's my poor smugglers again, is it? They ain't a ferry service.'

'You got Tom Paine away.'

'Paine, Paine . . .' The group she and Philippa had seen onto Jan Gurney's schooner at Babbs Cove had seemed amorphous in their mutual concern for their necks and their politics. '. . . was he the one with the carbuncles?'

Beasley sulked. 'He's a great man.'

'He's a great drinker,' Makepeace said. 'The bugger toped most of our profits that trip. Oh, get on and eat, and let me think.'

She left Jenny to serve the men and took Philippa into the hall. 'I'll have to go with them to Devon. They won't make it on their own, not even with Sanders driving. Every guard post and turnpike will be on the lookout for 'em.'

'Oh, Ma.'

Makepeace patted her daughter's extended hand. 'It's not that much. I was going to go down to Bristol to meet your Uncle Aaron next week in any case. It's just a matter of leaving earlier.'

'I wasn't thinking of the inconvenience, it's the danger.'

Makepeace shrugged. 'I'll talk my way through the stops, I've done it before.'

'I'll come, too; it will look more convincing if there are two women in the coach.'

'No. You stay here with Jenny. I need you to go bail if I end up in clink.'

Philippa realized that her mother looked better than she had for a long time; the despair had gone. It wasn't that Makepeace was enjoying the risk but there was a purpose to her that hadn't been evident since Andra died. We have to be useful, she and I, Philippa thought. Aloud, she said, 'Give my love to the Gurneys.'

Back in the kitchen, Mr Glossop was still wondering what his wife would think of all this. 'We were planning to go to America together,' he said.

'The ferry don't go that far,' Makepeace said. 'It's France or nothing.'

'You can go on from there,' Beasley told him. 'I'll see your Lizzie gets a passsage, Tom. She'll join you in Boston.'

Makepeace stared at him. 'Why? Where will you be?'

'Me? I'm staying.' She might have insulted him. 'Soon as I've seen Glossop's missus and told her what's to do, I'm giving myself up.' He looked around at their faces. 'Somebody's got to stand against the bastards.'

'They'll put you on trial,' Philippa protested.

'Certainly, they will.' In his glum way, he was looking forward to it. 'They'll say it's sedition. I'll say how can publishing a democratic tract be seditious? We'll see what an English jury makes of it.'

'They'll hang you, you silly bugger,' Makepeace said.

Beasley took an untidy bite of his bread and goosemeat. 'Let 'em.'

Makepeace pleaded, wasting her breath.

Philippa wondered if those who had been prepared to die for their beliefs, whose names sang down the ages, were as lumpish and grubby and stubborn and not a little pleased with themselves as this man. Were the great martyrs made of such stuff? *Yes*, she thought, *they probably were.*

And as brave, God protect him.

Tenderly, she filled up his tankard.

S TEPHEN arrived late the next morning. He had tramped the woods on his way down from London to pick holly and ivy and arranged them into a surprisingly attractive bouquet for her. 'Evergreen,' he said, kissing her, 'as our marriage will be.'

He said he'd called in on his mother in Mayfair to tell her the news.

'Was she pleased?'

'Yes.' He was always guarded when talking about his mother and had not yet suggested that Philippa meet her. 'She offered an emerald pendant of hers to be made into an engagement ring for you.'

'That's nice of her.'

'I suppose it was, but I refused. The token between us must be new—anyway, you are not an emerald person.'

She wondered what jewel he thought her to be but didn't ask; he was in a hurry. 'I have to take a meeting at noon.'

'So have I,' she said.

'Really? What meeting is that?'

She nearly said, 'A women's committee' but changed it at the last minute. 'Just a ladies' meeting.'

He nodded. 'Where's the missus?' He was looking towards the top of the staircase and she realized that John Beasley had chosen this moment to emerge from his bed.

Philippa said, 'She's gone to the West Country. She will be meeting my Uncle Aaron at Bristol.' It was more *supressio veri* than *suggestio falsi*; she didn't think her fiancé was yet ready to be apprised of Makepeace's smugglers—even less of what they would be smuggling.

She tried to lead the way into the morning room but Heilbron was fixed by the apparition on the stairs. She couldn't blame him; Beasley was wearing a blanket over one of Hildy's nightgowns, his hair straggled from under a tea cosy and unlaced boots flapped on his unstockinged feet.

'Stephen, may I present Mr Beasley. Uncle John, this is Mr Heilbron.'

Stephen bowed. 'Mr Beasley.'

Beasley mumbled, 'Ayoop,' or something like it and slouched off towards the kitchens.

'He's an old friend of Ma's,' Philippa said apologetically.

'Yes.'

They went into the morning room, which was full of the crystalline light of a sunny frosty morning.

'I love this room,' Stephen said. 'Simple grace, like you.'

It smelled of the apple logs burning palely in the grate and of lavender-scented beeswax. It possessed little in the way of style; Makepeace had none when it came to furnishings and had anyway been too desolate to bother. Philippa had gathered pieces more for her mother's comfort than their cohesion but their quality provided a certain unity. She had avoided clutter and the deep, reflective, dark shine of side tables, bookcases and a little walnut writing desk looked well against the matt white walls.

Only about the ceiling design had Makepeace expressed a view and Philippa had hired a skilled but somewhat horrified plasterer to execute it. If one looked carefully at the plasterwork it was to see that between the ribs spreading out from the cornices were the shapes of little coal wagons and that, instead of roses or mythical creatures, the bosses were decorated with pit ponies.

Andra's son by his first marriage now ran the mine for his stepmother but Makepeace was not ashamed to display to the world where her money came from.

Stephen had noticed it on his first visit and approved—it was what Philippa had immediately liked about him, that he wasn't one of those who looked down on trade.

He went to the long windows overlooking a garden that had been outlined in frost as if by sparkling chalk. 'I wish we could go for a walk,' he said. 'I wish we had time.' He turned round. 'We need to know each other better, we need to plan our wedding.'

'We can go tomorrow,' she said.

'Ah, but we can't. I'm bound for Liverpool so that I can get the report prepared for the House of Commons. I shan't be back for at least eight days. Do you mind?'

'Only that you may be hurt.' His activities were getting too well-known. When he'd been on the Bristol docks asking question and taking notes, the slave traders had given him a drubbing that broke one of his ribs.

'The real hurt is discovering the viciousness of man to man. God help us, Philippa, the chains, the manacles . . .'

She squeezed her eyes shut against the images. 'When you come back then.'

'Yes.' As if he was reluctant to go, or didn't know how to say goodbye, he began picking through a little pile of books left on the window seat. His face changed and he held one up. 'Do you read this?'

She peered at it. 'Mary Wollstonecraft? Yes, I've read it.'

'The woman leads an irregular life, Philippa. And anyway, she advocates revolution, a female Thomas Paine.'

'Not revolution, Stephen,' she said, gently, 'just equality.'

'And we see what that has led to in France.'

Keep calm, she told herself. Aloud, she said, 'France has at least abolished slavery, Stephen. You are fighting against the ownership of one human being by another. Miss Wollstonecraft merely points out that women are property, too.'

'How can you think that?' His face had regained the disappointment in her it had worn when she'd upheld Condorcet. If he were not the man he was, he would be showing anger.

This is for when we have time, she thought, *when I'm not angry.* She touched his hand. 'We can discuss these things when we take our walk.'

'Yes.' She'd reminded him of something. 'I was going to say . . . when we take that walk, perhaps it would be better if Marie Joséphine accompany us.'

Marie Joséphine was her French maid. 'A chaperone, do you mean?'

'Yes. I know your mother is unmindful of such matters but I think it would be better.'

She smiled. 'Stephen, are you afraid you might jump on me in the woods if we're alone?'

He laughed. 'I might. No, I just think it's up to people like us to be above reproach. There is too much laxity before marriage everywhere and if we don't restore some rectitude by our example, who will?'

'Very well.'

When she'd seen him out, she went back to the window seat to pile up the books he had scattered. Stubbornly, she put *A Vindication of the Rights of Women* at the top.

How could he not see the parallel? Once we're married, I shall have no right to my own money or my own children. He could turn me into the street to beg my living and I should have no recourse.

He wasn't that sort of man, thank God, but he *could*—and there were men who did.

Beasley came up behind her, chewing on a sausage. 'What you say his name was?'

'Heilbron, Stephen Heilbron.'

He grunted. 'One of those bloody hypocrites out to stop vice, ain't he?'

'And abolish the slave trade,' she said tartly. 'He's no hypocrite and I'm going to marry him.'

'More fool you.' He looked down to where her hand still rested on *The Rights of Women*. 'I bet he's overjoyed to see that in your library.'

She tucked the book at the bottom of the pile. Before she went, Makepeace had suggested Beasley stay at Reach House for a week in order to build up his strength for prison. It was going to be a long seven days.

'Met her once at one of Joe Johnson's dinners,' Beasley said. 'He publishes her. Tom Paine was there as well, that's who she got the idea from—*Rights of Man, Rights of Women*. He seemed to like her, so did Blake. Personally, I thought she was a bit fuckish.'

Philippa turned on him. 'Why do you say that? Is she living in sin? Did she dance on the table? Did she do anything at that dinner other than express an opinion?'

'No.'

He was taken aback but Philippa pursued him. 'Because my reading of history has led me to believe that any woman who is not content to sit by the fire and knit is immediately labeled a whore and a Jezebel. Not once, not *once*, when Miss Wollstonecraft's name is mentioned by a man have I heard anything but sexual denigration of her.'

He blinked at her. 'What's put the wind in your bellows?'

She had, she realized, displayed anger towards him when she had withheld it from all the other men who had thwarted her lately, which was unfair because he was the only one with whom she was sufficiently at ease to show it. 'Oh, never mind. And *why* are you wearing our tea cosy?'

'Keep me head warm. Hildy didn't give me a nightcap.' He finished his sausage, staring at her with calculation. 'If the bastards remand me in prison, I need somebody to write editorials for *The Passenger*. You'd better do it.'

'Write edi— I can't.'

The Passenger was Beasley's own weekly paper, a defiant little terrier of a publication that kept nipping at the government's backside. It had been suppressed more than once and its press destroyed, merely causing its proprietor to bring it out again at a different print shop.

'Why not? You're opinionated enough. One thousand words, scribble it down and take it to Inky Jones in Grub Street; he'll set it in type and Bob's your uncle. Don't need to sign it.'

'I couldn't possibly.' She'd never written for publication, and besides, Grub Street was an unsavory area, so Stephen wouldn't approve . . . What a strange man this was; slandering Mary Wollstonecraft with one breath, and in the next, offering his beloved editorial space to a woman's thinking as if it were an everyday thing to do. 'Could I?'

He shrugged.

'Grub Street,' she said, musing. 'Uncle John, by chance do you know any forgers?'

Chapter Four

Mindful of Stephen's regard for her respectability, Philippa took Marie Joséphine with her to the meeting, though on most occasions she was used to going about Chelsea on her own, the village itself being small and friendly and she now a well-known denizen of it.

In fact, with Marie Joséphine in tow she was subject to more embarrassment than if she had been alone since people, shopkeepers especially, braced themselves at the sight of the Frenchwoman as if glimpsing a hornet heading in their direction.

Passing the draper's, Marie Joséphine shook her fist at its proprietor who was in the doorway. 'I 'ave not forgot the cambric.' There'd been an outbreak of hostilities over a bolt of the stuff when Marie Joséphine discovered a miniscule fault in one edge of the weave and Mr Clark had unwisely said it didn't matter.

Mr Clark hadn't forgotten it, either. 'I *said* I was sorry,' he shouted after them.

The anticipation men showed on hearing the words 'French maid' was disappointed when they encountered Marie Joséphine, who was squat, dark, mustached and of evil temper.

Mistress and maid had met soon after the establishment of the Revolutionary government in France. Philippa was staying with the Condorcets who had moved into the Hôtel de Monnaie, the French mint, on Nicolas's appointment as minister of finance.

It was a time when, owing to years of Bourbon rule, countrymen and women were being forced to leave their homes and search for food and jobs in the big towns. Some eight thousand a year were migrating to an already overcrowded Paris and it had seemed to Philippa that a large proportion of them was being accommodated at the expense of the Condorcets in the vast and august halls of the Hôtel de Monnaie.

Sophie had converted one wing into a temporary hospital for mothers with their babies. Her husband, loathing the Church as he did, refused to allow a nun near the place, and the work had fallen on Sophie, Philippa and like-minded women, threatening at times to overwhelm them.

Among one set of new arrivals had been an ill-favoured woman clutching a bundle. 'See what you can do to help her,' Sophie had begged of Philippa. 'She won't let go of her baby and the poor mite is dead.'

The woman squatted in a corner with the baby clutched to her chest, not tragic, not defiant, not anything, merely looking at nothing, as if the crowded, noisy room were a quiet forest and she a wild animal in it, listening to the leaves fall.

Not knowing what to say and consequently saying nothing, Philippa cautiously lowered herself alongside the woman. After a while she stretched out her hand and cupped her palm around the tiny, cold skull and kept it there. Her arm was touching the woman's and it seemed to her that some small realization of the child's oblivion leeched from the mother's body into her own, slowly silting up, petrifying her as she stared into the Medusan eyes of the future. This is mother-love. How can they bear it? How shall I bear it if this happens to me?

An hour later, the woman looked at her and nodded, and they were able to take the baby to the Hôtel's chapel while Philippa went in search of a suitable coffin and a priest, her instinct telling her that, Revolution or no, the funeral must be in accordance with the rites of the Catholic church.

Evidently, the child, a little boy, was unbaptised and she had to resort to bribery to have him put in holy ground but eventually the interment was conducted by an indigent curé in the presence of the minister of finance in the graveyard of the deserted Convent des Récolettes nearby.

Marie Joséphine's surname was Mellot and she came from Poitu; apart from that she told them nothing about what had happened to her. Nor did they ask; the history of Paris's immigrant women was drearily uniform—they had either been raped on the road or had reached the capital unscathed, found poorly paid work as a maid, become pregnant, lost their job and been forced onto the streets in order to feed the child. Such babies as couldn't be cared for were left on the steps of convents and hospitals. It was reckoned that during Louis XVI's reign there were forty thousand new foundlings in France every year.

When it was time for Philippa to return to England, Marie Joséphine announced that she would accompany her. There was now nothing for her in France, she said. Philippa was lacking a personal maid at the time, her old one having been lost to marriage, and she, too, felt the bond that had been forged between them.

It was brave of them both but it worked out reasonably well. Marie Joséphine's insertion into Makepeace's household had stormy moments, especially with the cook, but the ferocity that characterized the Frenchwoman was applied to learning how to increase Philippa's comfort and woe to anyone who threatened it.

In the distance the clock of Chelsea parish church sounding midday carried frostily through the air as Marie Joséphine and the incurably punctual Philippa turned into Don Saltero's Curiosity Coffee House in Cheyne Walk.

Even when it was empty of customers, the downstairs always looked crowded; the walls were shelved with glass cases holding the curiosities that had made the place famous in the earlier part of the century, ancient firearms, stuffed exotic birds, relics from Jerusalem, Knights Templar dice, a petrified crab from China, a full-sized image of a cannibal. A pickled serpent that had attacked a ship's keel in the West Indies writhed across a ceiling studded with foreign coins between the dangling dancing shoes of Queen Elizabeth, a hummingbird's nest and other objects too darkened by tobacco smoke to be identifiable.

The café's great days were gone, as was Don Saltero, but it was still popular with the locals and the air was already full of the rustle of newspapers, conversation and the smell of coffee and mulled punch.

Mrs Hall, the don's granddaughter, escorted them up the creaky staircase to an upper room, lit a fire and brought them coffee. The room served as an overflow for the museum downstairs and Marie Joséphine, who was seeing it for the first time, circled it, clicking her tongue at the mummified head of an Egyptian, the Pope's infallible candle, the jaws of a wild boar that had starved to death by his tusks growing inwards . . .

Philippa stood at the window, looking across the river to the whitened Surrey hills and wondering how many members of the Chelsea Ladies' Charity for Foundlings would turn up.

England's record on caring for abandoned children was little better than France's and on her return to England in '89 Philippa had founded a local group to raise money for Thomas Coram's Foundlings Hospital in London. But the women she'd managed to attract to the cause had been of a caliber to recognize the deeper problem underlying the immediate need and, while raising funds, had applied their thinking to the desperation that caused a mother to abandon her child in the first place and, then, to the situation of women in society generally.

Such thinking was frightening; *they* had been frightened. They came from comfortable homes, they were not abused, few of them had outright conflict with their fathers or husbands. The realization that they were chattels, as were all women, something they had not been forced to consider before, was like wandering down a pretty garden path and opening the door in its wall to find wholesale rape and pillage in progress outside it.

Many retreated and the charity lost members who hastened back up the garden path to safety. Philippa had to make up the loss of their contributions out of her own money so that the foundlings didn't suffer.

Those who remained to view the new, alarming world learned that there was an alternative. They became cognizant of what was really happening on the other side of the Channel rather than the version of it peddled by their own propertied class. They used their schoolgirl French to read Rousseau's *Social Contract* and Linguet's *Memoirs of the Bastille*. They watched English performances of Beaumarchais's *The Marriage of Figaro* with fresh eyes. New names became familiar to them; that of Mme de Genlis and Olympe de Gouges whose *Déclaration des Droits de la Femme et de la Citoyenne* made them gasp with its supposition that marriage as an institution had failed and should be replaced by *'une sorte d'union libre.'*

One calm, reasoned French voice, however, commanded their attention more than these, saying clearly that all citizens irrespective of sex or rank should receive free state education together and that women were as entitled to the vote as men.

Their landscape changed. The vote was too distant to be spied; they knew they would never enter a polling booth, nor, perhaps, would their granddaughters.

Education, though. Universal literacy. Independence. Seeds sown into fallow minds so that laboring women were not chained to the distaff or the factory bench, that there was some other resort for the desperate than prostitution.

They retained their status as a charity but secretly they became the Condorcet Society.

We should have declared ourselves, Philippa thought, *we were timid.* Yet the inevitable vituperation against these ideas by friends and relatives, the hostility of the genteel society to which they belonged, had been perturbing; they would be condemned—worse, they would be ridiculed.

A woman, braver than they were, spoke out on their behalf in *A*

Vindication of the Rights of Women. They responded by renaming themselves the Condorcet and Wollstonecraft Society but, again, they did not publicly own it.

Then, in September of '92, news came from France of the massacres. True, royalist armies were advancing on the capital—Verdun had already fallen to them—and a defenseless Paris had panicked, fearing that the royalist sympathizers in the prisons would rise up to join the enemy. That might have been the reason why violent men had hacked fourteen hundred prisoners to death but it could never be the excuse.

And now the Terror . . .

The door of the room opened to let in two women and then, almost immediately after, a third. Their eyes went hopefully to Marie Joséphine. 'A new member?' asked Kitty Hays.

Philippa shook her head. 'I fear not.' Marie Joséphine restricted her world to what was around her at the time, as if she moved in the light of a single candle; events outside its circle remaining in ignored obscurity. Efforts to read her news of what was happening in France were met with disinterest. '*Le roi, le révolutionnaire* . . .' A shrug. '. . . *c'est toujours le même chose.*'

'But she's trustworthy,' Philippa added.

Georgiana Fitch-Botley said, 'Did you get it?'

'No.' She told them about Blanchard's procrastination in supplying a forged *certificat*.

'Damn, *damn.*'

'We must delay any further discussion until the others arrive.' Eliza Morris was today's chairwoman.

They sat down to wait round the central table, watching Marie Joséphine as she exclaimed at a case containing William the Conqueror's sword, a Chinese flea trap, a dolphin with a flying fish in its mouth and several pieces of the Holy Cross.

All of them were in their twenties and comfortably situated. They could have met in each other's parlors but from the first it had seemed more adventurous to hold their gatherings in a rented room, like men did. Saltero's Curiosity Coffee House was convenient to their homes, its proprietress sympathetic and, anyway, as the society became increasingly radical, somehow fitting; they were curiosities themselves.

Eliza's father was a Whig MP and, though concerned not to do anything to affect his position, she had cut her hair as a gesture of solidarity with the laboring classes; it made her look like a worried Joan of Arc.

Kitty Hays, the daughter of a well-to-do landowner, was the oldest, wore a divided skirt and smoked cheroots during the meetings to show her daring. Georgiana, cousin to Viscount Glenny, swore like a trooper in their company in order to show hers and adopted a Turkish headdress. She had the face of a marble Venus, and had once met Marat whom she described as an 'interesting little bastard.'

When at home they were different women; Philippa noticed that in the company of their menfolk, Kitty shed her cheroot, Georgiana her headdress and bad language, both adopting a mawkish attentiveness to husbands who were less intelligent than they were but on whom they were financially and emotionally reliant.

Eliza was quieter and equally attentive to her father who, though a kindly man by most standards, had stopped her allowance for a month when she'd cut her hair without his permission.

Only Philippa was assured enough in her family life not to be different when she was away from it. At home and at meetings, she looked and dressed like a conforming society woman but, as Kitty had once told her: 'You are the most radical of any of us, which makes you the greatest curiosity of the lot.'

At one o'clock it became apparent that there would be no others.

Eliza sighed and tapped her coffee cup with a spoon. Dutifully, they discussed charity business first, a sale of work in the parish hall next week, the form of letters of appeal to be sent around the neighbourhood.

'Now then,' the chairwoman said. 'We are agreed that M de Condorcet must be rescued, are we not? In view of Sister Dapifer's disappointing news, how is that to be done?'

Kitty said, 'What's the use of him to us if, when he gets here, he's regarded as just another blood-drinker? English opinion refuses to differentiate between the revolutionaries.'

'Fact is, my dear,' drawled Georgiana, 'the Revolution has done for all of us. The vote? We'll be lucky if we're not put back into chastity belts.'

'We need him,' Philippa said. 'We need a leader.'

'I thought we had one,' said Kitty. 'I thought we'd agreed to ask Mary Wollstonecraft to come and talk to us once she's back from France.'

'I have news of Miss Wollstonecraft. She also has done for us, damn her,' Georgiana said. 'Or, rather, has done for herself in more ways than one. While viewing the delights of the Revolution, still unmarried, she has managed to become pregnant. While in France, my dears, as the venacular has it, she has been jumbling her giblets.'

After a while, Philippa said, 'How do you know? And, Ginny, if you use that disgusting phrase again, I shall leave.'

Georgiana waved her elegant hands in apology. 'I'm so put out. It's so . . . so *careless* of her. I know because Lady Mountcashel told me—Wollstonecraft was her governess, if you remember, and Margaret has always kept up with her. She's had an affair in France with some American. Margaret says he has no intention of marrying her.'

There was another silence. After a while, Eliza said, 'God help us.'

He was likely to be the only one who could. Wollstonecraft's book had spoken for them all, not condemning men but pointing out that the bondage of women was to humanity's disadvantage; one half of the population was being dragged in chains, a dead weight retarding the advance of the other half.

Only let women be free, she'd said, allow them full education, strengthen their bodies and their understanding so that they can contribute to the partnership. Society could never fulfill its potential until it was founded on reason. If man regarded himself as the only creature capable of reason and its uses, she wrote, 'women have no inherent rights to claim and therefore, by the same rule, their duties vanish, for rights and duties are inseparable.'

Instantly, she had been portrayed as a slut. '. . . a philosophical wanton,' one ladies' magazine called her, 'who would break down the bars intended to restrain licentiousness.' A speaker in the House of Lords warned his fellow peers not to allow their wives and daughters to read this 'hyena in petticoats.' Smoking-room jokes in the clubs somewhat confusingly attached a penis to her while at the same time attributing to her a voracious sexual appetite for men.

There had been brickbats in plenty and now this, the most shining prophet of female emancipation, had herself supplied the enemy with its ammunition.

'She's done for us,' Georgina said again, quietly.

There was no doubt that she had. *And yet*, thought Philippa, *only a free-thinking and uninhibited woman could have written as Wollstonecraft has done; why, then, are we blaming her for being what she is?*

Kitty Hays stubbed out her cheroot in her saucer. 'Damn her,' she said. 'And damn Robespierre. They've put us back to being a charity. That's all we'll ever be, carriers of nourishing gruel to the poor. It's all they'll let us be.'

Marie Joséphine had taken the curious flea trap out of its case and carried it to the window to inspect it—a good flea trap was worth having—and a long slant of winter sun cast the shadow of the thing's mechanism over their table in a shape unnervingly like that of a guillotine.

It was Eliza, the sweet-natured, who kept them in line. She tapped her cup again. 'To return to the original proposition, I see no reason why we should abandon M Condorcet to his fate. For one thing, he is too good a man to be killed by those monsters and we owe him much. For another, he would command attention. Father says that he was the only one of the revolutionaries the House of Commons would have given a hearing to. What do you say, Philippa?'

'He's no orator.' She had been on a balcony in the Tuileries with Sophie when Condorcet had outlined his proposed revolutionary constitution to the Legislative Assembly and found herself nodding off to sleep, along with most of the 745 deputies. It was in small groups that the man's intellect and essential goodness became apparent. 'But Eliza's right. He has great influence when you meet him. Women would listen to him as they wouldn't to us. Men, too. He never wanted France to declare war on us and I am sure that if we could get him an interview with Mr Pitt . . .'

'We ain't even got him to England yet,' Kitty pointed out.

'Ah, well, as to that . . .'

Walking home with Marie Joséphine, Philippa thought how ridiculous all of them must have seemed to the Frenchwoman if she'd had good enough English to understand what they were talking about, how ridiculous they all seemed even to themselves.

'Marie Joséphine, wouldn't you like to be equal with men?' she asked.

'With *him*?' They were passing the draper's shop again and Marie Joséphine gave a vicious little nod towards it.

'With all men.'

'I am better than Sanders,' Marie Joséphine said, offended. 'He is a coachman, I am a lady's maid. And 'Opkin is only a footman.'

Why do we bother? We are like little boys aping grown-up men with our swearing and our smoking and our fantastic ideas of rescue, Philippa thought. *None of us really believes Nicolas can receive his* certificat *in time, even if we can get one to him, even if he can use it should we do so. It is mere bravado.*

Emancipated women? When we call on a man to speak for us because we are too frightened to speak for ourselves? And that man a native of a country at war with our own?

Where was an Englishman of sufficient stature to stand up and demand emancipation for his wife, daughters, his female servants, the washerwoman who came, unseen, at night to fill her tubs ready for twenty-four hours of scrubbing for pennies, the girls lured into brothels for lack of any other occupation?

In this age of enlightened men fighting for reform she could not think of one who championed the cause of women for women's sake.

Stephen, why couldn't it be you? You command the respect of respectable men, you could shatter the complacency of our generation. Why can't you fight for the abolition of all slavery?

She asked herself if she could love him then—and knew it to be a useless question.

No, it would have to be Condorcet because he was all they had.

And at least, she thought, *he can't get pregnant*.

Chapter Five

THERE was only a limited amount of speculation Makepeace
could expend on what Mrs Glossop might think of her husband
escaping imprisonment in going to France, and by the time they
reached Basingstoke she'd exhausted it.

It was a thing she'd noticed about dedicated reformers, they took
any help they were given for granted, as if it were a privilege for the
helper. Glossop was putting her to a lot of trouble and expense, not
to mention risk, and so far had said nothing in recognition of it.

She was sorry for him, especially as there were reminders of his
plight in the effigies of Thomas Paine being burned by gangs of rioters along the first bit of the Great West Road. Nor did she necessar-
ily want gratitude, but she didn't expect to get bored to death, either.

After Basingstoke, which they reached without enquiry or any
more burning effigies, she put him outside on the driving box with
Sanders. 'Nobody looks at coachmen,' she told him. Which was
true. 'Except other coachmen.' Which was also true. 'And they'll be
going the other way.'

It took over four days—she could not ask Sanders to do more
than fifty miles a day in this weather—but, apart from the usual vex-
ations of winter travel, it was an uneventful journey. If the hue and
cry had been called out after Glossop, the coach was ahead of it and
tollgate-keepers were too mindful of the cold to stand in it asking
questions.

Better if they had; it might have roused her. As it was, inactivity and a landscape of monotonous white and gray allowed her to reflect on her losses. It seemed to her that whether she went north or south in England, she followed a signpost that led to a death. In Northumberland it was Andra's, in Devon it was the Dowager's.

She didn't go north at all, while her trips to Devon had become rarer as the remembrance entangled in it refused to yield its pain. Makepeace had made only three female friends in her life; Betty, her nurse, and Susan, both of whom were American—and Diana, Dowager Countess of Stacpoole. All of them were dead.

The last friendship had been the most unlikely. Once the owner of T'Gallants, the great house at Babbs Cove which was now Makepeace's property, the Dowager had been chalk to Makepeace's cheese: lofty, elegant, aristocratic, seemingly supercilious. They'd disliked each other on sight; only circumstances and a mutual regard for freedom had brought them together to help a contingent of American seamen who landed on their doorstep during a mass escape of prisoners from Plymouth during the War of Independence.

A strange time, but the even stranger alliance between the two women had outlived it.

Diana had been a little older than Makepeace was then, a widow, and she'd subsequently married the man responsible for the French end of the smuggling relay between Babbs Cove and France. From then on, she and Makepeace had met every year, either at T'Gallants or the chateau of Gruchy where Diana, who became Mme de Vaubon, had enjoyed a happiness she had never known before.

It was short-lived. When she'd conceived at the age of forty-three there had been rejoicing in the villages on both sides of the Channel but the birth of her son, Jacques, had been difficult. Makepeace was with her when she died a week later from septicemia occasioned by a piece of placenta that had refused to come away.

Even the death of Andra seven years later had not swamped that particular grief, indeed had exacerbated it, like a hook still tugging at the mouth of a landed fish, with its reminder that the last female contemporary who could have comforted her was not there.

The best she could do for her dead friend had been to look after the baby until its stricken father procured a suitable nurse. Afterwards she'd regularly gone back and forth to Gruchy to keep an eye on the boy. When de Vaubon, with his friend Georges Danton, entered the fraught world of politics in opposition to Louis XVI's regime, young Jacques had spent nearly as much time with her in England as he had with his father.

For his sake, she might have roused herself from despair after Andra's death if the boy's visits had been kept up but by then Guillaume de Vaubon was a celebrated figure of the Revolution and, anglophile though he was, decided it was unwise for his son to seem too much at home in a royalist country. It had been Philippa, in her frequent trips to Paris, who'd kept up the connection between the two families and ensured that the boy retained his fluent English.

It was late by the time they reached the crest of the steep hill down to Babbs Cove; Makepeace had rejected the idea of stopping for another night on the road; there was a good moon, the ground was dry and Sanders was familiar with the way.

Against the sound of dragging brakes as they went down, she heard Glossop ask, 'Who owns that house then?' Below them, frost on the dour, slated, multiangled roof of T'Gallants was gleaming in the moonlight, the only indication that the house wasn't part of the cliff on which it stood.

'It's the missus's,' Sanders said.

No, it ain't, she thought, *not really.* To her, it would always belong to the tall, ivory-haired ghost who still haunted it, its face before her now, as she'd last seen it, fighting against incoherence, eyes going from hers to de Vaubon's, lips trying to shape words and managing only, 'Care . . . care.'

Makepeace had leaned over so that her face was only inches from the suffering woman's. 'He'll be the best cared for baby you ever damn saw.'

A twitched smile, peace, a terrible howl from de Vaubon . . .

She was afflicted by the thought of how little she had done for

Diana's child in the last two years. True, the boy now lived permanently in Paris with his father and Paris had become increasingly unwelcoming to all foreigners except those most dedicated to its Revolution, which Makepeace was not. In any case, last year France had declared war on England.

But we could have met at Gruchy, she thought. De Vaubon had left the *manoir* of Gruchy in the hands of his steward and its villagers but it was still his and its trade with Babbs Cove still carried on.

Wars had never prevented the activity of smuggling during the many conflicts between France and England in the past, never would. Gruchy on its lonely, wind-wracked Cotentin shore was, like Babbs Cove, isolated from government both geographically and temperamentally and in its view, which was also Babbs Cove's, government, whatever its color, imposed starvation taxes that it was the individual's duty to avoid. Government, said Babbs Cove and Gruchy, were enemies but the two villages had been trading with each other for centuries, trusting each other, sometimes intermarrying, always making a profit from their association. Therefore, government could both bugger off and *fous-moi la paix*. Gruchy, like Babbs Cove, decided who was friend and foe and over the years 'ze missus' had proved herself a reliable member of their company and was proud to be so.

Yes, she thought, *the boy and I could have met at Gruchy. Should have*.

They'd arrived. Sanders opened the coach door and let down the steps for her to descend onto the apron of the Pomeroy Arms, always Makepeace's first port of call.

The night was frigidly still apart from the sigh of water on sand. The looming T'Gallants cut off the westerly moon's light from half the cove so that only the eastern cottages made a defined pattern of roofs and dark doorways, their fishing nets strung between them like spider webs. Behind them, a hunting owl swept optimistically over steep, white fields.

The scene never failed to move her, though nowadays a sense of excitement was missing, as if the pungency of sea and seaweed had been taken away.

The Pomeroy Arms smelled the same, though. A mixture of fresh whitewash battled with the old wood in its crazy, crisscrossing beams, logs burning in the huge grate, good cooking and the liquor ingrained in the tables of its booths.

Every time she entered it, Makepeace thought that if the inn were on a coaching route it would be celebrated and she thanked the Lord that it was too far off the beaten track to be known to any but its locals. Even so, it prospered well enough, acting as it did as church hall, dispensary, meeting house, grog shop, refuge for locked-out husbands, courthouse, assembly room and funeral parlor. It was the place where the village men sat every night and their women, coming to fetch them home, stayed for a glass of something. It was wormed with hidden cupboards and passages where contraband was disposed until the ponies came to distribute it through most of southern Devon. It was the beating heart of the village. And it was a secret.

Dell, shrieking, and Tobias, smiling gravely, advanced on her. Two children with pale, freckled negroid features were ushered out to 'tell Jan Gurney that Herself has arrived.' Another was dispatched to help Sanders, an old friend, with the horses.

A chair was shoved under her bottom, her feet tipped onto a footstool towards the fire and a beaker of rum and butter put into her hand, another given to Thomas Glossop who was told, 'Drink that now, it'll drive the Divil from your soul and the snakes from England.'

Makepeace gave a stage groan. With a dubious past behind her, Dell's marriage to the quiet, elderly black man who'd once been the Dowager's servant had been happy for them both, and contentment had enlarged the woman in more ways than one, allowing her Irishness full rein—along with her figure.

Knowing the inn's importance to the village, Makepeace had

wondered if she was doing the right thing when she'd made this odd couple proprietors of the Pomeroy. But the choice had been a success; Babbs Cove might be isolated but few villages in England were as familiar with foreigners. Generations of illegal trading with other countries had brought it into contact with the polyglot world of seamen. French, Dutch, Irish, Lascars, Chinese, Turks, Russians, Africans, West Indians . . . what were another couple of oddities? Especially when their ale was good, their secrecy assured, their cooking excellent and, for all the landlady's Hibernian ebullience, it was the lisping but dignified and efficient Tobias who ruled the roost.

Dell ignored Makepeace's protest. 'Are ye for France?'

'He is,' Makepeace said, nodding at Glossop. 'I'm not. I'm staying a couple of days before Sanders drives me to Bristol to meet Aaron. Will you put us up?' Preparing T'Gallants for occupation in this weather was a big undertaking; anyway, she preferred the inn.

'Need ye ask? I'll do some lobscouse for supper, the way you like it.'

I was lonely, Makepeace thought. She was still lonely but at least, in this inn, she was among those who'd known and loved the dead as she had. A beautiful drawing of the Dowager, sketched by Betty's Josh, hung on one wall. Upstairs was the room where de Vaubon had been nursed to health by his future wife. There was the false wall, mended now, that excisemen had stoved in during the search for French brandy . . . the bastards.

That was one thing she'd done by buying into the Cove's smuggling trade; she'd bought the local excise as well. Once the swine who'd been chief customs officer at the time had been gotten rid of, the rest had proved insufficiently paid to resist the considerable *pourboires* she'd offered them to let the pony trains go into the night without investigation. Philippa said it was corruption, Makepeace regarded it as insurance . . .

'And there's a surprise for ye . . .' Dell was saying. A blast of cold stopped her as the door opened. 'Here's himself now, he'll do the telling.'

Apart from his yellow hair turning white, Jan Gurney had

changed very little; he still had to stoop to pass under the inn's lintel, he could still pick Makepeace up and swing her round. 'Did young Philippa get the letter?'

'What letter?'

'Gor damn, I took un to Plymouth, put the bugger in the post bag myself. Should've reached Lunnon by now. They handed it to us at Gruchy, trip before last. Come from Paris, so they did say.'

'Who sent it?'

'Ah diddun read un, did I? Reckoned it might be from that Sophie Condorcet as we brought over that time. Nice little woman, she was. How *be* our Philippa, anyway?'

In the interchange of news about families, the fate of the letter was forgotten.

''Tis as well you've turned up,' Jan said. 'Us only got back from France three days since and 'twere a puzzle what to do about young Jack; whether send for ee or take un to ee in Lunnon.'

'Jack?' She was fuddled from the tiring journey.

Dell called from the kitchen. 'She don't know yet. He's gone to his bed.'

'Jacques?'

'As ever was,' Jan said. 'Only safe when he'm asleep. Rest of the time he's as like to blow up the Pomeroy as not, ain't he, Toby?'

'Exthperimental young gentleman,' Tobias said.

'Will you tell me, for God's sake?' hissed Makepeace.

Jan sat her down and squatted on a stool opposite. He looked grave. 'Reckon things must be pretty bad for our Gil, missus. Him and Danton has got upsides with Robespierre, so they told us at Gruchy. Tryin' to stop that evil bugger cutting everybody's head off, so they did say, which puts 'em both in line to losing their own according.'

'Guillaume has sent Jacques over? Jan, it *must* be bad.'

Jan shrugged. 'The boy ain't been told the extent of ut. Still thinks his daddy's Lord Muck and Muck of the Revolution along of Danton. Which he may be, I don't know. Just looks nasty, that's all I'm saying. Better have a word with the tutor when you get un alone.

Weedy little sweet'eart but clever enough I don't doubt. Where is he, Dell?'

'In his room.'

'It must be bad,' Makepeace said again.

The intricacies of the French situation, who was in, who was out, had become too entangled and fast-moving for her understanding. Like almost everybody else in England, she regarded Robespierre as the Terror and the Terror as Robespierre. If de Vaubon and Danton were opposing that deadly little man, they were indeed risking their heads and the risk was obviously so great that Guillaume wanted his son out of danger.

'They wouldn't guillotine an eleven-year-old boy, just because of his father,' she said. 'Would they?'

Jan spat. 'I don't put nothing past them buggers. Nobody do know what they done with that poor little lad of King Louis's, do they?'

Probably, they wouldn't kill Jacques, she thought, *but he would lose the de Vaubon land, which, if it were deemed to belong to a traitor, would revert to the State. He'd be penniless and stigmatized.*

And the thing was, she thought, *that by ensuring the safety of his son, de Vaubon had quadrupled the danger to himself.* From the first, the revolutionaries had called themselves patriots so that, increasingly, the label 'unpatriotic' had become a slur. Not to wear the red, white and blue cockade was unpatriotic, Philippa had told her, so was the use of *vous* rather than *tu* and the deferential *Monsieur* rather than *Citizen*. Under the new Law of Suspects, the appellation was now a death sentence.

And if sending one's son to safety in an enemy country was not unpatriotic, Makepeace didn't know what was. *Oh, Gil.*

'Things must be bad,' she repeated.

Taking a candle, she went upstairs and quietly entered Jacques's room. The boy didn't stir from his sleep and she stood for a long time, looking at him. The same dark hair as his father, though somewhat less curly than Guillaume's, the same excellent sallow skin, long nose and planes of the cheeks, and, yet, in that strange way of physical heredity, the parts combining to look like his mother.

At rest, he appeared younger than his eleven years, a little boy, but at the same time Makepeace glimpsed for the first time the man he'd become—if he was allowed to.

Why, for all their puffing and bravado, did boys seem to her so much more vulnerable than girls? Andrew Ffoulkes, Josh . . . now Jacques de Vaubon, a poignant line of male humanity, sons she'd never had, for all of whom she felt a ferocious, protective impulse.

A hiss told Makepeace that her tears were dropping on the candle flame as she inclined over the figure in the bed. There was so much love encapsulated in it; Diana's love, the boy's love for his father, the father's sacrifice for the boy.

She wiped her eyes angrily—bugger it—and went outside to slam on the tutor's door and tell him to come downstairs.

When he joined her in a corner booth of the taproom, she could see why he'd earned Jan's description of 'weedy sweetheart.' The smugglers of Babbs Cove suspected the sexual proclivity of any man unless he looked as if he could shin up a topmast in a nor'easterly, hold his liquor, spit five yards and wrestle a customs officer to the ground.

Quintus Luchet did not. He was misty, the sort of person one had trouble remembering afterward, with die-away eyes, slight frame, colorless complexion. His high-collared black coat needed a brush, like his long hair, and his shirt and loosely-tied cravat were grubby— a condition which, had it been the result of his travels, Makepeace would have forgiven, but she instead suspected to be the latest revolutionary fashion. Clean linen, Philippa had said, was unpatriotic.

He had a book in his hand and one finger was holding it open at the place where his reading had been interrupted. Very irritating.

Impassioned by the emotion she'd undergone upstairs, she felt an immediate impulse to bully him. 'Well, young man, and what's this about?'

His response was slow and sweetly kind, as if he had to drag his mind away from higher things. 'You are Madame Hedley?'

'I am.'

Still holding the book, he fumbled in an interior pocket of his coat for a letter, dropped it, picked it up and handed it to her. 'From M Vaubon.'

She nearly snapped at him again but, of course, Guillaume had discarded the *'de'* as too suggestive of rank. Philippa said that ordinary people called Leroi or Leduc were hastily changing their names to something ridiculous, like Egalité. *God help us, what had happened to French common sense?*

Even the stamp on the sealing wax was plain where his device had once been an elaborately entwined dV. She broke it carefully.

He'd written one line. *'I trust him to you, missus.'*

She pressed her knuckles against her mouth.

It was the message of a dying man. *God, oh God, he knew he couldn't win.* They'd kill him.

Suddenly, he was in the taproom, where he'd been so often before, one foot up on a stool, his enormous voice roaring out the latest escape from the customs cutters to an appreciative audience, the most alive person she'd ever met.

I trust him to you, missus.

Fine bloody time for you to be quiet spoken, she sobbed at him.

Jan Gurney had come over and was patting her on the back. She handed him the letter, wiped her nose on the back of her hand and turned back to Luchet. 'Well?'

'The excuse is give out that the boy is ill and needs sea air,' he said.

'*Given* out,' she said. His English was almost accentless and, to give him his due, he was quick to understand what she wanted to know.

'*Given* out. Where Paris is concerned, Jacques is at Gruchy for his health.'

Well, that was one thing; his people at Gruchy would never give him away.

'What's happening to M de Vaubon?'

'When we leave him, nothing. He has make a great speech in the Convention, defending himself and Danton against the charge they are responsible for the massacres of September and would have save the King and Queen from execution if they could. He shout them all down. But he is too close to Danton. The *enragés* say the two are sorry for the State prisoners and they are against the Terror, and Robespierre suspect them of lack of virtue, that they are careless in the matter of money, corrupt.'

They're probably all those things, Makepeace thought. She'd never met Danton but Philippa had described him as de Vaubon's virtual twin, large, loud, generous, a lover of good food, drink and women. What Danton's approach to the making of money was, she didn't know, but if it was like de Vaubon's with his smuggling, it would hardly accord to the purist Robespierre's idea of virtue.

But Luchet was saying that sympathy for the Terror's victims was the gravest charge against the two men. 'In the Convention, Robespierre says, "I suppose a man of your moral principles would not think anyone deserve punishment?" And Danton leap up and shout: "I suppose *you* are annoyed if none do!" '

Yes, Makepeace thought, that's the difference between men like de Vaubon and Danton and men like Robespierre. Perhaps it's the difference between men everywhere.

'Well, I know what side I'm on,' she said and was irritated by Luchet's lack of response. His report had seemed disinterested, patronizing, as if he were describing the struggles of flies caught on sticky paper. *Perhaps he is*, she thought, *perhaps they are. But one of those flies is his employer and my friend.*

'And now,' continued Luchet, still remote, 'M Danton has go back to his home in Arcis and M Vaubon take me and Jacques to Gruchy and tell me to bring the boy to England. Perhaps they should not be absent from Paris at this time. It is a mistake to turn the back, I think.'

'Oh, you do, do you? And I'm supposed to look after you, am I?' She couldn't help it, the man inspired aggression.

He gave a shrug that was purely Gallic. 'M Vaubon trust me with his son.'

'*Trusts,*' she said, automatically. 'You don't want to go back to the Revolution, then?'

'The Revolution has turn ugly,' he said. 'I am concern only for beauty.' Dreamily, he tapped his book which, she saw, was a collection of Virgil's *Eclogues*—in Latin. 'Before you call me here, madame, I wander the Tuscan hills in the company of genius.'

'Better get back to them, then,' she snapped.

When he'd gone, Jan Gurney took his place opposite her. 'Told you.'

She shook her head. 'He's no molly,' she said. 'He's a romantic. That's worse.'

S HE was woken the next morning by the noise of tapping coming through the window of her room overlooking the inn's backyard. Jacques was hammering a piece of metal on the well head. A fire burned under what looked like an old metal wash bucket, small pieces of some machine were scattered about the cobbles.

'What are you doing, you blasted boy?'

He looked up apologetically. 'I try to muffle the hammer, missus.'

'Not enough. What are you *doing*?'

'I try to make a steam pump. It would be good. To pump water from the well for M Toby and Mme Dell.'

'You'd need a surface condenser,' she said out of her years of marriage to Andra, and received a look of such affection it made her smile; her stock had just gone up. 'I'll get dressed and we'll go for a walk.'

When they met, they kissed on either cheek, French fashion, but he wasn't too old to hold her hand as they went through the village.

Out at sea, gulls made livid parentheses against dull, snow-laden clouds but in the east, where the sky was clear, a wintry dandelion of a sun was coming up, reflecting full on window panes so that they seemed to blink, casting a path across the cove and lending such an improbable gold to water, grass, rock and the lines of little cottages, that they might have been painted by a sentimental watercolorist.

The air was crisp and women were hanging out bedding to blanch it rid of fleas. They nodded companionably at Makepeace, as if they'd seen her only yesterday; all the news she'd given Jan last night had already been disseminated. Rachel Gurney called out, "Morning, missus. 'Mornin', Jack. Step in for a zider on the way baack.'

'I like England,' Jacques said.

'May have to stay for a bit, so your pa says,' Makepeace told him. 'He's very busy.'

'Papa is busy always.' It was said without rancor.

She wondered at the boy's lack of inquiry but it appeared that he was used to being left in other people's care during de Vaubon's many absences. Jacques said, 'He is going on mission to the Loire, you know, and may be away a long time. It is why I come here.'

That was the story, then, and he seemed satisfied with it; he had little apparent awareness of the political situation; being sent to England was merely a reversion to the summers he'd spent with Makepeace in the past and he didn't question why any more than he had then. Obviously, de Vaubon had been able to isolate him from the worst excesses of the Terror.

He talked about the rented house in the quiet suburb of Saint Cloud where he'd been able have a workshop in the garden in which to build model steam engines. They were his passion, and part of his complacence in coming to England was that it was the home of steam power. 'I have brought my cylinders and a boiler,' he said, hopefully. 'They are in the stables. M Gurney said I would sink his boat but I think he joked.'

'I'd better get you a workroom then,' she said and felt him squeeze her hand.

'Have you met M Watt?' he asked.

'James Watt? Yes, he was a friend of Andra's.'

'Ohhh.' She might have admitted to a nodding acquaintance with God. 'What is he like?'

She didn't say she'd found the Scotsman suspicious, ungainly, penny-pinching and morose. She said instead what was equally true, 'Very clever.'

There was a sigh of envy. 'Will I meet him? I must ask him many things.'

They had reached the end of the village and took the path up to the headland that looked across the cove to T'Gallants. The sheep crunching the grass were dirty yellow bundles against the frost.

By the time they reached the top, Jacques had lain before her his plans to become a great engineer applying the motion of steam to everything that could be made to move by its power. 'I will build a steam carriage for you. You can go everywhere without horses.'

'Thank you,' she said, 'How will it get water?'

A wave of the hand, so like his father's. 'There will be water stations along every road. A Frenchman built the first steam carriage, M Cugnot. You hear of Nicolas Cugnot? Mine will be better.'

'What happened to his?'

A very slight twitch of the mouth, so like his mother. 'It knocked many walls down and King Louis put him in prison. But mine will be better.'

'How did you become interested in steam engines?'

'Andra.' He was surprised she should ask. 'He knew everything. Do you remember? When I was little he took me to Paris to meet Benjamin Franklin?'

He chattered on, talking about Andra without caution and she realized that everybody else sidled tensely up to her husband's name, thereby making him so much more dead. Here was Andra as he had been and she was grateful.

The view was tremendous. 'There's T'Gallants. That used to be your mother's house,' she said. 'Still is, really.' She'd told him this before but he might have forgotten. However, it didn't work by machine and so didn't interest him.

'Is that *Plymouth*?' he asked, pointing to a tiny cluster of sail in the far west. 'Does it use the shutter telegraph? *Brest* can send a signal to Paris and receive another back in a few hours if the wezzer is good.'

'You're ahead of us there,' she told him. 'The Admiralty's only just begun setting up relays to London.' She didn't approve; telegraph was excellent if it helped shipping but fast and accurate signaling between coastguards would do the smuggling business no good.

He climbed a few rocks and then came back to her.

'How does M Gurney manage to get past the blockade?'

'He waits for bad weather.'

It was why smugglers were first-class sailors; conditions that sent other boats scuttling into harbor were their opportunity. Even a blockade, such as the British were trying to impose on French shipping, had to be lifted in a storm or too much damage was done to vessels beating back and forth against a lea shore.

Mention of the war reminded her. For all their fluency in English, both Luchet and Jacques could not be mistaken as anything other than French. Even the boy, who had the better accent, suffered an occasional lapse of his 'th's.'

She raised her voice above the breeze that was coming up and beginning to pound the sea against the rocks below them. 'Jacques,' she said, 'don't forget England's at war with the French Republic. While you're in this country, you and your tutor are going to hear a lot of bad things said against revolutionaries like your pa. I don't expect you to agree with them but you mustn't *dis*agree, not out loud, you mustn't. If it gets known who your pa is, you'll be in trouble, you might even be arrested.'

She didn't want to frighten him, but this was vital. The British government was becoming as nervous of spies as the *Comité de Surveillance* in France. And if the French emigrés suspected that the son of de Vaubon, a man they hated, was in their midst . . . they could get him deported, they could even *kill* him.

She was assailed by an image of the boy brutally beheaded in a back alley, a note attached to his torso: *'Revenge for Marie Antoinette.'*

Complications piled up. 'You'll have to change your name,' she said, and added, as Jacques's nose wrinkled, 'Don't you cause no trouble. I ain't looking over my shoulder every minute for some royalist with a dagger. He might miss you and get me.'

She saw him laugh; his teeth were a pleasure against his olive skin. He'll be beating 'em off when he's older, she thought. He grew serious: 'Can I be Watt?'

'What?'

'Can I be Jacques Watt? Not ashamed of de Vaubon but like . . . like a nom-de-guerre.'

She saw his point immediately. He wouldn't be dishonoring his father, merely adopting a nickname. 'But Watt ain't very French.'

'No, but you see, Watt, Watteau, Water, Steam. I shall be Jacques Steam.'

'Watt it is.'

The wind was strengthening, blowing seagulls off course, ruffling gorse and the sheep's coats, livening the deadness of the cold with what could well be the first bluster of spring. Glossop would have a bumpy time of it across the Channel.

They started to go back down the hill. Makepeace was still worried. 'I've got to go to Bristol and meet my brother but perhaps you should stay here.' He would be safe enough hidden in Babbs Cove where strangers, if any, were immediately scrutinised and, often enough, sent away.

He stopped and looked away to sea. 'I would like to be with you,' he said, hopelessly.

He'd been left too often. Come to think of it, she couldn't bear to be parted from him now. *I trust him to you, missus.*

She put a hand on his shoulder. 'All right,' she said, 'but we're damn well going by horsepower.'

They went back to the village, relieved to be in each other's company.

B RISTOL was a beautiful city, a busy, bright, bustling, bullish, bouyant city and—as far as Makepeace was concerned—a bastard. She loathed it. Every visit she made, and those had been as few as possible, she loathed it more.

Its docks and harbors prickled with masts like toothpick cases, its shipping constantly setting sail for and returning from exotic ports, the foreign tongues chattering in its streets, should have reminded her of her American birthplace, Boston, though in fact Bristol's situation on the confluence of the rivers Avon and Frome was lovelier. It even smelled sweet, its air filled with the scent of chocolate, rum and sugar from its refineries. But to Makepeace's nostrils there always came the underlying stink of rottenness, an ineradicable base of filth such as became apparent when the tide went out to reveal the sewage on the bed of the Avon as it curved gracefully between steep, wooded cliffs.

Slavery.

To the innocent eye, Bristol looked like any other successful town in England. The slaves being landed at its docks were no more than the comparative few who were fetched up for sale to supply the wealthy with a fashionable black servant in London.

It was only after a while that you became aware that the ships' chandlers along its waterfront stocked a large range of strange goods among the usual marine provisioning—hand- and foot-cuffs, mouth bits, whips, branding irons, that the bottoms constructed in the ship-yards were being fitted with curious, small compartments into which human beings could be inserted like books into a library shelf.

It was only then you realized that Bristol's sweet air was the refinement of a trade that went on thousands of miles away, unseen by the ships' owners and builders and insurers who sent them out, in which seventy thousand souls a year were transported from Africa to work and die on the plantations in the West Indies. Next to Liverpool, Bristol ran the biggest slaving trade of any English port.

Makepeace knew about slavery. As a child, Betty, the best of women, had made the Middle Passage from Africa to Virginia as one of six hundred living beings spooned into its interior. Ordure from the bodies on the shelf above had dripped down on her and her mother, to whom she was manacled. A sailor used to come round every two days to inspect the cargo and give it water, his lantern the only light they saw. On the sixth inspection, he'd looked at Betty's mother and said, ''Nother one,' and they'd come and taken the body away to sling it into the sea.

'But I wasn't never certain she was daid 'cos I heard her moan,' Betty used to say. Then she'd wipe her eyes and add, 'Better the sea took her, mebbe, 'cos Ma was a proud woman and she couldn't never have stood nekkid in the marketplace when they come to sell us.'

Betty had survived it. She'd survived the branding and the beating and the work of the plantation and the swamp she'd had to wade through when she ran away from it. She always said her life began when she encountered the horse and cart in which Makepeace's parents were traveling north after another of Mr Burke's unsuccessful ventures in farming. Makepeace's father had his faults but he and his wife considered slavery an abomination in the sight of God.

So did Makepeace. To her, Bristol's merchants and their wives reeked of it, as if their finery and perfume could not be rid of the sweat from the black bodies that had paid for them, as if the sheen of fat on their skin had been squeezed from the marrow of other people's bones. The beautiful Queen Anne squares, the sugar houses, the carved gateways, the gardens, the churches, had been built with profit gained from vast and unimaginable suffering.

It was a slaving city and gloried in it. At the news that the latest abolition bill, for which Wilberforce and others—among them Makepeace's prospective son-in-law—had worked so hard, was defeated yet again in the House of Commons, the bells of Bristol had rung in triumph amid civic celebration.

Well, the damn place wouldn't get a penny out of *her*. She'd chosen an inn outside the city walls in which to spend the night and was prepared neither to drink nor eat while she waited for her brother. The trouble was, the packet from Wexford with Aaron aboard would only arrive at Bridge Street Landing when the tide came in— and at the moment the tide was out. It would be a longish wait.

In fact, of course, she'd have to spend some money; Jacques was agog at the overflowing confectionery shops, the international character of the streets, the fair advertising fluting snake-charmers from India, tightrope walkers, a two-headed lady, etc., and it was a shame to deny him. Sanders could look after him and Luchet while they saw the sights.

She, however, refused to accompany them. Nor would she so much as profit a Bristol coffeehouse by partaking of a cup in it.

'Where you going to be, missus?' Sanders said. 'We can't leave you alone.'

She was momentarily at a loss; the last time she'd visited Bristol had been with Andra, for a meeting between him and a Cornish mine owner investigating the use of drainage engines in his tin mine. They'd stayed in the house of one of Andra's Methodist friends who, like most Methodists, campaigned for abolition, but it had been years ago and she doubted if she could find the house again, even if the man still owned it.

However, there was one thing Makepeace knew well, and that was waterfronts. She headed towards the river, followed worriedly by the others, scrutinizing each inn and tavern as she passed, her dissatisfaction with Bristol not being improved by the occasional poster for runaways. *'John Fairbrook, sea captain and warden of Saint Mary Redcliffe Church, offers a handsome reward for anyone recapturing a negro man named James, a native of Jamaica, five feet six inches high, scar on left cheek . . .'*

'What you looking for, missus?' Sanders said.

'I'll know it when I see it.'

She found it, with its rear tucked against an escarpment overlooking the docks and a long stretch of the River Avon. 'Here,' she said. 'I'll stay here till you come back.'

Sanders was alarmed. 'You can't go in there, missus. It ain't even a tavern, it's a . . . an ale house.'

It was charity to call it even that. It was a mean little wooden building, isolated on its perch of land like a bedraggled, querulous owl. Its name board had half rotted and read THE KING'S . . . , leaving the reader to guess at what royal body part it had once aspired to. A flyblown notice in the window read: BED & BRAKEFST 6d.

'The landlord's honest,' Makepeace said, 'which is a wonder for this town.'

'How'd you know?'

She pointed to an upper window from which protruded a spy glass. As they watched, it described a slow arc that took in the view of both docks and river, then back again.

'He's got somebody upstairs watching out for the press,' she said. 'The other landlords round here, they're wicked bastards as get sailors falling-down drunk and then sell 'em to the press. Jan Gurney told me.'

Sanders looked around nervously. 'This ain't a naval town, missus. I didn't think it had press gangs.'

'It's got slaver gangs, they're worse.' Seamen were reluctant to serve on slaving ships, less from moral principle than from fear of dying. Slave captains were brutal and didn't spare their crews who, in any case, were open to the infections that appalling conditions created among the human cargo. And there was always the danger of revolt if slaves with nothing to lose managed to free themselves of their chains.

Being pressed into the British Navy was no bed of roses but being pressed onto a slaver was deadly.

Stephen Heilbron was preparing a report which, he'd told her, showed that the mortality rate among sailors aboard slavers was nearly as horrific as that of their human cargo. 'Perhaps the public will respond to that at least,' he'd said, wearily.

The door was warped and Makepeace applied her boot to it.

It was dark inside and smelled of ale, cheap tobacco and old sea boots. A stove threw out heat. The dozen or so men hunched over its central table looked up with suspicion at the figure standing in the doorway, its enveloping fur-lined cloak momentarily suggesting that a rather pretty bear had come to call—not, however, a cuddly one.

Makepeace threw back her hood and the sun flamed her hair into an aureole as she stalked in. 'Which of you's the landlord?'

A man rose from the table, his apron greasy enough to have stood up by itself. Makepeace crossed the room, took out her purse and slammed half a guinea in front of him. 'I'm waiting for the Wexford packet and I'm waiting for it here. The lad upstairs can tell me when it gets in. That suit you? Good.'

In fact, she was home. She knew these men, well not *these,* but men like them had been among her customers in the waterfront tavern she'd run for her father back in Boston. They, too, had hidden from British press gangs and customs men. The Roaring Meg had been bigger, generally more pleasant and definitely cleaner, but it and this King's Whatever were definitely cousins.

She turned to Sanders and with some ostentation handed him her purse, making sure the clientele saw her do it. Today she had deliberately worn no jewelry in case it attracted snatch thieves—a woman could have her lobes torn off in a grab for her earrings. 'Now, you take the rest of my money and go off to explore the town.' She looked round at the faces staring at her. '*What?*'

The eyes returned to examining their tankards.

'Go on,' she told Sanders, 'I'll be all right.' She looked menacingly at the landlord. '*Won't* I?'

The man shut his mouth and nodded.

'You might, missus, but will *we?*' Sanders was unnerved. 'I don't want us and the boy taken aboard no slaver.' Luchet and Jacques had followed him in and were staring around them with interest.

It was a point. Makepeace said more gently to the landlord, 'Will they be safe from the bastards?'

There was a sudden air of relief; they were all against the bastards. One of the men at the table became chatty.

'They'll be all right, mum. Slavers ain't got time to train men, not like the navy. They only got use for experienced sailors. He's a coachman, ain't he . . . ?' Sanders caped greatcoat gave him away.

'And the lad's but a tiddler and he'—this was Luchet—'don't look likely for anythin'. Reckon the gentlemen's safe enough.'

Makepeace nodded, told her men to take care and watch their pockets, before dusting a bench and sitting down to a pot of ale.

Two hours later, her cloak hung on a hook and her sleeves rolled up, she was washing pots that hadn't seen a soapsud since they were fired and she was engaging in an argument with two sailors called Chops and Toey on the advantages of a cutter as opposed to a sloop. Chops, who was black, had been on lookout when she first arrrived but his place had been taken at the spy glass by an elderly white man they called Bosun.

It was Bosun who called down. 'Tide's turned, missus, she'll be in soon.'

She went upstairs. The room smelled sour and was almost to-tally filled by six truckle beds. In the only available corner stood a brimming chamber pot. She had to shuffle on her knees across bare, tick mattresses to reach the window, where Bosun sat. The spy glass, a good one and therefore presumably stolen, rested in a sling hung from a hook in the ceiling. The old man swung its eyepiece towards her. 'Reckon that's the packet, right down river. Look, on the bend.'

Makepeace looked. The sweep of the Avon's silt was showing the sheen that argued the start of an advancing tide. When it came it would come quickly. The great difference between the river's high and low tide—about thirty feet—was a problem to the city.

If the tide was out, ships in the harbor or waiting to enter it were stranded in its mud for hours, leaving them lopsided and their hulks under considerable stress. 'Shipshape and Bristol fashion' was a phrase that had come to apply to boats incorporating sufficient strength to withstand the rigours of entering, docking and leaving the port.

It was a peaceful scene. The river bed was dotted with vessels slanted at a lazy angle as they waited for the tide to refloat them, some almost hidden in the shade cast by the hills on the right bank where the afternoon sun was beginning to go down. Makepeace could just see beyond them the stubby shape of the Wexford packet boat lying on its side in a patch of sunlight speckled by overhanging trees.

She smiled fondly, imagining her stately brother Aaron having to brace his legs against the bulkhead to stop himself sliding into a heap. There was no room for dignity at an angle of forty-five degrees.

Beside her, Bosun said, 'Hello. Trouble on *African Queen*.'

A large slaver that lay nearer to the docks than the other vessels wasn't waiting to discharge her cargo until she was upright. Two sailors, one of them with a whip, were standing in the mud watching a line of collared black men and women emerge on hands and knees from the hatch and clamber awkwardly down to join them. A chain ran from collar to collar.

'Naughty, naughty, her's got away, look,' Bosun said.

A woman was running from the vessel, hidden from the sailors by the angle of the mast, making for the bank away from the harbor. As Makepeace watched, the men saw the woman and began to chase after her, shouting. Their boots made heavier progress through the silt than did the woman's bare feet but she was weighed down by a bundle that she carried.

Makepeace applied her eye to glass and brought it to focus on the running figure. It was headed away from her so that she could only see it from the back, but the lens brought the bare black skin so close that she could see muscles taut with effort and the patches of mud thrown up as she splashed her way through the gaining tide. A head bobbed up and down over the woman's shoulder. She was carrying a child. For a moment the spyglass framed its face. It was about five years old and its eyes were white with terror.

'*Run*,' she said, without knowing she said it.

'They're like us some ways,' Bosun was saying. 'Don't like their young uns taken off 'em. Allus try and get away if they can.'

'Why . . .' Makepeace took in a breath. 'Why are they taking it away from her?' She knew. It was God she was asking.

Bosun was calm about it. 'Boy, I reckon. He'll go to one of they fancy houses uptown where they dress 'em up pretty and sit 'em on the back of their carriage.'

A voice behind them said, 'An' get rid of 'em when they ain't pretty no more.' Chop had joined them at the window and was watching the chase.

Bosun said, grinning, 'And she'll go to London. That's where Teast gen'ly sends 'em.'

'Cat house,' agreed Chop.

She couldn't look away, the spray the woman's feet kicked up as she ran was becoming irregular, she was beginning to stumble. The sailors were gaining on her. Makepeace's lips felt numb.

One of the sailors launched himself and tackled the woman, bringing her down. She fell awkwardly, sideways, so that she wouldn't crush what she carried.

They heard the cry she gave as they pulled the child away from her. It was a lost, inhuman sound, like a seagull's shriek, rising for a moment into an uncaring sky, an acceptance of hopelessness, before it was dissipated in the clamor of the city.

'Where they taking them?' Makepeace said. Her voice was thick from saliva, she could barely see.

'Teast's, won't they?' Bosun asked Chop. 'The *Queen*'s one of his.'

'Teast's Yard,' nodded Chop.

'Where is it?'

'Over Prince Street bridge and . . .' They had to shout the rest of the instructions after her; Makepeace was already running downstairs.

It was difficult to find the Yard; the wharves were busy. Cranes dipping cargo into holds or taking it out delayed her and she had to wait while gangs of puffing dockers manhandled crates across her way. She got lost and her requests for direction were answered by abstracted nods of the head. In order to get around one boat, she had to wade through water at the end of a slipway, got her foot caught in a rope and fell.

It was like one of those sobbing, running nightmares; the vital necessity to reach an object against obstruction. Like the time

Philippa had been lost in Plymouth when she was eleven. The woman's cry had looped Makepeace into a desperation that had also been hers.

At last she saw a large sign that read SYDENHAM TEAST & CO. It was a shipyard and looked normal; no sign of slaves. A large boat was being refitted, the name on its prow read HECTOR. She called up to a carpenter working on the deck, 'Where do they land the slaves?'

He pointed with an adze—farther along, he told her. She ran on.

There was a large warehouse standing back from the river but the landing stage in front of it was deserted except for a ragged black man who was throwing a bucketful of water onto its setts and sweeping them clean. A huge pillar had been set into concrete in the center, chains hanging loose from it like iron ribbons on a maypole. At one end of the stage there was a row of empty cages.

Once upon a time she'd wandered around the back of a fairground and into the area where they kept the animals. A troupe of performing dogs had been tied to a post, feline eyes had stared drearily out from cages . . . it had been like this; it had smelled like this. Except that here the animals were gone.

'Where's the owner?'

The negro looked towards the warehouse. Its doors were thrown back, showing neatly piled stacks of crates in the interior. A table had been put near the doors to catch the last of the sun and two men were sitting at it, one small, one large, working at some papers.

'Which of you's Mr Teast?'

The big man stood up, stretching. He wore a leather coat and a short-stocked whip stuck out of one pocket, its thongs trailing down to the floor.

'Are you Mr Teast?'

He showed large teeth in a grin. 'Wish I was, little lady. He's in Lunnon afeasting hisself and we're here, ain't we, Briggs?'

'Yes, captain.' The small man, who wore cuff preservers over his sleeves, didn't look up from the papers.

'There were some slaves just landed here,' Makepeace said.

'There was. I landed 'em. And now I wants to get home.'

'There was a woman ran away, with a child. You got her back.'

'What of it?'

'I want to buy her. And her little one.'

That got the attention of them both. The little man looked up, blinking, then gave a brief, unamused smile before dipping his quill into an inkpot and returning to his figures.

The captain settled one haunch on the edge of the table. 'You do, do ee? Well, you'm too late. They're all on their way to where they'm going. Can't delay in this business, can we, Briggs? Time's money. Longer you keep 'em idle, more they cost.' He leaned towards Makepeace. 'You couln't've afforded they anyway, ma dear. We deal in high quality here. What ee want? A nigger to help with the scrubbing?'

She was without her cloak, she realized, her sleeves were still rolled up, her skirt splashed with mud. She didn't look as if she had money. She hadn't; she'd given it to Sanders.

Behind captain and clerk loomed the vast capitalist enterprise that had infiltrated the country's bones, its fleets of ships, the banking houses, insurers, lawyers, dealers in stocks and shares; she felt as if she stood naked before a vast and efficient machine that had sucked the mother and child into its mechanism.

She knew then she wouldn't find them. Nor would the two of them ever see each other again. The knowledge robbed her of the power to be angry; she was beating on a door that wouldn't open. *Let me in. Let me find them.*

'I am a wealthy woman,' she said. 'I can send to Coutts Bank and have a draft for any amount you like within the week. I'll give you my note.'

He laughed, slapping his thigh; she'd thought only stage villains did that.

She could see herself reflected in his eyes, a tiny demented thing with pretensions—and something else—he'd taken a fancy to her. After a long voyage, any female would seem attractive but her powerlessness was the draw; helplessness provoked lust in men like these.

She said sharply, 'Where have they gone?'

Still grinning, without looking round, he said, 'Tell her, Briggs.'

Briggs tutted; he was in a hurry, but he was a correct little man. 'My dear lady, you must see that we cannot offend valued customers for the sake of a one-time-only buyer.' He drew a line under a column of numbers. 'There we are, captain, all accounted for. I must be off. Mrs Briggs will be waiting. Will you lock up?' He began taking off his cuff preservers.

'There y'are,' the captain said to Makepeace. 'The picaninny's gone to a good home, you don't want to worry your pretty head about him. As for her, that's for us to know and you to find out. You come along with me and maybe as I'll tell ee over a glass of rum.'

'You stinking pimp,' Makepeace said and watched his mouth go ugly before she walked away.

She paused by the black man, who was putting away his bucket and brush. 'Where did they take them?' she begged.

He stared at her and started to say something but Briggs had followed her. 'Time to go, Chalky.'

The man nodded and followed the clerk towards the boatyard. Makepeace ambled after them, to get away from the captain before he finished locking up the warehouse.

It was getting dark. The waterfront was emptying. The bare ribs of the *Hector* gaped at her as she passed it. Just before she reached the bridge, she sat down on a bollard, too dispirited to go on, grateful for the cold that pinched her.

You deserve it. All your money and you never thought of buying any of them.

I couldn't buy them all.

You could have saved another mother, another child. You never thought, never thought . . . you and your I-know-slavery. Now you've seen it.

I wanted to save that one, oh, I wanted to save that one.

The cry would stay in her ears. The picture of the running woman and the bobbing head of her child was etched into her memory with acid. It would burn forever.

After a while there were lanterns and exclamations but by that time she couldn't make sense of them.

Somebody with a deep and beautiful voice said, 'I'll carry her, Aaron. Ach, she's cold as snow.'

She was lifted and the somebody put the flaps of his coat round her so that she was pressed against his shirt and his body heat warmed her and melted the waiting tears. 'They took the little thing away from her. Oh God, her cry. I can't bear it.'

'It's a wicked world, so it is,' the voice said. 'We'll find her, now. Don't you worry, mavourneen, we'll see to that. There, there, *A Mhuire is truaigh*. Whisht, whisht now.' The nonsense was crooned at her through a miasma of whiskey but it was soothing, if Irish. Like the lullabies her father had sung her.

Aaron was limping beside them. 'Are you all right? At the inn they told Sanders where you'd gone and he told us. He's fetching the coach, ah, there it is. We'll soon have you tucked up in bed.'

'Where's Jacques?'

'I'm here, missus.' The voice came from the far side of the man who carried her. He sounded shaken, as the young are by the collapse of a respected elder.

Makepeace pulled herself together. 'You can put me down, sir. I am grateful, but I am capable of walking.'

'Thank the Lord for that, madam.' The voice had changed; it now drawled with the long vowels of upper-class English. She was put on her feet and her comforter, an enormous man, puffing slightly, made a bow involving a lot of hand-twirling.

'Makepeace, this is Sir Michael Murrough,' Aaron said. 'A very fine actor who has been good enough to join my merry band. He'll be coming with us to London.'

In the light of the coach lamps the man's face looked as round and flat as a clock.

Another actor, she thought, wearily. *A fat, overblown, Irish actor. The worst kind.* Ah, well, life was full of disappointments.

Chapter Six

THE two women were glad of the moth-eaten shawls covering their heads and shoulders to keep out not only the cold but some of the City's noise. On any weekday it was appalling. Iron-shod hooves and wheels rumbled on cobbles, cart drivers yelled angrily at each other through the congestion, animals mooed, baaed, clucked, squealed their way to market and slaughterhouse. Chestnut vendors, newspaper sellers, sweeps, all bawled their wares.

In Eastcheap a very large woman in a frightening approximation of Highland dress was playing the bagpipes badly and drowning out the competition presented by the more usual fiddlers and ballad singers.

Chadwell, the Fitch-Botleys' groom, who'd been brought along as protection but had never ventured into London before, had his hands over his ears.

As they approached the Monument, Lady Fitch-Botley paused out of habit to wait for the crossing-sweeper to clear a path for them through the horse dung and Philippa, unable to be heard, had to give her a shove as a reminder that crossing-sweepers, expecting to be tipped, did not extend this courtesy to women dressed as poorly as they were. Nor did traffic stop for them. Chadwell had to jump to avoid being run down by a brewers' dray.

It was quieter after Moorgate but they had to take to byways and expose themselves to a different sort of danger. 'Don't look around,' Philippa begged, 'Just scuttle.'

Georgiana Fitch-Botley was not a scuttler. Encountering a brawny gentleman in a blond wig and a rather fetching *robe à la polonaise* in Lad Lane, and discovering that Cat Alley offered services other than those of mouse catchers, she developed an appalled fascination with London's street names which kept her head turning this way and that.

'On this evidence, I suppose the Grub Street we're going to is infested with beetles,' she announced in her clear drawl. Some men who'd been conferring in a doorway looked up with predatory interest.

'Keep your voice down, will you?' Philippa muttered. 'They don't call this cut-through Floggers Alley for nothing.' She was relieved when they were through it without incident and waited until they were approaching the open space of Moorfields before she said, 'Grub Street's got woodworm, and it was described as the home of lice in the Lords the other day, but no beetles beyond the ordinary.' She couldn't resist adding, 'At one time it was called Gropecunt Lane but that was in the old days.'

'Lord, Pippy, they believe in calling a spade a spade 'round here, don't they.'

Philippa thanked God she hadn't let Jenny come with them. Even so, she'd miscalculated the effect that a walk through one of London's least salubrious areas would have on somebody who hadn't seen it before. Philippa herself found these places frightening but heartrending; as a child she'd been lost in the slums of Plymouth and only rescued from the fate awaiting lost little girls in a big city by the woman who was now landlady of the Pomeroy Arms at Babbs Cove. It had been an experience that made her less censorious than most towards the life of sin and those forced to lead it.

Georgiana, however, was being exposed to sights she hadn't dreamed of and if she was fascinated she was also appalled.

'The Society for the Suppression of Vice could have a field-day down here,' she said, 'and perhaps it should.'

'Suppression of poverty would be better,' Philippa said, bitterly. To her it was so obvious; she could not understand how other people didn't equate sin with desperation. Stephen, for instance, refused to see that extreme poverty was also enslavement. But then, he hadn't been exposed to it as she had. She wondered what effect it would have had on him if *he'd* been adrift and penniless in the back streets of a naval town. Then she wondered what effect it would have on him if he could see her and Lady Fitch-Botley now, in their shawls and patched petticoats and scuffed shoes.

It had been necessary to come on foot—to turn up on Grub Street in a coach or a sedan chair would have attracted an attention she wished to avoid—but that meant passing through places where even a good pair of boots was an incitement to theft. So they had dressed appropriately and come from Chelsea by water to London Bridge steps and walked up.

As protection, Chadwell was proving useless; he hadn't yet recovered from coming face-to-face with the fellow dressed as a woman in Lad Lane. He straggled bandy-legged behind them, gawping his innocence and being accosted by prostitutes, male and female. Eventually, Philippa had to take one of his arms and Georgiana the other and they'd walked him along between them to keep him safe.

They cut north across Moorfields—and desperation pursued them. What had been London's first recreational park where laundresses once laid their washing to dry on bushes, sheep grazed and yeomen had practiced at the archery butts, was now a few acres of scuffed bare earth edging the great brickworks where transient laborers, up from the country to earn a crust for the winter, had built huts for their families.

Men and women huddled in the cold by an open fire, carving clothes pegs out of twigs as they waited for work. Their ragged children pursued soldiers entering and leaving the grounds of the nearby Honorable Artillery Company, begging for pennies.

Georgiana swerved away to go and enquire solicitously of a woman who was crawling along a path on her knees and one hand, the other arm encircling a suckling baby, followed by a crying toddler.

She came back disgusted, trying to scrape vomit off her shoes with a twig. 'I thought she was ill, but she's drunk. Money for gin, apparently, but not for food.'

'Gin's cheaper,' Philippa said.

Grub Street had managed to escape the Great Fire and, therefore, Wren's project for a new, stone-built, airy London. Crazy-beamed upper stories still hung higgledy-piggledy over the unpaved roadway as they had in the days of the Tudors. Its name had changed, however, and its streetwalkers driven out to have their place taken by what successive governments had continued to find a greater evil—writers.

If you were a poor and radical hack, if you wanted to lampoon authority, had a complaint or a poetic bent—frequently the same thing—or merely wanted to transcribe the obscene to paper, if you wrote songs, polemics, wrote *anything*, you ended up in the cheap lodging provided by Grub Street and its surroundings.

Philippa had often accompanied her mother on visits to John Beasley's lodging at Number Eight, sometimes to go bail for him or bring him food—and had come to love the place.

It crackled with endeavour. The smell of paper and ink that came from its only shop, a stationer's with a delicious selection of notebooks, rulers, quills, editions of Dr Johnson's Dictionary, primers, examples of various print, easels, chalks, paper clips and blotters in its window, compensated for the sewage running along the gutters. A bottle shop and a tavern called The Scribbler's Arms suggested the street's other preoccupation. Abstracted men, and an occasional woman, stared out of the upper windows, chewing the end of their pens while, from downstairs rooms, came the screech of a printing press's weight being screwed tightly down onto a forme.

The air of danger was different again here, emitted by the risk the inhabitants ran. At any moment magistrates' men could appear to march into a house and drag away a protesting writer who had upset the government's sensibilities or, more often, his creditors.

Offending presses were supposed to be broken up, and more magistrates' men came with warrants to that effect—as they had for

John Beasley's after his arrest and not for the first time. One of Philippa's errands today was to ensure that his was rescued from destruction. Presses were valuable and, fortunately for the printers, magistrates' men were human. What usually happened was that they disassembled a press, took it to a pound where, once some silver had crossed their palms, the pieces were smuggled back to somewhere else in Grub Street and put together again.

Of its very nature, the street's literary radicalism had bled into its surroundings, as a splash of ink seeps more palely into wet paper, so that it was encircled not just by small associated tradesmen like paper-makers and stationers but by people of more dubious callings who also served it or required its services; struck-off lawyers, defrocked priests, agents provocateur, hunted men wanting to publish their innocence, apothecaries selling strange substances, Jacobite apologists and—Philippa hoped—forgers.

They passed Number Eight, where there was silence, on to the lopsided door of Number Twenty-seven and sounds of printing activity.

Philippa knocked and declared herself, adding her bona fides, 'Do you remember me, Mr Lucey? I am the missus's daughter.' People frequently forgot her but never her mother, she was used to it.

'Of course you are,' said a voice with enthusiasm, though a careful eye peeped out at her from behind a curtain before the door was opened. 'Come in, come in. My heart, what *are* you wearing? And who are these dear people?'

Philippa made explanations and introductions. 'Ginny, this is Mr Lucey who takes over editorship of *The Passenger* when John Beasley can't.'

They were led into a monochrome room, all lead, black beams, distemper and white paper, its light coming not from the street windows, which were curtained but from a large window at the back, overlooking a yard. The flat bed of a press that hadn't changed in design since the time of Gutenberg took up most of the space. In what was left, an aproned young man was squinting at a chapbook and choosing type from racks to set into a forme.

Mr Lucey provided the color; he was tall, abnormally thin and wore a brilliant turquoise tasselled smoking cap on his bald head, a pink and gold brocaded waistcoat and green breeches from the days when they still tied them at the knee with ribbons. His long, tapering fingers flirted constantly with the air and looked inadequate for the pressure all printers had to exert on the great lever of their press. Like most members of his profession, he had a bad back and his hand went frequently to his suffering lumbar region.

'You've heard the latest, of course?' Mr Lucey clutched at the press's handle for support as if transmitting the news was going to be too much for his legs. 'You know what they're accusing poor dear John of?'

'Sedition, surely.'

Mr Lucey's chin and eyes described a withering arc. 'High treason. *Treason*. Do you know where they took him and Horne Tooke and John Thelwall yesterday, the lambs? To the *Tower*.'

'Treason?' Philippa's shock was sufficient to gratify even Mr Lucey. She turned to Georgiana. 'Oh God, Ginny, they'll hang him.' Sedition had been bad enough but at least it was not a capital crime. She looked back at Lucey. 'How can it be high treason to publish a tract on reform?'

'Well, they *say* he and the others formed a convention and, as we know, thanks to our bloodthirsty Froggy friends, the word "convention" has become a tribal war whoop against anyone who disagrees with Mr Pitt.'

Mr Lucey had fetched down a book from a shelf. 'Here we are. I looked it up yesterday. High treason defined in a statute of 1351 as "compassing the death of the King or levying war against him."'

He shut the book with a slam. '*Well*. They raided Number Eight yesterday looking for arms, didn't they, Jamie?'

The young typesetter looked up and nodded.

'We all know our John, the dear heart. Breathes fire like a dragon but couldn't wield a hatpin, bless him. Anyway, they raided Number Eight and came away with a blunderbuss. Old Mr Prosser, he's got the rooms above John's, he told them it was his, he collects memorabilia from the Civil War. Didn't he, Jamie? Didn't he say it was his? Over and over, he told them but, no, they would have it the thing was John's. It's old enough to blow up in their faces if they fire it— and I do, *do* hope it does. *What* your dear mother will say when she hears, I can't think. Such a friend she's been to him.'

'A lawyer,' said Philippa, 'we'll get him the best lawyers.'

'Well, yes,' Mr Lucey looked dubious, 'though I always agree with dear Ollie Goldsmith who said: "Laws grind the poor, and rich men rule the law."'

Georgiana broke in brightly: 'Or Shakespeare who said: "First thing we do, let's kill all the lawyers."'

'Dick the Butcher,' exulted Mr Lucey. 'I've found a twin soul.'

Philippa interrupted their exchange of literary esteem. The sooner she could finish her business here, the sooner she could organize John Beasley's defense. 'I need a forger, Mr Lucey. It's a matter of helping a friend escape from France. Before he went off to get arrested, Uncle John said that you might know of someone who could make a French *certificat* for me.'

'*Look* at her,' Mr Lucey exclaimed to Georgiana. 'The very pattern of an English rose and can I find her a forger. So like her dear mother in many ways. Well, Miss Philippa, it so happens that I *can*, not that I've used him in an illegal capacity, of course, but occasionally one wants things authenticated that haven't been authenticated, if you know what I mean. Only the other day one got one's hands on a long-lost play by Ben Jonson which dear Ben had neglected to sign though one *knew* it was his . . .'

He caught Philippa's eye and bridled. 'Don't you look at me like that, miss. We all get inky fingers if we're to survive in this business.'

'You mistake me,' Philippa told him, gently, 'I am very grateful.'

Mollified, Lucey slapped the back of one of his hands with the fingers of the other. 'There I go, *such* a temper. I'm just a-tremble over this treason affair. All forgiven? Now, I'm not saying Scratcher's your man but he *is* foreign and very thick with our Froggy friends.'

'He sounds the perfect thing.'

'Not perhaps the best description of our Scratcher.' Mr Lucey went to an ink-stained shelf and scribbled some words on a scrap of paper. 'He's not the most salubrious member of our little coterie, is he, Jamie? Festering would not be too strong a word. And *cautious* . . . my dear, he suspects his own *fleas* of informing on him.'

'Perhaps you could let him know that I won't.'

'That's what I'm doing. Jamie dear, run this round to Scratcher and see if he's fit to receive. We don't want Miss Philippa encountering him in one of his turns, do we?'

While they waited, Lucey told them he had already been to the Tower to see if he could gain admittance to the prisoners. 'And got nowhere, of course. When I demanded to see the lieutenant, the beefeater I talked to was *unbelievably* rude, he told me to . . . well, I won't tell you what he told me to do but he wouldn't let me in. I said to him, I said: "I suppose I'll only be able to see my friends when their heads are stuck up on poles, will I?" But it was lost on that vermin, of course, simply *lost*.'

In the circumstances, Philippa thought it had been brave of Lucey to go at all, especially if he'd been dressed as he was now. But courage was all around. Hidden upstairs, Lucey told her, waiting for distribution, were several dozen copies of Paine's *Rights of Man*, which he had managed to retrieve from Beasley's print shop before they could be burned—'*Such* a worthy book'—and he was happy to accept some money with which to rescue Beasley's press from the pound. 'Do thank your mother,' he said, as he took it and, resignedly, Philippa said she would.

While the printer was out of the room fetching some refreshment, Georgiana explored, picking up one of the sheets that Jamie had been setting into type. 'Hannah More,' she said. 'Look at this, Pippy, he's publishing the enemy.'

'*Pirating* the enemy, I think.' It did not seem likely that a woman who was gaining fame as a purveyor of morals and education to the poor would use Lucey to print her tracts; it was hardly less surprising to find Lucey prepared to broadcast strictures echoing the hellfire that Old Testament prophets had promised to the Cities of the Plain.

'I'm sure dear Miss More would be delighted to have her work disseminated in these sinful parts, permission or no permission.' Lucey had returned, tray in hand. 'Those little chapbooks sell like Christmas beef at a penny a time. That only provides me with a ha'penny profit. Still, times are hard and a ha'penny is a ha'penny.'

He looked over Georgiana's shoulder. 'Ah yes, *The Story of Sinful Sally*—very popular. I've seen raddled old whores break down and cry at poor Sally's decline into sin and her eventual repentance. Of course, it has to be read to them . . .'

'I suppose if she's inspiring the lower classes to learn to read . . .' Georgiana said, doubtfully.

'I suppose so,' Philippa said. 'I just wish she wouldn't lecture them.'

Miss More's works had been urged on her by Stephen, who was an admirer. There was no doubt the woman wrote entertainingly for a public that was otherwise catered for by churchmen prepared to bore it into virtue, but Philippa disliked her insistence on telling the poor to be content with a position that had been designed for them by Providence, at the same time urging them to give thanks for an upper class good enough to bestrew them with charity.

'She lectures women as well,' she said, and picked up another sheet. 'She wouldn't approve of us, Ginny. It says here: "A woman's obligation to promote good works in her husband restores her to all the dignity of equality." I hope you're promoting good works in Sir Charles.'

'It's a good day's work if I can stop him raising hell at his club.'

'Then you must be resigned,' Philippa said, reading on, 'because Miss More further tells us that "to demand equality is to quarrel with Providence and not with the government. For the woman is below her husband and the children are below their mother and the servant is below his master."'

'Does she, indeed?' said Georgiana. 'Give me a pen.'

Jamie was back. 'Scratcher's a bit waxy, Mr Lucey, a-cause of he's missing his pipe but I reckon that's all to the good along of that'll make him agreeable to do what the lady wants.'

'Scratcher's an opium eater,' Mr Lucey explained. 'I wonder if I should come with you. I only hesitate because he and I had a falling out over our last transaction. Better perhaps if Jamie accompanies you. He's very sound in these matters, aren't you, Jamie?'

As he cupped his hand round the back of the boy's neck, Jamie preened with a mental and physical gratification. 'I'll see she don't come to no harm.'

'I know you will.'

Georgiana had got herself writing material and sat herself down on a stool with the absorption of one visited by a muse, so Philippa left her to Chadwell and Lucey.

As they walked down the street, she asked, 'Are you happy as a printer, Jamie?'

'Only a 'prentice yet, miss, but Mr Lucey, he says I'm comin' on wonderful. Never learned nothing but how to filch till Mr Lucey took me up . . . he's a tip-top man, miss. People laugh at him but they don't know.'

'No,' Philippa agreed, 'they don't.'

They turned into a narrow, fetid alley, empty for the most part and with its few windows shuttered. Philippa nevertheless received the strong impression of being noticed, as if they were passing a succession of blind men who turned to watch their progress when they'd gone by. She saw that Jamie stared aggressively at some of the shutters and tapped the side of his nose with intent.

They stopped outside a door so badly rotted at the base that it only filled three-quarters of the entrance. 'Do I call him Mr Scratcher?'

But that, it appeared, being the local term for a forger, was the man's designation, not his name which, Jamie said, started with Vladimir and ended in more consonants than was decent. 'Nobody don't know where he come from and I reckon as he's forgot but he talks a mort of languages and when his hand's steady he can copy a cully's signature so's that cully'll think he signed it.'

He gave one knock on the door, then slid his hand through a hole in the wood and lifted the latch inside. 'Me again, Scratcher, with the lady.'

They had to leave the door open in order to see the man whose upper body sprawled across a table which, apart from the stool he sat on, made up the room's only furniture. Philippa would have left it open anyway; the room was too cold to get any colder and its smell was strong and extraordinary—dirt dominated by the sweet scent of opium cut through by etching acid.

'Mr Vladimir?' asked Philippa.

He raised his head; he was so emaciated it seemed to take effort for him to do that much. 'What you want?'

Being unused to seeing one, Philippa was shocked by his beard but it and his hair were the only flourishing things about him, a tangled black bush surrounding a large nose and a pair of dulled brown eyes. His grimy, beautifully-shaped hands began rasping at the wooden tabletop, as if he'd been awakened to a gnawing pain.

She explained what she had come for in tones used to reach the deaf; she had to compete with a thumping on the ceiling so rhythmic that she wondered if a steam pump was in operation in the room above.

He addressed Jamie. 'She don't look like she got the canaries.'

'Canneries?' A thick accent was not aided in audibility by the banging overhead.

'Guineas, miss,' Jamie translated. He raised his voice: 'The lady ain't short, Scratcher, she's in disguise. She'll pay a fair price.'

'Yes,' Philippa said, and reiterated because she didn't know whether this scarecrow had understood. 'A passport and a *certificat de civisme*, a French identity card. I have my own here for you to copy . . .' She took a package from her sleeve and laid it on the table. During her last visit to the Condorcets she had been required, as a foreigner, to be issued with a *certificat*—an identity card and testimonial of public reliability all in one. Now, under the Law of Suspects, the requirement was applied to all French subjects.

'Yeah, yeah,' the Scratcher said. 'I do *certificats* whole damn time. What you want? Issued in Paris?'

'Section Thirty-One.' This was the section that included the Rue Saint Antoine; anyone coming from the area which had seen the downfall of the Bastille was likely to be regarded as above suspicion.

She was bewildered and relieved by the ease with which this man was accepting her commission; she'd expected greater difficulty. Indeed, originally she had intended to circumvent the whole unpleasant business of forgery by trying to buy a used passport and *certificat* from the French emigré community. Though the aristocrats, being personae non grata with the revolutionary government, were unlikely to have them, it was possible that their servants who had so loyally followed them into exile, would. But, again, awkward questions would have had to be answered.

In any case, traveling papers had to carry a description of the holder and she could not be sure of finding a man willing to sell her his who sufficiently resembled Condorcet by being in his fifties and six foot tall with brown eyes.

'Fifty canaries,' Scratcher said.

'One,' Jamie said firmly.

'Forty-five or go fuck.'

Jamie took Philippa's arm to usher her to the door. 'This way, miss. We ain't staying.'

Philippa was about to protest—she was unused to the niceties of barter—when a commotion broke out overhead; a series of choking grunts accompanied by a scream in dramatic coloratura.

What was terrible was that the two men took no notice. Scratcher was beckoning her with a limp hand and saying something, while Jamie teetered with her on the threshold.

'There's been an accident . . .' she said.

'Don't you worry about that, miss,' Jamie told her, and to Scratcher, 'Two, and that's generous.'

They continued to bargain. A curtain Philippa hadn't noticed was flung aside at the far end of the room to reveal a tiny staircase and a large man. He was buttoning his front breeches flap. He passed them without a word and went out.

'Thirty.'

'Two and a half.'

A woman came down the stairs, tying the strings of her grubby bodice. She said, 'Twenty-five and he ain't doing it for a penny less.' She looked at the astonished Philippa. 'Oh, I heard,' she said with aggression, 'Don't think I weren't listening for being otherwise engaged. That's a thin ceiling. You want a passport and a certificker you bloody well pay.' She began to count on her fingers. 'There's the type—that's got to be damaged special so it looks like the cheap print the Frogs use—there's the Froggy ink, we got to find a press, there's copying the committee signature . . .'

'If he's done 'em before, you got this stuff already,' Jamie pointed out.

'Got? Got?' The woman's voice went up in a crescendo of desperation. 'He sold it. We got to buy it all over. He sells ev'ything, *ev'ything*. Moment we got anything, the bastard pawns it for a pipe of bloody poppy. Look. *Look*.' She circled the empty room, whacking the man at the table across his head every time she passed him. 'We had furniture once. Where's it now? Down the bloody fulker's, that's where.'

She seized the Scratcher by his abundant hair and pulled his face up from the table, twisting it around so that they could stare at it, like Judith exposing the head of Holofernes. 'See? He don't care I got to whore to keep us, he'd filch the shillin' I just earned if he could. Woul'n't you?'

She shook the man's head back and forth as if she were scrubbing something with it. '*Woul'n't* you, you Polish pig?'

The man's face, what could be seen of it, didn't change expression as it flopped back and forth. His eyes remained indifferent.

The woman let go of her husband's hair and went to pound on the wall instead, crying.

'Two now,' Jamie said, 'and three on delivery.'

The woman's weeping quietened.

'Two now and *ten* on delivery,' Philippa said. She brought her purse out from her sleeve and crossed the floor to insert two guineas into the woman's hand. She set her own French papers and the instructions for Condorcet's in front of the forger. 'Dependent on it being done within the week.'

As they went back, Jamie lectured her on overgenerosity but she was unrepentant. 'Mrs Scratcher needs the money,' she said. 'I think she's a faithful woman.'

Jamie rolled his eyes. 'She ain't Mrs Scratcher and nobody couldn't call her faithful.'

'I think she is,' Philippa said. 'She could have left him.'

At Number Twenty-seven, Grub Street, Georgiana's muse had just released its grip. 'There,' she said, waving the paper she'd been writing under Philippa's nose. 'So much for Hallelujah Hannah. I'm inspired. Gervase here says he'll give it front page on *The Passenger*, won't you, Gervase? Oh ho, Miss More, just you watch us apples swim.'

'A remarkable piece,' Mr Lucey nodded. 'I salute a new talent.'

Georgiana was dancing. 'Read it, read it.'

Philippa read it. The handwriting was schoolgirlish, the spelling bad and its punctuation nonexistent but, as an attack on Hannah More and her insistence that society's status quo should be maintained, it was telling. The title alone, 'More of the Same,' was inspired.

The article's thrust was that change was vital for Britain's health; society had to change and *had* always changed '. . . or would we not even now be paying our tithes to the Pope, Miss More? Would we have rejoiced at the glorious Revolution, Miss More?

'We change our clothes and our bedsheets for cleanliness, why then must we not allow fresh air into a system that will allow those laboring in darkness to breath it . . .'

Slavery, Georiana had written, was soon to be consigned to the pit that had conceived it but other slaveries must go with it, that of women for a start . . . There had to be reform at all levels of class.

'Nor should we be so frightened by the Terror that we refuse to contemplate change. Because Scylla has wrecked the ship of France, must we assume that Charybdis is a less welcoming shore?'

Philippa clutched the paper to her and flopped down onto a stool. 'Oh, Ginny,' she said, 'you're a *writer*.'

Lady Fitch-Botley was still hopping with self-gratification. 'Ain't I just? I'll tell 'em. I can tell 'em every week, can't I, Gervase?'

'Delighted,' said Mr Lucey.

So was Philippa. She had reluctantly prepared a somewhat dry editorial, though on a similar theme, but she recognized that she'd been surpassed—and was happy for both *The Passenger* and her friend that this should be so. There was an animation to Ginny that she'd never seen before.

They said their good-byes and went out into Grub Street, Georgiana floating on triumph. 'I always wanted to write, Pippy. I knew I could. I used to pen stories for the boys when they were little but Charles disapproved; he didn't want them brought up on fairy tales. But now I have an outlet . . . Oh, hello . . .'

Philippa turned. 'Who are you waving at?'

'I saw . . . I was *sure* I saw Sir Boy. You know Boy Blanchard, Pippy.'

'Are you certain?' She looked in the direction Georgiana indicated but saw only two women bargaining with an onion seller.

'My dear, you don't mistake that gentleman. So attractively vulpine. Of course I saw him. And I *think* he saw me.' Her face changed. 'Lord, what if he tells Charles?'

Sir Charles Fitch-Botley was not a man to be amused at his wife inhabiting an area like Grub Street dressed as washerwoman.

'If it was him, he can't have recognized you,' Philippa said, more in comfort than belief—Georgiana's beauty was not usually found among washerwomen, who lost theirs early. 'But surely, Chadwell will tell Sir Charles.'

'Oh no, Chadwell is *my* man.'

Philippa wondered at a household where husband and wife kept their secrets and their servants had different loyalties. Then she thought, *I shan't tell Stephen about this visit, either.*

Then she thought, *But when we are married, I shall do nothing behind his back. Once Nicolas has his* certificat *and has escaped, there will be no need to.*

They went on down to the river, Chadwell looking nervously around him, Georgiana still chattering, Philippa in thought.

It wasn't until their boatman was rowing them past Westminster that Lady Fitch-Botley left the subject of her literary achievement. 'I did so take to Gervase Lucey yet, oh dear, I have a dark suspicion that he and that boy are . . . you know . . . lovers.'

'They probably are.'

'But it's a hanging offense.'

'Yes.' Philippa thought of John Beasley locked in a dungeon of the Tower facing the death penalty, she thought of Mr Lucey and Jamie whom the law could persecute for being what they most happily were.

'What isn't?' she asked, bitterly.

A letter came from Makepeace to tell her daughters that the journey to Devon had passed without incident and that Tom Glossop had left for France. 'All well Babbs Cove,' it read. 'Dell fat. Expects again. Sends affectn as do all. Yr Uncle Aaron arrived safe, also fat, but have to wait for rest of troupe that did not catch same boat. ACTORS . . .' This last word underscored several time. 'Also accompanied by fat Irish player who don't like. Am putting on play on return. Much to tell. How Beasley? Expect in two weeks. Yr loving mother, M Hedley.'

Makepeace's letters always promised more than they delivered.

'Putting on a play?' Jenny remarked. 'Ma hates the theater.'

'But Uncle Aaron loves it and she loves Uncle Aaron, so I suppose he's suborned her.'

'Oh, Pippy, what joy.'

The sisters clasped hands at the thought of it.

Makepeace, with her American Puritan background and, even more, her belief that acting was no job for a mature adult, refused to countenance attending any play other than her beloved brother's, which meant that, since his was a touring company, such occasions were rare. She herself couldn't pretend to save her life and generally distrusted those who made a career of doing so. It was not, however, a prejudice she passed on to her girls. If they wished to see grown-up men and women, most of them no better than they should be, dress up, clown, and speak words not their own, then so be it.

Her daughters did. Jenny, Sally and their aunt had a permanent box at Newcastle-upon-Tyne's excellent Theatre Royal. And, though keeping her mother company in Chelsea had made Philippa a less regular playgoer, she went to the theater whenever she could.

Twenty-six years earlier, Sir Philip Dapifer's death had brought Makepeace to mental and economic destitution. With the newborn Philippa to support and accompanied by Betty, the former slave who had come with her from America, and Tantaquidgin, her Huron servant, she had found sanctuary for the four of them with Aaron's troupe, then a band of ill-assorted thespians forced to perform in market squares, inns and any barn they could beg from a local farmer. Baby Philippa, earning her keep, had been floated on a paper stream as the basketed Moses in *The Pharaoh's Daughter*, been clutched to a bosom and speared in *Macbeth* and had generally raised tears to bucolic eyes from Land's End to John O' Groats.

'And never missed a cue, bless you,' her uncle had told her. He'd tried to prevail on her to take up the profession ever since but she'd refused; she knew her limitations. Nevertheless the smell of theater reawakened an excitement in her blood, as if she'd imbibed greasepaint along with her mother's milk.

'I haven't been to a play since . . .' She stopped.

'What was it?'

'It was Mrs Siddons in something. *Richard II*, I think . . .' Her memory was imperfect because, for once, the play had been of less importance than her companion.

Andrew Ffoulkes, just back from another rescue mission in France, had turned up at Reach House, bringing noise and bustle like a sea breeze into its grieving interior. 'Right y'are, missus. Come along, Pippy, get your traps, we're off to see the divine Siddons. Do you both good.'

Makepeace had refused to be done good to but she'd urged her daughter to go and, guiltily but faintly resisting, Philippa had gone.

Wonderful, wonderful. All the way to London, he'd talked of the excursion he and The League had made to France. She could remember *that* perfectly, every word. This time they'd snatched most of the de Précourt family almost from the gates of prison. 'Couldn't get the poor old Count, though,' Andrew had said. 'Only persuaded the Countess to come away for the sake of her children. Brave little devils, too. When I gave the eldest something to eat, she said: "Thank you, m'sieu, *now* I can admit I am hungry." Wouldn't complain before, d'ye see.'

He'd glanced at her. 'All right, all right, Pip, there were thousands of hungry little 'uns before the Revolution but I didn't know them, did I?'

All the way back, she remembered now, they'd argued about the character of Richard II. She thought him tragic; he thought the king 'about as useful as marmalade. All that sittin' about tellin' sad stories.'

Unlike Stephen who became perturbed if she disagreed with him, Ffoulkes enjoyed their arguments though he pretended it was *lèse majesté* for the godchild to contradict the godfather.

He'd been interested by a young actress playing one of the queen's ladies. 'Did you see her, Pip? Frail little thing, fair hair, sorrowful look.'

Like his mother. Like his first wife.

She'd said, 'I knew you'd notice her, you are always attracted by that complexion.'

He'd protested, genuinely surprised, but she'd known that she was stealing that night from the ashy-haired, delicately boned female of piteous appearance, whoever she was, that he would eventually marry.

As he had.

It was a week of letters. There was one from Stephen Heilbron. He spared her from descriptions of the abominations he was uncovering, merely saying that God must weep to see them. He said he was facing more ferocious opposition from the slave traders of Liverpool than any he'd encountered before. 'A hopeful sign, for it shows they feel the threat of the Society's activities.

'One slave trader, a great man in this city, had the impudence to tell me that a negro on a slave ship has nearly twice as much cubic air to breathe as a British soldier in a tent, that he had never heard of a slave being treated cruelly and he wished the English laborer half as happy. He tried to throw me with the old fallacy that abolition will turn the country into a scene of bankruptcy and ruin. I told him: "This or that measure is always supposed to ruin commerce—it never has, nor will."'

He didn't mention that he had again been physically attacked, though she'd read in the *Morning Post* that 'Mr Heilbron was well pummelled by adherents of the merchants of Liverpool for his interference in their legal trade.'

His courage brought tears to her eyes; as ever, she felt how he deserved more of her than she could give. Writing a letter back, she wracked her brains for incidents with which to amuse him since, as she knew, her excursion to Grub Street would not.

Instead, she included news of Makepeace: 'We have had an intriguing missive from Mama who has successfully met up with Uncle Aaron, and talks mysteriously of putting on a play after her return from the southwest.'

The reply was affectionate but carried a sting in its tail. 'Though I have ceased to be surprised by your mother's adventuring spirit, I should be sorry if she should involve herself in the theater and sorrier yet were you to admit yourself to her enterprise. I confess that as a heedless youth nobody enjoyed a good play more than myself but I have been awakened to the theater's innate folly and its occasion for vice of all kinds, since then I have eschewed it like the plague. Philippa, my dear love, let our minds dwell constantly on Eternity and the future consequences of our conduct.'

The next day she heard from Andrew Ffoulkes. His letter had been posted in Birmingham and was written in the usual scrawl that suggested he was rushing off to do something else. The stewards on his various estates complained constantly that to read his instructions took especial training.

'Milady wishes to be remembered to you through chattering teeth, wrapped her up in fur like Baby Bunting but the north proved too cold for her French blood, which was not even warmed by new engine sheds in Telford foundry, so on way home though must visit Norfolk first to see how turnips proceed. Hope B obliged with *certificat* for C.'

'What does Andrew say?' asked Jenny, watching her sister's face.

'He's coming home.' She tried to keep her voice matter-of-fact. 'Félicie doesn't like the cold. I think he's hoping to divert her with his turnip experiment.'

Jenny said, 'Lady Ffoulkes don't strike me as a turnip-lover.'

Philippa grinned at her. 'Nor me.'

Jenny didn't smile back. She reached over and touched Philippa's hand. 'Dear, *dear* sister,' she said.

Her compassion was shocking. *She knows*, Philippa thought. *And this is how she sees me, as someone who picks up crumbs from the rich man's table, waiting for a smile, a conversation left over from another woman's feast. A barren little planet so far outside the sun's warmth that its summer is but a snatched minute or two.*

She crossed to the sofa to sit beside Jenny and kiss her. 'Does Ma know?' she asked.

'I think she does now. I . . . may have mentioned something.'

'But you've always known?'

She realized with a jolt that Blanchard knew as well; during their first few minutes in Andrew's library on the night of the ball, he'd looked at her with the commiseration for the wounded that Jenny was showing now.

It was unsettling that two such disparate pairs of eyes, one gentle, one hard, had pierced the coconut shell like skewers. *Was it so obvious? Do I wear a placard*: HERE IS A LOVELORN MAIDEN?

'Always,' Jenny said, 'and I'm so sorry. So sorry, Pippy dear.'

Philippa kissed her again. 'I shall be all right, you know.'

'Will you?'

'Oh, yes. I'm not the Maid of Astolat and sure as taxes Andrew Ffoulkes isn't Sir Lancelot. Once I am married to Stephen and have a thousand children, think how happy I shall be.' She smiled. 'And I shall chase all your suitors away so that you may stay a perennial aunt and help me with them.'

But Jenny was dealing in truths this evening. 'I shall marry,' she said, 'but I shall not love anyone like you love Andrew. I couldn't love any man like that. It isn't helpful.'

Philippa smiled ruefully. 'Obviously not, but one can't help one's nature.'

'I can,' Jenny said.

K INDLY neighbors had awoken to the fact that the two sisters were without their mother and deluged them with invitations it would have been churlish to decline. The week passed in morning coffees, afternoon teas, soirées and suppers. They were generally feminine affairs, most of Chelsea's menfolk spending their days pursuing foxes, stags, otters and pheasants before the season ended, and their evenings in further masculine pursuits at their London clubs.

It was a surprise, therefore, to Philippa and Jenny, even to its hostess, when Sir Charles Fitch-Botley turned up at his own house in the middle of an evening card party given by his wife—with a friend in tow.

He kissed his wife noisily and announced to the company: 'Blanchard here thinks I don't spend enough time by my own fire, so I came to give it a poke.' He giggled; he was drunk.

His companion was not.

'Sir Charles needed no persuasion to pass the evening in civilized company for once,' Sir Boy said. 'Lady Fitch-Botley, your servant, ma'am. We are fortunate to find you at home, but it is to be supposed you do not venture far these cold days.'

'Oh, she don't go much beyond Chelsea, do ee, Ginny?' her husband said.

Philippa saw that Georgiana was immediately floored and fumbled the introductions.

So it *had* been Blanchard in Grub Street. She'd wondered all week if Scratcher was the same man he used for League business—after all, the number of forgers in London who could duplicate French papers was surely limited. That, therefore, was what he'd been doing in the vicinity and how he'd glimpsed Georgiana. Had he also seen her?

Not, she thought, *that it mattered*. He would have inferred that she was there; it would have been too great a coincidence otherwise—Lady Fitch-Botley was unlikely to have ventured into such an area on her own initiative.

Yes, he had. When it was Philippa's turn to be bowed to, the eyes raised to hers were knowing. 'Ah, Miss Dapifer. Have you solved that little puzzle we talked about the other day?'

She took the offensive. 'I believe so, thank you, sir. Have you solved your own? A matter of a dentist, I believe?'

'Yes, indeed. We shall have to see which case has the quicker outcome.'

He gave the thin smile other women found attractive; she saw only the acid in it. She was disturbed that his hostility to the rescue of Condorcet was so personal. What difference did it make to him that another soul, even one whose politics he did not agree with, was snatched from the fire? Yet he was prepared to lie in order to ensure that it was not. He'd told her that his forger had been put *hors de combat* by an injured hand consequent from beating his wife.

But if Scratcher was the man referred to—and he must be—his hands had appeared uninjured. In fact, as she'd seen for herself, the only beatings likely to have taken place in Scratcher's household were those inflicted by Mrs Scratcher.

The man was unfathomable, but if there was battle between them, she had outflanked him. In two days' time she and Lady Fitch-Botley would return to Grub Street, Ginny to deliver her next article for *The Passenger*, she to pick up Condorcet's *certificat*.

She smiled at him with the generosity of a victor, especially one who had good teeth, and joined him at a table to partner Ginny in a game of whist against Blanchard and Eliza Morris.

By the end of the evening, she was left wondering whether she had been reading too many gothic novels and had *mis*read him. The glimpse of the wolf had gone. Sir Boy Blanchard was better than charming, he was *nice*; not patronizing, but with an assumption that they were as well read as he was, showing an intimacy with charity work that won Eliza's heart, an endearing impatience with himself when he forgot which cards were not yet out and an unflowery admiration of his partner's and opponents' play.

Had she been superstitious, though, it might have concerned Philippa that, notwithstanding, he and Eliza won every rubber.

'IT was good of Sir Boy not to mention seeing me to Charles,' Georgiana said when they embarked for London Bridge two days later. 'It is not as if I were committing a sin, but I fear Charles would not approve of my journalism.' Her eyelashes fluttered at the last word, amused at her own pride in it.

The article she was to deliver today was a progression on last week's, an attack on those who refused to countenance change, but this time concentrating on the cause of women. She had drawn heavily on Wollstonecraft's *Vindication* but, wisely, did not mention her source.

'Women are urged to be modest and obedient,' she'd written, 'yet these terms are used in order to ensure their thralldom, for what passes for virtue nowadays is only a want of courage to throw off prejudice.'

It was an admirable piece. Philippa thought that, however minutely, it would help to push society's thinking beyond the boundaries, even while inflaming it. But she, too, was sure Fitch-Botley would not approve.

She said: 'In any case, Sir Boy has no reason to connect an anonymous editorial in *The Passenger* with your presence in Grub Street. He must merely think that you were there on my account.'

'So he must.' Georgiana was relieved.

Philippa was less reassured for herself. There had been a curious incident the day before when, minutes after Marie Joséphine had set off for the village for her afternoon off, they'd heard her shrieking.

Running down to the carriage drive to the archway, Philippa and one of the footmen found the Frenchwoman still shouting imprecations and shaking her fist at the Thames's apparently empty embankment.

When they crossed the lane to look over the rail, they saw a man in a skiff hastily pulling away upriver.

Marie Joséphine's imprecations echoed across the water after him. '*Voleur! Va-t'en, cambrioleur!*'

'What did he do?'

'*Il se cachait derrière le voûte*. He thinks to thieve the house. He will kill us while missus is away. *Va chercher les chiens de garde.*'

What passed for the Reach's *chiens de garde* were probably on Sanders's and Hildy's bed, their usual place when Sanders was away. The two friendly retriever spaniels had been bought as a present by Makepeace for the coachman, the only member of the household who liked to shoot game. Hildy and every other female member of the family spoiled them dreadfully, much to Sanders's chagrin.

Philippa managed to calm her maid down. 'He is here two days,' Marie Joséphine explained. 'Yesterday I think he makes pee-pee in the entrance and I shout him to go away but today again he is here. *Il reste caché* to murder us.'

'Just takin' a breather out the wind, I reckon,' Hopkins said with a shrug at female French dramatics.

But Philippa, watching the skiff shoot past the grounds of the hospital, was inclined to trust Marie Joséphine's instinct that the man was up to no good. True, March had come in with a slicing wind but it would be curious for a rower to beach his boat and clamber up an embankment in order to get out of it.

However, there was little to be done but alert the Watch to a prowler and make sure that all shutters and doors in the house were securely bolted at night.

Philippa had lodged the incident at the back of her mind, but just now, as their waterman took her, Georgiana and Chadwell upriver, she'd turned to glance at the view from the stern—the slope of Chelsea Hospital's gardens down to the river was worth a look—and saw a skiff some two hundred yards behind their boat, on the same course.

It was a blustery day but sunny and the choppy water was speckled with reflections that bothered the eye so that detail at a distance escaped it, yet Philippa received the impression—as she had previously—that the skiff was a good one, a racing craft such as gentlemen used in their competitions, and that its rower, in rough clothing, his head and mouth hidden by a scarf, looked as much out of place in it as would a farmhand mounted on a thoroughbred.

She told herself that suspicion was the penalty suffered by those pursuing secret activity, as she was. There were hundreds of such skiffs on the river and no reason why some of them should not belong to a working man. Strange, though, that such an ill-fitting combination of boat and rower should crop up twice in three days on this particular stretch . . .

She kept an eye on it until, nearing the City, she lost sight of it in the traffic of the river which, in Londoners' efforts to avoid the throng of the streets, was becoming almost as congested. They had to wait in a cluster of other boats lining up to approach the landing steps. Once ashore, they were sucked into the maelstrom of the City's crowds where the man from the skiff, if he were indeed following her and Georgiana, would be one among a thousand.

She shrugged. Why *should* anyone be following them?

But the chill of suspicion struck again when they reached the print shop. Mr Lucey, it appeared, had talked to a male caller.

'He was *struck* when I mentioned that a lady had written the latest editorial. "We must not underestimate the fair sex," I told him. "Shakespeare says in women's eyes are the books, the arts, the academes, that contain and nourish all the world." And he agreed.'

'Did you tell him who the lady was?' Philippa asked.

'Oh, no. One does not break the anonymity of a leader writer.'

'When did he call?'

'Let me see, when was it, Jamie? The same day last week that you ladies did . . . yes, it was—not long after you went.'

'Was he a rough-looking man?'

'Indeed not.' Mr Lucey was offended. 'Quite the gentleman and obviously a free-thinker, put himself down as a subscriber to *The Passenger.*'

He fetched the subscription list and pointed to the name: 'S. Smith, Esq.' The address was Boodle's Club.

Philippa's eyes met Georgiana's. Blanchard was a member of Boodle's. But, then, so was nearly every man of fashion. And S. Smith, according to Lucey, had been very fashionable. 'Plain cloth, you know, but the *cut*, my dear, and the *fit*. How he dared venture in these parts . . . but he'd heard of my work, he said. In any case, he looked like a man who'd acquit himself well against any of the brutes around here.'

Definitely Blanchard.

Georgiana shrugged. 'Very well, he knows what I'm up to. Even nicer of him to keep it from Charles, most enlightened of him.'

Apparently, she accepted the man's right to inquire into her business; Philippa found it sinister. As she and Jamie walked on to the Scratcher's house, the image of a spider collecting flies in its web for later consumption kept occurring to her.

Mrs Scratcher was out or, at least, not at work today. The hovel was quiet. An iron pot from which issued the smell of stewing meat hung over a fire in the tiny grate.

There were other improvements, a good candle on the table lighted several quills with variously cut nibs, ink bottles and two small pieces of paper on one of which Scratcher, wearing a pair of mended spectacles, was carefully inscribing.

He pushed the spectacles up so that they disappeared into his hair as Philippa and Jamie entered. His eyes were sharper today but even less welcoming than they'd been the week before. 'Tell her go fuck,' he said to Jamie. 'I got other work.'

'Ain't you done it?'

'Busy,' Scratcher said. 'Tell her go fuck.'

Jamie was incredulous. 'You're never passing up ten canaries?'

'Busy,' Scratcher said, 'Tell her go fuck.'

Philippa snatched up the papers on the table. One was a bill 'for work done' amounting to £70. The other might have been an exact copy except that its total was £200. Somebody had commissioned Scratcher to make him a profit. All in a forger's day's work and nothing to do with her.

Jamie was arguing. After a bit Scratcher reached into a filthy pocket and produced the original two guineas down payment which he flung on the table at them. 'Now go fuck.'

'I'll offer you more,' Philippa said desperately. 'I'll offer you anything,'

Jamie, however, pulled her to the door and out into the alley. 'No good, miss. Twelve guineas is more'n he'll see in a month o'

Sundays, if he won't do it for that . . . I don't understand it, I *don't*. But it ain't the money, that's for sure. It's some'ing else.'

'What?'

'Dunno. For certain he ain't gone honest.'

'Are there any *other* forgers around?'

'Plenty, miss, but none of 'em don't do French.'

The wind blew the alley's detritus around their legs, a sodden piece off a poster lodged itself against the hem of Philippa's coat; an incomplete headline read, 'WANT . . .'

She felt shriveled and angry, not at Scratcher—one did not blame detritus for being what it was—not even at Blanchard whose refusal to help had put her in this situation, but at Sophie. *Why did you ask me? I am not fitted to deal with these things.*

Then, even more shamefully, came relief. The difficulty had proved insurmountable; she had been absolved from a duty that had cost her anguish and sleepless nights; she had tried her best, it was not her fault she'd failed.

The burden slipped from her shoulders. She thought, *I'll wait for Andrew to return home and he will see to it.*

Sophie's face rose up at her but Philippa was firm with it. *I know. The delay may be fatal and I'm sorry but there is nothing more I can do.*

Redeemed, she took Jamie's arm and started back.

At the corner of the alley they bumped into Mrs Scratcher. The intervening week had worked wonders on the woman; she was inadequately dressed for the weather but her face had shed its despair; she was almost jaunty. On her arm was a basket filled with groceries.

She even smiled at them. 'Got it, then?'

'He ain't done it,' Jamie told her savagely. 'Don't intend to.'

'He what?'

'Gave us our money back.'

'Can't've. I been spendin' it.' She indicated her basket.

'Got it from somewhere then,' Jamie said. 'Show her, miss.'

There was no need for Mrs Scratcher to see the returned

guineas. With a 'Stay there,' she was off towards her home using a stride that boded badly for Mr Scratcher.

They stayed where they were commanded; even so they could hear the screeches and thumps emerging from under the Scratcher door—they could have been heard in Grub Street. Then it quietened.

After a while, Mrs Scratcher emerged. She glanced up and down the alley, though Philippa and Jamie were the only people in it, before hurrying towards them and ushering them round the corner into a backyard, empty except for the corpse of a dog that was interesting some rooks.

She put a hand on Philippa's shoulder and another on Jamie's to draw them close like a stage conspirator but her face was pale. 'He'll do it,' she said. Her breath smelled of bad teeth and porter. 'But it'll cost you fifty.'

At Jamie's flinch, she glared. 'Fifty and we can flit. Go abroad, maybe. He's scared. What you been up to? Some'un's give him the cash *not* to do it *and* put the frighteners on him an' all. Some'un's told him he'll see him lagged if he does it . . .'

'Transported,' Jamie translated for Philippa's benefit.

Mrs Scratcher nodded. 'S'right. And they don't serve no poppy on a transport. I tell you, he's shittin' on his shoes.'

'Who?' Philippa asked. 'Who's frightened him?'

'Don't know, do I? I'm us'lly otherwise engaged when they come.' The woman became angry. 'An' if he thinks I'm spending another year on my back a-cause he ain't got no spine, he's got another think coming.' She took a deep breath. 'He'll do it. But it's fifty.'

Philippa nodded and reached into her sleeve for her purse. 'Here's five on account and I'll agree to forty-five more if you tell me who frightened him.'

Mrs Scratcher lifted her skirts to slide the coins behind a grubby garter. 'Give us a week. But don't you come to the house; Vlad reckons you been followed. Meet you in Saint Mary Axe round noon next Tuesday an' you make sure you looks behind you. He ain't much I grant you, but he's no bloody good to me in Botany Bay.'

She waggled her petticoats into place and made to leave but Philippa held on to her arm. 'You know, don't you?'

'No, I don't.' Then she sighed. 'It might be the one talks Frenchie to him. I only hear the voices. This one . . . he's a special. Lovely pipe he's got yet he ain't, if you know what I mean. I reckon Old Nick'd talk like him, crummy but nasty . . . sort of treacle with poison in it.'

'Thank you,' Philippa said.

Mrs Scratcher cocked her head in inquiry. 'Know him, do you?'

'Oh yes.'

The woman nodded. 'You stay here till I gone. I ain't bein' seen with you.' They watched her hurry away, ill-fitting shoes flapping on her feet, shoulders hunched; the picture of a woman nearing old age. Yet when she'd smiled at them, less than half an hour before, she'd revealed herself to be no more than twenty.

T HE arrangement this time was that Philippa should call for Georgiana—the Fitch-Botleys' house was the nearer to London—and go in by road with Chadwell driving the trap as close to the City as the traffic would permit, at which point the ladies would descend, use some reputable inn in which to don their disreputable cloaks and shawls, and proceed on foot.

'And our friend in the skiff can scull up and down the river until he sinks, God rot him,' Philippa had said.

Kitty Hays was to come with them. Whey they'd reported their doings to the Condorcet Society, she'd said: 'If you think you're leaving me behind, my dears, you're mistaken. Pursued by villains in boats—with poisoned daggers under their cloaks, no doubt. Too, *too* Elizabethan.'

Eliza Morris had been intimidated. 'It seems to me the man's prepared to do anything to stop that *certificat* reaching M Condorcet. Don't you see? Once you have it, he could set ruffians on you before you can post it, and get killed even. It's a lawless part of town.'

'I can't go to the magistrates, though, can I? I'm as lawless as Blanchard—more. I am accessory to a forgery and if I succeed with it, I could be arrested for treating with the enemy.'

'Just think though, Philippa, how vulgar to be murdered in Moorfields.'

'Then I shall contrive not to be murdered until I'm back in Chelsea.'

But the vulgarity of being murdered at all bothered Eliza and would, she said, upset her father. She did not offer to come.

There was no doubt, however, of Blanchard's earnestness to thwart Condorcet's rescue. The intervening week had proved that he was prepared to expend the time of more than one employee on it.

Philippa and Jenny had been followed on their various visits to friends, three times on trips to the village as well as to church on Sunday.

Mercifully, Jenny had remained unaware of what was behind her, but a gypsy woman who trailed them twice was not expert enough to escape the notice of the now very alert Marie Joséphine who tapped Philippa on the shoulder and muttered, *'Regard l'indigente salle en arrière. Elle nous suit.'*

Philippa had turned round to see only a tree. 'Are you sure?'

'Bien sûr.'

'Ignore her.'

The weedy fellow who followed them to church was even less accomplished. He was not up to the pace Philippa set and was occasionally to be seen resting with one hand on a signpost while easing his boots with the other.

The situation was farcical, the more farcical because it was happening in the demure bowers of Chelsea, which rendered it not so much sinister as undignified. Philippa felt ridiculous, like a hen that some particularly ugly ducklings had mistakenly attached themselves to.

Nor could she divine the object of the exercise. Having put the fear of hell into Scratcher, Blanchard should have assumed that her attempt to rescue Condorcet had been nullified once and for all, yet obviously he did not. In which case he was crediting her with resources she did not have.

In a curious way her fear of Blanchard, which had been building, was diminished by what she regarded as an inept exercise in offense. That the man should send these clowns to dog her footsteps displayed not just rascally intent but vulgarity.

Incidents and matters of style that she had overlooked in him were now recalled; a too-slavish imitation of Ffoulkes's and the others' dress, overmuch use of French and Latin quotations, a jarring ferocity at the gaming tables, an unfastidiousness in referring to female acquaintances. Even to have penetrated the secret of her passion for Andrew Ffoulkes showed an unsuitable feminine trait in him.

Her mother had spotted him from the first. Makepeace could sniff out sham like a hound scenting a fox. She wondered why she herself hadn't been so acute and why his friends were still not. He spoke of inheriting a thousand Irish acres from his father but nobody had ever seen them and he had arrived at Eton—where he had performed brilliantly—without the train of English ancestors that weighted the others.

You don't belong, she thought. *Nothing wrong in that, of course, except your frantic imposture to prove that you do.*

Why he perceived her efforts as endangering him, she couldn't understand, but he was obviously prepared to go to considerable lengths to thwart her.

And if she succeeded in getting the *certificat* . . . what lengths would he go to then?

She dismissed Eliza's fears of violence; trickery seemed to be Blanchard's style; to pile her path with obstacles. Perhaps the very ineptitude of the people he'd sent to dog her was a deliberate maneuver on his part; she was to be made aware she was being watched—and be frightened off.

In that, he was failing. The possibility of getting hold of the forgery had once again landed on her shoulders like a yoke but with it had come determination. *If it can be done, it* will *be done.*

Every day Philippa scanned the names of those guillotined, carried by the English newspapers. At the beginning of the Terror the registers had been bordered in black and appeared prominently under the banners in large type that Mr Lucey called 'scareheads' but, as the toll drearily continued and the victims increasingly included people without titles and those nobody had ever heard of, the lists, though still bordered in black, were moved to less prominent positions.

So far Condorcet's name had not appeared on them.

Don't give way, Sophie. We'll save him yet.

The weather cheered her on. As she and Kitty walked up the carriage way to the Fitch-Botleys' house whence Chadwell was to drive them and Georgiana to London, it was one of those March days that always came as a surprise, a sudden release of a countryside and every creature in it from the imprisonment of winter.

Although early, the day was bright enough to warrant the parasols both women carried in anticipation of the open carriage ride. Birdsong was back in the air. Water splashed untidily in the bowl of the fountain as starlings preened themselves, blue tits darted among the trees with wisps in their beaks. A green woodpecker, its plumage incredible in the sun, pecked for grubs in the lawn. Farther off in the park, fallow deer posed in speckled elegance beneath the beeches.

There was a hint of green on the trees and against the stone of the stables a huge laburnum writhed in serpentine anticipation of the flowers to come.

Philippa even found herself moved to song. 'Jackie Boy,' she sang.

'Master,' Kitty sang back.

'Sing ye well?'

'Very well.'

'Hey down, Ho down, derry, derry down,' they chorused together.

With the sun warm on her back, Philippa climbed the steps to the portico, raised the heavy knocker and let it fall. The door opened. 'Good morning, Partridge. Tell Lady Fitch-Botley we're here, would you?'

'No, he damn well won't.' The footman was pushed aside so that he almost fell and Sir Charles Fitch-Botley stood in his place. He was in his shirtsleeves, his face puce from some exertion. The top buttons of his breeches were undone to allow for the swell of his considerable belly and he had a rattan cane in his right fist. 'Lady Fitch-Botley's locked in her room and there she'll damn well stay. And you, miss, can get off my step.'

His eyes bulged and spittle trembled in one side of his mouth. His looks had always been porcine but anger had stripped away sophistication and left an enormous boar standing there, about to charge.

He advanced on her, lowering his head to be nearer hers; he smelled of sweat and brandy. Philippa was too shocked to move.

'Oh, yes, I know about it. Coming here with your mimsy ways, your yes-Sir-Charles, no-Sir-Charles and no better than you should be.'

He caught sight of Kitty in the drive and shook his cane at her. 'And you, you monster, get back to that poor bastard you married. Had my way, you'd both be ducked for the hags you are. Leading that addlepate upstairs to think she can go against her husband and her country. Oh, yes, I had the truth out of her.'

His anger was feeding on itself and enjoying the feast. 'Well, there'll be no petticoat revolution in this house as the bitch has found out. Stay there.'

He stepped back into the entrance hall and gave a grunt as he stooped to pick up something lying on its floor. He came back waving it; he was out of control now.

'And *this*,' he shouted. 'This trash is handed to me in my own club. *My own club*.' It was a crumpled copy of *The Passenger*. 'I have to read the ravings of *my* wife in *my* club.' He showed his large teeth. 'Know what I did with it? What it deserved. I wiped my arse on it.'

He stepped forward and rubbed the paper against Philippa's front.

'Now get off my land, the two of you, and don't come back or I'll set the dogs on you.'

Somehow Philippa's legs took her down the steps to where Kitty was standing immobilized, her face clownish from the bloodless area that had formed around her mouth. She would have liked to put her arms around her, as much for her own comfort as Kitty's, but her coat was smeared and stinking. Instead, she took the woman's hand and led her away.

There was another yell from behind them. 'And I sent that damn groom off with a whipping. Taught him who's master in this house.'

They heard the door slam shut.

After a few yards, Kitty vomited. Helplessly, her own hand shaking, Philippa patted her on the back and waited until the retching was over.

A movement in one of the upper windows of the house caught her eye. Georgiana. Her hair hung loose. A red weal across one cheek accentuated her pallor. When she saw Philippa look up, she covered her face with her hands and turned away.

At the bottom of the drive, Kitty began moaning. 'I've never . . . he, he was so . . . Pippy, he'll tell my husband.'

Philippa tried to steady her breath and speak normally. 'Tell him what, dear? You've done nothing wrong.'

'Of course I've done wrong. All that secret plotting, the club. He'll tell Arthur, oh God.'

'We'll go to my house. I've got to change. We can take Mama's trap instead.'

Kitty stepped back. 'You're not still going?'

'*Kitty*. I'm to collect that *certificat* at noon. We have to hurry.'

'You're not still going. After *this*?'

'I have to. Nothing's changed.'

But it had and she knew it had.

It had been more than a brute shouting at them, horrible as that was. They had witnessed a truth. Everything they depended on for decency, the charity of men, poetry, chivalry, the hand-kissing, the everyday courtesies that pretended women had value . . . these things had been blown aside. As he'd stood in his doorway, Sir Charles Fitch-Botley had revealed the reality behind the mist. It was as if they had been picking flowers in a meadow and looked up to see the giant who owned it breathing fire. He had loosed the thunderbolt of the God of Abraham on the unrighteous. His was the huge figure that stood behind society's prettiness. He it was who came forth, weapon in hand, when his pygmies crossed the line drawn for them.

They had known it in theory but to come under its fire had broken their line. Georgiana would never be the same again, her talent stamped into obliteration under her husband's boot. Kitty's attempts at defiance had been shredded; she was running from the field like a panicking soldier in a rout.

And when it became known—as it would—not a soul would say it hadn't served them right. *'Good for Sir Charles, I'd have done the same in his place.' 'Well, my dears, you shouldn't have provoked him.'*

As for the assault on herself, there wasn't a magistrate who would sentence the man. The clubs would love it. *'Spread her with shit, eh? Serve the baggage right.'*

Oh, yes, it had changed everything. She didn't have time to analyze the alteration it had made in herself but she knew it was there.

'At least let me take you home,' she said, gently.

Kitty almost hit her. 'Get away from me. It's you . . . you and your ideas. Leave me alone.'

Philippa watched her blunder away in the direction of her house and then turned towards her own, walking quickly. There was a big oak beyond the gates with some dirty fingertips just showing on the nearside of its trunk. As she passed it, she thwacked them with her unopened parasol as hard as she could.

'Aaah,' somebody gasped faintly.

'Give your master a message from me,' Philippa told the tree over her shoulder. 'Tell him to go fuck himself.'

She'd never used the old Anglo-Saxon word as an imprecation before and if she hadn't been suffering from shock already she might have startled herself. As it was, Fitch-Botley had demonstrated that the ground they stood on was the dry and bloody dust of an arena. The iron fist prevailed; all gloves were off—hers, too.

A cowherd driving his beasts to the water meadow blinked as his 'Morning, miss,' was greeted with a snarl of bared teeth. Philippa thought she was smiling.

At home, she raced upstairs to her bedroom and stripped naked. Pouring water from the stand ewer into its basin, she began washing herself.

Toweled and in clean clothes, she was struggling with back buttons when Hildy came in and took over. 'What's oop, pet? Hopkins said tha came lowpin' in like a hooligin.'

Briefly, Philippa told her.

'Jist t'let me at the beggor,' Hildy begged of the Almighty. 'Ah'd finish the sod. Ah wish t'missus had been thor.'

'I wish she had, too.' Philippa leaned back and angled her head so that her cheek lay against that of the woman who'd dragged coal trucks through the Northumbrian mine in harness with Makepeace. 'She'd have told him, wouldn't she?'

'She'd've scalded his bawbels for pig-feed,' said Hildy, grimly.

'I miss her, Hildy.'

So much, and never more than today. Things happened when Makepeace was around but they happened right. Yet she had always needed her mother more than her mother needed her.

'Back amorrow, pet.'

Too late. Philippa Dapifer, you are a twenty-six-year-old woman with things to do that only you can do; you don't need your mother. 'Where's Jenny?'

'Sale o' work down the raa, at the Reeds' wi' Marie-Jozyfine.'

'Good.' She fetched down a hold-all from its cupboard and began packing. 'I'm going away for a while.'

Hildy watched her with concern. 'Howay, pet, tha's nivvor runnin' awa acause o' that dorty buggor?'

Is that how it would look? That she was too embarrassed to face people? Well, it would have to.

It was galling to leave the field to Fitch-Botley but she had a bigger battle to wage against a bigger foe. Even by the rules of this dirty fight, Blanchard had committed the inexcusable; he'd stepped aside from the main engagement to wound an innocent civilian. It had been nothing to him that Georgiana contributed an article to a publication few people read, yet he had taken the trouble to see she was whipped for it.

And, by God, Philippa Dapifer would hurt him for that.

She said, 'No, but I thought I'd go up to Raby for a visit. See Sally. Poor thing, she'll be missing Jenny.' She looked full at Hildy. 'And I'm going now.'

Hildy hissed with resignation. 'Joost lak yer Ma.' She watched Philippa's brisk movements around the room. 'What foor d'ye tak yer old claes?'

'They're comfortable. Go and ask Petrie to ready the trap and take me into London.'

'Tha's missed the stage north.'

'I'll get the night coach but I've got to go to Lincoln's Inn first— I have some legal business to settle.'

'Jenny not coomin' then?'

'No. She must stay for Ma and keep her out of trouble with this play.'

Hildy bent down, picked up the discarded clothing from the floor and sniffed them with distaste.

'I'll take those down,' Philippa said quickly.

'Get on wi' what ye're doing, lass, and leave summat for me.'

When the housekeeper had gone, Philippa forced herself to sit for a moment. In fact, she had plenty of time; the little ormolu clock by the side of her bed said ten o'clock. The incident on the Fitch-Botleys' steps had taken place little more than thirty minutes ago. Her body still trembled from it but her mind ran with limpid clarity. *What else was there to do? Ah, yes.*

She got up and went out of the room to the landing. 'Hildy.'

There was a call down in the hall, then Hildy's voice. 'What noo?'

'Fitch-Botley's groom, Chadwell. Do you know him?'

'Sanders do.' Nothing, probably not even the intimacy of their bed, would induce Hildy to call her husband by anything other than his surname.

'He's been dismissed. Ask Sanders when he comes back to find him a place.'

She went back to the bedroom, opened her escritoire and scribbled a note to Jenny, took out some papers from one of its pigeon-holes and inserted them neatly into the hold-all's pocket.

Is that all? Yes, I think so. Then let's be off.

O N their way along the river track, they passed a man limping Londonwards, the fingers of one of his hands being nursed in the other.

'Splash him,' Philippa told Petrie. As the trap's wheels spun yesterday's mud over the man's breeks, she bowed. What he shouted after them brought a blush to young Petrie's cheeks, not to hers.

Whether the horseman on a piebald who emerged from under a tree near the Physick Garden and cantered after them was another of Blanchard's myrmidons, she didn't know. She didn't care much.

H AVING been Makepeace's lawyer for years, George Hackbutt was used to the unusual. Once he'd heard Philippa's request, he sent for Mr Muddie who, he said, was the most discreet and reliable of his clerks.

'Ah, Muddie. Miss Dapifer requires you to step along to Saint Mary Axe right away and give this package of money to a lady you will find there. In return she will hand you a document to return to us here.'

'She's rather poorly dressed,' Philippa said. 'Quite young, though she looks older. Dark hair. And she may be suspicious but if you will explain to her that I dare not come myself for fear of pursuit, she will understand.'

Mr Muddie accepted both package and instructions without a blink. He was an elderly, stooped little man with mild eyes and it was Philippa who was taken aback when he asked his employer, 'Should I go armed, sir?'

'Should he go armed?' Mr Hackbutt asked her.

'Oh no, I don't think so.' How quickly men prepared for violence—but, then, violence could break out at any moment, as she'd found this very morning. These two expected it from the poor; it had come to her from a member of her own class.

However, it was unlikely to arise here, unless Mrs Scratcher was being followed, in which case she was sorry for whoever was doing it.

She had told the solicitor the truth so far as it went; she needed false papers to get somebody out of France. She hadn't mentioned the somebody's name. Her precaution, she'd said, was because she thought she was being spied on.

Mr Hackbutt took that in his stride as well; he not only assumed that the putative escapee was a royalist, but he shared the general belief that England had been infiltrated by a thousand agents of the Revolution.

Spies were being blamed for everything from a fall on the stock market to unrest in the Navy. An outbreak of cholera in Whitechapel had been put down to evil Frenchmen poisoning the water with rats-bane concealed in their snuffboxes. Poor rank and file émigrés who arrived in England without the connections possessed by most of the nobility were frequently likely to fall under suspicion and be imprisoned until they could prove their bona fides. One harmless Parisian hatmaker, fleeing the guillotine, had been picked up by the

Houndsditch Watch 'because he looked a villain' and was only released after a month when one of his former clients spoke for him.

From a window on the third floor of the building that housed Mr Hackbutt's offices, Philippa watched the foreshortened figure of Mr Muddie emerge from below, only to lose him immediately among the ant-runs of other paper-clutching clerks, lawyers and barristers going about the business of the Inn.

The grass of the square had not yet been cut and a wash of spindly pale mauve crocuses drifted across its lawn in lazy contrast to the black begowned figures scurrying around it.

There was a piebald among the horses tied to a hitching rail on the far side of the square; she noticed it because it was the only one—the legal fraternity, like most gentlemen, preferred monochromatic mounts.

She shook her head in disbelief that Blanchard had paid a horseman to wait on the London road in case she came by. But if he had, the rider's sojourn here would be fruitless.

She turned back to Mr Hackbutt. 'And how do things go in the matter of Uncle John?' she asked.

'Ah yes, Mr Beasley.' Mr Hackbutt spoke with distaste. 'I will not hide from you, Miss Dapifer, that my long experience of that young man leads me to believe that he will not help his own case.'

Philippa's did, too. Mr Hackbutt and 'the young man'—she thought how expressive it was of Beasley's permanent and sulky adolescence that he should be so described by an elderly man little more than ten years his senior—could never see eye to eye on politics. George Hackbutt was at heart a hunting country squire who happened to be an excellent lawyer; the near-black paneling of his office was decorated with the heads of foxes and cases of stuffed fish that had met their end on his estate in Surrey. His sympathy lay with Whig landowners like himself and not at all with the anarchic Beasley who, to add to their differences, loathed the outdoors and a nature which, he felt, was out to waylay him.

Their long and unlikely connection was Makepeace, for whom Mr Hackbutt had a high regard and who had used him to release her friend from the coils of the law in which he so frequently became entangled.

But, though they might interpret it differently, both men had a concern for the principle of justice. When Philippa had approached Mr Hackbutt to take on Beasley's defence, it was to find him already appalled that, against sound legal advice, the Attorney General was to prosecute the radicals for high treason, of which they were certainly innocent, rather than sedition, of which they were probably guilty.

'A rash and violent decision,' he'd told Philippa. 'Won't do at all, ain't fair and won't work. Can't see what Mr Pitt's about, bringin' down a deer with artillery. Juries don't like it.'

'Did they let you into the Tower to see Uncle John?' she asked now.

'They did, though not without considerable persuasion. The fools'—thus did Mr Hackbutt refer to the government—'have suspended habeas corpus, did ye know? Is this a way to fight the Terrorists? To abandon every principle achieved since Magna Carta? We'll be settin' up a guillotine in Parliament Square next.'

'How was he?'

'Beasley? Enjoyin' his martyrdom, I'd say. The others less so. My terrier could've nipped a dozen rats in the cell they're bein' held in—place hasn't seen the light of day since the late unlamented Bloody Mary was on the throne. Now, now'—he patted Philippa's shoulder—'we must not give way. And though it's me as says it as shouldn't, I am to be congratulated—I've bagged Erskine for the defense.'

'A good thing?' asked Philippa.

'Thomas Erskine? Finest counsel in England. Set Erskine on the scent and he'll run the varmint to the kill.' Mr Hackbutt flourished a hunting horn that acted as a paperweight on his desk.

'Uncle John's lucky to have you,' Philippa said, and meant it. 'Ma will be grateful.'

'Ah, well, your mother, you know,' Mr Hackbutt said, as if that explained everything. 'But I'll tell you this. I'd've taken the case even so, not for Beasley, not even for your mother, but because I'll not stand by to see the law twisted in a plot to convict men on a wrong charge.'

He leaned back in his chair and grimaced. 'It ain't makin' me popular around the Inn, I can tell you. "Sidin' with Paine-ites against your king and country, Hackbutt? Where's your patriotism?" they ask me. "Where it always was," I tell 'em, "on the same side as English justice."'

It was an unsought reminder that there was still decency to put on the scales against the weight of men like Fitch-Botley. Philippa found herself comforted to the point of tears.

Mr Muddie returned soon after. He carried a package wrapped in a dirty scrap of cloth, which he handed to Mr Hackbutt who handed it to Philippa.

'All well, Muddie?'

'The transaction was without incident, sir.'

'Well done.' He turned to Philippa. 'Is that what you wanted, Miss Dapifer?'

She was holding in her hands a cardboard passport stamped with the insignia of the French Republic made out to Jean-Pierre Brosse—the most forgettable name she'd been able to think of. Tucked inside it was a *certificat de civisme* declaring M Brosse's right to French citizenship, his address, 42 Passage de Lappe, Paris 31, his age and description, and it was signed on behalf of the *Comité Révolutionnaire, Paris Section Trente-et-un* by a squiggle which, since section heads were constantly changing, didn't matter.

Small wonder that Andrew and his League had been able to make rescue after rescue while they carried papers like these. If forgery was an art, Scratcher was its Rembrandt—both passport and *certificat* reeked of poverty-ridden bureaucracy; the type was worn at its edges by apparent overuse, and the written details attested to the hurried, jaded hand of the Watch Committee member that was supposed to have filled them in.

She could practically smell a section headquarters, nearly always a requisitioned church, hear the hubbub resounding against marble walls, see the queues of applicants for food and fuel tickets, destitution relief, *certificats* for this, for that.

'Thank you, yes,' she said. 'This is what I wanted.'

She still had business to transact. The excellent Mr Muddie, duly authorized, was sent to her bank to withdraw specific monies, and she asked for a copy of her will.

Mr Hackbutt settled her in what he called his counsel-chamber, a surprisingly large room on the next floor up where his clients could consult with him and their barrister. She was provided with writing materials, a glass of madeira and some biscuits, and left alone.

Solitude in daytime was something she was rarely permitted; it was as if there were an unwritten law that women should never be left to their own thoughts; they must be constantly attended, never walk by themselves, keep perennial company over embroideries, card, tea and coffee tables. On arrival from the north, Jenny had automatically assumed that she would share her half sister's bedroom as she did Sally's at home and had been hurt when Philippa pointed out that there were plenty of bedrooms in the house and she must choose one of them for her own.

She allowed the room's quiet to soothe her for a moment, the luxury of it accentuated by the muffled sound of far-off traffic.

Crossing to the window, she looked out. It had turned into a golden afternoon; a group of young clerks had taken off their coats and were being lectured by a gowned senior into putting them on again. The rail on the other side of the square held half a dozen horses—none of them piebald.

She sat down, settling her feet on the wide sill so that she was angled in its corner, only the glass of the casement between her right side and the drop below.

Why Fitch-Botley's ravings had determined her to go to France and deliver the documents herself, she still wasn't sure but it was time to let the decision, made during that encounter, catch up with her and assemble its logic.

Reasoning was elusive; the sight of Georgiana at the window, ashamed, a weal across her face, kept dragging itself across her memory like wire across raw flesh. Fitch-Botley's voice still blared in her ears, always now to be associated with the smell of feces: *'There'll be no petticoat revolution in this house as the bitch has found out.'*

Suddenly, it gave way to another, gently dogged. 'Don't you see, Philippa, liberty is indivisible or it is not liberty.'

Yes, there it was.

Men like Fitch-Botley tore liberty into pieces, taking a bit for themselves, calling it democracy and denying the rest to everybody else. Even Stephen wanted to give only some of it away. When he'd freed the slaves, would he complete the process and allow them the vote? No more than he would allow it to women and the rest of the unpropertied class.

The two men, one bad, one good, had this in common; they both apportioned freedom and, in doing so, destroyed the thing itself.

Liberty was whole or it was nothing.

Only one person she knew had ever said that. 'Either no individual has rights or else all have the same rights. Anyone who does not grant the rights of another person, whatever that person's religion, color or sex may be, has by the same token forsworn his own.'

In her possession Philippa Dapifer held two pieces of paper which might, with luck, grant liberty to Condorcer, who wanted to give it to everybody in the world.

And you didn't put universal liberty in the mail.

She was amazed at herself for ever having thought she would, knowing, as she had, that it might be lost, discovered, delayed, not reach him in time.

Cowardice on her part, that's what it had been. An unacknowledged and shaming compromise between a high-minded gesture and a wish to continue the life she was living.

For what? What sort of life *was* she living? A limbo, except for occasional moments spent with the man she loved? Marrying one she didn't?

How very sordid, she thought. In the Principled Life Stakes, she was running a long way behind the admirable Mrs Scratcher.

A loud clunk and a *whirr* that not only startled her ears but set up a vibration in the seat below her hocks, causing her to scramble down before she could attribute them to the bronchitic overture of the great clock set in the masonry just outside the window. It began to strike the hour and, as if they had been woken up by it, so did the other thousand or so mechanisms in church towers and public buildings from Whitechapel to Westminster.

She was fanciful today. In the pandemonium of chimes that had once called Dick Whittington to London, Philippa Dapifer heard the summons to a higher duty. *Go to Fra-ance. Rescue hi-im. Rescue hi-im. Go to Fra-ance.*

And-get-on-with-it, they said. It's five o'clo-ock.

The coach left in two hours, and she still had letters to write.

She hurried to the table, sat herself down, pulled a sheet of paper from the pile Mr Hackbutt had put for her use, dipped a quill in a silver-chased inkpot, wrote 'My dearest Ma'—and stopped.

Best to leave that to last. She set another sheet in front of her, wrote: 'Dear Stephen'—and stopped again.

'Dear Andrew . . .'

Why on earth was she bothering to write at all? By the time these three people learned that she had not turned up in Northumbria— and, since Aunt Ginny and Sally didn't know she was supposed to be coming, that could be three weeks or a month from now—she might very well have returned from France.

Or not.

Slowly, she put down the pen.

Dear God, I am engineering my death.

It was as if she had been split into two people. One, the accuser, backed the other into a corner: *You know you'll get caught. You* know *it. It's what you want, isn't it?*

The suicide wriggled, not wanting to admit what it was. It's concern was Condorcet, it would get the papers to him somehow. *I have my own* certificat *and an American passport—the French like Americans.*

And then? If you are seen with him?

It was like looking at her own intestines and seeing the squirming, innermost gut that processed her being. All the healthy, sweet-smelling principles were reduced to this: *you* want *to be caught.* By entering the Terror that lay across the Channel, she was seeking an end to an existence that had become too difficult for her. She could not bear to marry Stephen but neither could she bear the thought of childlessness. She was ensuring that her head was laid on the block so that one fall of the blade would rid her of both intolerable futures.

She looked at the three pieces of paper she'd written on. These weren't intended letters to dear ones, they were to be last notes, pitiful, brave farewells hiding her rage that those same dear ones did not love her enough.

Did all suicides feel this savagery, this you'll-be-sorry-now, as they departed the world?

In her case, how sorry would they be? Not too much. She lived on other people's periphery; to nobody was she the fulcrum. Makepeace's grief would be sharp for a while but she would survive it as she had survived so much else; she had never let her children interfere with the things she had to do; the loss of her eldest wouldn't change that. Jenny, whose main life was also elsewhere, would be on hand for her if necessary.

Andrew Ffoulkes would grieve for her, yes; miss her, perhaps, as one missed a pet dog, experiencing a wry pang as some circumstance brought it to mind.

And Stephen? He would miss her least of all. She found that a comfort; the poor man carried the fate of slaves on his back, why should he be burdened further? She had been suitable; he had caught her in passing, rather as one hailed a boat that would carry one in the direction one wanted to go. There would be another along shortly.

One by one and slowly, she took the pages of her unwritten letters between her hands and crumpled them.

Well, well, she was of no real significance to any of them. It was incredibly painful to know it, yet at the same moment she felt curiously untrammeled. There was no time to spend on self-pity; she was free to concentrate on saving Condorcet without worry for those she left behind.

And I damn well will—had she known it, Philippa looked suddenly very much like her mother—*somehow or another I'll reach Paris.*

Working swiftly now, she took another sheet of paper and redrafted her will. It had been drawn up years before and, apart from bequests to servants and personal items to her mother and sisters, who had fortunes of their own, the bulk of her estate had been donated to various and somewhat unmuscular charities. Now she divided it between Coram's Foundlings Hospital and the Society for the Abolition of Slavery.

She asked that five hundred guineas each be bestowed on her friends, Lady Fitch-Botley, Mrs Kitty Hays and Miss Eliza Morris. Marriage automatically endowed a woman's fortune on her husband to do what he liked with, but a personal bequest such as this would allow the three women some independence should they wish it.

Smiling at what he would make of it, she asked Mr Hackbutt as her executor to give another five hundred guineas to the female she knew as Mrs Scratcher. She wrote: 'Mr Lucey, Number Twenty-seven Grub Street, is to be trusted to know the person I mean and will provide you with her address.'

Who else? Of course, Marie Joséphine. Perhaps, in the end, it was Marie Joséphine who would miss her most of all.

She bent to the paper again, wrote and shook sand over it to dry the ink. Now at least the Frenchwoman would be rich enough to nurse her sorrow in comfort.

She wished she could have seen Marie Joséphine to say good-bye. And it would have been nice to have had her company on the journey, but she would not run the woman into danger.

A female traveling a long distance on her own was a mark for men's unwanted conversation, innuendo and harrassment, sometimes even assault, which was not something Philippa looked forward to during her passage through England and France.

How ironic that she, the Saint Joan of female liberation carrying the banner of freedom and independence into dangerous territory, should wish for a chaperone in order to do so.

Blowing the sand from her last will and testament, she said aloud, 'Well, I didn't make the world, did I?'

She took a deep breath and stood up to put on her coat. 'I'm just going to improve it a bit.'

Chapter Seven

I T was unfortunate that, on entering Reach House, Aaron should fall heavily on a doorstep that rain had turned slippery and, as it turned out, should break his ankle. It was even more unfortunate that the step's slipperiness was not the cause of his fall.

Since he made no sound apart from an initial grunt, Makepeace, tired from her long journeyings, was about to tell him sharply to stand up when light from the hall fell on her brother's face as it lay against the stone flags. It was gray; only white showed under his flickering eyelids.

'He's ill.'

Hopkins was immediately despatched for the local doctor and Sanders, even more tired than his mistress, whipped up again and set off for London to fetch Dr Alexander Baines, the only one in whom Makepeace—not an admirer of the medical profession—had any faith.

'Get him upstairs.'

'I should not move him yet,' the man called Sir Michael Murrough said. 'It may be his heart. Best to let him lie a while.'

'His heart?' She was more alarmed than ever.

'In the coach, wasn't he complaining of a pain in his chest?'

'I thought he was indigestive. He ate too much at the inn.' Because she was frightened, she became angry. 'Are you a damn doctor as well as everything else?'

The long days in the coach coming back from Bristol had been passed mainly in listening to Murrough's experiences of mastering various skills across the length and breadth of Europe while simultaneously bringing vast audiences to their feet with his acting.

The actor was unrepentant, 'Madam, I did Molière for the Théâtre-Français. Let us just loosen his necktie.'

Molière. Her brother was dying before her eyes and this buffoon was quoting some damn Frenchman.

However, she loosened Aaron's collar and coat and sent Hildy for a cushion to put under his head. The rest clustered around, getting in her light and on her nerves. Jacques was looking frightened, his tutor as imperturbable as ever.

'Where's Philippa?' Philippa would organize them.

'She's gone to Northumberland, Ma. Very sudden, it was.' Jenny, woken by the kerfuffle, was hurrying downstairs in her nightrobe.

Damn. Just when she needed her.

'Take Jacques to the kitchen and get him something to eat. And . . . him.' She kept forgetting the tutor's name. 'And him.' She avoided using the actor's name. 'Good girl, Hildy.' Tenderly, she slid the cushion beneath her brother's head and stroked his hair back from his face. 'It's all right, Aaron. You'll be well soon. Prepare beds for everybody, Hildy. We'll use Philippa's when we get him upstairs, it's narrow.' If he were to need a lot of nursing, a narrow bed would make it easier.

'Makepeace.'

'Yes, dear. I'm here.'

'Where's Mick?'

The actor squatted down. 'Me, too, me old son. You took a toss but you'll be grand. Rest now.'

Aaron nodded, said, 'It hurts,' and lapsed back into semiconsciousness.

Makepeace glared around at the rest of the company. 'Git.'

They got. The actor stayed and Makepeace let him since Aaron seemed to draw comfort from the man.

$\star \qquad \star \qquad \star$

D R Perry, dispenser of healing to Chelsea, with whom, since her own health was excellent, Makepeace was unacquainted, wore the red coat, satin breeches and powdered wig of a doctor in the time of Queen Anne which, from the look of him, had been his heyday. He was accompanied by an apprentice who appeared to be in the last throes of depression.

He tottered in and blearily regarded the body on the floor. 'Can't bend down there,' he said.

Since Aaron's color had improved slightly, Hopkins and Murrough had carried him upstairs to Philippa's bed where Dr Perry took his hand, palm up, in one of his own and traced the lines on it with a dirty fingernail. 'Liver,' he said. 'Clear as ninepence. Undress him, he needs blistering.'

And such was the authority with which he spoke, and so desperate was she, that Makepeace nodded, though she was reluctant to expose Aaron's back to outsiders; he hated anyone seeing it. The best she could do was send Hopkins out of the room and leave the handling of Aaron to the actor, who was showing a tenderness she hadn't suspected in him.

They had trouble taking off Aaron's boots; he cried out when they tried. Murrough produced a knife and cut the leather, exposing a bruised right foot that looked out of true.

'Sprain,' piped Dr Perry.

When they removed the shirt, Makepeace saw Murrough's eyes flicker at the state of Aaron's back. He turned to the old man, interestedly. 'Would you tell me, doctor, how you arrived at the conclusion that my friend suffers from his liver?'

'Are you a doctor, sir?'

'I am not, sir.'

Dr Perry sighed with exasperation and picked up Aaron's hand again. 'Do you see this?' His talon traced the line at the base of Aaron's wrist. 'Deep, uncommon deep. It is the Lineamentum Iecuri and to those of us who are expert, it tells us the condition of the patient's liver.'

'Does it now? I'll tell you what it tells me, it tells me you're a gentleman who hasn't read a medical book since Hippocrates was a lad. It tells me we'll not blister a man who's been blistered enough already and it tells me that we'll be dispensing with your services. I understand there's a doctor on his way, a *doctor*, sir, so with this lady's permission we'll wait for him and say good night to ye.'

He ushered the old man to the door and held it open while the apprentice, who lost his depression enough to grin appreciatively at him, followed his bleating and protesting master out. Murrough shut the door and came back to sit by the bed opposite Makepeace. 'There's too many murderers carry a doctor's bag,' he said.

There was a heavy silence, made heavier by Aaron's labored breathing.

He was right. Makepeace knew he was right, it just hadn't been his place to do it.

After a while she said reluctantly, 'Aaron was tarred and feathered. When he was a young man. We were in Boston. It was just before the states rebelled against the British. They poured boiling tar over his back.'

Each sentence was an effort; it had been her fault.

'The British was it?' The actor directed his sympathy at Aaron. 'That's another t'ing we have in common then. For sure, haven't I weals on my own back from their whips.'

'It wasn't the *British*,' she said savagely; he always had to bring every topic back to himself. 'It was American patriots—that's what the bastards called themselves—the revolutionaries.' Men who'd been her countrymen, her friends, customers of her waterside inn, men she'd agreed with about the bloody British rule, men she'd helped with their avoidance of British custom duties, fellow smugglers.

And she'd done one thing, that's all. They'd thrown an Englishman into Boston Bay *because* he was an Englishman and she'd fished him out. Wonderful fish, too, as it turned out, titled, the man who was to become her first husband and Philippa's father, but she hadn't known it then; she'd fished him out because she couldn't see a fellow creature drown, saved him and hidden him. And so the patriots had turned on her, burned her inn and tarred and feathered her brother.

'Don't you talk to me about revolutionaries,' she said—she had a deep suspicion that she was addressing one. 'Don't you damn dare. Look what they did to Aaron, look what they're doing to France. *Causes . . .*' If her years in polite society hadn't taught her not to, she'd have spat. 'All they do is hurt people.'

If Makepeace could be said to have had a philosophy, this was hers—formed unalterably on the night in waterfront Boston when a voice had called out, *'Here's your brother, Makepeace Burke,'* and a prickled, black *thing* had staggered towards her, mewing with pain as it came.

He'd been her responsibility, always. Penitence Burke, already worn out by the worry and work her husband's fecklessness had imposed on her, had died giving birth to him. Makepeace had been a child herself but not too young to know the baby's life depended on her.

She'd brought him up, her and her old nurse Betty, sat all night in steam-filled rooms when he had the croup, starved themselves so that he could eat well, scrimped to give him the education they lacked.

And in one drunken incident they called patriotism, some men had taken the young body of which she'd been so mindful and stripped it and kicked it until it lay curled like a fetus at their feet and poured scalding pitch over it.

They'd nearly destroyed him, physically and mentally. Only Dr Baines, who'd treated him, and his own unsuspected courage had enabled Aaron to walk upright again with a mind less scarred than his back.

But it had destroyed something in Makepeace. When the bugles sounded and the drums took to beating, she was deaf to them.

When politicians—who weren't going themselves—flourished young men off to war against other young men, or when the revolutionaries waved a banner and said, 'Go get 'em, lads,' when they demanded that everybody pay duty to *their* cause, *their* country, she only saw the hacked limbs and skin that weren't theirs to sacrifice.

She heard noises in the hall and went to the door to greet Alexander Baines as Hildy hurried him up the stairs.

In the quarter of a century since, as a ship's doctor, he'd first been presented with the moaning, tarry hedgehog that the patriots had made of Aaron, he'd hardly changed at all. He was still skeletal, precise, irritable, his old-maid Edinburgh accent unameliorated by years of treating the complaints of the rich—and the poor—at his Harley Street practice.

Philip had set him up in it when they all reached England, knowing by then it had been the grace of God that had happened to make Baines the surgeon on the British warship that had sailed them away from Boston, the smoke from Makepeace's inn still dirtying the sky behind them.

'Pairhaps ye'd let me look at the patient,' he said now, removing the gabbling Makepeace's hands from his arm. And to Aaron, more gently, 'Wail, Wail, my laddie, what've ye done this time?'

Murrough watched carefully as the bone-clean fingers lifted one of Aaron's eyelids. When the doctor put his ear to Aaron's chest, he nodded and left the room.

'What is it?' Makepeace begged after an age.

Carefully, Baines put the covers back over the top half of his patient and raised them over the lower half to begin examining Aaron's foot. 'His hairt has an incompetence.' He sounded judgmental.

Makepeace said quickly, 'It's not his fault.'

'I use the tairm in its medical sense, but, aye, since ye mention it, the fault is partly his. This is not the corpus of the young lad ye brought me on the boat, it's turned flabby and unconditioned. Too much rich food, too much liquor . . . Is he still in the theatrics?'

'Yes.'

Baines nodded. 'Then too much aggravation and excitement and maybe a touch too much wickedness, I dare say.'

'Stop lecturing. Is he going to get well?'

He didn't answer as fast as she'd have liked. 'I'll not haver with ye, woman, he's taken a jolt to the heart and if there's another I'll not answer for it. There's an irregularity. But if he sairvives the next day or two, it'll maybe settle—as long as he obeys the three great doctors . . .'

'Dr Quiet, Dr Diet and Dr Sleep,' she said; he'd taught her well.

'Ay. And this ankle's broken which is maybe a blessing; he'll be doing nothing til it mends.' Alexander Baines finished bandaging and then closed his bag with a snap. 'I'll retairn tomorrow.'

'Have something to eat.'

'Na, na. I have other patients. A dram, maybe, to keep out the cold.'

She called Jenny to sit with Aaron while she took the doctor to the dining room to pour him a glass of whisky. The actor was already at the table—he was a tremendous eater—talking to Hildy and making her laugh. She introduced them and turned to other business.

'They've battened and gone to their beds,' Hildy said of Jacques and Luchet.

'I'm sorry Sanders is driven so hard, he'll have to take the doctor home.'

'Howay, he can tak hisself to his bed termorrer.' She blushed helplessly; after forty virginal years, Hildy had discovered the pleasures of the flesh. The shares Makepeace had given her in the coal mine would have enabled her to retire but she'd preferred to stay on as housekeeper and it had been to everyone's pleasure when she and the widowed Sanders had married.

'An' ye're not tewin yesel' sitting wi' Aaron tonight, neither,' she said. 'Ah'll stay by him.'

Baines overheard. 'Sound advice.' His unlashed eyes, like an intelligent crocodile's, regarded her. 'Are ye well, Makepeace?'

'I'm always well.'

'Baitter than the last time I saw ye,' he said. Philippa had called him in after Andra's death to try and arrest what had seemed like a terminal decline. 'But ye'll not be sairving your brother by exhausting yeself. Sit ye down to yair meat, I'll see myself out.'

She went with him to the front door. 'Thank you, Alex.'

'Yon seems an informed fellow,' he said, nodding towards the dining room, 'Would he be in the line of science?'

'He's an actor,' she said, shortly.

'Is he now? Ah well, that's a pity.' Dr Baines shook his head at mankind's duplicity and went away.

She teetered for a moment between returning to the dining room or immediately making up a bed in Aaron's room in which to sleep. She didn't think she could stand any more of Murrough tonight; she lost energy in that man's company. There was too much of him; his bulk and his voice had dominated the journey from Bristol, which had, in any case, been delayed at the start by his absence in the city for a whole day on what, he'd said, was 'a matter of business, dear lady.'

That was another thing; he never addressed her by name. It was always 'madam' or 'dear lady,' robbing her of identity. Makepeace was used to making an impression, not always a good one, but people at least responded to her one way or another; this mountebank made her feel she bounced off him like an ignored and ineffective balloon.

That he had intruded on her at her most vulnerable—the lacerating memory of the running slave with the child cut and cut through her sleep—was another resentment. Who was he to comfort her? Or she to him? Another example of playing to the gallery, no doubt.

And he was vain; she'd caught him looking at his reflection in the coach window and stroking the underside of his chin as if admiring a still-tight jawline.

Which it wasn't.

As for cadging—he'd have the cross off a donkey's back. On the way he'd spent liberally enough—'*There, landlord, that's for a dry bed and a wet bottle*'—but she'd discovered it was Aaron's money, a loan, he was bestrewing on all and sundry.

And Aaron didn't *mind*. He was besotted with the man.

'*My dear girl, he is the greatest actor I've ever seen.*' Standing in the hall, Makepeace waggled her head and shoulders as she mouthed her brother's admiration.

He damn well was. He put on like he was the king of Eldorado but as far as she could make out he was escaping from some wrong-doing in Ireland. The reason that Aaron had slipped into England via Bristol and without the rest of his company, with whom he usually travelled, was now explained; he was accompanying a renegade.

'We thought it better not to go through the bigger ports—in case,' Aaron answered when they were alone. 'Somebody who knows his face from over there might have recognized him. He's very slightly persona non grata in Ireland just now, he needs to stay in-cognito.'

'*Incognito?* I seen parades of elephants more incognito than him.'

'That's why they won't suspect him. Who'll notice another ec-centric knight up from the shires?'

'Suspect him of what?'

'He's a United Irishman, Makepeace.'

'What's that?' She'd collapsed onto a chair. 'Oh God, Aaron, don't tell me he's another bloody revolutionary.'

He'd sat down beside her then. 'A radical, not a revolutionary and not a bloody one. They call themselves a brotherhood of affec-tion. They merely want the Irish Parliament thrown open to all Irishmen, regardless of rank and religion. At the moment it's a Protestant oligarchy.'

Was it? Makepeace's knowledge of the Irish political scene was hazy—deliberately so. An upbringing in Puritanical Boston had in-stilled in her its repulsion for the Roman Catholic religion and, since Ireland was full of Papists as well as Protestants who behaved little better, she'd closed her mind on it as a place too queasy to dwell on. Nor had the fact that her father had been Irish Catholic endeared the country to her. In her mind it floated sunlessly in a sea of ill will, its people emerging warped from its bogs into the sun of nicer lands.

'You've changed your tune,' she'd accused her brother.

Even before the punishment the American patriots had visited upon them both, while she was still a sympathizer with their cause, Aaron had always regarded himself as a loyal subject of King George the Third and had held the English establishment, its style, its dress, as an example to be copied.

'If you'd played to audiences all over Ireland as often as I have, you'd damn well change your tune as well,' he said. 'The real Irish . . . they're treated like cattle, their language and education stamped on, no positions open to them . . . I tell you, Makepeace, it makes you ashamed, it makes you want to shout *this can't go on*. If there isn't a revolution there soon, there damn well ought to be. For the first time I've begun to have fellow feeling with our father.'

'You didn't have to cope with the drunken old bugger.'

'Makepeace, we toured Mayo. Fat estates, starving peasantry. God, no wonder he left it for America.' Then Aaron had put his arm round her shoulders and she'd known what was coming. 'I thought perhaps we, you, could put Mick up while he's here, keep him out of harm's way.'

'How long?'

'Oh, until Viceroy Camden stops seeing a revolutionary behind every shamrock. Things will have calmed down by the time we've put on the play.'

And that was another thing . . .

She went upstairs to see to Aaron but Hildy and Jenny were with him, making up a bed on Philippa's divan for whoever would watch him through the night. They told her to go and eat. She *was* hungry and Aaron *did* look better.

She stumped back downstairs again and into the dining room

to seat herself at the other end of the table. Constance, one of Sanders's daughters by his first marriage, hurried in with a dish of chicken and rice, helped her tenderly to it and, at a nod from Murrough, recharged his plate.

'His heart, then,' the actor said.

'So it seems.'

'Too large, bless him.'

It sounded like an epitaph and she was immediately on the attack. 'He's got over worse; he'll get over this. I'll see he does.'

The actor raised his glass to her—Hildy had left a decanter of the best claret on the table for him, now, she noticed, half full. 'Let us drink to that, ma'am.'

She was too superstitious to ignore such a toast, so, though she was not a great drinker, she poured herself a glass and raised it in return.

'My presence must be a distraction at such a time,' he said. 'Dear lady, I shall remove it from under your roof tomorrow.'

More posturing, she thought; *he doesn't want to go, probably can't afford to.* This was merely a gauntlet thrown down for her to pick up.

She let it lie. 'You must do as you please, of course.'

Then, because it sounded so bald, because Aaron had asked her to let the man stay, because the Puritan ethic of hospitality she'd inherited was as strong as any desert Arab's in his tent, she was forced to add, 'But you will be no distraction, sir. You are welcome to stay.'

He was on it like a dog on a rat. 'Very kind, ma'am. I thank you.' He bowed courteously from his end of the table and she, sorry that she'd given way, nodded somewhat less courteously from hers.

I've got enough with Aaron, she thought, and there's John Beasley to be saved from the damn gallows, and now I'm burdened with this, this . . . whirligig.

Trying to find the essence of the man opposite her was like clutching at wet soap, her inability to grasp it deepened her distrust. He talked to Aaron in a slight and not unattractive brogue; to her he used the remoteness and long *a*'s of upper-class English which, when she rebuffed him as she frequently did, thinned into the acidity with which it was addressed to inferiors.

Even his looks were a contradiction, she thought; his face might have been a round of cheese into which a child had poked a finger to make the eyes and mouth but when he spoke, ah well, then, you heard a voice capable of calling shepherds from their sheep to set them running towards a Bethlehem stable.

And she distrusted it. Either he was so unsure of himself that he eddied in the direction of any prevailing current—and she suspected his self-regard was too high for that—or he was a plain fat liar and he was hiding something. She examined his every statement for the motive behind it.

Why did he profess affection for Aaron? Why had he been so concerned when she wept for the slaves? Was he really an Irish patriot or was he running from a more dastardly deed in a land of dastardly deeds? If he was such a marvellous actor, why was he penniless?

To punish him for his tergiversation, she said, 'Of course, Oroonoko is out of the question now.'

That hit home. His hand came up to cup his chin and his forefinger tapped against his lips as he considered.

Actually, she was rather sorry herself. To have indulged in the wickedness of the theater while expunging its wickedness, making trumpery serve a fine cause, had been an intriguing prospect. She'd actually been enthused. And Aaron had been so excited by it . . . So had Jacques . . .

The project had arisen while they were all at supper in the inn outside Bristol. Murrough had just returned from his day of doing whatever it was that had kept them waiting for him (and what could that have been?).

They'd taken a private room and Jacques was sitting next to the actor, whom he seemed to admire, listening to every word spoken. His tutor was eating with his usual disregard for anything else. She'd still been wild, talking of expending every penny she possessed on buying slaves and setting them free.

'Dear girl, you can't buy them all,' Aaron had said.

The actor agreed. 'Unfortunately, ma'am, there's not that much money in the world.'

'You didn't see her,' she'd said. 'You didn't see the child. You didn't hear her. If I buy enough, maybe they'll be among 'em.'

She hadn't been able to stop talking about it, sketching the captain and the clerk for them. Oddly enough, it was the memory of the clerk Briggs that obsessed her—the captain she set aside as mere brutish clay.

But Briggs . . . She'd drawn him well because she'd encountered him a thousand times. In Boston, he'd been in the British customs sheds, incorruptible and exacting to the last penny. She'd come up against him in prisons, in tax offices, in harbor masters' huts where he ignored the entrancement of sea and sail and concentrated on his figures, the epitome of bureaucracy everywhere, neat, dutiful, going home to his wife and children and small garden, attending church on Sundays.

'I'll wager he has a hobby,' she'd said. 'He collects coronation medallions or grows pumpkins. He counted those slaves in and he drew a line on the list when they'd gone. He didn't think it was wrong. He was doing a job.'

And the actor had said, 'I know him. We have him in Ireland. The banal functionary. Cruelty *en masse* couldn't do without him.'

Which, she had to admit, described the man exactly.

'I've got to do something,' she said.

'There's the Abolition Society,' Aaron said, doubtfully.

'I've joined. But it ain't enough, they're too slow, and they're preaching to the converted half the time. It'll take years for Parliament to vote in abolition. If it ever does.'

It was then the actor had turned to Aaron. 'Your sister saw it, d'ye see? Not three thousand miles away in the slave ships and the cotton fields, it was in front of her, she heard the cry. She *saw* it, Aaron. What if we make thousands see it, hear it?'

And Aaron's eyes had widened and the actor had smiled and both together they had uttered an owl's hoot. *'Oroonoko.'*

'What's that?' she'd demanded, irritably.

'It's a play. Listen, Makepeace . . .'

They'd been offered the use of a playhouse; it was why they had come.

Lord Deerfield, an Irish peer, had seen the *Othello* Aaron had put on in Dublin—with Murrough as Othello. Joining them in the Green Room afterwards, his lordship had mentioned that he'd bought almost an acre of the City of London's decrepit alleys near the river as a speculation with a view to knocking down its buildings and raising on it a club and a square of gentlemen's houses.

'He's bribing every alderman he can get hold of for the licence to build but in the meantime he's losing money on his investment.'

'Ye-es,' said Makepeace, dubiously.

The actor chimed in. 'And on that blessed, dingy piece of land, dear lady, there stands an ancient altar to Thespis, the father of Greek tragedy. . . . *Thespis, the first professor of our art, at country wakes sang ballads from a cart . . .'*

'It's called The Duke's Theatre,' interrupted Aaron. 'The Duke's Company played there before they joined up with the Theatre Royal. It's been renovated since, of course . . .'

'Betterton strode those boards, Kynaston, Gwynn . . .'

'Nell Gwynn?' asked Makepeace, sharply. The name of Charles II's mistress had always been synonymous with the Whore of Babylon for Puritan Boston and, for her, still carried an automatic charge of disapproval.

'The point is,' Aaron said, 'it's been empty for years but we persuaded Deerfield to let us have it at a reduced rent and a share of the profits until they pull it down.'

'And what better opener could we have to touch minds and consciences than a tragedy whose hero is enslaved . . .'

'Thomas Southerne dramatized it from a book written in the days of Charles II—this will attract you, Makepeace—by a woman.'

It didn't attract Makepeace; she hadn't got over Nell Gwynn.

The two men kept on, however, overlaying an image of oranges and bare breasts with assurances of *Oroonoko*'s Christianizing effect on audiences. 'It's a certain touchstone. Tell her, Aaron. Didn't we do it in Cork and didn't it have them in tears and didn't a bunch of them rush off to free Captain Bulmer's second coachman who was black?'

'That's it, you see, Makepeace. There'll be no change for the better until the mass of the public *demands* a change; people have got to be affected. We could have petitions in the foyer for when the audience comes out . . .'

'What happened to that second coachman?' Makepeace wanted to know.

'Well, actually, he went back to Captain Bulmer; turns out he was content in his job. But the point is . . .'

They made it again and again. With the Abolition Society pushing and *Oroonoko* pulling, audiences, people, could be brought to see slavery for the evil it was. The outcry would force Parliament into submission.

'We'll invite the King and Queen to the first night . . .'

'To hell with the King and Queen . . .' This was Murrough and, actually, the moment when Makepeace was caught. 'It's Mrs Briggs we want at the first night and every night. When we've done London we'll tour the country, Bristol, we'll play to the Mrs Briggses, the women, that untapped force of true persuaders . . .'

Yes, she thought. *The mountebank's right. I suspect his reasons but he's hit the nail.* The transformation must be made in the home or not at all. Mrs Briggs, wife to the bureaucratic clerk, was the slaves' secret agent. She has children; no mother could hear the wail I heard and not be ashamed to the stomach. If Briggs's conscience lies anywhere it is in his hearth, which can be undermined.

And the neighbors, she thought. Mrs Briggs won't like her neighbors looking down on her husband's job.

Makepeace was no upholder of women's rights; she thought Philippa's enthusiasm for them misguided. Like anybody who'd achieved a privileged position through hard work, she discounted the luck that had also attended it; if she could do it, so could others; it only needed a bit of spirit. But she did not underestimate, indeed she lauded, the influence of the wife and mother in the home. There lay woman's true dominion, in loving persuasion, in example, in nagging, in, as a last restort, shunning the offending mate's bed until he'd purged the offense—Makepeace hadn't heard of *Lysistrata* but she'd have approved the method.

She was also a businesswoman. 'Will it pay for itself?'

Ah, well. It *would*, undoubtedly it *would*. If the play ran long enough—and that was a given—it could make a small fortune. They would put on other popular plays during the course of the season and, well, a season at Drury Lane, for instance, could make a net profit, *profit*, of £6,500, and had. Naturally, there would be an initial outlay . . . just to get the theater into fettle after its long disuse . . .

'A little dusting, maybe,' the actor said.

'A lick of paint,' Aaron assured her.

'And mine's the initial outlay, is it?' Makepeace asked acidly. They weren't peddling the play to her this energetically just to get her blessing.

'A hundred pounds here or there,' Aaron said, airily. 'My dear girl, a minute ago you were going to spend all you had on a venture that could not have been maintained. Ours will alter the stars in their courses.'

The stars would probably stay in their courses but public opinion could veer slave-owners from theirs—they had convinced her of that much. And if this outlandish-sounding mummery would help to do it . . .

At this point Jacques broke in. 'The theater, missus. It is full of mechanical devices—Papa took me to the Comédie Français and a demon rose from the floor and there was magic, *toute mécanique*. How I should adore to work in the theater.'

'It ain't run by steam,' she said. If the boy thought he was going to imperil his immortal soul by going anywhere near a playhouse, he could think again. But his enthusiasm emphasized the draw the theater had over the young. The next generation must also be persuaded.

'You sure it's a Christian play, Aaron?'

It was the actor who answered. 'Madam, it was the first outcry against slavery and still the best. It gives voice to the pain. You can't be more Christian than that.'

With a rich part in it for yourself, she thought. Always the double motive with you. 'It's your troupe, Aaron,' she said. 'Why ain't you taking the lead part?'

Her brother nodded towards Murrough. 'Because I saw him play it.'

She'd sighed, showing more reluctance than she felt. 'I suppose you'd better go ahead, then.'

And, as they'd traveled homewards, their ceaseless discussion of the subject had drawn her further and further in so that, now, with Aaron *hors de combat*, with only anxieties for him and for John Beasley to contend with, the future looked unlit and flat compared with the flare that had so briefly illumined it. Now she must discover some other means of combating slavery.

The only comfort she could draw from the loss was that the play actor was more cast down than she was.

So much for you and Nell Gwynn, she thought and, excusing herself, went upstairs to bed.

ALEXANDER Baines was at Reach House early the next morning and pleased to find Aaron better. 'But he's sore afraid,' he said, when he and Makepeace consulted outside the sick room door.

She knew that. During the night she'd been attentive to her brother's every movement, every moan. In the candlelight his eyes had beseeched her for reassurance that he would not die. He was afraid to move in case it instigated another attack on his heart—and it tore at her own to see the years roll him back to the days when it had been a possibility that the tortured muscles of his back might not allow him to walk normally again, and, almost as bad from his point of view, that the boiling tar had so scarred the back of his head that hair would never grow on it again. He'd had to wear a wig ever since—even now, when false hair was out of fashion.

He'd done so well. True, he'd not achieved the eminence he might have liked, but he had overcome pain and humiliation to keep himself contentedly afloat in one of the most uncertain of professions.

'There's no cairtainty it won't happen again,' Dr Baines said when Makepeace begged him for it. 'But we can employ his fright to his benefit; assure him that my regimen of diet and exercise will reduce the risk.'

'How can he exercise on a broken ankle?'

It appeared that he could and must. There were limbering motions that could be made while he was in bed, and crutches to be used around the garden when he was up and around.

'I'll no' have him traipsing to London nor any playhouse,' the doctor told her, 'Tranquillity in the Lord's sweet air is the order of the day.'

From that moment the entire household was put on a diet of boiled fish and greens so that Aaron's nose should not be tortured by the smell of roast red meats rising, houri-like, from the kitchen. Philippa, who'd begun to be influenced by the growing movement for vegetarianism, would have been pleased but, as well as her care for Aaron's health, Makepeace's satisfaction lay in the restriction it would give to Murrough's gluttony. However, neither that night at dinner, nor any subsequent night, did he complain. Indeed, it looked as if the presence of the man might even prove an advantage; he seemed content to relieve herself and Jenny by sitting with Aaron, talking and reading in between the patient's bouts of sleep.

With her first panic over, she was now able to investigate Philippa's sudden departure for the north.

'He did *what*?'

'The dorty sod smeared the lass with his own sleck,' Hildy said. 'That Kitty Hays was there.'

'I'll kill him. Why?'

Hildy shrugged. 'Ah've not fathomed it yet. Summat about leading his missis astray.'

'*Philippa?*'

'Ah said the syem, but afore Ah could get the sense o't, she was packed and off, all hell for leather.'

'The bastard frightened her away?' That sounded even less like Philippa.

'Naa, naa.' Hildy considered. 'Ah'd not say she was feared, more determined like. Like she was set on summat.'

'Something that meant going up to Raby?'

Hildy shrugged.

Makepeace's questioning of Chadwell, the newest recruit to her staff, cast little light on the reasons for Philippa's departure but somewhat more on the cause of Fitch-Botley's attack. Such illumination took time since Chadwell tended to dwell with appalled relish on the sights he'd seen during his two visits to the capital. Somewhat tactlessly, considering his situation, he put the blame for his and Lady Fitch-Botley's exposure to them on Philippa, as he did his own punishment and Georgiana's at the hands of Sir Charles.

'Her poor Ladyship's flighty, I admit, but she'd never've gone to them places on her own account, not never. Nor she wouldn't've written they things if Miss Philippa hadn't put her with that newspaper chap—and him, well, talked like a woman he did, looked a bit like one, too. Shockin' it was. I seen Sir Charles angry but I never seen him in the rage Her Ladyship's scribblin's brought him to. Cut her across the face he did and as for me . . . see these stripes?' He pulled down the back of his collar to show the scars left by the lashes of a whip.

'What newspaper chap? Show me them weals one more time, Chadwell, and I swear I'll give you more to go with 'em. *Where* did you go? And *why?*'

To the why, she got no more than that it was something to do with papers. As to where . . . 'Grubby place 'twas, name and nature.'

'Grub Street? Was it Grub Street? Which number?'

It might have been Grub Street but as to the number Chadwell's memory failed him.

'Well, I'm going to London tomorrow and you can take me there.' Aaron seemed to be progressing well enough to be left to Hildy, Jenny and Murrough, and she needed to see Mr Hackbutt about John Beasley's defense.

On the way, she called in on the Fitch-Botleys. Chadwell was too afraid of another lashing at the hands of his former master to take the trap within view of the house so, as had Philippa and Kitty Hays a few days previously, Makepeace walked up the carriage drive, determined to get an explanation and an apology for what had been done to her daughter.

She received neither. She was kept standing in the pleasant entrance hall while the footman went upstairs with her request to see either Sir Charles or Lady Fitch-Botley. A male voice, deliberately pitched to reach her, said, 'I'll have nothing to do with any relative of that harpy. And you may tell the person below that, in any case, I do not receive tradeswomen.'

On the way to London, Makepeace only once interrupted the reverie that occupied her. 'Tell me, Chadwell,' she said. 'Does Sir Charles use coal or wood for his fires?'

She received little more satisfaction at the chambers of her old friend Mr Hackbutt than she had at the Fitch-Botleys'. Philippa, it seemed, had already done all that could be done for John Beasley at this stage. And, no, she could not see Mr Beasley in the Tower; he and the others were not allowed visitors other than their legal representative—and even that, grudgingly.

Mr Hackbutt extended himself on the government's perfidy in suspending habeas corpus, then asked after Philippa. 'I thought she looked peaked when she was here—a trip to the north is maybe just what she needs.'

'Did she mention why she was going?'

'No, she finished her personal business here and set off.'

'What personal business, George?'

Mr Hackbutt wagged a finger. 'Now, now, missus. Miss Philippa is my client as much as you are and just as entitled to confidentiality.'

At Grub Street, Gervase Lucey was delighted to see her and more forthcoming. He was devastated to hear of Georgiana Fitch-Botley's mistreatment at the hands of her husband. 'The *brute*. Poor dear thing, such talent. And I was depending on her for *The Passenger*'s next editorial, the matter of women's rights has attracted a deal of attention—not all of it complimentary, but at least it sells.' He cocked an eye at Makepeace. 'I suppose, dear Missus, that you couldn't . . .'

'No, I couldn't,' Makepeace told him. 'Don't believe in it and can't put two words together if I did. Was that why Philippa came here? So's the Fitch-Botley female could write for *The Passenger*?'

'Oh, no, dear. Initially it was to find a forger. Didn't she tell you?'

'I was away. *A forger*?'

'My dear, I was as surprised as you. There she was, bless her, butter absolutely *refusing* to melt in her mouth and it was by-the-way-do-you-happen-to-know-any-good-forgers-dear-Mr-Lucey. Apparently, she intended to send counterfeit travel passes to a friend of hers to enable his escape from France.' Mr Lucey tapped his chin. 'At least, I think it was a him, might have been a her. What was it, Jamie?'

'A him.'

Mr Lucey smiled fondly. 'Jamie knows. Jamie took her to the Scratcher, didn't you, Jamie? Scratcher's our local forger and quite excellent in his villainous way. There were some difficulties but I believe the business was eventually conducted to the satisfaction of all parties, wasn't it, Jamie?'

'I'd better go and see this Scratcher,' Makepeace said, drawing the strings of her cloak.

'He's gone,' Jamie told her.

'Almost immediately afterwards,' Mr Lucey confirmed. 'He and his doxy, off to Australia or America or somewhere.'

'Tell her about the man,' Jamie reminded him.

Mr Lucey flapped his hand as if snapping shut an invisible fan. 'Forget my own head next. A man came here enquiring about the ladies—quite the gentleman or I should not have entertained him—and Jamie is convinced that he'd followed them and was up to no good.'

'Nor he weren't,' Jamie said.

'We speculated about it, didn't we, Jamie? A French spy? A government spy? However, in view of poor Lady Fitch-Botley's experience, one must now conclude that it was some creature of her husband's, if not her husband himself.'

It was the more likely explanation; Fitch-Botley tracking his wife. Not for the first time, Makepeace thanked God that both her husbands had valued her freedom as highly as their own.

Further questioning gained little more information so, with promises to inform them of the date of Beasley's trial once it was fixed, she took her leave.

Before going home, she stopped in Chelsea to conduct some business and, finally, called on Kitty Hays. Who was not pleased to see her.

'It's no good, Mrs Hedley, I'm sorry, but I'll have nothing more to do with it.'

'Do with what?'

Mrs Hays, a woman Makepeace had often derided as 'mannish' had now gone so far in the other direction that her face peered through the flounces of her cap like a mouse drowning in a bucket of bubbles. Her neckline was low and the clinging muslin of her gown followed lines that, Makepeace thought, had been better left undefined.

'With the Society. I see now how foolish it was and I have confessed all to Arthur—and been forgiven, I am glad to say.'

'Would that be the Condorcet Society?' Philippa had tried to interest her in it and failed.

'That man.' Kitty shuddered at the name. 'How wrongheaded we were. Arthur says that if Philippa *does* succeed in bringing him to England, he will inform the authorities.'

Condorcet. Of course. She'd never met the man but Philippa put him only a little lower than the angels and had been distressed at his fall from Republican grace. Of *course*. And the Marchioness de Condorcet who'd spent a summer with them—an exceptionally nice woman. That's why the girl had wanted the travel documents—to send them to her friends.

And why shouldn't she? Makepeace became angry. 'Is that why Fitch-Botley covered my daughter in shit?'

Kitty's over-exposed bosom waggled as she shuddered again. 'Oh, no, he didn't know about that and it's to be hoped he never will. It was terrible, terrible. No, he was angry because Philippa encouraged Ginny to write those awful things in the newspaper. It was Philippa all the time, you know, Mrs Hedley. I'm sorry to say it, but she was the one who led us astray. Arthur says she brought it on herself. Arthur says he wouldn't have used Sir Charles's methods but he'd have corrected her, too.'

'Does he?' Makepeace gathered herself for departure. 'If I were you, I'd advise him not to try.'

Aaron had survived her absence without being set back, though he was beginning to complain about boiled fish—which his sister took as a good sign and, as a celebration, said he could dine on boiled chicken instead. But it was typical of life, she thought, that as one concern began to ameliorate it was replaced by another. After they'd dined, she and Jenny repaired to the parlor, leaving the actor to his port and cigar and herself free to discuss the disquieting thought that had occurred to her.

She recounted the events of the day. 'Jenny, do you think . . . I suppose Philippa *has* gone to Northumberland?' she said.

'What do you mean, Ma? Where else would she have gone?' It was an unusual experience for Jenny to see her mother uncertain.

'She wouldn't . . . this sounds ridiculous and, no, she wouldn't . . .

I was wondering whether we should write to your Aunt Ginny, see if she's arrived at Raby . . . it just crossed my mind she might have gone to France.'

'*France?*'

'Marie Joséphine thinks she has.'

'Why? Marie Joséphine was with me when she went; we'd gone to a sale of work.'

'She says she feels it.'

'Yes, but she's French.' Jenny spread out her hands palm upwards, casting the heated imagination of the French into the air, where they belonged.

'Well . . . yes, very well, it's silly—but if she wanted to make sure the Condorcets got away . . . No good-byes to anyone, it seems queer.'

Jenny's face assumed the self-satisfaction of the young who, unexpectedly, have the right of it over an elder. Kindly, she took her mother's hand. 'Philippa has gone to Northumberland, Ma, and it has nothing to do with French passports or what that horrid Fitch-Botley man did to her.'

'Hasn't it?'

'No. She's gone because she's in a taking over her wedding to Stephen and because Lord Ffoulkes is coming back with his bride earlier than expected. They may all arrive together and, poor dear, it's too much for her. We were in this very room when I got her to admit that she loves Andrew, always has and always will. I am sure she has gone to Raby to walk the moors—you know she takes comfort from them—and clear her head whilst she decides what to do.'

Makepeace, convinced, sighed and nodded.

Jenny sat back, smiling. '*France*, Mama. What an idea. You might go galloping off in such a manner but Philippa has a more circumspect character. No, her intention was to send the papers to Condorcet via Babbs Cove and Gruchy. She told me so. Now that's done, she's at liberty to consider her future.' Jenny sighed. 'And she is in agonies over it, poor lamb. I know her.'

And Makepeace, who was not sure that she did, bowed to her middle daughter's greater wisdom.

S HE had further business in the village the next morning. Having been virtually in a purdah of mourning for the last three years, she was only recently fully acquainted with Chelsea. She liked it. Though it was becoming popular as an address for an increasing number of London's professional class, its population was still not above a thousand and the rows of cottages behind the main street had not yet been pulled down to provide homes for the gentry. Barefooted children played in its lanes, women hoed vegetables in their front gardens. Cows traipsing daily from byres to the water meadows and back again kept up an odorous, bespattered link between it and deep country. Stags were known to come leaping down the village street with Lord Cremorne's staghounds on their heels, duly followed by Lord Cremorne.

The Chelsea bun bakery attracted customers from miles around but the sophistication of its shops, unusual in such a rural place, was due to the proximity of the two, almost conflicting, institutions—the Hospital for Wounded and Superannuated Soldiers and the Ranelagh Pleasure Gardens, the last of which, to the relief of Chelsea itself, was situated on the extreme eastern boundary of the parish and could be shrugged off as not belonging to it.

The hospital was a matter of pride; its great red brick Wren frontage added nobility to the waterfront panorama. Those of its five hundred pensioners who were still ambulatory were usually treated to a pint of porter when they hobbled down to the village green to smoke away their tobacco allowance, their scarlet coats and black tricorns looking as if the grass had sprouted benches of poppies.

The suggestion by an overenthusiastic parishioner, who purveyed cabbage to the hospital, that the village should put up a statue to Nell Gwynn for kindly persuading King Charles II into building it for his veterans, was turned down, however. Chelsea felt that there were some sorts of kindly persuasion that need not be commemorated.

Nor was Ranelagh approved of, except by those it employed and such shops as sustained a profitable visit from the gloriously accoutred, 'Oh how quaint'—shrieking gaggles of its guests who had drunkenly mistaken the way back to London and who were known locally as 'they damn pic-nickers,' not because they indulged in the new craze of eating supper on Ranelagh's lawns—as they did—but because they were prone to pick flowers from people's gardens in the middle of the night and nick trophies like door knockers and vegetables and subsequently throw them away, leaving behind a trail that suggested a troupe of high-spirited and destructive baboons.

Makepeace, like everyone else in earshot, had suffered disturbed nights from the noise of the fireworks with which Ranelagh accompanied its entertainments, and regarded the place, never having been there, as an English Sodom and Gomorrah.

Today, however, having called at the lord lieutenant's apartments in the hospital's west wing in order to borrow a pair of padded crutches for Aaron, she contrived to let fall that an open invitation to a subscription masquerade they were giving at the gardens the following night in aid of the army would not come amiss. The lord lieutenant and his lady were pleased to extend it; Makepeace was one of the institution's benefactors.

It was a pretty drive home. The weather was beautiful; still frosty at night but with daytime sun bringing out blossom on the blackthorn. Rooks were busy adding twigs to nests that looked as if the elms had sprouted dark untidy fruit.

She spent it wondering whom to ask to accompany her and Jenny to Ranelagh; they required an escort. Aaron could not, obviously, and she didn't think she could stand another evening with the Reverend Deedes.

She pulled up the horse in order to get down from the trap and examine the primroses speckling the bank of the stream that ran along the road. It would be nice to pick some for Aaron but they were still only in the tiny pale furled umbrellas of bud and had not yet developed the achingly sweet, elusive scent, the epitome of spring, that they would gain later on, so she left them to grow.

Back at Reach House, Hopkins came forward to help her down but, before going in, she couldn't resist using the crutches and swung herself along, past the kitchen garden to the walled yard at the back where Constance was hanging out the washing, pegs in her mouth, the stretch of her young body as she reached up to the line being dreamily watched by the tutor Luchet who lounged against a mangle, book in hand like a Hilliard miniature.

Undoubtedly, it was springtime; to Makepeace's certain knowledge he'd fallen in love three times at the inns on the way back from Bristol, once with a lady traveler and twice with serving wenches.

'Don't you ever do no teaching?' Makepeace demanded of him.

He was unperturbed. '*Madame*, the world is my schoolroom. I read poetry to this lady.'

'She's busy.' To Constance, she said, 'And don't you encourage him.'

Constance nodded after the Frenchman's retreating back. 'He's harmless. A right mooner, that one.' She gave an artificial sigh. 'I tried kissin' him but he still stayed a Frog.'

Makepeace shook her head at her. 'Where's Jacques?'

'He's with Sir Mick, blowing up things in the paddock.'

Sir Mick, Makepeace thought. *If that man was ever knighted by the king, I'm a monkey's uncle.* As she crutched her way past the stables, there was a loud bang and a plume of smoke with debris in it climbed into the air behind the trees.

The actor and Jacques, both in their shirtsleeves, were sadly regarding a cylinder of which the top had peeled back into smoking, blackened petals. 'Too high pressure,' Jacques said, as she came up. 'We reduce next time.'

'You get to your Latin,' Makepeace told him, 'or there won't be a next time.' When he'd gone, she turned her attention on the actor. 'The idea is to keep that boy alive. Perhaps you'd remember it. And he's supposed to get an education.'

'What do you think this is?' He nodded at what had once been decent grazing and was now littered with metal paraphernalia.

She was surprised; he hadn't answered her back before. She watched him put on his coat. 'It won't get him to university.'

'It will get him into the new age. As for the old one, he and I are reading the sonnets to Aaron tonight.'

Stop it, Makepeace told herself, harshly; *don't fall to his spell*. He may sound like a proper man but he's an *actor*. She watched him as he held up the tiny hand mirror that he always kept attached to one of his buttonholes by a ribbon and peered into it, smoothing his eyebrows. 'That's a relief, for a minute I thought I'd lost 'em.'

They walked back together to where Makepeace had dropped the crutches when she'd heard the explosion. He picked them up and swung himself along. 'We could play pirates,' he said.

She said stiffly, 'Jenny and I are attending a masquerade at Ranelagh tomorrow night, Mr Murrough. Perhaps you would be good enough to escort us.'

'I'd be charmed, dear lady.'

Whatever the moment had been, it had gone—reminding her of the primroses in promising scent yet possessing none.

R ANELAGH was a speculation from which a great deal of money, cleverly spent, was delivering a large return. It was *the* place to be seen; Vauxhall was nothing to it. The gardens were glorious and at their center stood the domed rotunda, a pretty circular shell which, inside, was fretted with white and gold pillared theater boxes overlooking a circular floor and, in the middle, a fat, gilded vermilion column that held up the roof.

To go in by one of the enormous pedimented doorways was to be immediately dwarfed to the size of an ant sheltering under an umbrella. Makepeace, determined to approve of nothing, thought the whole thing looked like an immense darning mushroom with a cotton-reel handle. But even she couldn't deny the seduction of the chandeliers hanging like golden snowflakes from the night blue of the dome and the music coming from an orchestra, fifty-strong, seated on the rising benches of a dais on one side of the room. Some two hundred people were already there and more arriving, but the great space allowed dancing in one area and supper tables in another without discommoding those who merely wished to parade and show off the latest art of their costumiers.

Most of the company wore masks, though Makepeace had forsworn them as diablerie for herself, Jenny and the actor. 'Hiding her blushes, I reckon,' she said acidly of one woman whose Venetian mask concealed her face but not the arresting body that showed under the gauze of her dress. 'If she *can* blush, that is. Don't she know there's a war on?'

But the excuse of raising money for the army had given Fashion the liberty to dress in its best and most fantastic, dance its shoes thin and eat a supper that would have kept a division of infantry fed for a week.

Chelsea, too, had also opted for patriotism rather than disapproval and its leading lights were out in force, including, Makepeace saw, the Reverend Deedes, his unmasked face carefully assuming a look of suffering in a good cause that would have outdone a martyr in the flames. London aristocracy had brought with it some of the French exiles, conspicuous from the contrast between their shabby, out-of-date Versailles dress and the brilliance of the masks borrowed from their hosts. From his lack of height and powdered wig, she recognized the Marquis de Barigoule, her former dancing partner on the night of Ffoulkes's ball.

She hurried through the throng, leaving Jenny to the care of the actor, and spent most of the evening alone in one of the boxes, partly hidden by its curtain and dividing her attention between the entrance and the swirl below her. And waiting.

Despite the crisp night air coming through the open doors, it was hot under the dome and most masks were soon laid aside. She watched the actor, with Jenny on his arm, go round the room, graceful for all his bulk, entering into easy and welcomed conversation with practically everybody, and within minutes being treated like an old friend.

Sir Mick-ing himself into favor, she thought, sourly. *Everybody talks to him; Sanders, Hildy, Jacques, they all tell him things; I bet he knows a damn sight more about my business than I know about his.*

He was attentive to Jenny, she had to give him that. Only once, while the girl was taken off to dance by the lord lieutenant's son, did he abandon her to go outside. Makepeace assumed it was to piss—the garden's bushes proffered less noisome accommodation than did the Rotunda's places of easement—but in the light issuing through the great portal onto the carriage area outside, she saw him talking to somebody.

Who it was, she couldn't quite see—the man was in shadow—but she got the impression that he wasn't a guest, more likely a servant attendant on one of the coaches that had come from London.

Only the day before, after she'd invited him to Ranelagh, the actor had asked permission to send Chadwell with a note 'to a friend in Saint Pancras.'

There'd been no reason to withhold her consent and the note had gone. There'd been no further explanation from him, which she found suspicious since he was usually an inveterate chatterer. Was he in touch with his radical Irish friends? Or merely, perhaps, making an assignment with a woman.

Nothing to do with me. But she kept an eye on him. His wonderful voice carried to her now and then as his perambulation brought him near her box so that she heard him talking charitable finance with the hospital's lord lieutenant, politics to the duchess of Gordon and even—God help him—joining in condemnation of the Vanity Fair around them with the Reverend Deedes. He reflected back the color of each, like a chameleon.

'And where are your estates, Sir Michael?' he was asked by the duchess of Gordon.

'Ireland, ma'am.' As if he owned half of it, and immediately changing the subject: 'Tell me, Duchess, what's your opinion on the Triple Alliance? Lord Camden was saying only last week, he feared Austria will make peace with France . . .'

Makepeace actually saw her own stock rise when it was learned this splendid newcomer was staying at Reach House. 'Yes, Mrs Hedley is my hostess, a most excellent person . . .' This was to Reverend Deedes: 'We were not acquainted before, but while her brother appears to take comfort from my presence in his illness, I must remain and render what assistance I can.'

The suggested reluctance, a man sacrificing better things to do by attending the sickroom of a friend, was excellently done, even if Makepeace translated it as reflecting on her competence. However, it also acquitted them both of what Deedes—who would suspect Saint Paul and the Virgin Mary if they were living under the same roof—might otherwise deem an irregular relationship. The tone implied that Sir Michael, with his estates in Ireland, would not consider Mrs Hedley, tradeswoman, as bed fodder if she were served up naked with parsley.

And it's mutual, Mrs Hedley thought.

A proper chameleon. They don't ask him what he does. Aaron's right; they assume he's somebody.

But then, very few of the glorious company below her actually did anything, they merely *were*. Other people made money for them, collected their rents, managed their land and handed them the profit. Only in manufacturing towns like her beloved Newcastle did people say, 'And what line are you in?' Up there they even asked it of women because you never knew which widow had taken over her husband's business or which daughter had inherited her father's or even, with so many men gone to the war, started up her own and was running it without trouble.

It was hot in her box; the red velvet with which it was lined smelled of dust and stale perfume. Suddenly this scented, golden globe nauseated her; what am I doing among this trash? I'm as bad as these wasters, battening on Raby, leaving it to young Oliver to run it. I'll go home, I can face it now. I'll stay for Beasley's trial and then I'll take Aaron home to God's own clean country.

The actor's moon face was directed at her—so he'd known where she was all the time. He was miming. Did she want an ice? Something to drink?

She shook her head and turned her attention to the entrance where there was a commotion. Sir Charles Fitch-Botley had entered with a crowd of friends. Georgiana, Makepeace noted, was not among them, although the group contained some women as well as Andrew Ffoulkes's friend, Blanchard.

They'd been drinking and were noisy. Fitch-Botley's boom to the lord lieutenant, 'Sorry 'm late, old dear. Been at m' club. When's supper?' could be heard over the music.

Makepeace got up, hitched her neckline into place, smoothed down her skirt and went downstairs. Making her way through the crowd, she bumped against Fitch-Botley and apologized with a Judas's kiss of a curtsey. 'Beg pardon, sir.'

Blearily, he bowed back; he didn't recognize her.

Makepeace went up to Jenny and the actor, positioned herself between them, taking each by the arm, and led them to where she had a view.

Fitch-Botley and some of the others had gone up to the orchestra in its white and gold stand and were demanding that it play 'somethin' lively.'

Two dourly-dressed men in heavy boots, who'd been standing in the entrance, began to cross the floor, causing some of the guests to raise their lorgnettes at them.

Jenny was chattering. 'You ought to have heard Lady Gladmain on the subject of Mr Pitt, Ma, she . . .'

'Definitely,' Makepeace said.

One of the men was tapping Fitch-Botley on the shoulder. 'Sir Charles Fitch-Botley?'

'I am. Who the hell are you?'

Afterwards, and it was a subject in Chelsea inns and coffee shops for some time to come, one of the men either produced a paper and was slapped across the face by Sir Charles, or was slapped first and produced his paper afterwards.

In any case, the result was the same; Sir Charles was being frog-marched round the pillar towards the door. The orchestra fell silent, leaving only an unaware flautist twittering arpeggios with his eyes shut.

Some of the Fitch-Botley coterie, trying to hinder their friend's unwilling, kicking progress, were loudly warned by the second man that to do so contravened the law. 'Legal arrest. He ain't paid his coal bill. Two years' supply. Forty-two pun and tuppence.'

Boy Blanchard stopped the procession by standing in front of it, waving a purse. 'There's no necessity for this, here's the money.'

'Debt to be settled at the compter,' the second man said. 'Arrest charges extra.'

There was a surge towards the doorway to watch Sir Charles put forcibly into a barred wagon such as was used for the transporting of felons, and driven away to the old round pigeon house in Cutters Lane that served as Chelsea's overnight lockup for drunks, criminals and debtors.

Makepeace waved.

'What's happening? Why have they done this?' asked Jenny.

'Looks as if the gentleman ain't been paying his coal bills,' Makepeace said equably. 'Ought to pay your tradesman, I always say.'

'Indeed.' The actor was looking at her. 'Remind me never to order coal from your mother, Miss Jenny.'

'*Ma.*' Jenny whirled round. 'Was it . . . ?' She began to laugh, half scandalized. 'Does Raby supply Sir Charles's coal?'

''Course not,' Makepeace told her, severely. 'We don't sell door to door.' Suddenly, she grinned, effecting a transformation that was breathtaking. 'But we supply the man as does.'

CONTENTMENT accorded by the spectacle of Fitch-Botley's public humiliation was tempered by the lack of Philippa to enjoy it. Jenny began writing an account of it to her sister but there was so much to relate and her own appearance at the rotunda had brought her so many invitations that the letter was still lying unfinished on her escritoire days later.

Makepeace, in high fettle from her triumph, was prepared to unbend a little to the man who had witnessed it with her and who had honored it with the deepest of admiring bows. With Jenny now attending so many entertainments, the actor's aid in sitting with Aaron and helping him make circuits of the garden by day was invaluable. She softened towards him sufficiently to join the rest of the household in addressing him as Sir Mick and privately absolved him of the various ulterior motives she had attributed to him.

It was a talk with Aaron that disabused her.

She and her brother were alone in the parlor that evening. Jacques and Murrough had gone to watch badgers in the woods; Luchet was in his room. She was knitting, a skill she'd picked up from Boston seamen—a working-class habit in the view of Chelsea's embroidering ladies but one which, since it was a useful handicraft and she knew no other, she saw no reason to drop.

Aaron was tired and querulous, worried that the walk they'd taken together had occasioned another assault on his heart. 'It hurts,' he said, rubbing his chest, 'I can't even walk lessen it hurts.'

'That's because you ain't used to the crutches yet,' she told him, praying that it was. 'Read your book.'

He was aggressive from frustration. 'We're going ahead with the play, you know, Mick and I.'

So all this time the actor had been goading her poor boy into risking his life—merely so that he should not be deprived of strutting the stage. 'There's a part in it for somebody who can hop, is there?'

'I won't be appearing, I'll be managing. I can sit in the stalls with my damn leg up.'

'No, you can't. You're not to disquiet yourself. Alexander Baines won't have it, nor won't I have it. I ain't lending you money so's you can kill yourself.'

Aaron tossed his book aside. He shouted, 'I'm sick of borrowing off you, don't you see? You've paid for me ever since I can remember; this was my opportunity to pay you back.'

She was astonished by his vehemence. Her early sacrifices for him, all the money she'd given him since, when she had it . . . these had flowed to him without her considering it anything but the natural course of things, like water running downhill. For the first time she tried standing in his boots to see this cataract of loving largesse from his point of view—and saw him drowning under it.

She went on knitting for a while, then she said, 'After Philip died, when they threw me and Philippa out on the street and you took me into the troupe . . . It'd been the workhouse for us else, me and Pip and Betty and Tantaquidgeon. You saved us, Aaron.'

'Did I?'

'You know you did.'

He was pleased. 'Remember Pippy as baby Moses? And sending Tantaquidgeon on as a spear-carrier, and him so taken by the applause he wouldn't come off?'

She did remember but it was painful for her; it had been a time when she hadn't thought she could go on living without Philip Dapifer.

Though you didn't think you could go on living without Andra Hedley, neither. Life continues but, Lord, what holes are left in it.

'I ain't going to lose you, too,' she said.

'Mick said you'd say that.'

'*Did* he?' Was all her personal business to be discussed with that man? 'If he's so almighty clever, let *him* put the bloody play on. He can do the acting *and* the managing.' She went back to her knitting. 'And while he's about it, stick a broom up his arse and he can sweep the stage as well.'

'You don't change, do you?' he said, grinning. He sat forward. 'Listen, sweeting, you've no conception what a plummy chance this is. There's only two theaters allowed under patent in London and the rest provide no competition. We've got three advantages over them: We've got a tried and tested play; we've got Mick—wait till you see what he can do on stage; *and*'—Aaron sat back—'we've got the blessing of the Lord Chamberlain. Deerfield's his brother-in-law.'

'That's good, is it?'

'It's practically unheard of. Makepeace, we must go ahead. Who knows, I could maybe establish a permanent company in London. Above all, we'll strike such a blow against slavery as'll advance abolition by years. Mick and I feel as strongly as you do, you know.'

She doubted it; Sir Michael Murrough felt strongly only about Sir Michael Murrough. 'Who *is* he, Aaron? What was he knighted for?'

'Well, you see, Makepeace, we must consider the *sir* a part of his stage name. It's not an uncommon practice among us theater people.'

'So he was never knighted at all. Is there *anything* real about the man?'

'Yes.' Aaron looked straight at her. 'His heart and his talent.'

It was her brother's heart that Makepeace worried about—and Murrough's talent for capturing it.

Well, he wasn't going to kill her Aaron; she'd out-maneuver him. She shrugged. 'Let him go ahead then. I'll advance him the cash—on the understanding you stay home and are restful.'

'Advance Mick the cash?' Aaron blew air through his lips to produce the sound more usually made to amuse babies.

'Run off with it, would he?' Makepeace was intrigued, this was the first breath against the actor her brother had uttered.

'Run *off* with it, no. Run *away* with it, yes. I yield to no one in my admiration for Mick the actor. But Mick the businessman . . . he has no conception of economy. He wanted real horses and half the Irish army for Richard the Third's last battle. He'd actually pay spear-carriers . . . *pay*, I tell you, when most of 'em are happy with a square meal. *"Ach, God, Aaron, we've used those costumes for two seasons, let's be having some new ones."'*

The imitation was exact but Makepeace didn't smile; she was shocked. She loathed waste. Early poverty had taught her that three pennies should do the work of four. She was prepared to cast bread upon the waters for this play but she damn well wanted it returned to her with advantage, not only for slaves but for Aaron.

He talked on, explaining the necessity for a business brain to cope with theatrical finance, how incapable Mick would be in running both production and management—a difficult enough job at the best of times; only Garrick had ever excelled at both—the eye that must be kept on actors and backstage staff alike if the whole thing was not to be an expensive disaster.

He loves it, she thought. Hopeless, now, to persuade him to lead a quiet life in the north; the strains of the theater might kill him but he'd find them a happier end than what, for him, would be a drawn-out death of an existence on his sister's charity.

And if this blasted play *could* establish him permanently in London it would at least obviate the added exertions of a traveling company.

She looked at him; he'd closed his eyes, worn out by expostulation.

He's not going to outlive me, she thought in panic.

'At least wait until your ankle's better,' she said. 'Baines said to rest your heart until then. It can wait, can't it?' She was begging for their childhood together, all the shared memories of a waterside tavern, Betty, Tantaquidgeon, Boston, the uniqueness of faraway sounds and smells and people that would go with him if he died. 'Please, Aaron.'

He opened his eyes. 'I'm awful tired.'

'There you are, then,' she said, relieved. 'Wait.'

'You do it,' he said.

'Do what?'

'You manage it. Till I'm better.'

'The *play*?'

He was smiling and she realized he was a smarter actor than she'd thought he was. 'Makepeace, I've seen you manage watermen on the Tyne that would have scared Genghis Khan. What did they used to say in Newcastle? That keelmen were frightened by nowt but a lee shore and Makepeace Hedley? What's a company of lily-sniffing actors compared to them? You do it.'

Chapter Eight

I T was such sunny weather and so warm that the driver of the Cherbourg-Paris diligence rolled up the side coverings and his passengers were able to look out on the countryside as they were lurched through it.

Only one, a neat, cheaply dressed little person, who'd got on at Valognes clutching a worn traveling bag, was going all the way to Paris—to help her sister-in-law with the children, she said, now that her brother was in the army.

Ah, yes, the army. Immediately fellow passengers were in sympathy. Everybody had a brother, a son, a husband, a cousin, in the army. Since the *levée en masse,* practically every young man in France had been called up to fight the British or the Prussians or the rebels or somebody.

It was the war, not the Terror, that occupied the minds of the people getting on and off the diligence; women going to see relatives, balancing a hen or baskets of preserves on their knees, the chemist traveling to Caretan to restock his store of drugs, the salesman with his case of scissors, the commune councillor on his way to report to the district chief at Saint Lô, the young widow taking her children to her parents' home in Beauvigny. That and prices.

Things had calmed down. The Revolution's soldiers who'd come last year to punish and repress Caen's insurrection had been recalled by a government realizing that they inspired more rebellion than loyalty. Madame La Guillotine was no longer thirsting for the blood of poor men and women of the Calvados who were only concerned with feeding their children.

The currency of the revolutionary assignat was regaining value after having threatened to become a worthless piece of paper. The law of the maximum, which was supposed to keep prices down and wages steady, was working a little better than it had.

If the men could only come home safe from the war, God would be in His Heaven again—here one of the market women looked nervously at the commune councillor. Was one allowed to mention God? Yes, one was—Robespierre had deemed atheism to be a concept of the aristocracy—although, strictly speaking, one should really refer to Him as the Supreme Being so as to cater for all tastes.

Paris. Did she really have to go there? Why not bring her sister-in-law and nieces and nephews to live in the country? The bloody Parisian sansculottes were more trouble than they were worth, thought they ruled France just because they controlled the capital. No idea of what went on outside; passing laws, decreeing this, decreeing that, most of it ridiculous.

Here, my child, have a bite of this sausage; my uncle makes them to his own recipe. Good, eh?

And yet, Philippa thought, as each new friend stepped down from the diligence to have his or her place taken by someone else, despite what they'd been through—upheaval, bloodshed, the reversal of everything they'd known—there wasn't one who mourned for the days of Louis XVI. Their eyes were brighter, their minds wider, they considered their prospects better, for the Revolution.

When the diligence stopped at Saint Lô to change horses, there was a rowdy crowd gathered around something in the market place. In the old days it would have been a dancing bear or a bull-baiting. Immediately she became afraid that she would hear her first blade drop. But she was told no, no, guillotining was done in Paris; this was merely a bit of fun, a priest being forced to marry a nun.

★   ★   ★

THAT apart, and against all expectation, it was an invigorating journey. While she'd been in England her mind had imagined France as clouded, as if its weather must reflect its political darkness. Instead, sun shone on a springing countryside, fresh and young. The chateaux she passed were windowless and gaping, their geometrically tidy gardens now grazed by sheep and bullocks—and they looked kinder for it.

She'd heard that awful desecrations had taken place on the altars of churches but at two, where the doors were open, men and women were peacefully rolling fat, round cheeses inside for storage, and she thought what a sensible use of a cool, spacious interior that was.

Nor was she harassed for traveling by herself. Though the shouts of the harpies in Paris demanding incredible things had been quieted, the part they'd played in the overthrow of the Bastille and the monarchy had raised the awareness of feminine power, not least among women themselves. Also, women were keeping everything going in the absence of the young men; farming, marketing, even working in munitions factories. There was a sense of comradery between the sexes she had never encountered in England; both were sliding together in this sometimes terrifying, sometimes exhilarating glissade to freedom.

In the overnight inns—and they were awful; not a patch on England's—she shared a communal bed with women on their way to join husbands and sons to become part of the immense train of camp followers that provided the army's nurses and, quite often, its sutlers. One woman, running a farm in her husband's absence, had secured a contract with the army to provide it with barley—and was actually being paid in cash, not assignats.

MEMBERS of the National Guard checking papers at the barriers were men too old or disabled to fight, too tempered by age and experience to be high-handed. Only one insisted on searching her bag and he was mainly teasing. 'It's the young innocents we got to watch, eh, Berthold? One as came through on this coach went and stabbed poor old Marat. No knife? Pass, then, citizeness.'

By this time she had been invited to sit beside Berthold, the elderly, taciturn driver. 'Did Charlotte Corday really travel to Paris in this diligence?'

'No.' He spat. 'She was on Georges's run. Quiet, respectable little thing Georges said she was.'

They traveled on, the hood over the driving bench protecting them from the sun. After a mile he added, 'Never liked Marat anyway.'

She knew she was seeing the results of the Revolution at their best; it would be different in Paris.

She wasn't sure, either, whether what she saw was having its effect on her spirits or whether she only saw what was reflecting her own emotions, but she was aware of a sense of liberation overlaying the frisson of danger. She was cut off, alone, responsible to nobody; the Channel had been her Rubicon and it was too late to go back. The intricacies of relationship had been left behind; she barely thought of them. She felt oddly clean, as if her mind had been swept of years of accumulated dust.

And it had been so easy.

When she'd disembarked at Gruchy, Jean Fallon, the man who ran both the manor and the smuggling business while de Vaubon was in Paris, had looked on her American passport and old *certificat de civisme* with disfavour.

'I should get through to Paris with these, shouldn't I?' she'd asked.

'Perhaps, perhaps not.' Not a talkative man, Fallon, his face resembled a piece of wood that had been twisted and hardened by the sea before being cast up on a beach.

He'd left her then and she spent the day shrimping with his grandchildren on the long white sands, their ears buffeted by the noise of surf and sea birds.

Even in the days when it had been legal to visit France, she had always used the smuggling route from Babbs Cove to Gruchy. For one thing, it avoided bustling immigration officials at the ports, for another, she'd liked the idea of slipping into another country unnoticed even then. Most of all she liked Gruchy and its people. Its harshly democratic relationship with its lord of the manor, de Vaubon, reminded her of that of Babbs Cove's with Makepeace. If you wanted respect for your class or position, it was not the place to come to, but if you accepted and gave friendship, you were home.

She often thought that, with nothing except sea between them and America, these people's ferocious love of independence had been carried across the Atlantic to be breathed in, like an infection on the wind which, when it had done its work, had been blown back again to be caught by all of France. Not that Gruchy had been affected much by the Revolution; it hadn't been affected by the Bourbons much, either. The only notice it took of the doings in Paris was pride that de Vaubon was now involved in them.

In the evening Fallon came back but said nothing until the family had sat down to a vast tureen of *soupe de poisson* and a plate the size of a wheel containing *fruits de mer*—a bland description for a plunge into battle with crustacea from which she emerged bespattered, exhausted and replete.

Only then, having lit his pipe, did he toss a new *certificat de civisme* into her lap. 'Jeanne Renard, schoolteacher, Rue de la Tour, Néhou, Normande.'

'How did you get this?'

He merely shrugged and she was left to gather that even commune committees consisted of local people and therefore of men who, Revolution or no Revolution, owed their living in this area to the smuggling trade.

It was strange. The name had changed her. The woman who was being carried southeast towards Paris was not the one who had left England. She was more cunning, careful, more hungry for her objective than Philippa Dapifer. Jean Fox had emerged from an earth in Néhou—a Cotentin village so far off the beaten track that even its nearest towns were unaware of it—as a creature which, though hunted, was also a predator.

She needed to be. She was entering Paris.

E NTRANCE from the west should have taken them along the Rue Saint Honoré but an overturned dray was blocking progress at that end so, with the rest of the traffic, they had to make a diversion in order to go around and return to it.

Without her being aware of it, the stink had been bothering her for some time, not because she didn't know what it was—she'd smelled it hundreds of times—but because it didn't belong here in what had been, and still seemed to be, the most expensive and sophisticated area of the city. It was like being in Saint James's Palace and coming across a cowherd fresh from the byre—a momentary displacement.

Then she recognized the huge and impressive open space they'd turned into, the Place de la Révolution, and knew why it stank of a slaughter house.

Even now, and it was evening, there was a man going back and forth to a bowser on a cart and throwing bucketsful of water onto the stones before sweeping a rusty result into a drain. It made no difference; a thousand men with a thousand brushes couldn't have swept it clean.

Dr Guillotin's invention had been in keeping with enlightened thinking; if there must be capital punishment, it should be a grim enough deterrent but also mercifully quick and efficient. So it was.

What they hadn't catered for was the amount of blood contained in the human body. Blood jetted from the necks when they were severed, splashing Sanson the executioner, spotting the uniform of the guards and the front row of the watching crowds. It permeated the boards of the scaffold and dripped between them, forming pools, then rivulets, then a river oozing its way down the Place's slight slope to the northeast towards Rue Saint Florentine, sinking into cracks, soaking into moss, feeding weeds, drying, impossible to dislodge.

She'd heard that local residents had complained of the smell so that, for a while, executions had been moved to the Place de la Grève but there, in the poverty of the city's east end, the spectacle had lacked the shock and awe accorded by the former place of kings, so the guillotine had been trundled back to it again.

And there it was. The enormous female statue of Liberty quite dwarfed it where she sat outlined against the Champs d'Elysée, her eyes directed above the scaffold and into the middle distance like a lady trying to pretend the dog shit steaming away near her shoes wasn't there.

The machine itself had been covered for the night in what appeared to be a giant black leather fingerstall, so that it seemed the more terrible for looking vaguely silly, as if it was a poorly finger stuck up for attention that nobody was giving it.

Nobody was. The place was almost empty. The sweeper whistled as he worked. A couple holding hands walked by the thing, their eyes only for each other. A woman who had earlier been selling something to the crowds was shutting up her stall.

They've grown used to it.

In the old days, the river edge of the Place had been part of the view from the Pont Royal. She had always stopped on her way to or from the Left Bank to catch her breath at the color and proportion between the palaces behind her and the palaces ahead, where various builders through the centuries had passed down a congenial sense of symmetry, one to another, where the bridges were like ropes of stone holding the great ship of the Ile de la Cité to its moorings between the banks.

It would never be the same now. It had been overprinted in red by a machine, lethal and ridiculously small against the plaster statue that loomed over it, an accepted part of the scenery.

Berthold didn't want to let her off at the stop for the Palais

Royale which, he said, was a place of *la vie dissolue*, always had been, still was, even if the Puritan Robespierre did eat in one of its cafés.

She pointed north: 'I go that way. My sister-in-law lives in the Grange Batelière section.'

'Take care, little one.' He'd grown protective. She was glad they'd taken on passengers at Neuilly or he'd have insisted on driving her to the door.

She waved until the coach was out of sight then turned south to slip into Rue Saint Honoré like a fox resuming cover, becoming immediately indistinguishable among the crowd. She'd taken the precaution to put a red, white and blue cockade in her cap and had dressed cheaply in case good clothes put her under suspicion but, amazingly, it was still possible to guess a person's class from their dress. Most working women had resumed the close caps, wide petticoats and aprons they'd worn before the Revolution, though a few, with a Phrygian cap and a ferocious expression, found it worthwhile to look as if they'd just paused in doing the washing to pull down the Bastille.

The rest, even in dowdy colors, mannish hats and a respectable fichu ensuring no part of the bosom was exposed, retained that very Parisienne *je-ne-sais-quoi* which had to do with confidence—that whatever the rest of the female world was wearing, they wore it better.

At the old church entrance to what was now the Jacobin Club, men in sober, high-collared coats were rubbing shoulders with what she supposed were the enragés all straggling, greasy hair and stained carmagnoles—as if patriotic fervor demanded that they be as unprepossessing as possible.

On those terms the shop, when she found it, was downright unpatriotic and would have caused perturbation in Chelsea. Its window frothed with lace-trimmed corsets and waists but, again, nobody seemed to mark it; the French had always been open about ladies' underwear, nor would a mere revolution change its frilliness.

In the corner of the display, under a branch decorated with garters, was a small, neat sign. PORTRAITS PAINTED, it read.

Inside, conversation came from behind the curtain of a booth that billowed with the efforts of a customer trying something on.

'I've a parcel for the portrait lady,' Philippa said to it.

'Upstairs. Fourth floor.'

Another curtain revealed a twisting staircase. Philippa went up it, counting the landings. The noise of the street quietened. No sound came from the apartments she passed and it was too dark to decipher nameplates. The stairs finished on the fourth landing where a dirty skylight enabled her to read the notice hanging on a nail in the unpainted door. PORTRAITS PAINTED BY CITIZENESS SOPHIE. ENTER.

It was a large attic, full of the light from another, bigger skylight and the window overlooking Rue Saint Honoré, bare and rather chilly now that the sun was going down. It smelled of oils and turpentine.

The far end was sectioned off by a red velvet, gold tasseled curtain; its twin hung as a backdrop to the dais by the door on which a soldier was standing in martial attitude. Opposite him, facing the door, a woman was applying paint with a long brush to a canvas on an easel that had been positioned to catch the light. The soldier didn't turn and the woman didn't look up. 'What is it?'

'I've come with a parcel for Citizeness Sophie,' Philippa said.

The brush stilled.

After a long moment and with only a flicker of the eyes in her direction, the woman resumed painting. 'Please to wait.'

Carefully, Philippa perched herself on the side edge of the dais so that she was out of the soldier's view—not that he was paying attention to anything but his stance—and tried to make herself believe that the woman opposite was Sophie Condorcet in the flesh and that she'd found her.

It wasn't that she didn't look the same, though she was much, much thinner, but, for Philippa, these last weeks had turned her into something fabulous, a rare bird, a statue that only myth said existed. Such traveling as it had taken to get here had been a journey of hard choices as much as distance, hacking through a jungle of the mind to reach a lost city.

However did I consider not coming myself?

Bless her, she looked so small in an overlarge powder dress which served as a painter's apron. There were lines around the mouth that made her seem older than her thirty years whereas, before, she'd always appeared young for her age—perhaps because of the snub nose that belied her aristocratic ancestry.

Charm had always overlaid Sophie's intellect—she could speak Latin, Greek, English and Italian, had done a translation of Marcus Aurelius's *Meditations*. People had never believed she was as fervid a revolutionary as any sansculotte in the Rue Saint Antoine, yet she and her husband had been republicans long before the Revolution got under way.

Once, when Condorcet had been verbally attacked by a monarchist, he said, 'It's my wife's fault, she persuaded me. Would you disturb domestic peace for the sake of one king more or less?' And he'd only been half joking.

As she watched her friend's intent little face, Philippa saw tears creeping down its cheeks. She had tears on her own.

Sophie Condorcet put up her brush and raised an arm to blot her face. 'The light is going, citizen. If you can return tomorrow, we will finish.'

'Let me see.' The man jumped down from the dais to look at his portrait. He was very young and very dashing, with an ostrich feather in his hat. His uniform coat was velvet and fitted perfectly, crossed by a tricolor sash.

An officer? Did the army still have officers? Were they wearing mustaches now? His was very curly. He was bothering Sophie . . . A little more emphasis on the sword, perhaps, citizeness, and the gauntlets, one should perceive they were best doeskin . . .

Oh go, she thought.

At last he did. The two women stayed as they were for a minute. 'You're mad,' Sophie said. 'You are a madwoman to come.' She ran into Philippa's arms. 'I am so glad to see you, so *glad*.'

Four-year-old Eliza, the Condorcets' only child, was asleep on a bed behind the curtain. They lived there, she and her mother, cooking what they could over a fire in a miniature grate.

Every day Sophie went downstairs and into the street with two buckets. She emptied the one they used as a lavatory at a midden on the corner, washing it out at the pump and filling the other with water.

'And they watch me,' she said.

'Who does?'

'The Committee of Public Safety. They want me to lead them to Nicolas.' She went to the window and closed the shutters fitted into its sides to the point where its bolt just met the corresponding eyelet. 'Careful.'

Philippa peeped through the gap. Across the street was a café with small tables outside it. The man sitting at one of them was talking to an aproned waiter without taking his eyes off Sophie's window.

'They watch all the time, everywhere I go,' Sophie said. 'They've got notebooks. If that one saw you come in, he'll have written you down. But he has to go inside to empty his bowels, thank God, so perhaps he missed you, or perhaps, if he saw you in, he may think he missed you coming out. Poor man, when the café closes, he has to stand in the street all night.'

Philippa put an arm round her shoulders but she went on jabbering. 'Getting the letter to you . . . the night I took it to Bercy . . .' She began to break down, as if she hadn't been able to cry about it before. 'I was followed all the way. And Eliza left alone . . . if they'd arrested me . . .'

'They didn't,' Philippa said calmly. 'And I'm here now. With the papers. Oh, and I've got this.'

It was an egg; one of the women on the diligence had given it to her. She'd wrapped it in every piece of spare clothing she'd had and prayed it wouldn't break.

'Eliza!' Sophie woke her daughter up. 'Look, look. Aunt Pippy's brought you an egg.'

Immediately, she began preparations to make an omelette of it while Philippa dispensed the other presents in her bag. She'd had to be careful not to arouse suspicion in a searcher but she'd been ingenious; paper and crayons were in keeping with her role as a schoolteacher, so was the picture book. There was also a doll for her mythical nieces, a plain wooden thing but some pretty clothes for it were hidden elsewhere.

It was pitiful to see the child in bliss from such things, pitiful, too, to see how thin she was, with a lassitude that sent her back to sleep when she'd eaten all the omelette.

'She gets so little exercise,' Sophie said. 'We go to the Tuileries when we can but I can't stay out long in case someone comes with a commission and finds I'm not here—there's so many of us doing portraits nowadays, competition is fierce. Mothers want a likeness of sons going into battle. Anyway, she's grown out of her shoes. And then . . .' her face tightened. 'I don't want her in the street when the tumbrels go by.'

Rue Saint Honoré was part of the death route. The carts with their human cargo rumbled over its cobbles every day on their way to the Place de la Révolution.

Except Sunday, Sophie said. 'Sanson won't work on Sundays, even though they've abolished them.'

She'd forbidden Eliza to climb up on the window seat to look out in the mornings, a penance for a child locked in an attic but better than chancing to see her father on the way to his execution.

'I haven't heard from him for two weeks. Sometimes somebody brings a letter from him—I don't know who. They leave it with Mme Hahn downstairs but not regularly . . . oh, Pippy, I go distracted until the next letter comes. I never know if they've found him. I can't see him, I can't even write to him.'

'You can now,' Philippa said.

'I know.' Sobbing, she clutched at Philippa's knees. 'I know. I can't tell you what luxury it is to go to pieces. I've been so brave.'

'Yes, you have. It's all right now, darling. I'm here. I'll get him away.' She soothed back Sophie's pretty hair. 'Will you be able to follow us to England?'

'I don't know. I can't think.' She looked round the attic. 'We can't go on like this. There's some property of my father's that I could claim and Eliza must have it; Nicolas and I haven't the right to take her to England to starve.'

'She wouldn't.'

'I know.' Sophie put out a hand to pat Philippa's cheek. It was as if by constantly touching her she was reassuring herself she wasn't conjuring up some phantasm. This, from a woman who had never been demonstrative, showed more than anything else how lonely she'd been.

She smiled; she was recovering. 'But we can't put her in debt all her life—not even to you.' She took Philippa's hand and kissed it. 'We're deep enough in that already.' She looked around helplessly. 'And I can't even offer you a cup of coffee.'

'Yes, you can. Have you any scissors?'

Using a tiny pair *à ongles* from a beautifully unpatriotic manicure set, Philippa started unpicking the hem of her thick, flannel under-petticoat. 'You liked Colombian, if I remember.' Smirking, she held up a packet of tightly stitched oilcloth. 'I was terrified somebody would smell it.'

'Oh my God.' Sophie fell on the packet and, denied the scissors, began tearing it open with her teeth.

Philippa went on unstitching. 'Sugar. Biscuits—oh dear, rather crumbled I'm afraid.'

Sophie hung a miniature kettle over the miniature fire, her head turned to watch packet after packet manifest itself from the petticoat.

'Rice,' Philippa said, smugly. 'Dried peas. I tell you, I was a walk-ing grocery. I barely staggered from the diligence to the inns and back again. One dear old lady asked if I was arthritic. Tea. No milk, I'm afraid. A lemon, though, a bit hard but not bad. Here are the doll's clothes. Oh, and these.'

'These' were a tube of leather containing five louis d'or. 'I pre-sume there's a black market where you can change them.'

Sophie nodded, past speech.

'I didn't trust the papers to a petticoat,' Philippa said. 'You'll have to wait to see those until I undress.'

Sophie had to be dissuaded from waking Eliza up again to regard the cornucopia; sharing everything, they'd been each other's only comrade. Philippa had already noticed that the child spoke with the gravity and awareness of one much older than four.

They sat on the edge of the dais drinking from delicate Sèvres coffee cups, two of a set that Sophie had brought with her from the Condorcet home in Auteuil. 'I had to have *some* necessities.'

The old days were too painful a contrast to dwell on and she steered the conversation away from them. She asked Philippa about her circumstances, what was happening in England, but the outside world was too vast and terrible for her; she kept reverting to essentials—Eliza could have new shoes, a coat, as long as they were careful not to attract attention to their sudden wealth. They could pay Mme Hahn the back rent. She must buy Nicolas new shoes as well; his last letter said his feet had swelled with inactivity.

She frightened Philippa with her happiness; she had waited so long for the documents allowing her husband to travel that they had become a touchstone; everything would be all right now. The journey that he, in disguise, and Philippa would have to make to Gruchy had become merely a corollary to his successful escape.

'Exactly what is he charged with?' Philippa asked.

Sophie shrugged. 'What would you? With being Nicolas Condorcet, with being honorable, framing a fair constitution for the State that has been rejected, refusing to vote for the King's execution—he was the only one, you know. But they *knew* he would not, could not—he's always been against the death penalty. That he was a republican before they had teething rings meant nothing; he stood there in the Assembly and the rest of them saw how fouled they were in contrast. He is the humanity they've lost. Sweet Jesus, Pippy, Marie Antoinette's trial . . . I held no brief for the woman, as you know, but she loved her children . . . They accused her of teaching the dauphin to masturbate. And where is that poor child now? What have they done with him? Whatever he is, he's still only a little boy.'

It was dark; Sophie had run out of candles and been unable to afford more. Philippa heard her move towards the window and fold back the shutters so that she was outlined against the glow from flambeaux in the street below.

She hammered on the window. 'What have you done to our revolution? What have you done?'

Philippa got up and took her away. 'Time to sleep, I think.'

Sophie insisted her guest share the single and only bed with Eliza while she took the floor. The bedclothes smelled grubby, for that matter so did the child and her mother. Philippa recognized it; the same smell that pervaded the cottages of old women denied the luxury of cleanliness by the effort of fetching water and the price of soap.

She was almost too tired to sleep deeply; when she dozed she was on the driving seat of the diligence with Berthold but this time traveling at supernatural speed. Trees and oncoming vehicles came towards them at a rate that made him swerve to avoid a crash, jerking her into consciousness so that she had to soothe back to sleep the muttering child pressed against her.

At one point, the street flambeaux sputtered out and were not relit.

Sophie's voice came out of the darkness. 'I have to divorce him, Pippy. They're going to condemn him as an outlaw and take Eliza's inheritance for the State. They can't if he's not my husband any more.'

She couldn't tell me while she could still see me, Philippa thought, *there are things that can't be spoken in the light.* After a while, she said, 'He'll understand.'

'He will. That's the worst of it, he will.' Sophie's voice went high as it began to break. 'But I don't know how to tell him.'

SOPHIE stood at her window, watching the man sitting outside the café over the road. Philippa stayed by the door, her eyes on

Sophie. They were waiting for the spy's bowels to move, an activity that caused him to go through the café to the privy over the stream that ran through its back garden. His pissing was done in the road's gutter so this was the only time during the day that he left his post. 'A very regular digestion,' Sophie had said of him.

Forty minutes went by. 'Constipated today.'

Another five minutes. 'He's gone inside.'

Philippa clattered down the stairs, nodded to Mme Hahn and left the shop. The man's chair was still empty. Even so, she took trouble to ensure that nobody was following her, turning into alleys, coming out again, dawdling before shop windows that gave an angled reflection of what was behind her.

She found a pleasure in it; her senses honed to a new sharpness—and a new hatred. If the fox could have turned on the hounds and killed them, it would have. She had tried to appear calm about Sophie's predicament for fear that her shock at it would, for Sophie, intensify the realization of how shocking it was. But it had made her very, very angry.

'I didn't love him when we got married,' Sophie had said. 'Admiration, reverence, all those things, but not love. And then one day—he was away—I suddenly knew I wanted him so much I could hardly wait for him to come home. Eliza was conceived that night, I know it. How to tell him I must divorce him for the sake of the child we made then? How to tell *her*?'

Listening to her, the Terror had seemed less terrible because it had become despicable. Condemning a man who had only ever ornamented his country was one thing, inserting its dirty fingers into his marriage another.

What have they done to our Revolution?

They've made it stupid, Sophie.

Its stupidity leaped out at her everywhere, tawdry against the towers of the city and the budding trees. Old and beautiful drain-pipes had been smashed where their ornamentation had included a fleur-de-lis or an escutcheon, gargoyles depicting the heads of cherubs had been torn off, only ugly ones allowed to remain. Above the list of occupants on every house door was scrawled, LIBERTY OR DEATH. Necessary, perhaps, if the householder was not to be suspect, but the graffiti's ubiquity made it not so much patriotic as ridiculous, a new way of keeping up with the neighbors.

Crossing to the Ile de la Cité, she paused in front of the cliff face of Notre Dame, because she always had. Axes had been taken to those saints whose niches were within reach but the doorway was still glorious, except for the almost overpowering smell of urine—as if every passerby had stopped to piss in it.

In the interior, under the great Gothic vaulting she could see that they'd set up a stage—Sophie said that Robespierre was planning some sort of Festival to the Supreme Being. A gimcrack structure of papier-maché was being erected in the resemblance of a Greek temple before which a lady in a toga was rehearsing a song about Reason.

Yes, she thought, the Church had oppressed them, taxed them, kept them in fear of hellfire for their misdemeanours, but their ancestors had built this out of passion and faith, harnessed themselves to carts to drag its stones into place. They had lived out their lives under its certainty. There was no certainty now. God had melted like wax under the command of a committee, his gaze replaced by the all-seeing eye of the *bureau de police*, the seven deadly sins multiplied into a confusion, last month's leaders becoming this week's traitors, yesterday's precepts today's shibboleths.

What have they done to our Revolution?

It wasn't just France's, Philippa thought, *it was mine and Ginny Fitch-Botley's and Hildy's and Mrs Scratcher's and John Beasley's, it was for people without rights, it was for women and men everywhere who work from dawn to dusk for two pence a day and have no say in the system that makes them do it. It was everybody's, it was the world's.*

And they've made it stink for all time.

She rejected her original intention of contacting de Vaubon. To have had a member of the National Convention up her sleeve for emergencies had seemed a good idea, now it did not. It wasn't that she didn't trust him, though from the start he and Condorcet had adopted different revolutionary tactics. Condorcet regarded him and Danton as too extreme and careless in their dealings; de Vaubon thought Nicolas Condorcet to be an old woman—and had said so.

He and Makepeace were of a kind, which is why they'd been immediate allies in the smuggling business; he would help Makepeace's daughter if he could because he was a man who put friendship above politics.

But Makepeace's daughter, at that moment stumping over the bridge to the Left Bank, was too furious to ask for help. She would not, could not, even talk to member of a National Convention that had turned the greatest advance humanity had ever made into a stain upon history.

Not, the careful Philippa thought, angry as she was, unless it was necessary.

Rue Vaugirard ran along the top of a hill with the railings marking the grounds of the Palace of Luxembourg on one side and steep little streets running off it on the other, like ribbons hanging downwards off a lance.

She counted the turnings. 'Rue des Fossoyeurs,' Sophie had said with that tight little grimace of hers. 'I am not superstitious, as you know—I just wish it had been called something else.'

Street of the Gravediggers.

It was narrow and damp, the sun hadn't reached it yet, would stay only a little while when it did. It looked blind, the windows of its tall, respectable houses shuttered, doors barred.

Number Fifteen was halfway down on the right. Two big gates with a wicket in them suggested that a courtyard lay on the other side and that the story above them was the upper floor of a lodge.

The prescribed list of occupants was nailed to the right hand gate.

Violette Vernet (propriétaire)
Manon Bercot

Jean Marcoz
Alain Sarret

One resident's name, she knew, was not on it.

She closed her eyes for a moment. Opening them, she looked up and down the empty street. Then she grasped the ornate door knocker, lifted it and let it fall.

Chapter Nine

MAKEPEACE Hedley and Michael Murrough stood together on the stage of the Duke's Theatre in Eastcheap, looking out on the auditorium.

'"A little dusting,"' Makepeace said, quoting.

'Did I say that?'

'"A lick of paint."'

'That's all, really, dear lady,' the actor said. 'A bit of restoration here and there.'

'How about bit of demolition?' Makepeace said, still horribly calm. 'Finish the job.'

'It looks worse than it is,' he said.

'Oh good.'

It looked appalling. Empty, neglectful years had done the theater harm but thieves had done worse; the proscenium curtain had gone, so had scenery and carpets and chandeliers and candle brackets and doorknobs with their escutcheons—in one instance an entire door. The boxes had been stripped of their gilt balustrades and stools, only scars showed where plaster cherubs and muses had once romped around the high, painted ceiling and walls. The orchestra pit was empty of chairs and music stands. The backdrop roller was broken so that a canvas of Venice's Rialto hung at an angle that threatened to tip its pedestrians into the canal.

A voice like a flute with a French accent came up from the stalls. 'It is not so bad, cherie. The seating is intact.'

'How can you tell?' asked Makepeace. 'Nailed down, is it? I can't see under the rubble.'

'But yes, it is.' The flute was undismayed. 'It need only a sweep.'

Another voice, slightly Irish, said, 'Will you look at this now?' A crumpled playbill was waved over the balcony of the circle. 'They put on *Romeo and Juliet* with Mrs Cibber and Barry.'

There was a sound like an organ roll from beside Makepeace. 'She speaks. O speak again, bright angel.'

'O Romeo, Romeo! Wherefore art thou, Romeo?' asked the circle. The stalls chimed in:

> 'Deny thy father and refuse thy name;
> Or, if thou wilt not, be but sworn my love,
> And I'll no longer be a Capulet.'

There were murmurs of approbation all round the theater.

'Look . . .' said Makepeace.

'How about the sound?' demanded Murrough.

'Not bad at all,' the circle told him, 'Bit sharp, fine with a full house.'

'Cherie, anything is better than the Abbey, it was an ear trumpet.'

'Will you all STOP?' Makepeace said. She gained silence. 'I'm sorry but there ain't going to be no sounds. There ain't going to be a play, not anything. Setting this place to rights would cost more than it's worth. *Look* at it.'

The silence grew deeper. 'I'm sorry,' she said, and meant it. 'I'd have liked to put the play on but it's got to pay its way for Aaron's sake. We'd be in debt before we started. This ain't a charity.'

'I thought it was,' somebody said, reasonably. 'For slaves or some such.'

'Yes, well, I'll think of something else.' Even to herself she sounded shamefaced. 'Perhaps you could put on a production in Hyde Park.'

There was a deep, reflective sigh.

'Bracey's making tea in the Green Room,' somebody said. 'We could give her some of that.'

'Excellent idea.'

They talked about her as if she were a recalcitrant horse.

There were five of them. It seemed like more. They'd got off the boat from Dublin at Holyhead and made their way from Anglesey—God knew how; they hadn't a penny to bless themselves with—to land on the doorstep of Reach House like a flock of parakeets. 'We're Aaron's players, dear lady. How *is* the poor darling?'

She'd let them settle in the parlor and had taken only one, the most insistent, upstairs to Aaron's room on the principle that en masse they would be too much for him, as they were too much for her. That one had been the French actress, Adèle de Beauregard, the one they called Ninon—they all had nicknames—and there'd been a lot of kissing and *cherie*-ings and 'my treasures' between her and Murrough and Aaron but Makepeace had seen at once that here was another of Aaron's women.

There'd been a number of them over the years, always the same as to type, but she'd only known well the two he'd married. At least, he'd called the second one his wife, being somewhat vague as to what had happened to the first—disappeared rather than deceased, apparently. There'd been a child by that particular Mrs Burke and, to Makepeace's distress, it had gone with her.

Andra Hedley had insisted that, however outraged her Puritanism might be, she must not only receive the second Mrs Burke but be nice to her. 'Which do ye want to keep to, pet? Your principles or your brother?'

So she'd kept to her brother, though why, if he'd had any choice in the matter, Aaron should have made the change was difficult to see; both marital peas might have come from the same pod. Both were actresses, slightly vulgar, thin, brunette, overexuberant and, to Makepeace's mind, overfriendly. Both had treated her as if she were as risqué as themselves, presumably because she'd had two husbands, one of them titled, rich and previously divorced. There'd been a companionable women-of-the-world winking from them; the second Mrs Burke had actually complimented her on having 'done well for herself'—a phrase that had enabled Makepeace to bear the eventual severance of that alliance with equanimity.

Ninon, being thin, dark and animated, went down immediately as another from the formula and there was no mistaking the mistiness of Aaron's eyes as she settled a silk-covered haunch on his pillows and smoothed back his hair in what Makepeace considered an unnecessarily proprietorial manner.

She had to leave them together in order to attend to the rest but, on the way, sought out Hildy. 'Send Sanders for Dr Baines. And tell Constance she's to go and sit in Aaron's room and stay there.'

'Is yon lad worse?'

'He will be if he's left alone with this one. She's *French*.'

'Aw deor.' Hildy had run for it.

Baines didn't arrive and Ninon had the grace to come downstairs after a short interval. The woman was reassuring though, again, irritatingly proprietorial. 'You look after *mon pauvre* ve'y well, *madame*. He mus' not be excited, no?'

Hospitality required she put them all up for the night. By that time the invaders, especially Ninon, had nearly everyone in the household eating out of their hands. Luchet bobbed in the Frenchwoman's wake like a lovelorn cork. She won Jacques by taking the rest to look at his inventions and showing baffled admiration.

Marie Joséphine, however, did not succumb. 'That one is no *grande dame*; she is a peasant, like me. *C'est une imposture.*'

'They're actors,' Makepeace told her. 'Imposture's their trade.'

Their gossip at dinner was so enchanting that Makepeace had to frown at the maids who gathered outside the slightly open dining room door between courses so that they could listen to it. Hopkins had to be reminded to serve the gravy.

They had enough politeness, or self-interest, to include Makepeace in their conversation and expressed delight that Aaron had persuaded her to be the company's business manager. Nevertheless her dining table had assumed the bulwarks of a vessel that sailed without her; she was reminded of the aristocratic dinner parties she'd had to attend with Philip Dapifer when, without one antagonistic word being spoken, she'd been left in no doubt that she was an interloper.

It wasn't that these players overrode her personality but that they changed it. As their patron and a non-thespian she must be pandered to; she found herself being altered into a sort of bountiful bookkeeper, an elderly aunt who had wandered into a young person's party, to be respected while she was present but oh-what-a-relief when she went.

Yet Murrough was of her own age, so was the stout woman they called Bracey. *And you won't see forty again either, you baggage*, she'd thought, looking at Ninon.

To her relief they intended only to stay the one night at Reach House; they had friends in London among whom they would scatter themselves. She thought Murrough might go with them, but he showed no sign of it.

The next morning they'd packed into her coach, arranging to meet her in two days' time at the theater to view it and begin making arrangements for the production. Ninon took a tearful farewell of Aaron but promised to come back often 'to keep up his spirits.'

'Long as that's all she keeps up,' Hildy said, darkly.

Now, sitting in the wreck of the Duke of York's Green Room, they wove Makepeace around with persuasion and charm, like Titania's fairies enchaining Bottom.

Jacques, who had enveigled himself into the outing, reinforced their argument that the theater could be made good, his eyes pleading; he had found wonderful mechanisms under the stage still intact.

Would she not admit that the theater's structure was sound, its pillared, pedimented outside impressive, only needing a lick of paint? Oh, very well, several licks, but that was nothing. Inside, they could do the clearing and cleaning themselves.

Makepeace regarded the smooth hands fluttering at her. Those of the two young men, Paul 'Polly' Armitage and Señor Distazio, 'Dizzy,' were as white as those of Jane Jordan and Chrissy Gardham, the ingenue. 'Carpenters?' she asked. 'Decorators? Plumbers? That's before we even start hiring stagehands.'

'Oh pish,' Mrs Jordan said. 'There are always little men just begging to be employed in that sort of work.'

'In Dublin, maybe,' Makepeace said. 'But there's a war on over here and all spare little men are in it. You employed an English plumber lately?'

She knew that by arguing with them she lost ground. Partly, she wished to be persuaded; it had been so long since she'd been as exhilarated by a project as she had by this. Nor did a day go by without her hearing the slave shriek for her child.

But it was hopeless; to restore the theater to a place of entertainment that competed for audiences with Drury Lane and Covent Garden, as it had to, would cost more than it could ever recoup—and would thereby deeply offend the businesswoman in her, besides putting Aaron in her debt forever.

Most of all, she was no longer convinced that the play would do what Murrough and Aaron had promised her that it would. They'd given her a copy of *Oroonoko* to study—unwisely as it turned out because she thought it was rubbish.

The two-dimensional words on the script read badly to her, silly and flat. By making the hero a betrayed African prince, the playwright had, she thought, used special pleading instead of portraying the enslavement of real people.

Worse, running through the drama was a comic tale involving a couple of English girls hunting husbands—to which end, for reasons Makepeace failed to grasp, one of them had to dress as a man. As for the sexual innuendo . . .

'It's rude,' she had said.

'It's funny,' Aaron said. 'It relieves the tension, audiences expect to laugh as well as cry.'

'I didn't.'

'Wait until you see it performed, dear lady,' Murrough had told her. 'That last scene, I shall reduce you to weeping rivers. Didn't it move you when Oroonoko kills the wicked governor and stabs himself?'

'No,' Makepeace said. 'I thought good riddance to both of 'em.'

They overrode her; she was unused to reading a script, she lacked the expertise to flesh it out with actors' speech, movement, pauses, dramatic effects. They promised her it would turn London audiences into wholesale abolitionists. In Dublin it had brought tears from the audience that flooded the stalls.

Oh, well, she was a newcomer to this business; she was reluctantly prepared to give way to professionals. But she'd concede to no one when it came to a balance sheet.

In the Green Room they pushed hard on their end of the scales. They were prepared to work merely for their keep—only when the play was a success and the theater established would they take a salary.

I'm keeping that damn Sir Mick already, she thought.

Look, look, they'd discovered a cupboard the thieves had missed, full of gilded plaster wreaths, garlands, pilasters and fretwork with which to decorate the auditorium, even the molds to make more.

Well . . .

It was Ninon who delivered the coup de grâce. She sprang up. 'But why do I not think of this? We do not need the carpenter, the scene-shifter, *les ouvriers*, always they are trouble. We have the emigrés.' She stood with her arms outstretched, waiting for applause. It was slow in coming; even her colleagues were doubtful. Makepeace was mystified.

'The what?'

'The emigrés, the nobility, the ones who fly to England from the guillotine. They are here, *des centaines des pauvres*, they are starving.'

'Ye-es,' said Makepeace patiently.

'But they will work for nothing, for their food, for two pennies an hour.' She turned to the others. 'I walk into a hat shop yesterday to look at *un chapeau de paille*. Who is selling it? The Comtesse de

Saisseville. I recognize her because once at *la Comédie* she talk all through my grand speech in *Le Bourgeois Gentilhomme*.' Ninon closed her eyes in bliss. 'Now she is brought down and well disposed to me. She ask that her daughter do my sewing. They all starve, I tell you. The ladies work, perhaps, the lords do nothing—they do not know what to do.'

She crouched down by Makepeace's chair. 'We tell them, eh?'

'Aristocrats? *French* aristocrats?' Makepeace had no high opinion of the English version; as for the Gallic . . . 'They'd be useless. They couldn't even run their country.'

'No, no. They are desperate. And . . .' Ninon's voice cooed into Makepeace's ear like a lover's. '. . . they have servants who are desperate even more.'

'Servants?' She was aware that Murrough was watching her with amusement, the rest withheld their breath. She ignored them all.

Tuppence an hour, she thought. *Servants, handymen, seamstresses . . . we could have every job in the theater filled at tuppence an hour.*

Murrough's voice said, 'A bargain, madam.'

'Whether it's worth making is another matter,' she said, detecting sarcasm. But *a bargain* . . . the word called to her like a siren. It would be something to create a little working world out of this hellhole, provide for Aaron's future, employment for the needy and light a flame that might, just might, start a fire to burn all the shackles and the whips, end a darkness . . . at tuppence per person per hour.

She tutted grudgingly, for the look of the thing. 'I'll see,' she said.

A T first she was sorry for the exiles; they were so brave. They arrived nonchalantly, the men striding, the women tottering in their threadbare shoes with that peculiarly French upper-class walk of theirs, toe first, heel after, their work-roughened hands delicately pecking the air as they talked.

They had heard . . . but what fun to be involved in a play . . . they had taken part in *beaucoup de théâtre d'amateurs* . . . if they could be of service to Madame?

Ghosts of the headless dead came with them, almost visible, like chains that couldn't be shaken off. Nostalgia gnawed at them worse than the hunger that was forcing them to shame themselves but they affected insouciance; they might have been viewing Makepeace and the theater to see if both were suitable.

She wondered why so many wanted theater work rather than other menial jobs that were better paid and came to realize it was because they'd be out of the public view. Exposing themselves within these confines—and this was a much later realization—didn't matter because actors were dross whose opinion didn't matter anyway.

She stood in the orchestra pit, her elbows resting on its rail, as each one took a seat before her in the front row. Ninon sat on a stool beside her, out of sight, ready to be consulted.

A few brought servants with them—for the sole purpose, as far as Makepeace could see, to have someone to announce them. The worst were those who brought their children . . .

'You see, Countess, we're not casting for the play, we want laborers.'

The Comtesse d'Arbreville indicated her seven-year-old son. 'We are most strong, are we not, Henri?'

'Indeed, Maman. I am like Hercules.'

Makepeace sank down below the partition. 'What do I do?'

'Send them away,' Ninon told her. 'They are no use.'

'I *can't*. He's so small. They're both small.'

Ninon shrugged.

Makepeace stood up. 'Can you sew, Countess?' They needed seamstresses to make costumes.

'I embroider, of course.'

Makepeace shook her head. There wouldn't be time to do other than suggest embroidery by putting on *appliqués*; what they wanted was cutters-out and good old fashioned sewers. 'Perhaps later . . .'

When they'd gone she called up to Polly Armitage, who was cleaning the stage so that rehearsals could begin, and put a guinea in his hand. 'Run after them, tell her she dropped this when she sat down.'

The toll on her pity and her purse grew. So did her irritation.

'Monsieur the Count, I'm afraid the work we're offering ain't suitable for you, but if I could talk to your man here . . .'

'I answer for Joseph.' The Comte de Penthémont had lost an arm somewhere, an empty sleeve was pinned to the tattered sash of his uniform. Joseph, on the other hand, had all his limbs and looked competent.

'Perhaps he could answer for himself. Now then, Joseph, what work can you do?'

Joseph looked at his master who gave permission in French; few of the servants spoke English.

'Je suis homme à tout faire de M le Comte.'

Makepeace bobbed down into the orchestra pit.

'A handyman,' Ninon said. She listened—Joseph was going stolidly on. 'Also he built huts in the royal army at Coblentz when they served together, also he saw to their drains, also . . .'

'Lord love him,' Makepeace said and bobbed up. 'Can he mend that ceiling?'

The Comte de Penthémont looked calmly upwards then down again. 'Only if I hold the ladder.'

'I ain't paying tuppence an hour for somebody to hold a ladder.'

'Then I fear . . .'

'Oh, all *right*. Threepence an hour for the two of you.'

'Four pence.'

'Three and a half. My final offer.' If Joseph lived up to his curriculum vitae, it was still a bargain.

'Done.'

As she leaned across to shake the Count's only hand, she said, 'You ever thought of going into business?'

'It would be beneath me, madame.'

She shook her head, watching him go. 'I don't understand these people.'

'It is your fortune you did not have to,' Ninon said.

Makepeace looked down at her. 'You're enjoying yourself, ain't you?'

'But yes,' Ninon said and Makepeace saw that not all the ghosts in the theater that day were being dragged in by the royal exiles. Already Ninon had vetoed the former abbé of a church in Montmartre. '*Non,*' she'd said on hearing his name.

'He's a priest,' Makepeace hissed at her. 'He says carpentry was his hobby. We need a carpenter.'

'His hobby was little girls,' Ninon said, which put an end to the matter.

The Chevalier Saint Joly, who wore the Order of Saint Louis on his breast, was hired instantly. A sensible-looking young man, he'd also served in the ragtag royal army that had been defeated so comprehensively by the Revolution's forces and where, he said, he'd had to turn his hand to anything.

One of the last to arrive was Makepeace's old waltzing partner.

'I'm very sorry, Marquis, we don't need dancing masters just now.'

He looked more dilapidated than ever but just as self-possessed. 'You will need musicians, Madame. I have some small talent in that direction.'

'Will we need musicians?' asked Makepeace, sotto voce.

'Yes. Who is it?'

'Marquis de Barigoule.'

Ninon was instantly on her feet. '*M le Marquis, vous êtes vraiment bien.*'

'*Mademoiselle Adèle. Suis enchanté.*'

France, Makepeace decided as the two chattered, was a small world.

'That is very good,' Ninon said when the Marquis had gone. 'Already he play in a sextet with friends for his own pleasure, now they play for us.' She looked sideways at Makepeace. 'I suggest sixpence an hour.'

'For *amateurs*?'

'Mozart has compose for him. Surely you have heard the "De Barigoule Sonata"?'

Makepeace, who was tone deaf, had hardly heard of Mozart. However, she assumed they must have musicians; from what she remembered of the theater there were always tunes. She'd have to consult Aaron. 'I'll see,' she said. Ninon was relishing her power over a class that had exercised power over her—obviously, in most cases, none too kindly—and getting above herself in the process.

Still, it hadn't been a bad day's work. She'd hired three seamstresses—one of them a lady-in-waiting who'd created costumes for Marie Antoinette—three and a half handymen, if one counted the Comte de Penthémont, and four of the more robust-looking nobility as plain laborers. Also, because she couldn't get the Countess with the little son out of her head, she had sent a note around to their lodging and hired them, too.

All of them, supposing they came up to expectation, were to begin work the next day. Since time was money, she'd decided that rehearsals for the play must start right away; the cleaning and restoration of the theater would have to go on around them.

'I want to open in three weeks,' she told Murrough and Jacques as they traveled back to Chelsea.

She'd expected the actor to ask for more time but he merely nodded. It was Jacques who said, 'As long as I can get the cannonballs.'

'What cannonballs?'

'Sir Mick wants a thunderstorm in Act Three, and I have had an idea superb.' He turned to Murrough. 'Do you remember at the armaments factory in Saint Cloud when we went with Papa, the noise cannonballs made when they rolled from the foundry? Like thunder?'

'I remember. A grand idea.'

Makepeace was silent for a while, then she said, 'You're not going to the theater again, Jack.'

'Please, missus, please.' The boy was distraught. 'Already I am working on the traps. It is an education much better than Latin, *oh please*. Tell her, Sir Mick.'

'It's a matter for the lady, Jack. I'd merely point out that with you involved in this production, your tutor'd be free to give us a hand as well.'

The thought of Luchet doing hard work for a change was a happy one but Makepeace was not to be seduced by it. She said, 'We'll see,' merely in order to gain peace for the rest of the journey in which to think.

So the actor and Jacques had met before; what she'd assumed to be instant liking rested on former acquaintanceship. He knew who Jacques was. He and de Vaubon has visited an armaments factory together.

She began collating her suspicions about the Irishman. She was sure he'd left Ireland because the place had become too dangerous for him. Only this morning when, because of the weather, she'd intended that the three of them be driven to London in the open carriage, Murrough had asked that they use the coach instead. 'My public, dear lady . . . recognition can be embarrassing, demands for keepsakes, that sort of thing.'

His public my arse, she thought. *The only keepsakes he's worried about are a pair of handcuffs and jail.*

The actor had closed his eyes, either in sleep or feigning it, and she studied him. A plastic face, like a piece of dough that could assume any expression. An actor's face. Or an agent's.

You're a spy, she thought, *that's what you are, a bloody spy. For which side?* Not that it mattered. He was dangerous whichever way the cards fell.

Ain't I got enough? There's John Beasley, there's Jacques and now there's you.

When they reached home, she sent Jacques off to his supper, invited the actor to join her in the parlor and closed the doors. She faced him, his size reducing hers. It wasn't that he was fat, it was the sheer bulk; there was a massivity to him which was menacing on its own account; he bled Philippa's demure parlor, made it lopsided, as if a rhinoceros had entered it.

She asked him to sit down so that he'd be less intimidating. She stayed standing and went hard into the attack. 'Are you a danger to that boy?'

'Your pardon, ma'am?'

'Don't you pardon me.' Pugnacity was ever her weapon when she was scared. 'You're up to some hocus-pocus and I've a right to know if it can harm that boy. He's my responsibility, his father put him in my care and I'm not having him put at any more risk than he is already.'

'Ah.' Murrough flicked a piece of lint from his sleeve. 'The armaments.'

'Exactly. You didn't tell me you knew de Vaubon.'

'You didn't ask.'

'I'm asking now.'

To show him that they were there for the duration, she pulled up a stool and sat in front of him.

He was considering. 'Dear lady, if I told you I'd not harm a hair on that boy's head, would that do for you?'

'No,' she said. 'It wouldn't. And I'm not your dear lady.'

'Are you not? That's a shame then. Well, it's like this . . . Could we be having a dish of tay? I bare me soul better when I'm not parched.'

She felt powerless to get through the veneer of banter, the mock politeness, whatever it was, that kept her from the truth of him. She sent for a tray of tea so that he'd have no excuse and because her own mouth was dry. When it came she poured them both a cup. 'Now,' she said. 'Talk to me. To *me*. Stop being so . . . so Irish.'

'I am Irish,' he said. 'Aren't you? Isn't Aaron?'

'No,' she said. 'We're American.' No law of marriage was going to take that identity away from her. 'And proud of it.'

'Rightly so. A people who chose freedom rather than pay British taxes. But in Ireland, now . . . well, taxes are the least of it. Aaron says your father told you. The Burkes of Mayo were never a clan to be silent on their grievances. Did ye listen?'

She'd listened. And listened and listened during endless maudlin sessions when her father had wept tears of pure rum. *'They made us cattle, Makepeace darlin'. Fokkers took our language, our education, advancement, our religion, our bloody souls. Cattle in our own land.'*

It had been his justification for failure and drunkenness; eventually she'd stopped listening and become irritated, as with a beggar that wouldn't go away.

'We Americans did something about it,' she said.

'Indeed ye did, indeed ye did.' Murrough waved a congratulatory hand. 'And, if I remember rightly, ye did it with the help of the French.'

She put her cup down. 'Dear God,' she said. 'Are you doing the same? You're planning an Irish rising. You're a traitor.'

She heard the word fly out of her mouth and buzz round the room like a blue-bottle fresh from the shit-house.

It didn't land on him. 'So I am,' he said. 'So was Jefferson, so was Benjamin Franklin. All traitors to the British in their day. So was Sam Adams—a gentleman of your acquaintance, I believe.'

'Yes,' she said, slowly. 'Sam used to come into my tavern in Boston.'

They were *different*, she thought. They were good, clean, intelligent men seeking liberty. But the Irish . . . Father, running footmen, double-dealers, Papists, potato-eaters, bog-trotters, the butt of jokes, always jokes . . . A drip, drip of prejudice that turned sympathy to stone.

He was watching her out of his little eyes, like an amused, intelligent pig's. 'Not the same? Independence too good for the Irish?'

'I don't know,' she said.

'Abolition will only stretch as far as the negroes, eh?'

'You're not slaves.' She was only nettling herself; she couldn't disturb him. She felt like a fighter unable to land a punch on a superior opponent.

'Was your father a lazy man, Mrs Hedley?'

Dear God, how much had Aaron told him? 'What's that got to do with it?'

'Mine was,' he said. 'Lord Altamont complained of him though, living mostly in London, he didn't know Dada, but he disapproved of not getting enough rent off him. And his overseer disapproved of him, too. "Will you not improve your land, O'Leary, so's we can kick ye off it and charge a higher rent to somebody else?"'

O'Leary? Not Murrough? The man hadn't even kept the name he'd been born with.

'They put the rent up anyway,' Murrough went on, companionably. 'I'll tell ye one thing your dada didn't do, you being born in Boston. He didn't give you up to the overseer's bed in exchange for rent. Mine did that to me sister. A pimp, you'd maybe call him and starvation for the rest of us no excuse.' He settled himself more easily in his chair. 'And, silly girl, didn't she go and hang herself?'

Her father had asked for too much sympathy; Murrough was shrugging it off, merely making a point on his way to whatever explanation he was giving her, a brief glimpse into the night, lightning transfixing a scene in rain.

She got up and went to the sideboard to get them both a glass of malmsey—again more for her sake than his. She heard his voice as she poured the wine into the glasses. 'It's grand training for an actor to be Irish. We learn it at the mammy's knee, d'ye see, how to mop and mow, how to please, tell the lords what they want to hear. Some call it blarney, others call it deceit. I call it acting.'

She went back to her stool and handed him his glass. 'And de Vaubon?' she asked.

He brought his eyes down to look at her as if he'd forgotten she was there. He said, 'Isn't that the coincidence? I don't know the man well, he was one of a succession of the bigger frogs in that revolutionary pond I was wading in . . . did ye know Robespierre has a greenish complexion? Green as a shamrock. Tiny fella, like a leprechaun. Came up to me knee. It was like asking the Little People for help.'

'But you got it,' she said.

'I got their promise,' he said. 'We'll have to see what that's worth.'

She persisted. 'So the French are going to help Ireland rebel.'

'They'll maybe help Ireland to its freedom.'

'Send arms, troops?' She was a woman who needed the words said.

'Such is the plan.' He swigged back his malmsey and slammed the glass down on the little table by his chair. 'If it's good enough for America, it's good enough for Ireland.'

He was saying there was no difference. But there is, she thought. Ireland's too close, too poor, too Catholic; the English have owned it for too long; it is a postern into their castle. They'd fight for it as they hadn't been able to fight for America—and to the death.

'When?'

'Not yet. When they're ready. And when we are.' He yawned. 'And that, madam, was me one and only foray into the dirty world of secret negotiation. No connection any more between Michael O'Leary, agent and courier, and Sir Mick Murrough, actor. You need have no worry on that account.'

He was reassuring her; he thought she was worried about him being a threat to the safety of her house. Come to think about it, she was.

'There is a worry, though, isn't there?' she said. 'Why did you slip out of Ireland like you did? Why don't you want to be seen in the streets?'

'A tiny precaution, madam.' His vast shoulders shrugged it off. 'There's maybe one or two double agents who saw O'Leary in Paris that shouldn't have. But they'll not connect him with Sir Michael Murrough.'

'And Mick Murrough capering about onstage in full view of some of 'em won't give them a clue?'

He was indignant. 'I'll be blackened, ma'am. And I'm an actor. Me own mother won't recognize me.'

If you had a mother, she thought, bitterly. She'd found out a lot about him, but merely as much as he'd chosen to tell her; at no point had he spoken to her as an individual, only as an audience. She knew as little of the essence of him now as she had when they came into the room. *Perhaps there is no essence,* she thought; *perhaps the actor's all there is. Even his spying for Ireland is just another role.*

'Well, madam?' he said. 'Do I go or do I stay?'

She looked up. He was smiling—and not unattractively. That had 'em lining up at the stage door, no doubt—Aaron had said women threw themselves at the man's feet. Lord knew why.

But she was surprised by her reluctance to tell him to go. He'd insinuated himself into the household; he'd leave a gap. Jacques would miss him, Aaron would be cross with her—though how much he'd told Aaron about his activities was something she'd have to investigate.

And how much danger was there? If he were discovered, which, as he said, was unlikely, she could disclaim all knowledge of what he'd been up to. And she would, oh she would.

One thing, he'd safeguard the secret of Jacques's connection with de Vaubon for fear of revealing his own. She had a hold over him there.

Immediately, it occurred to her that his hold on her was as tight. If he was in danger of exposure, so was Jacques.

All the more reason for keeping the bastard under her eye.

'I'll see,' she said.

'Good for him,' said Aaron.
'It's not good for him, it's not good for any of us. Every

revolutionary in Europe thinks he can hide out in this damn house. Government spies must be counting 'em in. Beasley, de Vaubon's boy, your Irishman. Even Philippa and her rights for women.' Makepeace flung out her hands. 'And I don't agree with any of them.'

Aaron grinned at her. 'But you'd fight for their right to do it.'

'Looks like I'll bloody have to. Now, about these damn musicians . . .'

M AKEPEACE and Murrough started quarrelling on the morning of the first day that *Oroonoko* went into rehearsal and restoration of The Duke's Theatre began. If Makepeace had wondered what was the essence that lay beneath the shifting character of Mick Murrough, it was made apparent to her then and in the days to come. At base, the man was a fanatic.

The war started with shouting but, then, it had to. The hammering and sawing, cries and orders, competed with the thump of Jacques's traps opening and closing that in turn competed with repetition of a phrase from de Barigoule's violins and trumpets, all of it rendering normal converse impossible.

'What?'

'I said stop this damn noise. We can't hear each other rehearse.'

'Go somewhere else then.'

'We need to be on stage, woman. I need to show them their positions.'

She won that one; the work couldn't be stopped. Watching him lead the rest of the players to rehearse elsewhere, she felt that she had established who was in charge.

An hour later, she erupted into the Green Room. 'Who said they could dismantle the boxes on the sides of the stage?'

Murrough flung his script onto the floor. 'In the name of God . . .' He turned on her. 'I did.'

'What for? They could hold twenty people. More.'

'They're old-fashioned, they're a damn nuisance and they're going. I need the space.'

Ninon who, for some reason, had been standing on a chair, got down. 'It is true, *cherie*. Stage box customers, they are *affreuses*. They drink, they comment. Also they come on stage . . .'

'They make advances, too,' Mrs Jordan said. 'I won't tell you where one of them grabbed me in *The Beaux Stratagem* but it was certainly strategic.'

'Remember when one of 'em climbed out and tried to throttle Garrick in *Macbeth*? Didn't like him killing Duncan?'

'They pay top price,' Makepeace said.

Murrough advanced on her, a finger wagging at her nose. 'I don't care if they pay their hearts' blood, I need the space. You can do what hell you like out front, but on stage I'm governor. Now, madam, will you kindly leave us in *peace*?'

She'd lost and she knew it. She made one last feint. 'Well, who are all these people?' The Green Room was crowded.

Murrough expired. 'They're the rest of the cast.' He picked up his script and waved it at her. 'See here. Thirteen characters. Didn't ye read the *Dramatis Personae*?'

Actually, she hadn't. She looked around at the newcomers, one or two bowed, a woman curtseyed, the rest waved and smiled. 'I wasn't consulted about hiring them.'

'No, you weren't. It's not your business. Did ye think we were putting the thing on with six? What do you want us to do, double up?'

Her chagrin directed itself at Luchet, who'd been standing behind Ninon's chair, trying to make himself thinner. 'What's he doing here?'

Murrough looked round. 'What *are* you doing here?'

Luchet regarded Ninon adoringly. 'I prompt?'

'Get out,' Murrough told him, and turned back to Makepeace. 'You, too.'

The rules were established; she was the practicality, he the artistry—which would have sufficed perhaps anywhere else, but in a playhouse the two mysteries overlapped and frequently conflicted.

That first day set the tone for the rest. Each saw the other as a hurdle deliberately set in his/her path to be tumbled over. Common decency went to the wall. Shouting rose to screams. Murrough's plastic face hardened, as if wind had blown away desert sand to reveal the rock beneath. The piggy eyes lost indolence and gleamed with the ferocity of an attacking boar. Makepeace's curled fists held an invisible, prodding spear.

'I want lamps on stage.'

'You'll have to do with rushlight; I'm keeping candles for when we open.'

'We can't see what we're doing. Dizzy can't read his words.'

'Tell him to learn his lines.'

'*I'll* decide when he must learn his lines. And if Your High and Miserliness would oblige, I want those bloody curtains up. They've got to draw back at just the right moment—Jack's going to work on it.'

'We're not having curtains, only false ones. We're having a drop. It's cheaper.'

'In hell we will. I get curtains or I go. A *drop*.' The stage shook as he stamped around it appealing to the gods. 'I've met some cheese-paring, miserly lickpennies in my day but this one . . .'

'Let me remind you, Mr Spendthrift, *I'm* the goose laying this golden egg, it's my cash you're lavishing on all this fiddle-faddle . . .'

'*Fiddle-faddle*? God save me from barbarians. It's vandals like you sacked Rome.'

'And a good job, too, if it had decadent bastards like you in it.'

The theater would fall quiet to listen to the two of them, but neither noticed. Jacques got upset at first, though the calm of the cast reassured him that this was normal chit-chat between manager and directing actor. The workmen cocked their heads with admiration, the émigrés with lifted eyebrows that suggested nothing less was to be expected of the vulgar.

Only Ninon and the Marquis de Barigoule, experienced in other passions, gave each other a sentimental wink. Makepeace, intercepting it, became the more angry. *It isn't true.*

In any case, the quarrel always ended in compromise. It had to; they might threaten, but neither would abandon the play now. He got his curtains, she retained her candles.

Their vituperation only flourished in company. The moment Sanders drove the coach to the stage door of an evening and they and Jacques entered it, an awkwardness fell, along with silence. With their ears burning from the punishment inflicted on them, and with Jacques regarding them nervously, the hellhag reverted to dear madam, the spendthrift to Mr Murrough. Not a word was spoken concerning the theater, and very few about anything else, though they occasionally touched stiffly on the weather.

It was Aaron who became the vessel into which each poured complaint about the other, *privatim et seriatim.*

'It's not going to work, Aaron. The man will bankrupt us . . .'

'Far be it from me to denigrate your sister, old friend, but she has no idea . . .'

And Aaron, who had occupied both pairs of shoes, declared that things must be going splendidly.

'Incidentally,' he said to Makepeace. 'Your neighbor the Reverend Deedes paid me a visit this morning.'

'What did he want?' She was tired.

'Not to be neighborly, I can tell you that. Came to persuade you to give up the play. I suppose the word has spread. Preached at me instead. Said it was his duty to save our souls from the perdition of the playhouse—it means whorehouse to him, apparently. I sent him away with a flea in his ear.'

'Oh dear.' Fleas in the Reverend Deedes's ears tended to transmute into a hornet's nest for the giver. 'You pointed out that I'm doing it for the benefit of the Abolition Society?'

'I did.' Aaron's mouth screwed into a purse. ' "*I think you will find the Society unwilling to accept charity from such a source.*" He's going to appeal to Caesar in the shape of Stephen Heilbron and the Lord Chamberlain. Don't worry about it. Nobody'll pay attention to a provincial little fart like that.'

Makepeace wasn't so sure and, had she been less occupied, she might indeed have worried about it but when she woke next morning, her head was filled only with what faced her at The Duke's.

To her, entering the theater was a plunge into a sea, the hoots of its denizens booming in her ears like a loud deafness. She couldn't strike out for an objective without being diverted by reefs and distracting schools of complaining fish. Every day brought some new difficulty threatening to drown her along with the entire enterprise. When she shouted at malcontents and idlers it seemed to her that her mouth must be moving soundlessly under water, like a guppy's, having no effect.

The seamstresses sent her mad. They had contempt for what they were doing. And they were slow.

'But we cannot sew this, it is *criard* . . . tawdry. See, it split under the needle.'

'Don't stitch it so fine, then. It'll look rich on stage, it's shiny.'

Though both controlled themselves vocally, Madame de la Pole's sneer said it would not have done for the Queen; Makepeace's grinding teeth said that Marie Antoinette was dead and good riddance.

'And sew faster.' She wished now she'd hired all the costumes as Aaron had told her to, but the financial point of no return had been passed.

Those who did their job and did it well became beautiful to her, like firm sand under her feet. Joseph was her rock, he patched the ceiling, widened the stage, mended the auditorium boxes—and cleaned up after each job, a deed for which she could have wept in gratitude. She was even able to put his ladder-holding master to work when it became apparent that Joseph, not trusting him, had lodged the ladder's feet securely anyway.

'I see you can still draw, Count.' She held up a scrap of paper she'd found pinned on the wall of the Green Room—a cartoon showing her and Murrough at loggerheads; him as a bull, herself as a yapping terrier.

The Comte de Penthémont, unabashed, lowered the copy of the

Courrier de Londres he'd been reading while leaning against the ladder rungs. 'I was not unknown for my watercolors.'

'Good, then you can whitewash the scenery.'

It cost her an extra halfpenny an hour but it was worth it.

The Chevalier Saint Joly was another on whom she relied and it was a blow when, after a week, he told her he had found other employment.

'I hope it's more worthy of you,' she said, 'but I'm sorry to lose you.'

'Better paid perhaps,' he said, kissing her hand—they'd got on well. 'How worthy I do not know but it comes with a little house so my wife and children and I can be together. I am to be butler to Lord Blakeney. He is a good man, I think.'

'So I hear. Good luck to you.'

He was to work out the rest of the day so she left their good-byes until later but that afternoon the leader of the theater's émigrés, the Comte d'Antrais, asked her if they might use the Green Room for a meeting for an hour. It was their social center in the evenings after work. Makepeace allowed it because all of them had lodgings too small and too sparsely furnished for gatherings, whereas the Green Room was large, shabby but comfortable, with plenty of chairs, and they could invite other exiles and bemoan the old days. To use it in daytime, however, was unusual.

'Naturally, we forgo our wage for that hour,' the Count said; he was a very correct little man.

Something was obviously up. She noticed that Joseph was left behind as the nobility trooped off. 'What are they at?' she asked Ninon.

'Something to do with the Chevalier, but what I do not know.'

An hour later, to the minute, the émigrés were back at work—the Chevalier had gone very white. Makepeace saw Ninon talking to him and waited.

'What was it about?'

'It was a court martial,' Ninon said. 'The Chevalier is not to be of their company. He has been stripped of the Order of Saint Louis.'

'For Lord's sake, why?'

'He is disgraced. He has taken work as a menial. He is to be a servant.'

They watched the Chevalier as he took off his apron and packed his tool bag. Makepeace thought of the dignity assumed by and shown to butlers she had known in the big houses. 'God damn them,' she said.

'He has already, has he not?'

Another rock, unexpected but as firm as any, was the elderly actress, Bracey. She was playing the rich and man-mad Widow Lackitt, a leading role in *Oroonoko*'s comic sub-plot but possessing fewer lines than most, and in her spare time she put herself at Makepeace's disposal as overseer to the costume-makers and general adviser.

Makepeace found her sympathetic and less of a show-off than the rest. It was Bracey who found a solution when Makepeace bewailed the potentially horrific cost of plastering the patched ceiling of the auditorium and of finding a modern-day Michaelangelo to paint it with scenes from the classics, as was done in other theaters.

'Cover it with material,' Bracey said. 'Cheaper.'

'It'll look so plain.'

'Not if you stud it with all those cherubs we found under the stage.'

The effect, when done, was impressive—plain but smart. 'Modern,' Bracey said. ' 'Course you'll need a lot of chandeliers. You've got to light the place.'

'Why?'

'The audience has to find its seats. Can't do that in the dark.'

'Yes, but after they're seated . . .' The cost of candles, of which drama seemed to use an inordinate amount, was becoming an excessive burden on the budget. 'The stage is lit anyway and there's all those oil lights along its foot . . .'

'The floaters.'

'Them . . . So why'd you need a lit auditorium? The audience ought to be looking at the play, not each other.'

Bracey was sent to put the idea to Murrough—Makepeace decided to avoid what would be their third quarrel of the day—and came back surprised at his acquiescence. 'He says even Garrick didn't think of that.'

At the chandelier shop in Bishopsgate they found a massive candelabra, going cheap because its size had frightened off everybody else, and Joseph hung it securely over the center of the stalls on a chain. Just before the play began it was to be lowered and its candles put out until the interval.

Not only was it a saving but it was one less fire hazard in a world that seemed determined to burn itself down. Makepeace had drawn up rules about the use of naked flame but had to spend time and energy seeing them enforced. The cast were fairly cautious—most of the theaters in which they'd performed had been destroyed by fire at one time or another—but the émigrés, used to committing their care into the hands of others, might have been intent on auto-da-fé.

That evening, Murrough congratulated her. 'An innovation, madam,' he said and, to Jacques's relief, they were able to discuss it and theater business all the way home without so much as a hard look.

Jacques's inclusion in the production had been decided on the grounds that the risk of him blowing himself up with one of his experiments if he were left at home in Reach House was more immediate than the possibility of his father's identity being discovered by the émigrés. Makepeace was under no illusion, though, that, if it became known to aristocrats that she was harboring the son of one of their enemies, the prime minister's attention would be drawn to the fact within the hour. Jacques would be sent back to France.

As a precaution, she enspanned Marie Joséphine onto the theater team, putting her in charge of the costume-makers and asking her to keep her ears open for any mention concerning Jacques.

The sewing ladies rebelled. 'We do not work with peasants,' Madame de la Pole declared.

'Her name's Mme Mellot,' Makepeace told her. 'And you don't have to work with her—you can go.'

There was a hasty conference in which the three aristocrats had to decide between indignity and their tuppence an hour, not to mention the plentiful food Makepeace brought in for everybody at midday from the pie shop next door. Food and money won. Harsh exchanges of French could be frequently heard coming from the sewing room but under Marie Joséphine's eye the rate of work improved and Makepeace was comforted by the thought that any gossip about Jacques would be passed on to her.

Luchet, who might have performed that service, was a broken reed; either he was languishing at Ninon's feet or he was writing poetry.

'Leave him alone,' Murrough told her when she would have spurred the tutor into activity by kicking his backside. 'The man has a gift for words, he's writing us a prologue.'

'He's got a gift for doing damn all,' Makepeace said, but she was forced to suffer the sight of Luchet lolling in the stalls, his eyes on Ninon, occasionally jotting down some well-considered word on his slate.

The hatred nursed by the exiles towards those who had brought them down was, to a large extent, what kept them alive; they could not, would not, believe their golden world had gone for ever. At one point, when Polly Armitage was overheard mentioning an incident as having happened '. . . about the time of the French king's death,' the Comte d'Antrais stepped forward. 'Pardon me, m'sieur, but the king of France is not dead. He lives.'

The sacred flame of kingship had left the headless body of Louis XVI to lodge itself in the breast of his nine-year-old son suffering God knew what God knew where. And if *he* was dead, then it now rested in the Comte de Provence, the child's paternal uncle and self-declared Regent, still trying to rally the reluctant courts of Europe to the royal cause.

Makepeace had introduced Jacques to them as Jack Watt, her orphaned ward, the son of an English friend who'd married a Frenchwoman and had spent time in France. It was a story the émigrés accepted without interest. She thought they treated him more superciliously than they would an ordinary English boy but, since Jacques was too bound up in what he was doing to notice, she let it be. In any case, along with everybody else, they were soon showing him the amused indulgence given to enthusiastic children and mad inventors.

Once he'd been persuaded that drama didn't run on steam and that ropes and pulleys were quieter and more effective than engines when it came to operating the traps, the boy devoted himself to creating effects for the play that would startle audiences with their novelty.

Some proved impractical, like his idea for wafting the scent of a rainforest—the action of the play took place in Surinam—into the auditorium by warming a combination of grasses and spices on strategically-placed hot plates. The principle was good, the execution was not. As Murrough said, coughing and wiping his eyes, 'It's usual to try and keep the audience breathing until the finale, my son.'

But Jacques got the traps to work silently and at different speeds so that an actor could apparently spring out of the ground or gradually materialize, like a ghost in a graveyard.

He had even acquired the much-desired cannonballs for the play's thunderstorm. An appeal and a promise of free tickets to a captain of the Honorable Artillery Company in nearby Moorfields had produced two that were damaged and four that had come warped off the production line. He and Joseph had trundled them back on a trolley and constructed a wooden chute backstage down which to roll them.

Their first trial brought work to a standstill. The noise was tremendous. The usual method of depicting thunder—shaking an undulating piece of tin—was outranked in reverberation like a penny whistle by a full orchestra. Makepeace had to cover her ears. Murrough said, 'That's God in a temper, sure enough.'

Jacques shook his head. 'The sound is good but it does not come from the right place. It is an earthquake, not a storm. The chute must go up. We have to suspend it above the stage.'

The cast's eyes flickered to Murrough. The idea of six seventeen pound spheres of iron descending on their heads had occurred to all of them. Purist, however, had appealed to purist. 'Up it goes, then,' Murrough said.

Jacques's greatest success was with the lighting. He invented a switch that could be operated by wires leading from the lanterns hanging over and around the stage, changing the glass panels in their sides so that they emitted different colors. At a touch, a brightly lit comic scene could be darkened with purple shadows at the entrance of the villain, or give the effect of the sun rising or setting.

Murrough promised that 'See the Dawn rise over Surinam' would be included in the playbills.

The playbills were another of Makepeace's tribulations. After a row with Murrough, which led to another journey home in silence, she complained to Aaron. 'He wants four thousand printed. Four *thousand*.'

Aaron nodded. 'Five would be better.'

'You won't see London for paper.'

'That's the idea. You've nearly a thousand seats to fill every night for a week at least. Every wall in the City must have a poster stuck to it and the prettier members of the cast should be distributing handbills in the street next week.'

'Next week?'

'You open in ten days.'

'Oh dear Lord.' Work on the theater had become almost an end in itself. 'We'll never be ready.'

'I could help, Mama,' Jenny said. 'I could hand out bills at least.'

'No you couldn't.' Makepeace was definite. 'No daughter of mine is soliciting strangers in the street.'

It appeared she had another rebellion on her hands. Jenny was envious of the favor shown to Jacques and Marie Joséphine. 'Half the family is having an exciting time and I'm here twiddling my thumbs.'

'You're being useful, you're looking after your Uncle Aaron.'

'No, I'm not. Chadwell drives him to Chelsea Hospital every day but he won't take me.'

'She might inflame the pensioners,' Aaron said, as Makepeace turned on him. 'It's just a work of charity. Arranging a pageant for the anniversary of the taking of Quebec. I was asked to organize it by the governor himself.' He smiled. 'Actually, I'm rather enjoying it. As the only thespian, I have an army hanging on my every word. I'm thinking of invading London.'

He did look better; the gray was out of his face and he was leaner. *He's behaving well*, she thought. Perhaps gentle, parochial occupation such as organizing an amateur pageant could do him no harm. She'd feared that talk of happenings at The Duke's would be a bugle that set him pawing the ground to rejoin the battle but the tap of death's finger on his shoulder had given him pause for reflection. Never having spent time in the country, or wanting to, he was now enjoying it, sniffing the scent of bluebells wafting from the woods with a pleasure he had previously accorded to the smoke of a good cigar.

Ninon visited him on Sundays and the rare occasions when Murrough allowed her time off. She was not invited to stay the night, nor did she ask to, but Makepeace had become resigned to what was obviously an affair that had been going on for a long time. Considering his past record, she decided that Aaron could have done worse. Despite her grande dame exterior, the actress had proved to be a sensible, hard-working, somewhat jaded woman. She flirted with anyone who would flirt with her but it was an automatic response and not designed to go further, more a habit of which she was tiring. Her affection for Aaron appeared genuine, as was his for her, and brought contentment to them both.

In fact, Makepeace's prejudice against the entire acting profession was undergoing a change. True, nearly every member of the cast had looser morals than she would have liked; Mrs Jordan, it turned out, was the mistress of Lord Radcliffe; little Mrs Gardham had an illegitimate child back in Dublin; Polly Armitage was having an affair with a married man. And only yesterday Dizzy Distazio had overnight gambled himself into a debtor's prison.

Yet there wasn't one among them, poor as they were, who would have traded their profession for the idleness of a kept woman or man that their beauty and sexuality might have gained them. They were devoted to the stage and, despite frequent squabbles, to each other. When news arrived of Dizzy's plight, Jordan had pulled a gold bracelet—a present from her lover—off her arm without comment and given it to Polly Armitage to pawn so that their colleague could be released.

Their language was salty, like their stories, but they curbed both when Jacques was in hearing distance.

Jenny, thought Makepeace, would not be harmed by being in such people's company—as long as it was only in daytime. After all, there were houses belonging to the highest peers of the realm in which vastly darker deeds were perpetrated than the sins committed by her poor band of players.

'You'll be needing a prompter,' Aaron said, artfully. 'I usually choose an intelligent young woman for the job. Her respectability's ensured by the fact that she can't be seen.'

'Can I, Ma? Can I?'

'I'll see.'

So Jenny, too, joined the workers at The Duke's.

The one impression of the dramatic art from which Makepeace could not be moved was that it was silly. Murrough squirming in Oroonoko's death throes, Ninon slapping her thigh and being taken for a young man when everyone else could see she was a mature woman, declamations of heroism or evil by men who then came off stage and read the paper . . . she wondered how they could do it without feeling foolish.

These were, of course, glimpses, caught as she hurried from one job to another; she hadn't yet seen the play in its entirety and worried that it didn't promise well.

'Aren't you . . . don't you feel embarrassed when you've done that?' she asked Bracey after Widow Lackitt had screamed her way through one particularly outrageous speech.

'Too loud was it?' Bracey was immediately anxious. 'Sir Mick wants her played broad.'

They were speaking in different tongues. Makepeace left it.

As they entered the last week, more things went wrong than went right.

A glaring misprint in the playbills—insisting that the performance was to be held at The Puke's Theatre—meant they had to be done again.

Mrs Jordan, who had a chill, lost her voice and Murrough his patience: 'Then bloody find it, and quick.'

Costumes were unfinished, so was the scenery. The émigrés, seizing their chance, sent the Comte d'Antrais to Makepeace demanding higher wages.

But it was the moment when the bailiffs came again for Dizzy and Makepeace, having paid them off, boxed the actor's ears for him, that the theater, figuratively and almost literally, came falling down around her own.

She was standing on the side of the stage at the time and developing her theme of 'You gamble again, you little bastard, and I'll chop your liver for pig swill,' in a voice that reached to the back of the stalls when she noticed three men coming down the aisle.

At that moment a succession of crashes shook the building. There were screams.

Simultaneously, Makepeace recognized two of the visitors—and knew with deadly instinct the purpose of the third—even as she took in the fact that Jacques's chute up in the flies had collapsed, allowing six cannonballs to plunge through the other side of the stage.

For a moment she stood between two worlds.

Each had its tableau. The one on the stage held Mrs Jordan with her mouth open to scream—the shot had just missed her; Ninon, who'd been trying on her costume, appeared wearing breeches and very little else; Jenny, assisting her, held her discarded bodice; Murrough was breaking the third commandment in a voice that blew candle flame sideways; Widow Lackitt had frozen in the act of waggling her backside at her supposed suitor, Polly.

The tableau held three men in the aisle justified in what they had come to do. Reverend Deedes's face displayed joyous horror. The stranger was nodding, yes, indeed. Stephen Heilbron, kind and wise, sorrowful.

She stood on the equator of two antipathetic hemispheres and knew to which she belonged.

Her rogues and vagabonds, ever ones to exaggerate a sensation, swooned and exclaimed around the hole in the stage without noticing their manager being handed a paper from the Lord Chamberlain's office that closed the theater down.

Chapter Ten

THE new maid at Number Fifteen in the Street of the Gravediggers scattered the remains of the grain in the back garden's
poultry run and watched its two hens run flapping towards it for
their last meal. Doomed, poor things. No more grain. The scraps
they once fed on were now the household's meals. The ax awaited.

Philippa was sorry; the hens made pleasant noises, little balloons
of sound popping in their throats. Two more living things silenced.
But, as she told them, shutting them in, 'Innocence is no excuse
nowadays.'

She returned to the scullery, crossed the kitchen floor she'd just
washed to reach the hall and went out of the front door into the
courtyard. A lovely morning, the emerging leaves of the vine on the
wall were translucent green in the dawn.

The silence was eerie. Difficult to believe it wasn't Sunday, which
it wasn't. Even on Sundays, the bells of the churches would have
been exercising their tyranny over the faithful; come to church,
come to church. Now they were only rung in the case of alarm.

No dogs barking. The order had gone out to have canines destroyed; they ate too much. No cocks crowing; a voluntary extermi-
nation, that—in case they alerted poultry thieves to their presence.
No cooing pigeons; even sparrows had to watch their step or they
ended in somebody's pot.

In the empty, aimless air, the buzz of a bee dodging among the
blossoms in the courtyard's plum tree sounded very loud. Ah, the

stationer opposite had opened his bedroom window and was coughing out of it. Paris would begin work soon.

She picked up the boots Citizen Marcoz had left outside the door of his lodge and took them back to clean with the rest. She liked cleaning boots; one had something to show for the effort.

In a moment she would prepare the breakfast trays for the household, crisping last night's leftover crusts in the oven to approximate toast, putting out pots of Mme Vernet's *confit des pruniers*, making the coffee from yesterday's grounds. She liked that, too. Orderly activity, a comfort in a world threatening to reel off its axis.

They'd executed Tom Glossop yesterday. *Don't think of it, don't think.* She'd been walking towards the underwear shop in the Rue Saint Honoré when the tumbrels came by. Two of them, both crowded. Hadn't wanted to look. Had looked. Seen the face she'd last encountered in her mother's kitchen at Reach House, Uncle John Beasley's friend, the little man fleeing arrest for distributing Paine's *The Rights of Man*.

He'd been so *frightened . . . don't think of it . . .* so bewildered. Only the aristocrats in the carts had known why they were there and stood up straight. The rest, shopkeepers who'd sold above the maximum perhaps, women who'd hoarded a few bars of soap, an old man who hadn't killed his dog, a disliked neighbor informed on by other neighbors . . . all these had huddled together in disbelief that they were to die for it.

And Mr Glossop, wondering to the last what his wife would say as they sliced off his head for advocating what they were supposed to advocate.

She'd wanted to call to him, supply one last friendly face in that avenue of stones. But he wouldn't have seen her, he was blind with terror. And she'd been too frightened; she had Condorcet's life to consider as well as her own. Face it, she'd been too frightened on her own account.

In Sophie's studio, she'd sat with her head in her hands. 'I wanted to apologize to him, *somebody* should apologize to him.'

'And to Tom Paine,' Sophie had said. 'He'll go by and I shall hide for shame. Nicolas thought him the greatest Englishman he'd ever met.'

'Paine? They haven't arrested Tom Paine? Why? He's a member of the Convention. *Why?*'

And Sophie had said, 'Why anybody?'

On the way home—already Number Fifteen had become home—she'd gone by the Conciergerie and looked at the list of the next day's guillotine victims on its great spiked gates to see if Tom Paine's name was on it.

> 'When, in countries that are called civilized, we see age going to the workhouse and youth to the gallows, something must be wrong in the system of government.
>
> My country is the world, and my religion is to do good.'

So far, the name of the man who'd written those things and had come to France to help transform it into that world, wasn't on the list. She didn't know if she had the courage to look for it again tomorrow. *Oh, God, how could they kill* him?

Don't think about it. Don't think.

She brushed Citizen Marcoz's boots until her elbow ached, polished them off with a soft cloth and took them back to the lodge door. In a moment—and she still had trouble believing this—Marcoz would set off for the National Convention of which he was a member, the same Convention that had condemned to death and proclaimed outlaw the man who was hiding across the courtyard from his own lodging.

'Do you think he knows you're concealing Nicolas?' she'd asked Mme Vernet. It seemed incredible that he did not, although he never entered the house itself.

And Mme Vernet said calmly, 'If so, he has not betrayed the fact.'

He was a dour-looking man, with black up-curled eyebrows, living alone, always frowning—unsurprisingly, Philippa thought, considering the things he was asked to approve in the Convention.

Perhaps, by not betraying Condorcet, he was salving some part of his conscience. He'd asked no questions about her sudden arrival and employment at Number Fifteen, didn't talk to her at all, merely grunted on the one occasion when he'd opened his door as she was putting his boots down.

He was rigidly courteous to Mme Vernet if they met in the courtyard but, Philippa thought, the devil himself would have been polite to Mme Vernet.

She went back to the house and prepared three breakfast trays, balanced them one on top of the other and carried them carefully upstairs. On the first landing she put the trays on the hall table, lifted one to put it outside Mme Vernet's room, knocked to let her know it was there, and took another to the next door behind which slept M Sarrett, Mme Vernet's distant cousin.

There was a connecting door between the two rooms which, according to Sophie, allowed the two to be less than distant, a liaison Philippa at first found somewhat shocking and then didn't. Both were widowed, at any moment they could go to the guillotine for helping Condorcet. The Terror was no time for middle-class morality.

If they *were* having an affair, it was decorously conducted. Everything Mme Vernet did was decorous. That first day she had invited Philippa into her parlor, sat her down in one of its uncomfortable chairs and listened, her hands neatly folded in her lap.

It was an ugly little parlour, typical of the French bourgeois; heavily furnished and dark, though very clean, smelling of beeswax and lavender sachets. But it was surprising. Other such rooms Philippa had known in the past had displayed a large and gruesome crucifix, this one had a statue—work of the late M Vernet, an artist who'd belonged to the affrighted nymph school of sculpture. Adding to the overcrowding, she stood in a corner, her marble hands upraised as if in horror at the hideous chiffonier next to her.

Sophie had called Mme Vernet an angel but it took time to recognize her seraphic qualities. She was angular, late fortyish, dressed in black, her thin hair pulled severely back under an equally harsh cap.

The most celestial thing about her was her calm. If it had not been for the loud tick of the ormolu clock on the mantelshelf, Philippa could have thought that time stood still, her own voice merely going around and around in the face of Mme Vernet's stillness.

Her explanations and intentions finished, the tick of the clock took over while Mme Vernet considered them. When she spoke at last, her mouth made prim little pecking motions, like that of her own hens.

'Eight months ago when my doctor, Dr Cabanis, asked me take in the gentleman now residing upstairs, I asked only one question: "Is he virtuous?" Dr Cabanis assured me he was. "Then let him come," I said. I have had no reason to regret that decision. The gentleman is not only virtuous, he is a man of genius engaged on a great work.'

'Yes,' Philippa said, slightly mystified at this departure from the matter in hand. 'But now we can get him to safety. May I see him?'

Later, she realized Mme Vernet was warning her.

As if she'd been making a social visit, she was left waiting while Mme Vernet went upstairs to establish that Condorcet would receive her. His permission having been given, the maid who had let her in was called to escort her to his room on the third floor.

Half an hour later Philippa had returned to the parlor, angry. 'He won't go.'

'No,' Mme Vernet said. 'Not yet.'

'There is no *yet*, madame.' Philippa's fury pitched her voice above the damn clock. 'He's in danger, you're in danger, and he wants to finish a *book*.'

'It is a great book,' Mme Vernet said quietly. 'I have been privileged to read its chapters as he completes them. *The Progress of the Human Mind*. It is a work of optimism. Mademoiselle, can you not admire the spirit that can envisage such a book at this time?'

'No,' Philippa said. 'Frankly, I can't. He can finish it in England without endangering everyone around him. Point it out to him, madame. He'd listen to you.'

'He has. He has wished to leave many times for fear of

endangering myself and M Sarrett. "Where will you go?" I ask him. "The Convention, sir, has the right to place you outside the law; it has not the right to place you outside humanity. Stay and finish your book." That is what I tell him. I set no limit to his stay. Will you take some tea?'

Even sentences, no more weight attached to one than the rest.

So she drank tea, not knowing then that it was the last of Mme Vernet's precious store, gulping cup after unnoticed cup as her resentment built—after all this trouble, all this way, progress of the human mind, progress of human cowardice more like, battening on this poor woman, stupid, stupid, obstinate man.

Mme Vernet questioned her gently. How was Mme Sophie? And the little girl? Would she return to England now? Had she somewhere to stay the night? Useful domestic questions made Philippa realize she was cross and hurt on her own account. Nobody had asked her to come. She had as good as erupted into this place yelling, 'Fly, fly,' nudging the wire on which Mme Vernet maintained her balancing act, carrying her household with her.

The prosaic little woman opposite her, she saw, was as magnificent as the man upstairs who wrote of hope while bloody death rampaged around him. Of course he must finish the book. Why should he drop a work of hope—and, God, if the world ever needed hope it was now—to accompany Philippa on a journey that he knew, and she knew, could be the death of them both?

She knew something else; she couldn't go home without him. *Yes, I was in France. I went to rescue somebody but he was too busy, so I came home.*

Another humiliating failure to add to a long list.

Somehow, during the course of that afternoon, it was arranged. She was to stay at Number Fifteen to await the completion of Condorcet's manuscript. She was to be its new maid—partly to explain her presence in the house and partly because Mme Vernet wanted to send the old one to safety and could not manage on her own.

The maid's name was Manon and she'd been in Mme Vernet's

employment for twenty-seven years and this, the occasion of her dismissal, was probably the first time they had ever quarrelled.

Manon's denunciation of her sacking was loud; everybody heard it and the little punctuations of quiet, which were Mme Vernet's loving but obdurate insistence.

'I will not go. Why should I go? . . . You think I am afraid? . . . We will go to the guillotine together . . . But that chit (*gosse*) cannot care for you properly. Can she starch your caps? Make M Sarrett's tisanes? . . . I am not going, you cannot make me.'

Mme Vernet could and did. The two of them embraced in the courtyard, Manon still weeping and pleading, while M Sarrett carried her luggage to the cart that was to take her to the Rouen diligence and the Normandy village of her birth.

Until then, Philippa had not been sure that Mme Vernet was fully aware of how great a danger she ran in hiding Condorcet. But the woman stood at the gate until the cart was out of sight; when she turned her face was that of one who had bidden an old friend good-bye for ever.

So the name of Manon Bercot disappeared from the prescribed list of residents at Number Fifteen, Gravediggers, and that of Jeanne Renard took its place.

The new maid and her mistress went together to register the change.

Philippa was frightened from the moment they left the house. The walk down the hill to the church of Saint Sulpice, now the administration headquarters of the Luxembourg Revolutionary Section, was like walking into jungle with nothing to protect her from its beasts. She could hear them baying.

In a sense, the noise in the church provided cover. It bounced off marble and stone to bewilder the ears; everybody was too busy and too harried to be on the watch for counterrevolutionaries. At the entrance, women were sorting a small mountain of donated shoes and boots awaiting shipment to the battalions fighting in the Vendée. A 'Down with Tyranny' flag was draped over a confessional box, swathes of tricolor ribbons hid such icons as hadn't been already chipped away. An out-of-date poster that hadn't kept up with the thinking of Robespierre declared, 'Liberty is the only form of Worship.' Others, more usefully, gave the names of the months and days in the new revolutionary decadal calendar for those still confused by it—practically everybody.

In a side chapel a choir of children was rehearsing the 'Hymn to the Republic,' while a small boy on a chair delivered the *Declaration of the Rights of Man* to the lines of people waiting at one side of the trestle tables for papers, permits, food and fuel stamps, *certificats de civisme*, destitution relief. Clerks, questioning and scribbling, sat at the other.

It seemed to Philippa, trying not to shake with nerves, that people would notice Mme Vernet, so neat, so cool, an eye of calm in this hurricane of hubbub and anxiety; composure like hers *must* be unpatriotic.

But Republic or monarchy, the Mme Vernets of France were eternal factors; anyway, most of the Luxembourg—an area she'd lived in since she was married—seemed to know her. The clerk who dealt with them called her 'Madame,' without being dragged off to prison, or anyone even noticing.

They returned home without incident, Philippa on legs left weak with tension.

The work at Number Fifteen was hard, made harder by shortages and Mme Vernet's refusal to deal with the black market. At first Mme Vernet did most of the shopping and cooking—miraculously stretching rations to include her unregistered guest—Philippa most of the cleaning and laundry. At nights she dragged herself up to her attic room almost too tired to undress. Yet living by Mme Vernet's immutable routine was her safeguard against fear; inside these walls, she could almost believe that God's purpose still ran and that, sooner or later, the jungle outside would achieve the harmony existing within. It was only in her dreams that reality broke through the defenses in a flood of blood, mingling terror and a horrible desolation; I don't want to die among strangers. *I want to go home. I want Ma.*

Curiously, if escaping the havoc of loving Andrew Ffoulkes had been one of her reasons for coming to France, she had achieved it. The love was there and always would be, but it had retired to the horizon, a crazy sweetness of adolescence to be remembered with nostalgia.

That much had been achieved, then.

But the best reason was Condorcet. She set his breakfast tray on the floor while she knocked on the door of the third floor room—and waited. After a while a voice said: 'Seven to the power of n . . . Come in.'

She smiled. So he was between chapters and relaxing his mind with mathematical problems the way other people took a walk, or a bath. It had been a foible of his, to speak his last thought before everyday life intruded on him, like putting a bookmark between pages. Still was.

The room was thick with the smell of tobacco smoke, books and bad feet. Philippa crossed it, put the tray in the fireplace—every other surface was covered with papers and his manuscript—planted a kiss on the head of the man sitting at a writing table and raised the window to allow air in.

He'd aged dreadfully. He'd hardly left this room in eight months and lack of exercise had made him flabby. His right leg had become ulcerated but he refused to allow Mme Vernet to send for Cabanis to treat it, saying it was too dangerous for the doctor to come, and anyway the discomfort was nothing.

'I'll be seeing Sophie today,' Philippa said and saw his eyes shut in happiness, though automatically he said, 'No.'

He feared for her; she brought him newspapers and he was therefore more aware of the jungle's dangers than she was—she didn't have time to read them. But if Philippa had a purpose here now, it was to provide the link between two great souls who loved each other and whom she loved.

His letters to Sophie made no mention of his discomfort; they spoke of plans for their future, drawings to make Eliza laugh, a small miracle of a book he'd written on a simple method to teach her mathematics.

Sophie's letters to him ignored her poverty and gave descriptions of her sitters, gossip, tales of their child and love, always love.

Oh, God. Philippa remembered that today she must deliver to him the letter on which Sophie was spending blotched, agonizing days of composition, telling him she must divorce him.

'I'm safe enough,' Philippa said to him now. 'Mme Vernet is even letting me do some shopping—it will look strange if she's constantly queuing while she has a maid to do it.'

'To queue' was the new verb. Somebody had likened the waiting lines of people outside the shops to a tail of hair and the word had caught on. You queued for everything, sometimes for hours, waiting for the rationed meat or bread to come in. Rumour went around: 'Fouquet's has a consignment of stockings,' and you queued for those. Sometimes you joined a queue not knowing what it was for but hoping it was useful.

For Philippa, the queueing itself was an education and not an un-happy one. For one thing, the weather was sunny though, as an old countrywoman she met in the bread line had pointed out, the per-sistent drought was worrying—it meant that the queues next winter would be longer and for less.

For another, it brought her in touch with the ordinary Parisians, mostly women, but sometimes men as well, and the latest cautious gossip—you never knew if a Committee of Public Safety spy was lis-tening in.

What it was like in the East End where extreme poverty and the Rue Saint Antoine enragés kept up the demand for more and more heads to roll, as if blood could feed the starving, she didn't know. But in the queues around the bourgeois sections of the Luxembourg and Quatre Nations dominated by the Cordelier Club of men like

Danton and de Vaubon, she detected a deep and growing sickness at the slaughter perpetrated in the Republic's name.

Fewer and fewer turned up in the Place de la Révolution to watch the executions, and those who did were people you wouldn't want to take home to mother.

Standing at the window, looking out at the back garden and the doomed hens, she said suddenly: 'Why can't it *stop*? Nobody wants it any more. They were muttering against Robespierre in the queue yesterday. What happened to our Revolution? I don't understand.'

'Neither do I.' He took off his spectacles and pinched the bridge of his nose. 'Perhaps the expectation was too high; people wanted more bread and more power than it was possible to give them immediately. They became a mob. An individual is of value above rubies, a mob is reasonless.' He shook his head. 'I am sorry for Robespierre; he didn't want this, either, he's on the back of a tiger and trying to direct it by pulling its ears.'

He isn't sorry for you, Philippa thought, *he wants to feed you to the tiger.* But she had already broken the rules; in this room the present was merely an inconvenience, one that might kill him but still just a passing wobble in humanity's steady march towards betterment.

Somewhere under that mound of papers lay the *certificat de civisme* and travel documents she'd given him, less important than the essay that covered them that charted mankind's progress from its earliest days, that prophesied, that *promised*, a world where men and women would have no master except their own reason.

'It will show that nature has set no bounds to the perfecting of human faculties, Philippa,' he'd said of it. 'Independently of any power that would like to stop it, as the Terror is trying to do, so long as our globe exists the tempo will differ but we shall never go back.'

Oh, she loved him. 'Don't let your coffee go cold,' she said and went to the door.

But today, because he was between chapters, he wanted her company. 'I've become a garrulous old man,' he said, 'whereas

you've told me very little of yourself. You lay this burden of gratitude on me yet I know nothing except that it cannot be repaid. Tell
me whys and wherefores. Speak English—I grow rusty. Have you
kept up with your mathematics?'

She smiled and sat down. 'No.' It was typical of him that this
should be the first question he asked. 'I've been too confused and
in love.'

She could tell things to this clear and alien mind that she kept
concealed from those they most closely concerned. She told him
about Ffoulkes and his marriage, about Stephen Heilbron, about the
Condorcet society and what Fitch-Botley had done to her, and threw
in some makeweight about her mother—though they'd never met
he'd always loved Makepeace stories.

Once she'd enumerated the portmanteau of problems that had
driven her to France in order that he would not feel so indebted, she
went back to the beginning, to the Ffoulkes's ball and her request for
papers from The League and Sir Boy Blanchard's reluctance to help
her. From this distance, the man's subsequent actions against her appeared ludicrous.

'He had me followed,' she said, amiably. 'Now there is someone
who'll go to all lengths to avoid England's pollution by your damn
republicanism.'

'Yes.' He was looking out of the window. 'He's a traitor, you
know.' He said it as if it were of passing interest.

'He's a what?'

'Hmm?' He turned from the window. 'Yes, Brissot used him.
Called him a flesh-monger, I remember. A shameful business but
there were some of the old regime, some aristos we couldn't allow
to escape; they were taking too much of the country's gold with
them. Blanchard would offer them transit and then hand them over
to the State.' Condorcet smiled apologetically. 'In return for a por-
tion of the gold, I'm afraid.'

'Blanchard? Sir *Boy* Blanchard?'

He nodded. 'Oh, yes.'

She stared at him; poor old man, his mind was wandering. But he'd been in the center of revolutionary government for three of its years; he'd *know*. 'Andrew wouldn't have allowed it. '

'Lord Ffoulkes? No, no, I doubt he was aware of it. His men seem to have run a most successful escape route. Certainly, we never caught them at it.' He smiled. 'Perhaps we didn't try too hard; the greater the number of our aristocrats other countries had to support the better we liked it.'

'But Blanchard . . . he sold some of them to you?'

'Yes, yes.' The perfidy of men didn't interest him, perhaps because he'd never understood it. Anyway, some factor to the power of n, or a new idea for the book, was now occupying him. He began fidgeting with his papers.

She sat on a while longer, then groped for the door and went out. On the landing she gripped the balustrade, listening to voices and seeing visions of a beautiful mouth hiding bad teeth.

'He's a schemer. He's jealous of everything Andrew has, without the goodness and money to have it.'

Ma knew, bless her.

'Imagine a Machiavelli that plays cricket and you've got Boy Blanchard.'

For a moment she was assailed by pity for both betrayed and betrayer; how terrible to be the trusting Andrew Ffoulkes; how much worse *not* to be Andrew. What a burden on the soul; in England to twirl in the light of adulation from those you helped to escape knowing that in France you peddled human beings to a contemptuous enemy. A flesh-monger.

She could almost smile, remembering their encounter; an insignificant woman asking his help to bring to England one of the few people who could reveal what he had done and declare to his adoring, betrayed aristocrats, 'This man is stained.' The energy he'd used in trying to stop her had been panic.

She stopped smiling. If he knew she'd succeeded, how much more would he do to stop her getting back? Her description would be sent to the Committee of Public Safety within the day.

He doesn't know. Nobody's even aware I'm in France.

Yes, they do. The smugglers know.

But he can't know exactly where I am, nobody knows where Nicolas is hiding.

Sophie knows and you told Andrew you'd received a letter from her.

Yes, but why should Andrew tell Blanchard?

He trusts him; why should he not?

'Jeanne?'

'I'm coming, Madame.'

She went downstairs, frantically trying to remember whether she'd given Andrew Sophie's address.

Chapter Eleven

THE council of war in the Green Room had only one defeatist in its ranks.

'I tell you they're going to close The Duke's down,' Makepeace repeated.

'Not at all, not at all,' Murrough told her. 'They're only going to refuse us a license to perform plays.'

'It's the same thing, aint it?' Her eyes were closed with weariness. She felt as if she'd rolled down an extremely steep hillside and was being asked to climb up it again; she wasn't sure she had the energy. The Lord Chamberlain, more especially Stephen Heilbron and his understanding pity, had taken the stuffing out of her.

Salvos of not-at-alls and certainly-nots were coming at her from all sides. They amazed her; they weren't at all cast down.

'We could turn *Oroonoko* into a burletta. We could . . .'

There were apparently several ways to get round Lord Chamberlain rulings. If there were not, virtually the only theaters in the country would be Covent Garden and Drury Lane, those two holders of the royal patent, whereas nearly every big town now had its playhouse, or at least some hall where drama could be performed by one of England's bands of strolling players.

You could use what was known as the 'snuff ploy;' get in some cases of snuff, charge the audience to sample it and perform the play free while it was doing so. 'Colley Cibber did that, do you remember? Turned Lincolns Inn Fields into a snuff factory?'

There was the similar 'chocolate ploy,' providing a cup of chocolate per person. 'And that's better,' Polly Armitage said. 'That way the buggers don't sneeze during the performance.'

Or, since the Lord Chamberlain couldn't forbid a concert, you could charge for a musical entertainment—'hire a fiddler or two, dance the odd hornpipe'—and invite the audience to watch you 'rehearsing' a play gratis during the interval. 'Goodmans Fields got away with that for three years.'

Or, on much the same principle, you could turn the play itself into a musical entertainment, punctuating it with song and dance and calling it a 'burletta.' In his early days, they assured Makepeace, the great Garrick himself had appeared in a *Macbeth* that included fifteen songs and a hornpipe.

She looked around at them. Dizzy's fine, long face flickered with persuasion, Ninon's lifted as if encountering an old enemy, little Chrissy Gardham kneaded her hand, trying to enthuse her through her skin.

Irreverent to church and authority. Vagabonds, all of them—literally. None of the statutes passed against them by Henry the Eighth, by Elizabeth, by the Puritans, by Walpole, had been rescinded. The laws that had clipped the ears of their predecessors, put them in the pillory, in prison, could still do the same to them; government hated mockery as much as it hated the transmission of ideas.

She contrasted their faces to the miser's purse that was the Revered Deedes's.

How sorry, he'd said, he was to see her, his neighbor, a widow and consequently in need of Christian protection, consorting with these, the lowest dregs of humanity, this nursery of impious immorality, contamination and damnation . . .

He's rehearsed this, she'd thought. *He trod the boards of his bedroom, practicing his alliteration and striking attitudes at his looking glass. He's as much a performer as those up on the stage.*

'. . . ribaldry and obscenity. I could not shirk my duty to one of my own flock. The Lord Chamberlain was informed out of the need to save you from yourself.'

'And I'm out to save slaves, you pious little pizzxle,' she'd shouted, not above some alliteration herself in her temper, 'so get out of my theater.' And she'd shredded the Lord Chamberlain's injunction and thrown the pieces after him.

Stephen Heilbron, however, had remained, kind and careworn as ever. 'I know Deedes can be insufferable,' he said, 'but he came to me when he heard I was back from Liverpool and, *dear* missus, as there is no man to direct your family, I—who will soon belong to it—hold myself responsible for you.'

'Well, you ain't,' she told him sharply. 'Of all people, you ought to see what I'm doing here.'

'I understand what you are trying to do and that I must seem pharisaical in your eyes. But, missus, the means are foul, don't you see? No matter what the end? Attitudes to slavery must be changed by bringing people nearer to Jesus Christ and only by that. A playhouse merely brings the Christian religion into contempt.'

'Why does it?' She didn't understand him; Christianity was strong enough to look after itself. '*How* can it?'

Gently, he took her by the shoulders and turned her round so that they both faced the stage and the splintered hole that Jacques's cannonballs had made in it. 'Were you not trying to imitate the Almighty's wonderful act of thunder? Oh yes, I know the tricks—dropping peas on a drum to make the sound of rain. Can you not see you are making mockery of him and his most blessed gifts?'

At which point Makepeace decided the man was mad. She'd left him and followed the cast's flight to the Green Room.

Chrissie Gardham said, 'Missus, the Marquis thinks it wouldn't take much to turn *Oroonoko* into a burletta, it's got songs already.' They were all looking at her. The Marquis of Barigoule was with them, now part of the team, nodding in confirmation.

Murrough was watching her. He always watched her.

They filled the shabby room liked a crowded flower arrangement, elegant even when they were troubled; the men placed like dark fronds between the overblown roses of the women balancing on the stalks of their pretty, white-stockinged feet.

Such good companions, she thought. Yet they made her feel lonelier, even jealous; she might long to be one of them but the footlights divided them; she could never enjoy the easy understanding they shared. Part of her belonged in the auditorium. They knew it, kind as they were to her, and she knew it.

'Missus? It isn't just that we've worked so hard, I promise it is not. It would be so *nice* if we could do the teeniest bit to help stop slavery.' Chrissie Gardham looked round. 'Wouldn't it?'

There was a round of clapping.

Chrissie the sinner, Makepeace thought. *They were all sinners. Small wonder Christ had preferred their company to that of Pharisees.*

'You can turn it into a pantomime for all I care,' she said. 'We open next week if it kills us.'

M URROUGH didn't go home with them that night, saying he had to see to the new arrangement; he'd beg a bed from somewhere.

Makepeace thought, *And who'll be in it with you?* She'd noticed Jordan's hopeful eyes; the woman was always waggling her hips at him.

So it was quiet in the coach back to Chelsea; Marie Joséphine asleep, Jacques figuring weights and stresses for a new cannonball run on his slate, Jenny unusually silent—until they were at Reach House and getting ready for bed.

'May I talk to you, Ma?'

'Come in. See to this damn bodice, will you?'

Jenny unhooked her. 'Ma, I don't think I should come to the theater any more.'

Makepeace turned round. 'What?'

'Stephen doesn't want me to. I was talking to him . . . when you were in the Green Room.' She smiled. 'He won't give up, you know, he says your soul is worth fighting for.'

'*Does* he? And who is Stephen to tell you what to do?'

'He's . . . he's goodness. He points the way. When he was speaking everything else seemed . . . I don't know . . . grubby.'

'Did it, indeed.'

'Oh, Ma, don't be cross. But he was so shocked that I should be there; he said he was worried for my reputation and he truly was, Ma. Concerned for me, I mean. He asked why I wasn't amusing myself with things like botany or astronomy instead.' Jenny's speedwell eyes concentrated. 'From which I could never obtain what was false or base.'

'Botany and astronomy.'

'Yes, Ma. Or helping the Society in its clerical work. That way I could come up in the coach with you to London every day.'

'Lot of botany in London, is there?'

'Ma, *please*. He's afraid that by being too close to the flame I may be scorched.'

'And the rest of us are burning in hell, I suppose.'

'Of course not. But he said I had my future to consider and that good men might judge me by the company I had kept. I know I agitated to come but I didn't realize . . . Stephen says no female can become an actress and remain an honest woman. And though Ninon and Mrs Jordan and Chrissie are charming . . . well, you know what they are.'

'Human beings,' Makepeace said. '*Human* human beings. Don't judge them, pet—it doesn't give you any leeway for what crops up in your own life. I've learned that much.'

She sat down on the bed. *What a preacher Stephen is*, she thought. *With one conversation he has taken Jenny away from me. Have I risked her morals? Have I been a bad parent? Her father would have known what to do.*

'I don't judge them,' Jenny promised. '"Judge not, that ye be not judged." But I see my own way now.'

She looked like Andra at that moment, fair-skinned where he'd been dark, but the same purposefulness giving her face character where before it had been just youthfully pretty. Yet Andra's road had been wide and taken in all human endeavour. Jenny was choosing a way that narrowed.

Makepeace put out her hand. 'Do you want to go home, pet?'

'No, Ma.' Jenny sat down beside her and hugged her. 'I want to stay with you, I just won't come to the theater anymore.' Like a modern day Mary, she began figuratively pouring spikenard onto the head of the absent Heilbron; how brave he was, how good, a modern saint. With all of which Makepeace was prepared to agree to a point though, like Martha, she thought the adulation overexpensive. Was it adulation, or adoration? Had Jenny fallen in love?

'. . . and I think it naughty of Philippa not to be here to greet him back. He was so disappointed. He'd told her when he'd be arriving. He wanted to know where she had gone. If only she would get over her calf love for Andrew and see that Stephen stands head and shoulders over other men . . . What is it, Mama?'

Makepeace was scrabbling at her writing case. 'We can post it tonight. Sanders can catch the mail at Slough and put it in the bag.'

'Who are you writing to?'

'Babbs Cove. Jan Gurney'll know.'

'Know what?'

Makepeace looked up, distracted. 'Whether she's gone to France.'

'Pippy? Ma, I told you. She's at Raby. Yes, yes, we haven't heard from them but you know what Sally and Aunt Ginny are like for letter writing.'

'I know what Philippa's like. She'd have written. It's been weeks . . . Damn the girl, I should have known, I should have known. I've done nothing. Oh, Pippy.'

'Ma.'

Makepeace threw off Jenny's restraining hand, scattering them both with ink. 'She's gone to France; she's gone to rescue the Condorcets.'

'Of course she hasn't, Ma. How can you think that?'

'Because it's what I would have done.'

* * *

EVERYONE thought her hysterical—except Marie Joséphine, who became hysterical herself. Hildy, Jenny and Aaron considered her conviction to be outlandish. Philippa? Too level-headed. It was merely bad manners on the girl's part not to have come back to greet her fiancé's arrival—obviously, she was still in two minds about the marriage.

Makepeace was persuaded that she had been overworking; she must rest, at least for today. 'I'll go in your place,' Aaron said. 'I've been meaning to look things over. Tomorrow you can take up the reins again. Makepeace, I am *well*, I shall not overreach myself. Jenny can bring me up-to-date; yes, you can, Jen, just for today. Makepeace, stay.'

So, because she had no proof and because she was in such a taking, she stayed, like a dog, watching them go off without her and, like a dog, not knowing what to do with herself.

Eventually, needing to breathe, she clapped a straw hat on her head and went for a walk by the river.

The countryside conspired to calm her down; the last of the bluebells rendered scent that mixed with the cow parsley coming into flower. The water meadows were striped with yellow-rattle and Saint-John's-wort.

It was all gray to her and she tired herself out by metaphorically pushing a distant mail coach into going faster.

Their lives are controlled, she thought, *even Aaron's. They think things proceed at the same pace but they don't. They haven't felt the winds that scatter normality in a second.*

No they don't know Philippa. I should have seen the warnings. She didn't send the forged passport; she took it. Why didn't she tell me?

She became angry. This was déjà vu. The blasted girl had done this before when the ship bringing her back from America had been sunk; Philippa was rescued but in the confusion had been lost on the docklands of Plymouth. And there she'd stayed, deliberately, waiting for Makepeace to find her. Aged eleven and using her adversity to see whether her mother loved her enough to come after her.

I passed that test. Is this another?

''Mornin' Mrs Hedley. 'Nother fine day.'

''Morning, David. Yes, it is.'

While she waited for the herdsman's cows to go past, she forgave her daughter. This time Philippa had gone where she knew her mother couldn't follow. Makepeace didn't speak French.

God, if they catch her.

Reach House was deserted when she got home and she remembered, resentfully, that she'd given everybody the afternoon off to go to a flower show at the hospital. It was so quiet she could hear Chadwell hammering something in the stables and the flutter of house martins' wings as they repaired last year's nests under the eaves for occupation.

She went into the parlor, taking off her hat, and somewhat self-consciously fell to her knees. 'Watch over her, dear Lord. Keep her from all harm. If I have offended thee in the matter of the playhouse, thou knowest it was done with the best intentions so don't visit it on my daughter's brave head. May she achieve her purpose and be on her way home. This instant, Lord, it if please thee. Your loving servant, Makepeace Hedley. Amen.'

The prayer was so strong that she got up and went to the window to see if the Lord had granted it and Philippa should be coming up the drive. She wasn't but Makepeace sat down, waiting for her—and for one other.

He came half an hour later.

Since the play had gone into rehearsal, he'd been limbering up. His exercises in the garden and refusal of the richer foods in the dining room had occasioned hilarity in the household, especially from Aaron, a fellow-sufferer. Makepeace had expressed scorn—another example of dramatic attitudes, more vanity.

'My body is my instrument, madam,' he'd said, making her scoff the more. 'Would you have a trumpeter let his trumpet rust?'

If it was ridiculous, it had been effective. The man who got down from the coach was trimmer than he had been. He said something to Sanders up on the box and strode up the steps.

She ran to the front door, pulled it open and threw herself at him. 'Mick, she's gone to France.'

'I know,' he said and picked her up. 'Come to bed.'

S HE was appalled at herself afterwards. The afternoon sun coming through the open window onto their bodies among the rumpled sheets was a reproach. A blackbird's song was the reply of innocence to the groans of satiety that had so recently drowned it.

She heaved his arm off her breasts. 'I'm sorry,' she said, stiffly.

His face was buried in the pillow but she saw one eye open and swivel towards her. 'What the hell for are ye sorry?'

'I was upset,' she said. 'I didn't know what I was doing.'

The eye closed. 'You did it fine all the same.'

'Oh, don't say that.' She untangled her legs from his; the skin sucked apart with sweat. An actor. In the afternoon, like a trollop, like an adultress while her husband was away. Which he was. *Andra, pet, forgive me.*

She must get up. What was she doing here? Give her a moment for her body's lethargy to release her and this interlude would be over.

The worst was, she'd betrayed Philippa. For intense and sordid minutes her mind had neglected its duty, as if the cessation of worrying had taken away what protection she could give her daughter.

'I don't know what to do,' she said. 'They don't believe me, but I know she's gone to France.'

'So Aaron told me. I'm unacquainted with the young lady,' he said, 'but I gather she has strong reasons and a stronger will. From all I've heard of the circumstances, I'm inclined to agree with you.'

'Oh, God.' That he found it credible added to its reality and her fear.

She began to get out of bed. He dragged her back and loomed over her on his elbows. 'Listen, when we know—and I mean for certain—I'll go and fetch her back meself, I'll maybe need to go anyway. Me sources tell me the lads I dealt with over there in that little matter of armaments are no longer the ones in charge. There'll have to be new arrangements made.'

He sat back, offended. 'I've offered to rescue your daughter, woman. A bit of gratitude wouldn't come amiss. What for are you smiling?'

'Andrew,' she exulted. 'He'll fetch her back. Why didn't I think of it? Where's his letter?' She rolled out of bed and scampered to her writing case. 'What's today?'

'The fifteenth.'

Makepeace scanned Lord Ffoulkes's latest scrawl. '"Return sixteenth." He'll be back tomorrow. Oh, God, thank you, God.'

'Andrew?'

'My adopted son, sort of. Lord Ffoulkes. He and his friends smuggle aristocrats out of France, they're experts at it.'

'Aristocrats,' he said, musing. 'No friends of mine then.'

'He's Philippa's friend,' she told him, sharply. 'He'll bring her home.'

She realized that the bosom to which she was clasping Andrew's letter had nothing else on it, a petticoat that had fought back when she'd tried to rip it off had rolled itself up around her waist. 'Oh, look at me. No, don't.'

He was, comfortably, his arms behind his head. 'I'm enjoying the view, woman. It's rare to see a natural redhead nowadays.'

Revulsion overtook her; he was comparing her to his other women. She was an incident that had been enacted in bedrooms across all Europe.

Through nausea the clear eyes of her children peered at their mama. Sir Mick and his fancy woman. She was ashamed, entangled, suffocating. Her body had lain only with good men, both of them with honorable intentions. This man was . . . God knew what he was. For one thing, he was silly—lying there, making silly faces at her as she picked up her clothes from the floor and struggled into them.

'I'm sorry,' she said again. 'This shouldn't've happened. I ain't that sort of woman.'

'When did your husband die?'

'Five years ago.'

'A long time for not being that sort of woman.'

Assuming everybody needed sex, as if it was a tonic to be taken regularly for one's health's sake.

'Get up and dress, for God's sake,' she said. 'They'll all be back in a minute.' She paused in pulling up a stocking as another horror struck home. 'What will Sanders think? What did you tell him?'

'I told him I'd heard you were upset and needed a good fuck to calm ye down.'

'You *didn't*.'

He got up, yawning, and began pulling on his breeches. 'I told him I'd left some papers behind. Since he could have fetched them himself, I doubt he believed me, but that's his business.'

Soon it would be everybody's. Groaning, she sat down at her dressing table to brush her hair.

'But the first explanation was the truth, wasn't it?' He'd descended into Irish ever since he'd got her to bed; his 'truth' was 'troot.' He padded over and took her head between his hands. 'Wasn't it? *Wasn't it?* You're feeling better, confess it.'

Well, she was, but not due to him, thank you very much. It was remembering Andrew that had done it; Andrew, the rescuer.

In the looking glass, she could see his fingers in her hair; his hands were the most gentlemanly thing about him; strong and nice nails. She closed her eyes to them and felt the warmth of the bare skin above his waistband against the back of her head.

'I was upset,' she said, stubbornly. 'I'm sorry.'

'Ah, well.'

She went on brushing her hair, listening to him dress and the door close as he went.

From the window she saw him emerge and walk off to the

stables, calling for Sanders to take him back to the theater. It was 'theater' now, not 't'eater.'

A shape-changer, a bog-trotter who'd learned tricks. Everything about him was wrong. He was a skulker. Time and again she'd caught him in the alley by the stage door talking—*in Irish*—with men who'd look better on a gallows. That bravado about fetching Philippa home . . . an actor's boast and about as honest.

The coach came crunching out of the stableyard and passed beneath her window in a spray of gravel. A hat was waved out of its window.

She didn't wave back.

She sat down again to finish her toilette, wondering how it was she'd been so sure he would come to her. And that he had. As if she'd called to him and he'd heard her. *'Ye're not denying what's been between us these last weeks?'*

I damn well am, she thought. *If you think it's the start of a liaison between us, Mick Murrough, you can think again. I'm too old and respectable for that, thank you very much.*

But the Makepeace in the looking glass had lost respectability, despite its tidy hair and a fichu that came up to its neck. There was a glow to skin that this morning had been haggard, a suspicion of prankishness in the eyes, a disorderly mouth. She was reminded of guilty little boys denying a raid on the comfit jar while sugar still stuck to their chops.

S HE had other things to do the next day than go to The Duke's. In any case, it was a day she'd known for some time that she must reserve for John Beasley.

The coach dropped the theater party at The Duke's and then crossed the river to Clapham to set Jenny down at a house Heilbron had told her was the latest headquarters of the Abolitionists. Makepeace, now very careful of her second daughter, wanted to inspect it.

She was surprised by its grandeur; in a rural setting like Clapham she'd expected a farmhouse. This was a mansion. She and Jenny were greeted warmly by a Marianne—daughter, it turned out, of Henry Thornton, a former governor of the Bank of England.

'You're Mr Heilbron's friends, he's spoken of you highly. How good of you, Miss Jenny, we need all the help we can get—we are trying to organize public meetings and petitions ready for the Commons debate. Mr Wilberforce and Stephen are lobbying the members but it is slow work; so many of them want gradual change. They talk of moderation, silly men. Was our Lord moderate when He saw suffering?'

Makepeace watched Jenny gathered into a drawing room full of paper, ink, good works and good women, and left her there.

She's chosen wisely, she thought. *Wilberforce, Heilbron . . . I must not forget these men are fighting the greatest crime of history. I am thankful for them, Lord, I am really. But, dear Lord, make them extend their humanity to everybody; don't let them strike off the black man's chains only to put them on women.*

There was a crowd outside the Old Bailey and she stayed in the coach while Sanders went in search of Mr Hackbutt. A new sessions court had replaced the one that used to accommodate judges and lawyers under its roof, leaving the far end open to the weather—an attempt to protect their lordships from the prisoners' diseases that had proved faulty when a Lord Mayor, two judges, an alderman and fifty others went down with typhus after one gaol delivery.

The frontage of this one reminded Makepeace of nothing so much as the box of toy bricks Andra had once given to their daughters, all arched windows, pilasters and pediments. The crowd waiting in clumps for admittance along the spike-topped outer wall had delineated itself into two groups that were being kept apart by a stolid line of court officials.

Quite plainly, the one to the left of the gates consisted of Paineites, concerned-looking men, some of whom reminded Makepeace irresistibly of Tom Glossop. (She wondered how that poor little man was getting on in France and if he had met up with his wife yet.) There were a few women amongst them and, here and there, a clump-booted, alert representative of the laboring class—a sort to which their constitutional societies were giving access.

Well behaved and worried, they nevertheless appeared to provoke passion in the smaller but louder group on the other side of the gates. Fists and the union flag were being flourished at them along with catcalls of 'Levelers!,' 'Traitors!,' 'Savages!,' 'Frog-lovers!' One of these had brought along a soapbox on which he was urging passersby to prepare themselves for the day when 'this lawless and furious rabble'—the Paine-ites blinked sadly at him—'would murder them in their beds.'

'Honestly,' Makepeace said when Mr Hackbutt came to usher her into court, 'you'd think that asking for universal suffrage was the same as wanting to cut the king's head off.'

'Ah well, you see,' he said. 'In France it has been.'

He'd reserved a seat for her in the public gallery. 'How is John?' she asked him. Instead of answering the question, he brought her up to date on the trial so far. The attorney general had opened it with a nine-hour speech of intricate detail, which, in Mr Hackbutt's opinion, had done his side more harm than good. 'Too labyrinthian.' Erskine, for the defense, on the other hand, had brilliantly poured scorn on the Crown's case that the men in the dock were traitors. He'd demolished the accusation that they'd procured arms with which to bring down the government, getting even the prosecution witnesses to admit that these were merely a few pikes and antiquated weapons with which to face the mobs attacking their homes.

'You heard of the assault on poor Hardy's house while he was yet in the Tower?'

Yes, busy as she'd been, she'd heard of that; the attackers had wrecked it while yelling, 'For Church and King,' and in the process caused the death of Hardy's wife in childbirth.

'Terrible, terrible,' Mr Hackbutt went on, shaking his wigged head sadly but keeping his legal eye on the legal fox, 'yet the tragedy may do for us what even Erskine's advocacy cannot—the jury were much distressed to hear of it. I scent a shift in the public's opinion.'

Which was more than Makepeace was able to do. For one thing, despite the open windows, Newgate, next door, had steeped the court's wood and walls in the smell of the filth in which it kept its prisoners; she could only scent the stink of humanity in terror and despair. For another, the man who now plumped himself onto the bench next to her was the one who had stood on the soapbox outside—she noticed that more anti-Paine-ites had been let into the public gallery than Paine-ites—and had come to see traitors confounded.

He was large, wore a round brown hat on top of a round brown face and a caped coat open to show a vast display of waistcoat banded in red, white and blue. Either he was copying the cartoonists' John Bull or was the original version from whom the cartoonists had taken their prototype. In view of the heat in the court and his coat, it seemed useless to hope that the perspiration, which was already dripping from his hair, would decrease.

'Ha, ha, madam, today's the day,' he announced. 'We can expect before nightfall to see these men of violence dancing from a rope.'

He was, he told her, a proud member of 'the Association for Preserving Liberty and Property against Republicans and Levelers,' and he'd come up to London from his farm in Budleigh Salterton specifically for the trial, an attendance that had turned him into an expert. 'Lord Chief Justice is being too fair to these would-be king-killers, in my opinion. They've all been given their say—which is just allowing their wickedness to find its way into the minds of the lower orders. We'd have every street beggar clamoring for a vote as good as mine, might as well give it to women. My way, they wouldn't have a trial at all, English justice too good for 'em. String 'em up, I say. Teach them to attack property.'

'Attacked yours, did they?' Makepeace asked coldly.

He was immune to sarcasm. 'Didn't get the chance, ma'am. Down in Devon, we strike back first. Ousted the local Leveler from his house and burned it afore he could get ours. Shrieking for the magistrate, he was—wonderful how they call on the law they have contempt for. "I *am* the magistrate," I told him . . .'

Makepeace looked around desperately but the gallery was full.

In any case, they were bringing the accused up from the cells and into the dock. Thomas Hardy, Horne Took, John Thelwall—all men Makepeace had met through Beasley—and others she didn't recognize. Men whose one crime, as far as she could see, had been to campaign peacefully for reform, men who wouldn't be on trial now if the British establishment hadn't been panicked into reaction by the Terror.

Perhaps it had cause to panic, she thought. If the men in the dock got their way, the propertied class of John Bull here would lose its power by act of parliament—hardly a less inviting prospect than being stripped of it by revolution.

All the defendants had the pallor and cough that their weeks in the Tower had given them but it was John Beasley—the last to come up—whose appearance shocked her most. He had to be helped up the steps by a warder; true, he shook off the man's hand when he reached the dock but he'd shriveled. The familiar sulk was still on his face but it was the glower of a sick man facing death.

She leaned forward and gripped the gallery's rail, hoping that he would look up and she could wave. He didn't, nor did he seem interested in the proceedings around him. *He's just trying to stay upright*, she thought.

The judge under his sword of justice, the wigged heads, the jury stacked like biscuits in their box, all lost Makepeace's attention—she spent the time trying to send strength into her friend by willing it.

At one point a burst of laughter interrupted her concentration. Erskine, the defending counsel was making his final speech. '. . . ridiculous that my clients' approval of some of the French Assembly's actions is evidence of their revolutionary sympathy. It is as well, my lord, that they did not say there were good things in the Koran or they might even now be charged with Mohammedanism.'

There was a disgusted grunt from John Bull. 'Wouldn't put that past the rogues.' But the jury was smiling. For the first time, Makepeace began to hope.

The judge had summed up—not unfairly if the fidgeting of Mr Bull on her left was any indication. It was time for the jury to consider its verdict. The twelve men trooped out, looking self-conscious, like communicants having taken of the bread and the wine and returning to the body of the church to think on their souls.

'Shouldn't be long,' John Bull said. 'Only takes seconds to say "Guilty"'

But Mr Hackbutt, when she found him, was sanguine. 'Erskine has been masterly,' he said. ' I have hopes, I have hopes.'

'I've got an errand to run,' Makepeace told him. 'Will there be time?'

He thought there would.

Whether there was or there wasn't, she had to see Andrew Ffoulkes.

But at St James's Square, Lord Ffoulkes's butler told her that His Lordship and his wife had not yet returned. They were expected later.

The jury was still out when Sanders delivered her back to the Old Bailey. John Bull had resumed his soapbox and was haranguing a crowd that had grown and, to judge from the heckling and the occasional egg he was receiving, was proving unsympathetic to his point of view.

George Hackbutt's right, she thought, *public opinion's shifting*.

But it was the jury's decision that mattered and it took three more hours before they made it. Makepeace spent them pacing the Old Bailey courtyard, sometimes going outside to sit in the coach, not being able to bear inactivity, and returning to the courtyard to pace.

What were they talking about in that jury room? What other verdict could they come to other than guilty? It was the one they were supposed to give; the lord chief justice, the attorney general, both of whom had advised prosecuting for treason, wanted them to give it. So did the prime minister, his cabinet, practically every peer in the land, most of parliament. So did the king.

'Jury's coming back.'

This time Makepeace took care that she was seated well away from John Bull.

The twelve men filed in as self-consciously as they'd filed out, looking at nobody. Was this a good sign or a bad? Were those twelve sober-suited, ordinary, undoubtedly property-owning men going to hang her friend of twenty-five years?

As ever, when she was nervous, Makepeace rubbed her hands agitatedly up and down her knees—and was asked by her neighbor to desist.

The procedure was taking forever. The men in the dock couldn't stand it, she couldn't stand it.

The clerk of the court asked, 'Gentlemen of the jury, what is your verdict?'

'Not guilty.'

Makepeace's hands went still. Amid the cry of 'Disgraceful' from John Bull, the cheers and hubbub of the court, the beat of the judge's gavel trying to stop it, a great and loving peace descended on her. There were times, not too frequent and not too many, but there *were* times when she was very, very proud of England.

By the time she got outside, it was to find that the Paine-ites had been joined by their supporters and a crowd less concerned with reform than rejoicing in what it regarded as an English jury's right to cock a snoot at government. Erskine was having to appeal to it to let the judge get to his coach. The best-known of the acquitted men were being carried shoulder high. Makepeace saw Hardy set in a carriage, its horses replaced by men, being dragged in triumph towards the West End.

She found Beasley cowering in the court doorway.

'Aren't you proud?' she asked him. 'Wasn't the jury brave?'

'So it bloody well ought to be.' It was automatic gracelessness; the fight had gone out of him. The ridge of his nose and cheekbones were almost poking through his skin; scurvy had lost him some teeth so that his mouth had puckered into an old man's. Lice crawled in his lank hair.

Sanders helped her to get him to the coach. 'You can drop me at

St James's Square,' she told him. 'Then take him home. Give him to Hildy.'

To Beasley she said, 'Young man, you're staying with me till you're better.'

'Ain't going to get better,' he said, for all the world like a small boy refusing to clear up his toys.

'Oh, shut up.' But he frightened her, and so did the tenderness with which Sanders settled him against the coach's cushions.

L ORD and Lady Ffoulkes had returned from their honeymoon— for the last half of which, it appeared, they had been joined by their friend Sir Boy Blanchard.

When Makepeace was ushered into the dining room the three were at dinner; Lady Ffoulkes and Sir Boy were teasing his lordship.

Sir Boy's fine eyebrows went up at the sight of Makepeace but he rallied, 'We were just saying, Mrs Hedley, could you conceive of any other man in England who would take his bride to a steel mill and a turnip farm on their *voyage de noces*?'

She ignored him. As Lord Ffoulkes hurried round the table to kiss her, she said, 'Philippa's gone to France, Andrew.' She turned on Blanchard. 'And it's your fault.'

'I *beg* your pardon?'

'Yes, it is. I heard it all from Jenny. If you'd given her Condorcet's papers when she asked . . . It took too long. In the end it was quicker to take 'em than send 'em.'

'I thought you'd arranged it for her, Boy.' Ffoulkes's voice was quiet.

Blanchard's was reasonable though his face was pale. 'My dear man, I had every intention of it. I told her so. It just could not be done on the instant—the estimable Scratcher was *hors de combat* from an injured hand . . . Anyway, are we certain the young lady has taken this dramatic step?'

'Yes, we are,' Makepeace was speaking to Ffoulkes. 'I got a letter from Ginny this morning. That's where Pippy said she was going, up north. She ain't there, Andrew. Ginny asks how she is.'

There was a silence. Blanchard filled it with silk. 'E'en so. One hestitates to suggest it but there are gentler reasons for a young lady's absence than a precipitate run into the cannon's mouth.'

Lord, how she hated him. And how he hated Philippa. Why he did, Makepeace didn't know, but Chelsea gossip put him somewhere behind Fitch-Botley's discovery of his wife's radical doings and the subsequent assault on her daughter.

You bastard, she thought.

Andrew was sitting her down, pouring her wine, asking for details.

Félicie said, 'Some food, Madame 'Edley? A little cheese, per'aps? No? Then forgive me that I retire, I am weary.' The conversation did not look like it would center on her. As she drifted past Blanchard, she touched his shoulder. 'You stay for cards, later?'

He put up his hand to cover hers for a second. 'Of course.'

Andrew, Makepeace saw, didn't notice his wife's going. 'Tell us, missus.'

She told them what she knew, Blanchard interrupting frequently but kindly to suggest that it was nonsense; Philippa's disappearance could be interpreted in a dozen ways, the most likely being a romance.

'I know her,' Makepeace spat at him.

'So do I,' Andrew said. 'God, missus, she's your daughter right enough. Now then, she'll have gone via the smuggling route, you agree?'

'Yes.'

'What's the smuggling route?' Blanchard asked.

Makepeace's eyes begged her godson to be quiet about it; add smuggling to all her other nefarious activities and her name would irretrievably be mud.

Andrew's eyes reassured her. 'A private matter between the missus and me,' he said. 'If I find she's gone, I'll follow her. All right, missus?'

'Oh, Andrew.' She'd wanted it; but now she was afraid for him.

'Yah,' he said. 'I'm the arrow you shoot after the one you've lost, ain't that right, Reynard? That's how you find arrows.' He laid his cheek against hers. 'Done it a hundred times, ain't we, Boy? Easy as lick a dish. It's what we do. London's teemin' with aristos we've nipped from under Robespierre's snout. I'll have that little baggage back in England quicker'n you can sneeze.'

'Thank you.' She put her arm round his neck and held him close.

'*No.*' Blanchard's chair scraped back. 'I will go.' He stood tall, looking down at them both. More quietly, he said, 'I go, Andy. It's only just. If it was my fault, it's my responsibility. Only tell me where she is—one presumes she was making for wherever Condorcet's holed up.'

Ffoulkes looked at him with affection. 'Good try, old man, but this one's mine. You're to stay and look after Félicie for me.'

'Oh no, my lord, Miss Philippa is my bag.'

'She's my goddaughter.' The words lashed; Ffoulkes had finished with pleasantries. 'She tell you where Condorcet's hidin', missus?'

'No.' Makepeace felt humiliated; Philippa had not confided in her. Blast the girl. And blast me, I was too tied up in myself.

'Nor me.' Ffoulkes began striding. 'She'd had a letter from Madame Condorcet . . . that's right.' He wagged a finger at the air and started walking again. 'What did she say . . . something, yes, that's right. The woman was earnin' her living painting portraits. Paris, somewhere. Where?' He banged the heel of his hand against his forehead. 'Damn, where *was* it?'

'Left Bank?' Blanchard suggested, softly. 'Lot of painters there.'

'No. Not the Left Bank.'

'Pont Neuf? Palais Royale? Montmartre? *Voisinage de la Comédie, peut-être?*'

Makepeace dragged her eyes off Andrew Ffoulkes. Blanchard was sitting as stiffly as she was, invoking the locations in a whispered litany. I've misjudged him, she thought; he's desperate to find her.

'No. NO.' The candles flickered as Ffoulkes slammed his fist on the table. He took in a big breath and let it out again. 'I'll think of it. Look here, I'll meander upstairs. I'll collect a passport or two, few false noses. I'm a master of disguise. Ain't I, Reynard?'

They were left alone. Blanchard took Ffoulkes's seat and leaned back in it, his hands clasped like a priest's, his eyes contemplating the gilded ceiling, the sheen from the table's candles caressing his chin.

'Will he be all right?' Makepeace asked.

'The September massacres of '92,' he said, gently. 'Did Andy ever tell you what the *canaille* did to the Princesse de Lamballe in that little rampage?'

The newspapers had. 'I don't want to hear.'

'She was Marie Antoinette's mistress of the household, you know. Pretty thing, blond curls. Andy and I dined with her more than once in the old days at Versailles. Lesbian whore, so they say, but loyal. Stayed with the queen when the others fled. They hacked her to death. Stripped the body and displayed her private parts to the mob. Stuck her head on a pole and carried it to the Temple to show the queen.'

It was like being in the room with an assassin; he stabbed at her with words.

'Andy and I and the lads of The League were out to rescue the Saint Galière children at the time. Which, I may say, we eventually did. Arrived in Paris the day after the massacres. There were still bits of Lamballe's pubic hair on sale outside La Force. Enterprisin' lot, your revolutionaries.'

'You hate her, don't you?'

'Not at all. Empty-headed little filly but she served the best champagne I ever tasted.'

'Philippa,' Makepeace said. 'You hate Philippa.'

He opened his eyes wide. 'Oh, your daughter. No, ma'am. Apart from the fact that she's like to cause the death of my best friend, I can't say I think of her.'

Hatred, she thought. *It isn't only me and Philippa; he just hates.*

Ffoulkes appeared in the doorway. 'Rue Saint Honoré. Came to me. That's where La Condorcet is, bloody Rue Saint Honoré. On your feet, missus, the carriage awaits. I'll drop you at Reach House on the way.'

Behind her, as she left the room, she heard Lord Ffoulkes's friend embrace him and tell him lovingly not to concern himself for his wife, Boy Blanchard would look after her.

HILDY had bathed John Beasley, shaved off his hair and put him to bed. She'd also sent for Dr Baines to come on the morrow. 'He's in poor fettle,' she whispered, 'but he's slumberin' at least.'

They looked down at her patient. The shaven head was that of a convict but his adolescence had returned to him in sleep.

'Does he nivver say thank you?'

'Never.'

Hildy said that Jenny had come back exalted from her day with the Abolitionists and had already retired. The theater party hadn't yet returned. 'Get t'bed yeself, missus. You look worse nor this beggor.'

Though Makepeace obeyed, sleep eluded her. The responsibility of having sent a beloved boy into danger after a beloved girl was almost as terrible as the likelihood that she might see neither of them again.

She's like to cause the death of my best friend.

No, it's me that's done that.

She attempted to overlay the dreadful day with remembering the trial jury's triumphal 'not guilty' but even there the cost to the acquitted was represented by the wreckage that was Beasley and she wept for it.

When she did doze, Blanchard came at her out of the shadows, a knife in his fist, and the head of a mutilated princess shrieked until she woke up again.

Some time after midnight, her door opened and a voice with depth to it said: 'I've been thinking you owe me another apology.'

Gratefully, she made room for him in her bed and apologized.

Chapter Twelve

Mme Mabillon was well known in the Cour du Dragon as a bruiser and the mother of six hungry children, in both of which capacities she felt herself entitled to arrive late and push herself into the bread queue ahead of those who'd been waiting longer.

Having invented the queue, Paris was still having trouble sticking to its principle. Waiting in line in the heat was bad enough but tempers became dangerous when the queue began to move as those at the front were served. The fear was that the bread would run out before you got to it. Tussles were frequent.

Today Mme Mabillon was using her bulk and vocabulary to overcome the objection of a comparative newcomer to the court's queue, somebody's maid by her appearance, and she was prepared, if necessary, to use her clogs as well. 'Fuck off, you snotty little nothing. I got six children. Who you got?'

'Six legal ration cards.' Philippa waved them. 'Think you're a bloody aristo?' She shouted at a National Guardsman who was talking to an ironmonger farther down the alley. 'Here, look at this *ci-devant* trying to get ahead of everybody else, thinks she's a fucking aristo.'

Ci-devant was *really* rude, once an adjective now a noun, the worst word in sansculotte vocabulary, and Mme Mabillon shrank back as the guardsman came lounging up. The suggestion that they'd been aristos, had aristo connections or even served in an aristo household, had been the excuse to get more than one queue-jumper guillotined. She protested. ''Course I ain't, you know me. I just got hungry kids at home.'

There was a chorus of so-have-I. Mme Mabillon's belligerence had won her no friends over the years. As the National Guardsman told her to behave herself, she retreated like a dog slinking away from a growling pack.

Philippa shuffled forward, shaking from the anger that had torched her like dry straw, but victorious. *Teach her, bloody woman.*

Then she was frightened at herself. Calling on a National Guardsman had been madness; her papers had stood up to scrutiny so far . . . still, you never knew.

But I am a dog now, she thought. *I snarl the language of the streets. I think in the language of the streets. I want to use every dirty word there is.*

War, the threat of the guillotine was as nothing compared to the everyday desperation that had reduced all of them to animals. Philippa Dapifer would have kept quiet and given way; Jeanne Renard could have torn the bitch's throat out. Nor would she have been sorry that she'd done it; she too had a child to think of. Sophie Condorcet was sick and Philippa was foraging for her and Eliza as well as those at Number Fifteen. Good manners and propriety belonged to those whose food arrived regularly on the table and in Paris you either abandoned them or returned home with an empty basket.

One of the reasons these women had welcomed the Revolution in the first place was that they'd had to spend their lives worrying about the price of bread while watching gilded carriages pass them by, seeing the *poudré*-ed wigged heads of lord, lady, coachman and outriders whitened with flour that could have been used to feed their children.

There was no regret for the old days; nobody wanted the king back. They were a republic and would stay a republic—but they were still hungry and even now they suspected that somewhere there was a cornucopia of brown-crusted, milk-white bread that they weren't getting and somebody else was.

The queue for the baker's went down the length of the court and out into the Rue de l'Egout. Philippa had joined it at dawn and was still well down the line. She and the others had seen the flour cart arrive and deliver pitifully few sacks, waited while the baker prepared and pounded the dough and endured the smell from his ovens. Would he sell out before she got to his counter? The bastard was known for having his favorites.

In the early days of the Revolution, a gathering of women like this—it was always women who queued—would have provided an occasion for some other woman to harangue them.

Sisters, this is our opportunity, come with us as we march with men to liberty. We, too, are entitled to the new world. Join the Society of Patriotic Dames/Women Friends of Truth/Citizenesses of Republican Revolutionaries. There had been a club for everything; women's education, divorce, hospitals, child benefits, political rights. Condorcet had spoken at nearly all of them, advocating not only female suffrage but that women should be eligible for election to governing bodies—a step too far for most of them.

All gone now. Too revolutionary for this Revolution. The Convention had banned them and the heads of women who'd spoken for women had fallen into Sanson's basket. Reason had gone with them; the only oratory now was the cry of the enraged. Kill the hoarders, kill the black marketeers, give us bread. Just kill.

And I don't care, Jeanne Renard thought. *I'm too bloody hungry. Somebody's got to pay.*

'Oh blessed Mother,' shrieked a voice ahead of her. 'The cunt's shutting up shop.'

M Raspail, the baker, was bolting his shutters as quickly as he could. The next minute his perspiring face appeared from the safety of an upstairs window—more than one baker had been hung from the lantern by angry women.

'No more, citizenesses. I'm sorry.' The National Guardsman had been joined by another and both were standing before the shop door, pikes at the ready.

How to say, 'Nothing to eat today,' to the faces waiting at home?

There was no way out. Like seeing lions pad into the arena, nothing between you and their jaws.

There was some screaming. And clattering—a couple of women were venting their frustration on the ironmonger's goods. The terrible Mme Mabillon was sitting on the stones, her head in her hands, weeping.

Philippa made her escape before the riot developed. It would have to be the black market, then—she still had a couple of louis d'or that she'd brought with her from England. Mme Vernet would not approve; it was not honorable for those who had money to buy on the black market; it was a betrayal of the women in Dragon Court; their food was being held back and sold to the privileged, a betrayal of the Republic itself.

But Mme Vernet didn't have to listen to Sophie Condorcet cough and watch Eliza grow thinner and tireder by the day. As for the Republic, the hell with it.

She began to go down the hill, heading for the Saint Germain market. According to the gossip she'd picked up during her days in the Dragon Court queue—and it was amazingly well-informed about things that mattered—there was a bastard in the market who, as long as people had cash, not assignats, but *real* money, could procure anything from a churn of fresh milk to an abortion.

'Why don't you inform on him?' she'd asked.

Well . . . but why bother? He's the Hydra. Cut off his head, there'd be a dozen to take his place. The high-ups didn't care, they probably took a cut anyway. The explanation had been accompanied by a shuffling of feet and she'd realized that in these terrible days— if you could beg or borrow enough—an abortionist sometimes came in handy.

It was a grubby transaction. She made it in an old, enclosed and empty slaughter yard behind the market with a thin-faced young man whose eyes were never still but whose assurance suggested that the local militia had been well paid to ignore what was going on. He would survive the Terror a dead man or a rich one; he was prepared to gamble. She had to show him her *certificat de civisme*, but she'd expected that; he'd need to know who she was so that if she betrayed him for profiteering, he could betray her for buying with cash. They balanced each other nicely on the scales of illegality.

She also had to lift her skirt to get at the coins sewn into her garter. 'Don't look,' she hissed at him. He shrugged; he'd seen legs before. Queue gossip said that if you didn't have cash, he'd let you whore for him.

Oh, a grubby transaction and it took one of her louis. But as she hauled herself up the hill with a basket containing a ham, a cheese, some leeks, two five pound loaves and a tin of tobacco she'd made the man throw in as makeweight, her only concern was that someone might ask her why it was so heavy.

Stooping through the wicket in the gates of Number Fifteen, she felt like a penitent regaining salvation; order and calm flowed from the house into the courtyard as into a convent cloister. In the kitchen she lifted the basket onto the table and collapsed over it, waiting for the mother superior's rebuke.

She felt Mme Vernet's hand rest for a moment on her shoulder before it took the ham out of the basket and started to saw it in half. 'And leeks, too,' Mme Vernet said. 'I'll make a broth.'

Gratefully, Philippa took the tobacco up to Condorcet's room; he was an inveterate pipe smoker and had been suffering withdrawal.

'Marvellous,' he said when she gave it to him. 'Where did you get it?'

She didn't tell him, though she was in a mood to say, *I sold my soul for it.*

We protect him, she thought. *He sits here writing his book, like a scribe in a monastery, fed and watered by others' hands, with no idea how dirty those hands have to be. Does he know what a danger he is to us all? Does he care? And that woman downstairs won't tell him, won't let me tell him, either. Oh, no, he's a virtuous man and must be protected.*

Sharply, she said, 'How's the *Progress* going?'

His beautiful smile. 'Still progressing. Not long now.'

She stumped downstairs and into the kitchen. 'He's never going to finish that damn book.'

Mme Vernet looked at her, then cut the crust off one of the loaves, sliced a piece of cheese to put on it and gave it to her. 'Sit down, my dear. Eat. Slowly.'

She tried to chew each mouthful but gulped most of them, feeling the sustenance soak up her resentment like blotting paper. 'I was cross,' she said.

'Of course.'

She had no right to blame Condorcet for putting the household in danger when her own presence in it had redoubled the risk. Though her hostess gave no indication of it, she was here on sufferance. True, she might one day be the means of getting rid of the millstone around its neck but in the meantime she added to its weight.

She watched Mme Vernet's long freckled hands as she chopped the leeks. The ham was already boiling on the stove, releasing the smell of bay leaves picked from the tree in the back garden. 'Don't you ever get angry, madame?'

'Indeed, I do.' Mme Vernet did not elaborate, just as she had not expounded on her definition of 'virtue,' the quality which had endeared Condorcet to her in the first place. Whether it was political, moral or religious goodness, Philippa still didn't know. Mme Vernet gave the word a standard that Condorcet had met, thereby qualifying him for her hospitality and, if it came to it, her life.

Just general goodness, Philippa decided. *And she's right*.

Resuscitated, she went back upstairs and planted a kiss on Condorcet's head. He looked up in surprise and then smiled. 'You've changed,' he said. 'France is having a bad effect on you, you're becoming demonstrative.'

'I know.'

She looked round the stuffy, overcrowded room with appreciation. In here, among the tobacco smoke, Condorcet's hands twisted the world first one way and then the other to reveal aspects she hadn't known it possessed, sometimes giving it the rarified atmosphere of the moon. At one side of his table, there were neat piles of paper tied with ribbon—a work on a universal language, a mathematical primer for schoolchildren, wonderful things written in between chapters of *The Progress of the Human Spirit*.

The man was a geyser of knowledge; without a library at his disposal, the first nine chapters of the book itself dealt with the advance of the human race from the primitive, the hunting and gathering groups, the beginning of towns, on to the genius of the Greeks, the coming of Christianity, Islam and the thousand years between the fall of Rome and the invention of printing.

Philippa found his view of Christianity rather shocking—a superstition spread by priests to increase their authority he said it was, like all religions. The inevitable march of men and women towards happiness and truth did not need it.

In his view, advances in hygiene, medicine, science, the discoveries of Copernicus, Galileo and Newton, the ideas of Descartes, Locke and Leibniz, universal education, must inevitably lead to a world of peace. National hatreds would end. People would learn they could not become conquerors without forfeiting their own liberty, that permanent confederations alone could maintain their independence and that their aim must be security, not power. Commercial prejudices would gradually disappear and the mercantile interest would lose its capacity to cause war and ruin nations on the pretext of enriching them.

He was watching her. 'Will you be seeing Sophie today?'

'Yes.'

'Only I have a letter I wish her to have in reply to hers.'

That would be the one in which Sophie'd told him she had to divorce him. Philippa had given it to him and left the room, unwilling to see him read it.

Delivering the reply wouldn't be fun, either. Even less amusing was *when* she must deliver it. Midmorning. When the death carts lumbered down Rue Saint Honoré towards the waiting guillotine, when she used them as her cover, walking beside them on the other side of the street from the agent who watched the lingerie shop, when his eyes, like all eyes, were on the tumbrels' occupants.

She did it regularly now, every time it was necessary to take food and messages to Sophie. It had to be done if she was not to be questioned, or followed, but each time she felt like a vulture flapping along beside the soon-to-be-dead.

'And then tomorrow I want you to return to England,' he said.

'Not without you.'

He smiled. '"With your shield or on it."'

'Yes.'

It was a regular exchange. She weighed terribly on his conscience; he told her to go every day.

When he was ready to leave she would have to, but in her mind—and, she sometimes wondered, perhaps in his—his book had become a Penelope's shroud which would never be finished; he would go on writing it until some cosmic Ulysses stepped in, swept France clean of its quarrelling suitors and put everything right again.

Curiously, for all the privation, she was content that this should be so. With death as a near neighbor, life narrowed down to an awful simplicity that was in itself a purpose. She was useful to people she cared for and who cared for her. England existed on a remote horizon, beautiful but also complicated by entanglements and emotions that it was a relief to be free of.

Had she been in love with Andrew Ffoulkes? She hardly thought of him. Had she been going to marry Stephen Heilbron? It took an effort of will to remember why. Children, of course; she'd wanted children. But here, now, with death so close, motherhood was an option she was hardly likely to be offered.

In any case—and this made her smile—Heilbron wouldn't marry her now. Even if he could forgive this foray to France, he would find her unsuitable. Jeanne Renard was not at all his kind of woman and Jeanne Renard, having emerged from the box, could not be put back in it again.

Strange, she thought, that in one of the most restrictive cities in the world she had been liberated; the ridiculous coconut shell had broken. Whatever the future held and however short it was going to be, she wasn't going to spend it hiding the things she felt and not saying the things she thought. If she felt like swearing—and how often poor Philippa Dapifer had—she'd bloody well swear.

Oh hell, she thought, *I've become Ma.*

Briskly, she went downstairs to see if Mme Vernet had made the broth.

Unless somebody famous was going to the guillotine, Rue Saint Honoré had lost interest. People looked up, of course—it was always worth seeing how others faced death—but crowds no longer lined the route. Even the number of National Guard that marched alongside had been reduced; there were no rescue attempts, people were too numb. Civilians, now allowed to accompany the carts on their way, were either the usual ghouls or family, friends and lovers who didn't care that their tears were noted. To begin with, Philippa had been ashamed to be thought of as one of the former and equally embarrassed at assuming the tragedy of the latter. Now she tried not to think at all and just kept to leeward of the tumbrels, blessing a lack of height that kept her hidden from the other side of the road.

On these days the Rue Saint Honoré, usually one of Paris's cleaner thoroughfares, became a stinking corridor. In their spare time the tumbrels were used to transport pigs and calves to market, nor was their straw changed very often, so that the droppings of the animals mingled with those of the poor humans whose fear made them unable to control their bowels. Yet it was a dignified progress. The frightened were comforted by the brave. Most of the faces were calm, their sight fixed on the sky as if they were seeing its beauty for the first time, not the last.

Philippa walked behind a girl whose hands reached up to clutch the skirt of an older woman with her own hands bound behind her who stood close to the cart's side edge. 'Go home,' the mother kept telling her daughter, 'Go home, dear. You must be the *maman* to the little ones now.'

'I can't bear it. How can I bear it?'

'Go home.' The woman's voice was desperate.

Philippa touched the girl on her shoulder. 'She doesn't want you to see it.'

The girl broke away and sat down in the road, her head in her hands.

And the woman said, 'Thank you, mademoiselle.'

Is that why you've got to die, Philippa wondered. *Because you couldn't remember to say* citoyenne? *What do I say?* Je vous en prie? *Think nothing of it?*

But the woman's gaze had gone upwards; she was praying. Behind her in the cart a man was swearing quietly and furiously to himself.

Oh, God, it's Lavoisier.

The energy was still there; dirty, unshaven, obviously ill, he still crackled with it. It had made dinners at the man's house chaotic, poor little Mme Lavoisier trying to rescue dishes that were being pushed aside, the smell of chemicals overpowering that of roasts. Her stepfather had taken her 'to meet the greatest chemist in France, in the world.'

And how Andra had loved him, sure that sooner or later this Frenchman would solve the problem of coal damp, that killer of miners; Lavoisier's book on the elements of chemistry had been his bible. She'd met Lavoisier again at the Condorcets', expounding his discovery of oxygen, incomprehensible words made more incomprehensible by the speed and excitement with which he delivered them.

She was dumbfounded. The Revolution was not only eating its own children, it was devouring the seed corn. Potential, wonderful discoveries were being tossed casually away, like trash into a basket, before they could be made.

Jesus, he mustn't die. He's a gift. Sometimes God opened his hand and let a Mozart or a Shakespeare or a Da Vinci slide into the world as a present to it. The Almighty had generously done it again with Lavoisier—here, my children, have this teeming brain, it will prove useful to your understanding of my matter.

And they had put this rare, extraordinary intelligence into a dirty cart and were going to kill it.

He seemed more cross than afraid, anger sparked round him like Saint Elmo's fire round a ship's mast. Later she heard that he'd begged to finish an important experiment before they beheaded him. They'd refused.

Robespierre's lodgings were farther down the street; did he watch the tumbrels pass or did he take care to be at the Convention when they were going by? Would he feel anything if he saw the mother? Or Lavoisier?

She was almost past the lingerie shop before she came to herself. Opening the door set its bell tingling. As she shut it, she clung on to the handle, feeling as if she'd been tumbling in space and waiting while the earth readjusted itself under her feet, listening to the rumble of infinite stupidity growing fainter as it made its way towards the Place de la Révolution.

Mme Hahn was arranging silk stockings in a drawer, releasing the smell of lavender from the sachets in which her goods were kept. 'Good day, mademoiselle.' She never asked questions.

'Good day, madame.' Philippa stood for a moment, grateful for the fripperies surrounding her; who had money to buy them, she couldn't work out.

Upstairs, Sophie and Eliza were asleep on the bed, the mother's body curved round that of the child's, a sheen of sweat on both faces. The air in in the studio was hot and sour; Sophie kept the windows shut when she slept, afraid Eliza would wake up before her, climb up on the windowsill and fall out.

Philippa crouched below the sill, careful not to be seen by the watcher opposite, and pushed up the sashes. The sudden noise from the street woke the two and their eyes followed every movement as she lifted the lid of her pail, took two bowls from the cupboard and filled them with broth. Slices of bread with melted cheese floated on the top—Mme Vernet hadn't spared anything.

When they'd finished the bowls, she filled them up again. 'It won't keep in this heat.' It was like seeing rainwater reach the roots of wilted flowers; Eliza began chattering, Sophie declared herself fit enough to begin painting again—the last time she'd fainted at her easel. 'Why aren't you eating?'

'I'm not hungry.' She told Sophie about Lavoisier.

Sophie had lost the capacity for astonishment. 'I'd hoped he would be spared. Marat hated him. He bought a taxing right years ago. He used the money on his experiments and he set up free schools for peasant children in his area but . . .' She shrugged. 'He was a farmer-general of taxes. I hoped with Marat dead . . . But "The Republic has no use for savants," is what they said. His poor wife. She was a child bride, too, we used to tease our men, say they stole us from our cradles.'

Her mouth became ugly as grief widened it into a horizontal band. 'And here we are,' she said.

And there you are. Wordlessly, Philippa took Condorcet's letter from her basket and handed it to his wife. Then she joined Eliza on the floor to play dolls. The child asked, 'Will you wait till the man goes and does pooh-poohs today?'

Philippa grinned at her. 'Will you watch for me?'

'Watch him do pooh-poohs?' Eliza had reached the anal stage.

Above them, Sophie was controlled. 'Nicolas says that of course I must divorce him.' Then her voice broke. 'He says: "I have served my country, I have possessed your heart. There is no greater happiness." He's saying good-bye.'

When it was time to go, Sophie, clasping Eliza close, stood at the window, and Philippa, on tiptoe like a sprinter, at the door. 'He's been constipated lately,' Sophie said. 'Too many croissants.'

'He's going pooh-poohs,' sang Eliza triumphantly. Philippa ran for it.

She was crossing the Pont Neuf when she realized she was being followed.

Any daytime walk through Paris was like strolling around an orchestra in full blast; ears assailed not by the symphony but by its component parts—strident piccolo from a cluster of newspaper sellers, a blast of brass from a foundry, the deep grumbling tympany of the queues, but through Philippa's progress there had sounded one constant and eventually nerve-twanging beat, like a ticking clock, like someone keeping time by tapping a metal triangle with a rod. Underneath the city's daytime rising and falling cacophony, it was this regularity that imposed itself on her attention.

She stopped halfway across as if to consider the view of the river and looked to her right but the perpetual busyness of the bridge, the second-hand stalls with their miserable artifacts, street painters, the stands of the barbers and tooth-pullers and the attendant people who loitered around them, made it impossible to pinpoint whoever was doing the tapping which, in any case, was momentarily drowned in the hubbub. Down on the mudflats, sand-carters and washerwomen were shouting to one another.

Overacting, she mimed the start of someone who's remembered an urgent appointment and almost ran across the rest of the bridge where she stopped in the shade of one of its lamps and turned.

Now she had him. The click came from the iron-tipped end of a walking stick in the hand of an old soldier. Paris was full of them—'old' in the sense of no longer useful, back from a war that had shattered a part of them, bearded, often decorated, with a knapsack on their back, invariably shabby and cynical. This one was typical, except that he showed more purposefulness than most. And *she* was his purpose; she saw him look around and assume nonchalance when he spotted her.

Then he made a mistake. In his hurry to catch up, he took two steady steps without the use of his stick. Now he'd remembered and was using it again.

A government spy.

She turned, shouldered her way through a group approaching the bridge and made as quickly as she could for Notre Dame. Her spine and the back of her hams had gone chilly. Minutes ago she'd been an ordinary Parisian, thinking herself and her friends hard done by; now she would do anything, *anything*, to return to that happy state. She was marked. The State knew about her; its terrible eye had fixed on her. The cat was extending its claws to pull her in.

Her breath sobbed as she hurried. Let other people die, not me.

The only decency panic left her was mere instinct: Condorcet would not go up the guillotine steps with her. *I'm not going home. You won't get him through me, you bastards.*

She was in the cool of the cathedral, running now, dodging from pillar to pillar, making for the north door. The place appeared empty and echoed to her own gasps.

No clicking.

Out into the sunshine again and a dive into the alleys of the ancient and sculptured labyrinth that had once been riddled by clergy, that Abelard and Heloise had walked five hundred years before. Deserted now; nobody about, gargoyles stared at her above little arches with Latin inscriptions.

Not through me . . . not through me . . . bastards . . . bastards.

No clicking.

She stopped and held on with one hand to a doorway's carved pillar while she bent over to get rid of the stitch in her side.

And she heard him coming up the alley at her back. She felt in her basket for the empty iron pail and swung it round behind her, catching him in the stomach. She heard the cough of breath as it left his lungs and turned, ready to swing again, prepared to batter him to death in her panic.

'Bloody Monday!'

The words stopped Jeanne Renard's arm in its arc, so that it lost its impetus and the pail only clattered onto the man's bent head.

'Ow,' the spy said. 'Stop hitting me, woman.'

Life encompassed her again; beneath the whiskers and dirt was the face of Lord Ffoulkes, baron, whom she had once loved.

And she was so scared again, *for* him, *of* him, of the untidy cataract of feeling he brought with him, that she became angry at his damn cheek in coming at all.

In fact, she was furious.

'Damn you,' she said. 'Go *away*.'

Chapter Thirteen

FFOULKES's letter from Babbs Cove came in the middle of the dress rehearsal. Sanders, who'd returned to Reach House, had galloped back with it to the theater.

'"Yes gone to France,"' Makepeace read, '"Not Gurney's fault. Would not take her. Sent her home with flea in ear. Thought she'd gone back to London till I said no. Investigated. Minx went along coast and paid Thurlestone pirates take her over. Following. Back soon. Missus do not worry. Yr devoted Andrew."'

'Don't worry, he says. Don't worry, missus, just following your daughter into the furnace. I'll kill her, Sanders. If the French don't do it, I will.' She clutched at his coat. 'What am I going to do?'

'Nothing else *to* do, missus, only wait. He'll get her out, will Lord Ffoulkes; damn Froggies won't down him.' Sanders belonged to the one-Englishman-worth-ten-Frenchies school of patriotism.

She must wait. But the 'nothing else to do' did not apply. She put the letter in her apron pocket where it weighed her down, like rock, as she scurried.

Oroonoko was opening tonight; the date on the posters said so, and the reason that they were holding the dress rehearsal on the same day was because the costumes had not been ready. Nothing was ready. There were still a thousand playbills to be handed out in the streets and none of the company available to do it, not one.

Murrough had co-opted every man-jack of her émigrés, dressmakers, scene-shifters, into the cast. Now they were Caribbean planters, servants, sailors, Indians, negroes and assorted extras and, it seemed to Makepeace, merely lolling about in the wings waiting for infrequent forays onto the stage in order for Murrough to shout at them.

She grabbed three of the prettiest, the Countess d'Abreville and her son and Mme de Césarine-Delorme and was urging them towards the foyer when a vast voice from the stage said, 'Bring them back.'

'Do you want these bloody playbills handed out or not?'

'Bring them *back*.'

Sullenly, she let them go. 'I thought they were supposed to stay behind the scenes.' It was why the aristocrats had taken work in the theater in the first place—to hide from the public eye their shame at having to work at all. But one sniff of greasepaint and the buggers had become stagestruck, though the two women were taking the precaution of wearing eastern veils, as if English planters in Surinam chose their wives exclusively from Arabia. Young Henri, now a delicious little black serving boy, was unrecognizable.

She scoured the theater for help. Luchet, as usual, could not be found. Jacques was sending Murrough mad by perfecting his effects and rolling cannonballs down the mended overhead chute over and over. The Comte de Penthémont, an apron over his sailor's costume, was too busy putting final touches of paint on a backdrop. The scene-shifters, Prince de Luxembourg-Turpin and Marquis de la Platière, now also sailors, said they had a quick scene change coming up and dare not leave their posts. Marie Joséphine was doing last minute repairs to the costumes.

She wished she'd brought everybody from Reach House but Hildy was attending John Beasley's sickroom and could not be left alone.

Joseph she didn't even ask; a man who could tackle anything was too valuable to leave the theater for a moment. She blinked at his feathers. 'What are you?'

'I am Indian, missus.'

'Good God.'

She peered hopefully into the orchestra pit. '*Non*,' Marquis de Barigoule said, before she'd even asked.

In the end, she enrolled Sanders. Such passersby as accepted the playbills took them from Sanders because they thought they advertised a new coach line, and from Makepeace because the paper was thrust at them like an assassin's knife and they were afraid not to. From their faces, the auguries for their attendance were not good.

When she got back two new figures were lounging in the stalls.

Blanchard got up for a graceful bow; Félicie ignored Makepeace's curtsey.

'Lady Ffoulkes received a note from her lord this morning,' Blanchard said. 'It appears he has indeed gone chasing off to Paris to find your daughter.'

'I know,' Makepeace said miserably.

At this Félicie turned on her. 'I am not content. Andrew promise me not go back, '*e promise*.'

Blanchard said soothingly, 'She is his goddaughter, my dear. And Andrew is an honorable man.'

'It is not honorable to leave 'is wife.'

'So you've heard from him as well, have you, missus?' Blanchard asked. 'I hope you will keep us informed if you receive news that we do not.'

'In the name of all Divinity, will ye be quiet down there?' A black-corked Murrough with a sword apparently stuck into his guts was glaring down at them.

Blanchard stepped forward. 'Mr Oroonoko, I presume? I do apologize. Her Ladyship and myself are by way of making a preliminary sortie—we're bringing a party to tonight's performance.'

'There won't bloody be one unless I get some peace in this house. Start again, Chrissie, from "Nay then I must assist you . . ."'

Since the couple showed no sign of going, and there was no one else to do it—Sanders was still handing out playbills—Makepeace went out to order them a tray of coffee.

She must show every kindness to Félicie. If it had been Blanchard alone, he could have gone thirsty. Apart from the way he'd treated Philippa, his reference to Andrew's honor had seemed designed to rub salt into Félicie's perfectly justified resentment at her husband's departure into dangerous waters for another woman.

Nor did she like the way he'd been amusedly polite to Murrough, as if to a yokel. She dreaded the party he would bring tonight; Aaron always said that aristocratic claques were the worst; the bluer the blood, he said, the lower the manners.

And what right has he got to call me 'missus'?

On the way back with the coffee she called in at the pie shop. 'Extra special this afternoon, Jerry. All the trimmings.' The least she could do for her company was send it on stage with a full stomach to face whatever it had to face.

She had an all-encompassing sense of disaster.

Later, when she had occasion to go again into the body of the theater, Félicie and Blanchard were still there. Luchet sat in the row in front, his chin on the back of his chair, regarding Félicie with the adoration of a dog expecting a biscuit. Ninon, it seemed, had lost the tutor's devotion to a younger, prettier woman—an outcome for which the actress would be grateful. It wasn't being returned here, either. Ignoring Luchet, Félicie was leaning close to Blanchard and laughing at something he'd said.

Undoubtedly, Andrew's wife looked heavenly. *With all Andrew's money to play with she ought to*, Makepeace thought. Then she castigated herself for being sour. Money, a lot of it, could buy the high-waisted cambric *robe en chemise*, the gold girdle, the hair plumes, but it could not buy the style with which Félicie wore them, nor the natural curl of her hair nor a skin that appeared to be lit from inside.

Boy Blanchard nodded to Makepeace and then at the stage. 'One hopes these little *balourdises* will be ironed out by tonight.'

If *balourdises* meant chaos, Makepeace hoped it would, too. The Widow Lackitt had just crossed too closely to the edge of the stage and her enormous skirt had caught one of the 'floaters,' setting light to its hem and spilling oil on the boards causing the lieutenant governor of Surinam to fall heavily on his arse, bringing Dizzy Distazio down with him. Jacques, running on with one of the fire buckets they kept all over the theater, had put out the flames but skidded and joined the others on the floor. Murrough, still with a sword hilt sticking out of his stomach, was cursing the lot of them in tones reminiscent of Jonah addressing Sodom and Gomorrah.

'It is a comedy?' Félicie asked hopefully.

'No,' Makepeace told her and called, 'Are you hurt, Bracey?'

Bracey said she was not; in a high, steady voice she also announced she was too old for this and that the play, Murrough and the Society for the Abolition of Slavery could all go and fuck themselves.

'It'll be all right,' Makepeace said. 'The worse the dress rehearsal, the better the first night.' Polly Armitage had told her this. She didn't believe it.

She organized orange girls, water- and program-sellers, ticket-takers, lamplighters, ushers—all hired from Drury Lane, which had closed for the summer. She was thankful for the hundred emergencies the day threw up to be diverted from the letter in her pocket, but a sense of impending doom stayed with her.

The best efforts of the pie shop were wasted. Even the dancers whose slim frames concealed enormous appetites—their arrival had almost doubled her costs—refused to eat, though the chief ballerina said she could be revived with cold soup in the interval. Of the rest, nobody but Luchet, Jacques, Marie Joséphine, young Henri d'Abreville and one or two of Marquis de Barigoule's musicians would touch the food. In the female walkers-on's dressing room she was waved away. The men's was the same; Comte de Penthémont had been given one line. Once ruler of a million French acres, whose sword had only ceased defending his king when the hand holding it had been cut off, he was crouched over a sick bowl audibly regretting that his head hadn't gone with it.

The professionals were no better. Trotting into Murrough's dressing room with her tray, Makepeace encountered a stare of such black hatred that she trotted out again.

Front of house reported that ticket sales were slow. With fifteen minutes to curtain up, there were less than two hundred people in a theater built to seat over a thousand. The only heartening thing was Jenny walking into the foyer with Sanders, who'd gone to Clapham to take her back to Reach House. 'Stephen said I might come, Mama. And I was to wish you *bonne chance* on his behalf in order to prove he is not the curmudgeon you may think him.'

Suppressing the desire to ask who was Stephen Heilbron to tell her daughter what she might and might not do, Makepeace kissed her and said she was grateful, which she was. Aaron hopped in on his crutches a few minutes later, and Chadwell was in attendance, too.

The boxes having been reserved by Blanchard's party, uncle and niece were sat in the stalls near the front. Makepeace told Sanders and Chadwell to find themselves seats—there were likely to be plenty to choose from—when the performance began but until then to stand by. 'Expecting trouble, missus?' Sanders wanted to know.

'Maybe.' The sense of disaster to come was so strong that the panic-cum-excitement she discovered backstage seemed as artificial as the play about to be performed. She might have been with savages worshipping in their sacred grove. Ninon and Chrissy crouched in prayer on a rug in the wings, and Mrs Jordan was muttering an incantation. The sensible Bracey was playing a grim and ritual pat-a-cake against Jacques's borrowed back.

Murrough, fixed and cold, was striding up and down the stage, clutching a bust of Molière, disregarding the dancers who practiced their pirouettes around him. When Makepeace crept by him to peer out through the curtains and count the audience, he woke up and almost threw her into the wings.

'What did I do?'

'It's bad luck,' Bracey said, still pat-a-caking.

Their superstitions defeated her; no whistling, no mention of *Macbeth* or Queen Anne. 'Can I wish you good luck?'

'No.' Murrough had come off stage. 'Go and watch the bloody *play*.'

It would be the first time; she'd been too busy to get other than glimpses of it at rehearsal and these had been so repetitious or so fractured as to be charmless.

As she took her seat, Aaron congratulated her on the auditorium. 'Very stylish. I've heard favorable comments.'

It does look nice, she thought. The enormous chandelier gave it an opulence without spreading light to the ceiling's small deficiencies; instead it gave the effect of a cluster of stars concentrated in a night sky. She wished it excited her more.

Aaron sniffed appreciatively. 'There's nothing like the theater's smell. Sets the old blood tingling.'

She envied him. All that the combination of fish glue, wood and paint did for her at this moment was make her feel sick.

The theater was fuller than it had been; there were only a few spare seats in the stalls. But the gallery boxes—known to the cast for reasons she'd preferred not to inquire into as 'spittoons'—were empty, as was the upper gallery with its benches for what the actors called 'the unwashed.'

'Don't worry,' Aaron said. 'They'll fill up at halftime at half price.'

'Stupid system. How can latecomers keep up with the plot?'

'If that curtain doesn't go up in a minute they'll know how it starts.' They were running late. Aaron had to hold his sister back from going to see if an emergency had arisen, but just then the huge chandelier was lowered. The lamplighters used their snuffers quickly—she'd made them practice again and again—leaving only a few strategically-placed lanterns. There was a murmur of surprise from the audience.

The back of the Marquis de Barigoule's head appeared just above the pit wall. He tapped his music stand and took his orchestra into the overture. He'd arranged a selection of popular tunes shame-lessly borrowed from other productions. The audience seemed to like it; being tone deaf herself she could only judge by the sway of others' feet.

'He should've taken a bow,' Aaron whispered.

'He's afraid of being recognized. All the exiles are.'

Aaron looked around. 'Who by? Nobody here'd know him from Adam.'

It was a sore point; there were enough émigrés in London to fill the Roman Colosseum and Makepeace had suggested to hers that, should there be sufficient seats, their friends be allowed in at reduced price. The offer had been rejected. French aristocrats did not accept charity from a lower class. Nor, while all of them might have to ac-cept menial work, did they want to see each other doing it. Yet, watching de Barigoule's bobbing *perruque* as he conducted, Make-peace felt a flush of affection for them. They irritated her, she could well understand the hatred they'd inspired in their serfs, they were cack-handed, unused to work, but there wasn't one who'd given short measure in anything she'd asked them to do. *Except Luchet*, she thought. But then, Luchet wasn't one of them—something they'd made very plain.

She saw him at that moment; the tutor was ushering a glittering Félicie into her box. Damn the man; he ought to be backstage help-ing Jacques. And damn Blanchard and his party; twenty or more of them, all beautifully dressed, all talking at unmodulated pitch, call-ing for service from the orange girls, bickering over the number of programs the usher was handing to them.

Around Makepeace, the audience stirred. From the comments, it seemed partly irritated at the interruption, partly impressed by the interrupters.

The Marquis de Barigoule lowered his baton and the music stopped as he stared up impassively at the latecomers.

'M'apologies, Orpheus.' It was Blanchard's voice. 'We're settled now—start again.'

'Out for trouble,' Aaron murmured.

'What do I do?'

He shrugged.

'That's Sir Boy Blanchard,' somebody said. 'He's a friend of the Prince of Wales.'

He would be, thought Makepeace.

De Barigoule tapped his stand again, the music began.

Being sat down for the first time that day, weariness overtook her. She hadn't yet shown Jenny nor Aaron the note from Ffoulkes; let them enjoy the play first—if enjoyment was to be had.

She was jerked to attention. A shrill and discordant shriek of brass cut through the music, causing it to stop. A voice equally as harsh on the ear cried, 'Hear me, you people, before ye take the downward step to vice and misery. Listen to the blast of the Lord and not to these debauchers . . .'

The Reverend Deedes had brought a trumpet that he was waving and a box he was standing on before the orchestra wall. 'Go home,' he was shouting, 'go to your prayers. Countenance not the filth of mountebanks unfit for Christian burial . . .'

Makepeace stood up, looking for Sanders but he was already on the move, Chadwell after him.

'. . . ye will be damned that watch as surely as these emissaries of the devil that perform Satan's works.'

Sanders grabbed one of the man's arms, Chadwell the other, pulling him off his box. He went limp so that he had to be dragged to the side exit, still yelling, under a shower of oranges thrown by Blanchard's party and cheers from other sections, though whether for Deedes or his expellers was uncertain.

Aaron clung on to Makepeace's shoulder. 'Sit down. He's gone.'

'I'm going to slit his throat.'

'You're not. Sit down.'

For the third time, the Marquis raised his baton and started the overture. Few heard it; the theater was in uproar. Some people were leaving. Most were staying to see if there was more fun to come.

Gradually, the music and then the dancers calmed things down a little but the auditorium was still restive when Polly Armitage came on to speak the prologue and he was given a hard time of it, especially by the Blanchard boxes.

By then Makepeace didn't care. Not content to take Philippa and Andrew away from her, the Lord was manifesting a dozen fists with which to knock her from one side of the arena to the other in punishment for stepping into it in the first place. She had wasted her money, her time and this sad company's efforts. In the flurry of the last weeks, she had forgotten their purpose. The slave and her child stood before her, real and stark, against the tawdry background she had prepared for them.

I'm sorry, I'm so sorry.

Aaron nudged her.

She was surrounded by silence. Blanchard's voice, amused, trying to urge his companions into jeers, was being ignored and trailing away. The curtain had drawn sideways and up in the effect Murrough had wanted and Jacques had achieved, so that she was looking at a picture, no, through the porthole of a ship taking her in to a foreign shore. The sunlight was not from lamps or an English summer, but a thicker, hotter light, infusing color into strange foliage.

The curtain was gone now, she was drawn in, the ship had landed her on scorching sand. Either her eyes were tricking her nose or Jacques had concocted a blend of aromatic grasses for his hot plates that sent out the smell of raffia and spices. From the depth of the jungle at the back of the beach came the wail of a pan-pipe and the insistent beat of a drum.

She was where she had never been before.

It was odd to hear English spoken, and the setting gave emphasis to the two young women—Chrissy, very pretty; Ninon, very dashing in young man's attire—in their plot to hunt out and capture husbands from the unsuspecting wildlife. It didn't matter that Ninon regretted in a French accent the fact that they'd had to leave their native London in order to do it. Here, everything was strangeness and expected to be so.

Makepeace heard Aaron draw in a deep breath. 'That's my woman.'

Even when the Widow Lackitt hustled on, familiar in her sex-starved monstrosity and causing laughter, one was not allowed to forget that she wasn't the only man-eater in this wilderness and that other predators lurked in the grasses.

How have they done it? Makepeace wondered. Flat forgettable words on a page, a ridiculous plot, had been dilated into three dimensions and given substance. This was not a life reflecting hers nor anyone's in the audience but a glimpse of demigods and goddesses flirting and bickering and deceiving each other in a Caribbean Olympus.

And she had derided them.

Was that Polly Armitage, who fainted into the arms of his male lover in a pretence of overwork at the end of the day, this square-jawed, iron-headed bastard of a governor? Yes, it was—because he said he was. Could Dizzy, an inveterate gambler and pain in the backside, be dependable Blandford, that hero and friend to the slaves? Yet he was, because Dizzy said he was.

Here was skill, more than skill. Insubstantial dross was being transmuted into insubstantial gold. She was watching alchemy.

A pillar of ebony seven foot tall strode onto the stage and Makepeace knew that, like the Queen of Sheba at the sight of Solomon, behold, the half was not told her. A woman sitting behind her gasped, 'Oh, my.'

A red robe had been wrenched off one shoulder showing gleaming black muscles, the creature's feet griped at the boards like prehensile hands as it paced restlessly back and forth on the end of its chain. It should not be chained; splendor like this was masterless.

Makepeace and Murrough had argued over the play. 'It's not about slavery,' she'd said, 'it's about one exceptional slave.

Oroonoko's a prince, he's as contemptuous of his fellow slaves as any white man.'

'He's the spirit of Africa,' Murrough had said. 'It may not be the great play but, by God, I'll show our temerity in enslaving a continent.'

And by God he's doing it, Makepeace thought as she watched. Africa stood there on stage. The shame of capture was not Oroonoko's but that of the colorless pigmies who'd inflicted it on him.

From that moment the play was Murrough's, in his mouth uninspired lines became the deep cry from a million yoked throats. The laughter of the audience at the antics of Widow Lackitt was near frantic because it knew they were mere interludes in something terrible. Even in the romantic moments of Ninon and Chrissy and their swains, it was kept aware of the pulse of Oroonoko's blood by a barely audible but unceasing drumbeat.

And there was another continual presence, this time silent—a thin black woman and her child, unacknowledged by the other characters yet always onstage, sometimes driven by whips from one side of it to another, sometimes curled in a corner, never leaving hold of each other, watching tragedy and comedy with the same dull faces.

When Murrough had told her the Countess d'Arbreville and Henri were on the payroll at the highest rate, she'd demurred. 'They don't have speaking parts.'

'The loudest,' he'd said.

The audience wasn't allowed to forget the two figures; they were the heart of the matter. The broken heart. She couldn't bear to look at them.

At the interval Aaron turned on his sister with the greatest compliment of one impresario to another—envy. 'They're doing you proud,' he said.

'Shall I go to them?'

He shook his head. 'Let 'em keep the bit between their teeth.'

Jenny said, 'I can't bear it, Ma. What do they do to Oroonoko? What will happen to the woman and the little boy?'

'They aren't in the script.'

They walked out to the foyer to listen for compliments. 'Wonderful!' 'Isn't he magnificent?' 'My dear, I've been transported!'

Makepeace thought of the letter in her pocket; even enchantment couldn't make problems go away.

In the street outside, a crowd had gathered to buy the half-price tickets for the rest of the performance and was growing as passersby were attracted to the unmistakable buzz of success. The doorman was bringing it up to date on the plot so far. 'He may be a savage but he's more Christian than those what caught him. They've got his poor wife an'all, an' she's going to have a baby an' I don't know what's a-going to happen . . .'

Snuffy Throgmorton was struggling through the crowd followed by a footman with a tray of ices for Blanchard's party. 'Fine play, Mrs Hedley. Makes one sorry the pater ever invested in West Indies sugar.'

She glowed. 'Does it? Does it really?'

'Too late now, though.' He put his head down to hers. 'No news of . . . I suppose?'

'No.'

'She'll be all right. Ffoulkes pushin' that end and Blanchard pullin' this end, can't fail.'

A little man was tugging at her sleeve; she couldn't think why her heart sank at the sight of him.

'A fine musical entertainment, Mrs Hedley, a truly splendid concert.' He winked at her and with the excitability of a convert tore across a piece of paper he had in his hand. 'Had it been a play, I should have presented you with this, but no, no, the dancing . . . the songs . . . most musical, most musical. The Lord Chamberlain will be so informed.'

'We're legal?'

'Yes.'

He was lying, bless him; they both knew it. This was a play with songs and dances and Murrough had incorporated them in order to enhance the story, not interrupt it. A love song that had no purpose in the original script, where it had been inserted for its own sake, he'd given to Ninon to sing apparently as part of her seduction of Widow Lackitt, but in fact, achingly, to the man she'd fallen for. When the players exited, leaving the stage empty except for the figures of the slave and her child, dancers rose from the undergrowth like plants come alive and curled back into the grass when they came on again.

Makepeace went back to her place. Félicie, she saw, like the rest of the audience, was settling for the second half even before the third bell was rung.

Jacques's lanterns were darker now, the drum beat faster; the native Indians were becoming dangerous. Imoinda was reunited with her husband and again torn from him.

On paper, Makepeace had thought her a ninny. 'She's always swooning or weeping. I'd have kicked that damn governor in his credentials.'

'I've no doubt ye would,' Murrough said, 'but you've never known slavery.'

Under his direction, Betty Jordan played Imoinda as a young Amazon, a bow in her hand, a quiver of arrows on her back, a princess of the forest, bewildered into naiveté by the disaster come upon her. Her scenes with Oroonoko widened the audience's eyes at the palpitating physicality of their love for each other. For this savage Romeo and Juliet, clothes were another enslavement they would have got rid of if they could.

'Oh, my,' whispered Makepeace's neighbour as Imoinda struggled free of her captors to run across the stage and jump on Oroonoko, wrapping her legs around him and taking his face between her hands.

Aaron murmured, 'Thanks be the Reverend Deedes ain't here.'

But Makepeace's shock was at the strong preference she felt at that moment for slitting Mrs Jordan's throat rather than the Reverend Deedes's. *Leave him alone. He's mine.*

Dear God, was that how she felt about him? An actor? An Irishman? Two unreliable personae rolled into one? Look at him; how could you feign passion like that? He was projecting the lust he showed in her bed. Or perhaps he feigned it there, too. Either way he was betraying her. Heilbron was right; capturing the audience's pity for the silent slave and her son was showmanship. It degraded the reality.

And I'm degrading me, she thought, sitting here and slavering for that swine. I am a middle-aged woman; I've been many things but a slut wasn't one of them. He's made me one.

Her husbands had been nice men; the excitement she'd experienced with them had been lambent in mutual trust, not this dark and unedifying dependence. In company, she was distant to him—a drunkard pretending to ignore the beckoning bottle. At nights she could hardly wait for him to open her bedroom door. He was her drug; when the ecstasy wore off, she foreswore it. Never again. Until the next time.

'Nobody must know,' she'd say to him.

'I know.' An answer that was equivocal, like everything else about him.

Of course he'd slept with Jordan, *look* at them. *Lay off, you bitch, you bitch. He's mine.*

The light onstage flickered; a far-off roll of thunder was one of Jacques's cannonballs rolling down a chute with a lining of wool. She knew this; it was a trick; she'd seen it, but the approaching storm carried a menace that raised the hairs on her arms.

Then the terrible end came. Thunder cracked the ears. As Imoinda assisted Oroonoko's dagger into her belly and the child she carried in it, there was a whoosh of protest from the audience.

We've gone too far, Makepeace thought.

But Oroonoko's grief held them. '*Soft, lay her down, we will part no more.*' Nobody moved. There was another sigh—this time of good-riddance—when the evil governor fell to the same dagger.

Silence as Dizzy spoke the last lines over Oroonoko's body. Silence as the actors waited for applause on their corpse-strewn stage.

They don't like it.

Silence as the curtain came down. Silence as Murrough came from behind it to give the epilogue. Which had been changed from the apologia Southerne had written for it to Cowper's poem, 'The Negro's Complaint.'

'It's doggerel,' she'd said.

'Not the way I'll do it,' he told her.

> '*Is there, as you sometimes tell us,*
> *Is there One who rules on high;*
> *Has He bid you buy and sell us,*
> *Speaking from His throne, the sky?*

In this mouth the hip-hopping lines became a howl of accusation. Behind him the slave mother and her son walked on quietly, hand in hand.

> *Ask Him if your knotted scourges,*
> *Fetters, blood-extorting screws,*
> *Are the means which duty urges,*
> *Agents of His will to use?*

From the wings appeared two of the hooded slavers who had sailed Oroonoko and Imoinda from Africa to Surinam. One took the mother by the shoulder, the other took the child—quite gently, ritually—and led them off, the woman to the right, the little boy to the left. For a moment their black pleading arms could be seen stretching towards each other from the opposing wings before they disappeared.

Aaron told Makepeace later that it was almost a minute before the cheers began. She didn't notice. Neither did the woman next to her; she'd abandoned wiping her eyes and had spread her handkerchief over her chest to let the tears flow as they would.

There were twenty-two curtain calls, Aaron said, and fifteen of those broke with tradition when Murrough commanded the entire cast to come on rather than allowing the leading actors to hog the applause. Aaron said Countess d'Abreville and Henri, black mother, black child, who hadn't spoken a word, received the greatest cheer. People were still crying, he said.

'Better now?' he asked her.

'Yes.'

'Not like you to break down.'

Ah, but he hadn't seen the real thing, only the representation of it. *Yet that will do,* she thought. *It's as near as we can get.*

They were waiting for her on stage when she finally made her way to it. All of them, looking at her.

They're expecting me to make a speech, she thought, to tell them how wonderful they were. She opened her mouth and lifted her arms, trying to find the words and found none that could reach even the edges of how wonderful they had been.

She dropped her arms, closed her mouth and shook her head.

'She's speechless,' Dizzy shouted. 'That's how bloody good we were. The missus is speechless.'

They carried her in triumph to the Green Room.

She'd laid on champagne for them with cold salmon and cucumbers, game and salad, wondering in what mood they would eat it and drink it, and was glad now that she had at least been prepared to honor them for hard work. Abandoning economy, she'd also laid out a purse, known in the theater as 'a firing,' of double wages for each one. It seemed scanty in view of a triumph that might well, given good reviews and word of mouth, run long enough to make a profit. Oh well, she could always add more purses.

Speechlessness could not prove sufficient congratulation for long; actors, apparently, needed complimenting again and again. Bracey, you were so funny. Jacques, there never was such thunder. Monsieur Luchet, the songs were very, very pretty. Yes, Dizzy, I could have hated you, I nearly did, you were astounding. Monsieur le Comte, the scenery was alive. No, Countess, nobody could have recognized you but you should consider the stage as a career. And you, Joseph . . . Ninon, my *dear* girl . . . Henri . . . Thank you, thank you.

She became smeared with makeup from their kisses, pink, white and black. She watched them dwindle into everyday and wondered at the artistry that could raise them out of it, grateful to her boots for it.

This wasn't being fair. Gritting her teeth, she approached Mrs Jordan.

'Betty . . .'

'I was good, wasn't I?'

'You were marvellous.'

'It's Sir Mick, of course. He carried us all to the heights.' The actress regarded her straitly. 'I hope you know what you've got in that man.'

What did she mean? 'I hope I do. He acts and directs extremely well.'

She hadn't congratulated him yet. Looking round, she saw that he'd gone. She found him in his dressing room, sitting in front of the looking glass, wiping off burnt cork with oiled wool and bewailing the effect on his complexion. He looked up at her reflection.

'Thank you,' she said.

'Thank *you*.' He patted a stool beside him and she went and sat on it, watching him. 'D'ye love me best when I'm black? Or white?'

'As long as it's not parti-colored,' she said. 'You've left a bit by your ear.' Her nails cut into her palms with the effort of not mentioning Mrs Jordan. I won't, I *won't*. She said, 'The scenes between you and Betty were very affecting, very realistic.'

'The woman's a fine actress.' He stretched. 'And I'm the greatest actor and wouldn't Shakespeare have worshipped me? Didn't I take that sow's ear of a play and turn it into something they'll tell to their grandpups?'

'Yes.'

'And made the buggers think?'

'You did that, too,' she said.

'You've been crying.'

She nodded. He was drunk, on champagne, on achievement . . .

He said, casually, 'You do love me, you know.'

'Do I?'

'And I'll tell you somepin', Makepeace Hedley. I've known a lot of women and I've loved a lot of women, some of them me wives, but there wasn't one I found weeping because a slave's child had been taken away from her.' He swiveled round to face her. 'It was your play, missus.'

The door of the dressing room hit the wall as it was flung open to allow revelers in. 'Come on, come on, there's more champagne. We've got guests.' The guests had already followed them into the room.

'The Lady Félicie wants to meet the black buck she's been droolin' over all night,' Blanchard said. 'And there he is. My good sir, what a performance—not a dry seat in the house. When he has time, Pellew here's going to send to have all his slaves in Jamaica released immediate, ain't you, Kit?'

With it all, he managed to sound charming and nobody except Makepeace was listening to him anyway; he and Félicie and the others were hauled into a wild celebration that threatened to go on all night.

When it became too wild, Makepeace decided to save an exuberant Jenny from herself and ordered all those who wanted a ride back to Reach House to the coach. Murrough declared himself in need of beauty sleep and came with them. Only Luchet could not be inveigled from the presence of Félicie and was left to spend the night in the theater.

With her arm round Jacques, who'd nodded off to sleep on her shoulder, Makepeace spent the journey listening to Aaron and Murrough perform a postmortem on the play and wondering if she had the strength to take Ffoulkes's letter out and show it to Philippa's sister and uncle, adding their concern to her own.

As it turned out, that effort was left to the next day. When the coach drew up at the front door, Hildy was waiting for her.

John Beasley had died that afternoon.

Chapter Fourteen

Lord Ffoulkes was aggrieved. 'That wasn't very nice,' he said.

'It wasn't meant to be,' Philippa said. 'What are you doing here, anyway? Rescuing somebody? In which case, go away and do it.'

'I'm rescuing you, blast you. I don't think I will now.'

'Good.'

Since it was likely to be a long and heated one, Ffoulkes had expressed a need to have this conversation where nobody could overhear it and, if possible, sitting down. 'Tirin' work, limpin' all the time and I've been hoverin' all day in Rue Saint Honoré—do you know how many portrait painters there are in that damn street? Kept bumpin' into Robespierre. Congratulated me on fightin' for the Republic, bless him. If I hadn't spotted you comin' out of the petticoat shop, he'd have taken me home for tea.'

He'd arrived in Paris only that morning, having taken a diligence as far as Neuilly where he'd changed into his old soldier's garb at a safe house then walked through the dawn into the city.

The two of them had crossed to the Left Bank and the Luxembourg Gardens, a tic of irritation twitching in Philippa's cheek at every click of Ffoulkes's stick. She nursed her aggravation against a man sent to fetch her home as if she were a child skipping off school.

They found a bench away from the trees with a long view in either direction and sat down, sweating under the exposure of the late afternoon sun. 'You've worried the missus horribly,' Ffoulkes told her in English. 'Goin' off like that, not a word. She was frantic.'

Philippa stuck to French. 'Then go back and tell her I am safe and well. I shall return with Nicolas when he's finished his book.' And was instantly aware that she sounded childish, as did Condorcet. It made her crosser.

He expired. 'God save us. Has anybody pointed out to the mad old goat that this is no time to write his memoirs? You're coming home with me, Pippy. Now.'

'No. Go back to your wife.'

He thumped his stick on the ground with both hands, which, she saw, were suitably calloused and had broken nails as befitted a conscript soldier. He'd always had nice hands; still had, despite the wear of their disguise. She felt the need to punish him for having nice hands.

'You look ridiculous in that beard,' she said, 'And I can see the glue.' *Dear, dear, more childish by the minute.*

'Skin trouble if anybody asks,' he said. 'Pip, stop it.'

The Luxembourg Gardens, like the Tuileries, were surprisingly well kept. Now that they were open to the public, they were required to be in the same order that the palace's owners had previously enjoyed. The first roses were coming into bloom and a gardener was weeding one of the beds.

Yet the Terror was here; you couldn't get away from it. The huge paling fence that hid the lower half of Marie de Medici's palace, a reminder that the place was now a prison, took away symmetry, making incongruous the children floating paper boats on the lake, their watching, chatting mothers nearby. Beneath its bulbous slate roofs, prisoners' faces lined the upper windows like wilting poppies. At nights their friends gathered on this side of the fence to shout and receive messages.

'Had some rare times there in the good old days,' Ffoulkes said, breaking the silence, 'Look at it now.'

'Good old days,' she repeated harshly. But she was defending the indefensible; at nights the calls going back and forth between the free and the condemned carried to the Street of the Gravediggers. They sounded like the cry of nightjars and kept her awake.

'Time to go home, Pippy,' he said.

'No.'

He began urging her, the professional pointing out dangers to the amateur. She could tell she shocked and puzzled him; he was trying to reassess her but he couldn't get beyond their old relationship and stayed patiently in his role as friendly, amused and amusing godfather.

That won't do for Jeanne Renard, she thought.

'Come on,' he said, getting up. 'I'd better see the old boy for myself. Where do we go?'

She stayed where she was. She didn't want him to meet Condorcet. He would intrude on Mme Vernet and the orderliness of Number Fifteen, contemptuous of it, unsettling it, unsettling *her*.

'For all that's holy, Pip. What's got into you?'

But, of course, there was a better, a *vital* reason to keep him away—she was amazed she'd forgotten it. 'Did you tell your friend Blanchard where Condorcet is?' she asked.

'I don't *know* where he is, do I?' His stick hit the path, making gravel fly. He forced himself to quieten. 'You're all *right*, are you, Philippa?'

'*Je n'ai pas mes règles à ce moment*,' she told him, shocking him further. Menstruation was mentioned in whispers, if at all—and then only to other women. 'Did you tell Blanchard where Sophie is?'

'Good God, girl, I can't remember. One was in something of a rush. I might have mentioned Rue Saint Honoré. What's that got to do with the price of fish?'

'Because if you told him, he'll tell the Committee of Public Safety.' She repeated what Condorcet had told her.

'Sir Boy Blanchard, informer to the Frogs.' He was grinning. 'And I'm the Queen of the May.'

'I don't care,' she said, 'Condorcet's been safe for nearly nine months where he is, I'm not risking him now. I hope you've got somewhere to stay because I'm not taking you to him while you've got friends like Blanchard. '

He was still amused. 'Thank you for asking, ma'am. As a matter of fact The League's got a cozy little house not far from here. Belongs to a graphite dealer—that's me in my other *chapeau*, incidentally.'

'Let's go there.'

'What?'

'You say Blanchard knows about the house. Let us go there. See if anybody's watching it.' It was the only test for proof she could think of.

'My dear girl . . .' But he was prepared to show her how deranged she was, so they walked out into Rue Vaugirard—almost past the mouth of Gravediggers Street before they turned left then right, down the hill, Ffoulkes's stick striking sparks from cobbles laid on the foundations of a castle built by Philippe Auguste, that greatest of England's enemies.

In a sense, it was still in the hands of Britain's enemy. It was the Revolution's seed bed; the Cordeliers Club, rival to Robespierre's Jacobins, was in the next street; farther down the hill were the homes of Danton, Desmoulins and the late Marat.

But it was a softer Revolution that had been spawned here and Philippa always felt less oppressed in its midst than on the Right Bank. Here Sanson's tumbrels couldn't negotiate alleys and corners that might have been crazed into the hill by gigantic, drunken snails. If they did, their vibration would bring down palsied houses that leaned on buttresses and each other for support and from which caged canaries sang on balconies trailed with ivy and washing.

He made her cling on to his arm like a soldier's woman—the first time she'd touched him except with the pail—and pressed on his stick with the other, grumbling through his beard about army generals for the benefit of passersby. She could hear the tension in his voice; he was the one irritated now. He refused to believe that Blanchard was an informer but the assertion had disturbed him.

In the Rue de la Liberté, he nudged her and cocked his head towards the ancient, engraved medallion on the corner that declared that it had once been Rue Monsieur-le-Prince. She found herself smiling back at him; this was the territory of students, writers, lawyers, journalists, publishers and academics, people who knew that history was ineradicable and lived more easily with its royal manifestations than did the rest of Paris.

When he'd nudged her, she'd felt moving muscle as hard as wood beneath his sleeve. *No*, she told herself. *Stop it. Be free of him.* 'What have you been doing to get your hands in that state?'

'Digging turnips.'

'Ah yes, the honeymoon.' Damn it, she must not slide backwards into jealousy and heartbreak, the emotional paraphernalia she'd been glad to leave behind. Stay free of it. 'I hope Félicie enjoyed turnip-digging.'

'Can't say her heart was in it,' he said. 'No appreciation of life's pleasures, that one. You know this is damn ridiculous, don't you?'

She was afraid that it was but *if* Blanchard had betrayed her, he would also have to betray Ffoulkes. He must view the knowledge Condorcet had of him as an infection that had been passed on to her and from her to Ffoulkes. The man could not allow them to ruin him by bringing it back to England where he would be damned as a traitor. She supposed it all depended on whether he put his friend's life above his own. From her experience of the man, she doubted it.

Of course, he would have had to have acted quickly and so would the Committee of Public Safety if it was to have laid a trap outside The League's Paris lair. But Ffoulkes had come by the long route of Babbs Cove to Gruchy. Blanchard could have sent his letter or his agent the quickest way, via Dover to Calais.

Oh, God, he might even have come himself.

'There it is.' They were approaching a shaded alley leading off the other side of the road. 'House on the corner. A small thing but we call it home.'

She made him pause while she inspected the place from across the way. It was safe enough to do it; the lane they were in was congested with people, some looking up to where a poet was declaiming his ode to the Republic from the overhanging window of a café, some listening encouragingly to a mother who was dictating a letter for her soldier son to a street scribe. A man leading a donkey cart down the narrow street was having a sweaty altercation about his right of way with two others who were rolling barrels up it. The noise was such that she and Ffoulkes could confide into each other's ears, like lovers, without behind overheard.

From what she could see of the house, The League had chosen well. There was a front door leading into the alley and a side door that gave on to the street she was in. A window above a gable showed that there was yet another escape route, this one leading to adjoining roofs.

Ffoulkes's beard tickled her ear. 'Satisfied? Can't ask you in, sadly. Have to change into my business clothes. Old soldiers ain't expected to call in on graphite importers. I'm away at the moment, in Canada, negotiating for some. Graphite's good business, actually; I'm thinking of going into it in real life.'

'Mmm.' It looked well enough but from here she couldn't see down the alley; there might be a dozen watchers in its depths. If there were, did they have Ffoulkes's description? On the other hand, even she hadn't recognized him at first. 'Let's just walk past the door, make sure.'

'God Almighty.' But he crossed the street with her and they ambled into the alley together. It was rather charming; a dusty but willing fig tree splayed shadow over the dipped stones. The narrow terraced houses on both sides prickled with signs displaying the trade carried on in their ground floors—a huge, leather boot, a barber's pole, an enormous pair of spectacles. Down the far end, at a small smithy, a horse was being shod, its reins attached to a ring in the wall, watched by a man in shirtsleeves sitting on a bucket. They might have stepped into a tiny village.

Philippa felt silly; the place was a cul-de-sac—by entering and leaving they would attract suspicion. Then she thought, I've lived in fear too long. Ordinary people aren't suspicious.

Ffoulkes solved the matter by advancing towards the man on

the bucket. 'Hey, *copain*, where in hell's the bloody section house around here?'

'Next street, bottom of the hill.' The yelled exchange made the horse nervous and the man had to get up to help the smith calm it. '*Holà*, you bugger. *Holà*.'

They walked off, Philippa feeling silly. 'Well,' she said, defensively, 'there *could* have been somebody there.' As a recompense, she would have to take him home to Mme Vernet. There would be no danger in harboring him while he changed into his business clothes. *And I don't mind so much now. I don't want him to go. Damn.*

They went back up the hill, making for Gravediggers by cutting through the deserted square outside Saint Sulpice. As they crossed, he swerved and sat down on one of the benches.

'What is it? What's the matter?' she asked.

'There was,' he said.

'There was what?'

'Somebody there.' He looked up at her without seeing her. 'Fella on the bucket. He's a Sûreté man. Seen him before. Had to give him the slip once. Followed me and Snuffy Throgmorton through the length of Les Halles.'

'Are you sure?' She couldn't believe she'd proved her point, now couldn't bear it that she had.

'Bloody great mole on his upper lip.' He had a hand over his forehead and was gasping, like someone who'd just been sick. 'Jesus,' he said, 'Jesus God.'

Philippa sat down and put her arm round his shoulders, holding him close. An elderly woman came up to them, full of sympathy. '*Le pauvre. Un blessé de guerre?*'

'*Oui, madame.*' He was, after all, badly wounded. '*Mais il se port bien mieux maintenant.*'

'*Cette guerre, quelle peste, quelle peste.*' The woman walked away, shaking her head sadly.

After a while he managed to control his breathing but he still wouldn't move, just stared sightlessly at the Florentine frontage of the church—an ugly thing, Philippa had always considered. 'We ought to go,' she said gently. She had to get him indoors before Citizen Marcoz came home—it wouldn't do to load that conscience by presenting it with yet another man with a price on his head.

Ffoulkes got up at last and she guided him into the lane that crossed the bottom of Gravediggers, looked to see if the street was empty and tried to hurry him up the hill. They'd left his walking stick on the bench, she realized; just as well he'd forgotten it, since he didn't seem to be aware that he was walking at all.

She had to prop him against the wall, like a drunk, while she unlocked the wicket gate and went into the courtyard to see if Citizen Marcoz was in his lodge. The deputy kept his door key under a flowerpot by his door. It was still there; he wasn't home yet.

She returned to the street. Ffoulkes hadn't moved. 'Jesus God,' he said again.

'Get in,' she said, and pushed him through the wicket, holding his head down so that he didn't hit it, went in behind him and took him to Mme Vernet to be mended.

S HE had been afraid that he would interrupt the ordered tenor of life at Number Fifteen and he did—for her, at least.

Mme Vernet took him in her stride. There was, of course, little else she could do. Since this stranger knew of Condorcet's presence in her house, it was better that he, too, be sheltered in it rather than risk arrest by the National Guard while wandering the streets. Philippa had presented her with a fait accompli—he was here, the damage was done—but she accepted it gracefully.

She asked to interview Ffoulkes alone in the parlour, a session he later described as 'like being questioned by the Inquisition, without the thumbscrews.'

Afterwards, Philippa, who was preparing supper in the kitchen, heard her escort Ffoulkes upstairs. She waited with trepidation. When Mme Vernet came back, she began setting the table, only the pecking tic of her lips showing that she was disturbed. 'I have put your young man in the attic.'

'Not my young man,' Philippa said, hastily. 'A family friend. Madame, I am sorry. I didn't know what else to do.'

Mme Vernet ignored that. 'It appears that M Collet has aided others in avoiding execution,' she said.

'Collet?' From the first she had been anxious that her hostess be aware that she was taking in a guest equally as dangerous as Condorcet himself and had told her that he was English and a wanted man.

'Geoffre Collet, corporal, is the name on his papers,' Mme Vernet said without emphasis. 'I am required to know nothing more about him other than the fact that he helps to take those in danger out of the country.'

Philippa marvelled that Ffoulkes had told the woman that much. The boots of most of The League's clients had stamped too hard and too often on the faces of those they ruled to meet Mme Vernet's requirement of virtue. Perhaps he hadn't gone into detail.

Anyway, Mme Vernet, it appeared, was making the best of a bad job, her mouth pecked away at what could be salvaged. 'I have elicited his assurance that when the time comes he will assist both you and the gentleman upstairs to England and that until then he will do nothing to put us in further danger; he will not, in fact, leave the house.' For the first time, she sighed at the burden she carried. 'It will not be long, I believe. We are on our last chapter.'

Daringly and with gratitude, Philippa kissed her. Even more daringly, she teased her. 'Did you find him virtuous?'

Mme Vernet did not smile back. 'Competent,' she said.

In a way, Philippa decided, Mme Vernet was relieved that Condorcet would be in experienced hands when he went and, furthermore, in those of a man. For all that she upheld the ideal of liberty, fraternity and equality, for all that she could wipe the floor with most of the male sex, Mme Vernet still believed that men were the lords of creation and was happier to leave them in charge of it.

Nevertheless, there was no doubt that, while he remained,

Ffoulkes's presence had sharpened the knife edge on which the household balanced.

'He has retired for the night,' Mme Vernet said, 'He refuses supper. I suggest you take this tray up to M Condorcet and tell him about the new arrival.'

Ffoulkes might not have been hungry but he hadn't gone to bed. Nor did he. As she reached the landing with Condorcet's tray, Philippa could hear him pacing in his attic room above her. He was still pacing when she went to her own bed.

His world has changed, she thought. Betrayal was a wickedness that, for him, had existed only outside the enchanted circle in which he'd had his being. It was to be expected of lesser mortals, the French, the lower classes, politicians. But this plunge of the knife had come from Brutus. Now everything must be reassessed; school days, university, the adventure of The League, *especially* The League. When had the poison entered the bloodstream? How far had it spread?

Looking back on his behalf, Philippa saw a telltale stain that went back years; not betrayal as such, but perhaps the envy that had led to betrayal. She remembered that Blanchard had challenged Ffoulkes to a wager on almost everything—which raindrop would reach the sill first, how many apples on a coster's barrow—and won more times than not. If they played for something with the cut of a card, he'd won every time.

Cut you for it, Ffoulkes.

Trivial things sometimes, others not so trivial. In her presence Ffoulkes had lost a cricket bat to Blanchard and a loved pointer bitch. Snuffy Throgmorton had told her of a prize bull that had passed on the turn of a card and he'd wondered, though without suspicion, what the town-loving Blanchard could possibly want with such an animal.

Damn, Boy, not again. Bloody Monday, you've the devil's own luck.

Because Andrew, rueful, trusting, had not questioned his friend's honesty, she hadn't, either. What she *had* questioned was how a friend could dispossess another of valued things with such amused callousness. She had put it down to her own lack of understanding of the rough-and-tumble of an exclusively masculine playground.

He's jealous of everything Andrew has.

You knew, Ma.

And now he knows, too, she thought, listening to the floorboards of the room down the corridor crack and crack again as the pacing went back and forth.

Is that how it began? Had selling Ffoulkes's trust been the start of a glissade that led to selling people and, in the end, to selling Ffoulkes himself? Or had it been plain old lack of money, to keep up the style of life that other members of The League had inherited and Blanchard had not?

Don't feel sorry for him, she told herself. Yet how terrible to struggle in the mental quicksand that sucked at Blanchard every day. The man was his own punishment; he had imagination beyond anything Ffoulkes would ever experience. He'd recognized her love for Andrew and sympathized for a moment. Loved him, too, probably. And, with mud clogging his own nostrils, hated him for the innocence of the air he breathed.

He's killed people, sold them to their death, sold Andrew, sold you.

Let him roast in hell, she thought, and went to sleep.

T HE next morning Ffoulkes was offhand with her—as if it were her fault, as if, without feminine interference, he and Blanchard could have continued their old relationship. When Mme Vernet offered to take him to Condorcet's room and introduce him, he gave a stiff refusal. 'Perhaps later, madame.'

The old Philippa would have seethed inwardly, the new one waited until they were alone in the kitchen and faced him with his own illogic. 'It's not fair. You're blaming me and Condorcet. You'd rather have gone to the guillotine than know that Blanchard was prepared to send you there.'

He was furious. 'I don't know what's got into you. That's ridiculous.'

By the afternoon he was more reasonable. He begged Mme Vernet's pardon and asked humbly to be presented 'to the great man.'

Mme Vernet, being occupied in doing something interesting with beans and an onion, gave the job to Philippa.

As she tapped on Condorcet's door, they heard the verbal bookmark—'n equals nine is provable'—being put into place on the other side of it.

Ffoulkes rolled his eyes. She glared at him; she was nervous. It was necessary to her that the two most important men in her life should like each other—and she didn't see how they could. Ffoulkes was of the opinion that Condorcet was a dangerous weakling hiding behind women's skirts. She'd made it a condition of his tenancy in Number Fifteen that he be polite. 'If Mme Vernet is content with the situation, and I am, then it is nothing to do with you.'

As they went in, she had to admit that Condorcet did not show to his best. He was sitting in his *bergère* with his bad leg up on a stool, puffing at his pipe, for all the world like an idle old man with nothing better to do. Only the slate on his lap, covered with mathematical symbols in chalk, suggested a busy mind.

He was superb. 'Lord Ffoulkes, how charming. We've met before, of course. At the de Staëls', wasn't it? Sit down, my dear fellow. Forgive me for not getting up. I believe you know my old friend, Philip Stanhope. How is he? We were masters of our respective mints during the same years.'

Ffoulkes said he did indeed know the Earl of Chesterfield and that, last seen, he was well.

Philippa left them cantering together through fields of highborn acquaintances.

The two men remained talking until supper. Condorcet's was taken up to his room as usual; Ffoulkes would have been happy to have supped with him but as a matter of courtesy came down to be introduced to M Sarrett and to eat with the household.

It had been decided he should remain a soldier for the time being; if by chance Citizen Marcoz should discover him the story would be that Mme Vernet was employing this army veteran and had not yet had time to register him.

With his beard and worn carmagnole he looked outlandish in the small, cluttered and essentially bourgeois dining room but he'd regained his energy and manners and set himself out to make amends. He complimented his hostess on her beans, her hidden guest and her courage. 'Which shall be tested only a little longer, madame. M Condorcet tells me that he will be ready to leave in a week.'

'I told you not to harry him,' Philippa said. 'You promised.'

He swallowed a mouthful hurriedly. 'I did not harry him. For your information, he brought the subject up himself. The book's nearly finished, apparently. I'm going to read it.' An explanatory fork was waved at them, like an admonition. 'He's damn clever, you know. I was telling him, no good talking to me about mathematics, I said, they tried beating sums into my backside at Eton and failed. So he gave me this little book he's written for his daughter, *A Sure Method of Learning to Count*, he's calling it. I tell you, one chapter and I've mastered the decimal system. Lucid, that's what it is, lucid. Man's a genius.'

Mme Vernet's eye sought Philippa's and, amazingly, winked.

It's effortless, Philippa thought; *Nicolas doesn't even know he's doing it.*

For a moment she wondered what was wrong with her, then realized that for the first time in years she was . . . content. For that moment she was relaxed in body and mind. *I can enjoy the next seven days. And the journey home.*

Then, of course, it would stop. There she must pay duty on him and let him go. She, once the great planner for the future, would not think beyond that; perhaps she would return to England, perhaps she wouldn't. It didn't matter; what mattered was the next seven days.

In fact there were only five but they were the best of her life so far.

It was as if he had been enlarged. He'd always known that he was privileged and tried to alleviate the unfairness of that position by making life better for those who were not. He was a Rockingham Whig, even though Rockingham was dead and his radicalism out of fashion. His love for Makepeace, who'd become his unofficial guardian when he was seven, had introduced him to a wider philosophy, undreamed of by his fellow barons.

Nevertheless, he was rich, a peer and a man; his education in all those capacities had been to reinforce them. He'd recognized the need for improvement in France but the Revolution, when it came, had concerned him by, in his opinion, throwing the baby out with the bathwater; the masses needed good leadership, not equality. The Terror had only confirmed his fears.

Again, though Makepeace had given him a high opinion of women, his male friends formed the preserve in which he breathed most easily. The League had only made closer a bond that had been welded by the rigours of Eton and the depravities of university. Philippa, whom he counted his best woman friend, had known that she, along with his wives and the rest of the world, was merely peering over a fence at a Garden of Eden where Eve wasn't a problem because she wasn't there.

The serpent Blanchard, however, had been.

She watched him grapple with the knowledge, becoming grimmer but at the same time humbler. It was as if the breaking down of the fence had not only proved that it wasn't Eden in the first place but had allowed entrance to ideas and people that it had until then excluded.

Constancy became more valuable to him—in whatever form it took and whatever the class of person who displayed it. She realized he must be comparing Blanchard to Mme Vernet and her refusal to betray a man who was yet a comparative stranger to her; Blanchard to Condorcet, who had stayed loyal to a principle and would not vote for Louis's death though it meant his own; Blanchard even to herself who, though he might think it wrongheaded, was risking her head for a friend. Suddenly, those who'd been outside the magic fence were proving more valuable than one who had existed within it.

What he would *not* do was change towards her. It wasn't that she expected him to fall in love with her—there was no chance of that—

but she wanted some recognition that she was a woman of twenty-six and he a man of thirty-four.

She puzzled him; she knew that. She'd gone up in one part of his estimation but she'd come down in another. The tough speaker of her own mind, who called a spade a bloody spade, was not the composed and reticent girl he'd known, even less the clinging, delicate flower that was his ideal of femininity. Yet to him she remained his goddaughter, to be teased, placated, a child he wanted to stay on friendly terms with. It was as if he refused to let go of the old Philippa to recognize the new, finding some sort of safety in it, even a taboo.

Well, that was up to him; it was an irritant but she could do nothing about it. Being what men wanted her to be was another trammel she'd left behind in England. He could take her or leave her but damned if she'd be forced back into the mold he'd made for her; she hadn't come to France to be his pet dog.

'And you can make yourself useful while you're here,' she told him. 'There's the boots to clean and the silver needs polishing and while I'm out I'd be obliged if you'd take the clothes out of the washtub and put them through the mangle.'

'What in hell's a mangle? And what are you going to do?'

'I queue.'

In fact, Ffoulkes had brought money with him, sewn into his knapsack, and, while she queued in order not to arouse suspicion in those who'd shared queues with her in the past, she bought extras on the black market. It was a risk but the gain in everyone's health was not to be forgone.

When she got back it was all done, though the mangle—a monstrous and modern machine of which Mme Vernet was exceedingly proud—had given him trouble. 'Tried to eat my damn fingers,' he said. He pretended exhaustion and shame. 'Oh that I, a peer of the realm, am cleaning revolutionary boots. They'll never let me back into The Lords.' He tapped the pair belonging to Citizen Marcoz. 'You say our esteemed convention deputy knows Condorcet's hiding here?'

'Yes.'

'And hasn't given him away?'

'No. But you'd better make his boots shine.'

Ffoulkes found M Sarrett another oddity. He was a retired surveyor and a poet *manqué* who kept irregular hours and roamed the house in a fez, a velvet smoking jacket and turned-up Persian slippers, muttering and posing as the muse took him. Philippa liked him; he was kind.

He bewildered Ffoulkes. 'Is he a . . . you know?'

'No.'

'Oh.' That was a relief. 'Then are he and Mme Vernet . . . ?'

'Probably.'

'Oh.'

It was M Sarrett who went out for the newspapers every day and read them aloud to the company after dinner. The *Vieux Cordelier* was particularly hopeful that night. Desmoulins was advocating an end to the Terror.

'*Mon Dieu*, listen to this.' Sarrett had to get up to read it.

> ' "*Do you want to exterminate all your enemies by guillotine? But this would be madness. Can you destroy even one on the scaffold without making ten enemies from among his family and friends? Do you really believe it is women, old men, the feeble, the 'egoists' who are dangerous? Of your true enemies, only the cowards and the sick are left.*" '

He clasped the paper to his chest. 'That is Danton speaking. Desmoulins writes but it is Danton. *En avant, mon brave*. Let us begin the march towards sanity.'

He started to dance. Mme Vernet's eyes were closed and her hands clasped as if in prayer. Philippa made no bones about it. *Please*, she thought, *please, God*.

Then she noticed, because she was aware of every move he

made, that Ffoulkes wasn't joining in; he'd picked up one of the other newspapers and was reading it.

As they went up the stairs together that night, he said, 'I didn't say anything, but don't expect too much. They've challenged Robespierre; it's a straight fight now, Danton versus Robespierre. Robespierre will win.'

'But everybody loves Danton, even Robespierre. They're friends.' She saw his mouth twist and remembered the friend called Blanchard. She said, 'He's like de Vaubon, Ma's old partner; he's *human*, he makes people laugh.'

'The other papers have got a new word for him,' Ffoulkes said, '"*Indulgent*." It's code for anyone opposing the Terror. Danton's a human being, you're right, but, like the missus's smuggling friend, he's got human weaknesses. He's been lining his pockets with public money since the Revolution began. Robespierre can throw him to the wolves any time he finds it necessary. If the Paris mobs keep shouting for blood, it *will* be necessary. Desmoulins and de Vaubon'll go with him.'

She sat down on the stairs. 'I don't understand all this, I don't *understand*. Is it going to go on forever and ever?'

'Not according to our philosopher in there.' Ffoulkes jerked a thumb towards Condorcet's door. 'Sooner or later the mobs must quieten, the guillotine'll be packed away in lavender, Pitt and Robespierre will kiss and make up and we'll all live happily ever after. God, he's a fool.'

It was a new bitterness and, while she knew its cause, it had a clang of truth that sent her to bed in a hopelessness against which there was only one appeal.

She knelt on the bare floorboards of her room. *Let him be wrong, Lord. Let Condorcet be right. Let something wonderful happen. And, Lord, spare my mother's good friend, de Vaubon. Spare everyone in this dear house.*

The silence contained a negative. When she pinched out the

rushlight and opened the window to let in the night air, He sent her His answer through the cries of the prisoners in the Luxembourg.

She knew then that they weren't going to get away.

NUMBER Fifteen revived. It had become tired from the strain of keeping its secret; every sound of marching boots echoing down Gravediggers Road, coming closer, had stilled movement, stopped breath, until they went past. A sideways glance in the queue set the heart jumping, a word out of place from a neighbor had to be analysed.

Ffoulkes's energy fed it like a drooping plant. He tackled housework like a military maneuver, expounding theory and practice once he'd mastered them as if nobody had discovered the secret before. 'Look, you've got to allow the polish to *dry* first—comes off better then.' 'See, glasses need *very* hot water. By God, the housemaids better look out when I get home.' He made Mme Vernet laugh and she introduced him to the mystery of omelette making—he watched them eat the result with the ferocity of a midwife unsure that the baby's parents appreciated it.

For all that the man amazed and horrified him, it was Condorcet who intrigued him most and he spent the spare time between his duties and Condorcet's writing in the smoke-filled room.

'What do you two talk about?' she asked him.

'You, mostly. He's got a high regard for you, thinks you're as insane as I do. Women in general, really. Oh, and rights—got a lot to say about rights.'

Condorcet told him the Revolution had finally failed when the Convention closed down the women's clubs. 'It negated women's rights without seeing that it had negated its own,' he'd said. 'Rights must be universal and extended to every living soul—that is the meaning of the term. They cannot be delivered to one group and not another. If they are, they are not rights but privileges, and the purpose of the Revolution, my revolution, Philippa's Revolution, was to rid the world of the privilege of the few and extend rights to all.'

'Mad as May butter,' Ffoulkes told her. 'Do you know he wants women to have a vote?'

'Yes.'

'You do? But let's face it, old thing, what do you need it for? You ladies have all the power as it is, look at Mme Vernet, rules the roost here, don't she? And the missus? God help the man who tells her what to do. Look at Félicie, leads me around by a ring in my nose. What would you do with the vote?'

'Use it,' Philippa said.

On the third day he remembered Heilbron. He was helping her fold the sheets she'd brought in from the washing line, a matter of leaning back at their different ends to pull them into shape, come together, fold, back, come together, fold. 'Last time I saw you, madam, you'd just plighted your troth to a worthy gentleman. Did he sanction this little jaunt of yours?'

'He doesn't know about it.'

'*Pull*, woman. This side's not straight. I bet he does now.'

'I bet he does,' she said ruefully.

'Ends together.' They came close, transferred the ends and retired. 'What'll he say when I deliver you back to him?'

'I'm afraid he'll say I'm not a suitable wife for him.'

'And I don't blame him. Now, the next one, *pull*. It's like a minuet this, ain't it? What will you do then?'

'Oh . . . find another wittol to marry me. There's plenty of them about.'

He nodded. 'Well, I can't dance with you all day, I've got me cutlery to clean. It's smeary. I've had to talk to Mme Vernet on the subject.' As he left for the kitchen, he said, 'About Heilbron.'

'Yes?'

'He'd be an idiot.'

H E began to hate her leaving the house. 'Where the hell have you been?'

'I had to take Sophie some eggs.'

'You didn't have to take her anything. It's too bloody dangerous.'

'Oh, stop interfering.' She was tired; the tumbrels had been more crowded than ever that morning.

Furiously, he lectured her; he had a right to interfere; she wasn't to go again, not even to say good-bye. 'You can write her a letter from England. And wipe your feet before you step on my floor.'

That night, it was the fifth, the two of them were tidying the kitchen after supper. Mme Vernet, who had a cold, had gone upstairs, M Sarrett had folded his newspapers and followed her.

They heard Citizen Marcoz come in from his day at the Convention and then, as she always did, Philippa went out into the courtyard to bar the gate for the night.

It was one of those summer evenings when light is reluctant to fade and a near-full moon showed against the clarity of the sky like a pale replica of sun.

As she passed the rose on the wall, Philippa dead-headed a fading bloom and put the petals in the pocket of her apron—Mme Vernet didn't like them falling; she said it encouraged black spot.

She lifted the bar into its slots and turned to pick up the boots that Citizen Marcoz left outside the door of the lodge. And jumped—Citizen Marcoz was standing in the doorway.

'Citizeness.'

'You gave me a fright, citizen.'

He was in shadow and she couldn't see his expression. He cleared his throat; it sounded like gravel shifting. She thought, *he's nervous*. So was she; he'd never talked to her before.

He said, 'Today I was vouchsafed a sight of the list of houses to be searched for saltpetre. This house was on it, for tomorrow.' He cleared his throat again. There was a pause. Far away a dog barked. 'You should inform Mme Vernet. It is as well to be apprised of these things.'

From the Luxembourg the first cry of the night traveled through the warm air. 'Papa, Papa.' An answering shout, quite clear. 'I am here, my dear.'

'The Republic has need of saltpetre, citizeness,' Marcoz said.

She heard herself say, 'Yes. Yes, thank you.'

He shut the door and she ran for the house.

Ffoulkes fetched Mme Vernet and M Sarrett down to the kitchen.

Sarrett was in his nightshirt, a pink crochet shawl clutched round him for decency; with his fez still on he looked oriental and absurd. Mme Vernet hadn't undressed yet but her hair straggled over her shoulders; a hairbrush was still in her hand. For the first time since Philippa had known her she was distraught. 'Shall we tell him? Shall we tell him?'

'Of course, we've got to tell him,' Ffoulkes said, then more gently, 'The time's come, Madame. You knew it would.' He turned to Philippa. 'When will they be here?'

'I don't know. Tomorrow was all he said.'

'Is it just this house? Do they know about Condorcet? Or a general search of the area?'

'I don't know, I don't know.'

Saltpetre, that essential ingredient of gunpowder, grew in crystallised form in dank, dark places, on cellar walls, in outbuildings. The demand for it was pressing, and patriotic Parisians, finding it on their property, were happy to do their bit for the war by alerting the authorities so that it could be scraped off and delivered to the munitions factories.

Just lately, however, it had been made the excuse to break into any house under suspicion. It had happened to a bookkeeper living in the next street in an apartment so new that its walls had barely dried out, let alone developed a fungus. He'd been discovered to possess a snuffbox with the royal arms on it and had been taken off for questioning.

'We'll get him away tonight.'

'You can't. What about curfew?'

'Tomorrow then, at dawn.' Ffoulkes looked around. 'I'll go and tell him.'

'No.' Mme Vernet had recovered her poise. 'That is for me.' She put her hand on the table for a minute, to steady herself before going quietly upstairs.

M Sarrett watched her go. 'The poor dear,' he said. 'My poor, poor dear.'

There'd been a plan for this; Philippa had made it herself, though at that moment she realized that somehow she'd never expected it to be implemented; that something marvellous would happen to prevent the need of it. She'd intended Condorcet and herself to leave in the evening, mingling with the homegoing crowd of workers streaming out of Paris for the outskirts, to pass the night hidden among the trees of the curfew-deserted Bois de Boulogne—and board the northwest bound diligence at Neuilly in the morning.

With luck, its driver would be her old friend Bertholde. She'd tell him her brother had been killed and she was taking her distressed father back with her to Normandy.

Ffoulkes had approved the plan and improved it; they would all spend the first night at his safe house in Neuilly itself.

Now they would have to go *against* the stream of people coming into the city; they would not reach Neuilly in time to catch that day's diligence but would have to spend twenty-four hours waiting for the next.

'Can't be helped,' Ffoulkes said after they'd discussed it, raggedly. 'It'll be all right.'

Mme Vernet came back, very pale, but with her head now neatly capped.

Philippa thought, she tidied herself before she went to tell him.

'He is prepared,' was all she said. 'I shall get some food ready for you to take with you on your journey. Jeanne, M Collet, go now and get some sleep.'

They left her and Sarrett filling the soup pail with provisions.

Candlelight came from the crack under Condorcet's door as Philippa passed it but she didn't go in; he'd be putting the finishing touches to his manuscript. They'd have plenty of time together on the journey. She wondered if he was in as deep a fright as she was.

In her room, she washed, changed into fresh clothes and folded the ones she'd been wearing into the battered traveling bag. It distressed her terribly that she wouldn't be able to say good-bye to Sophie and Eliza; she'd tried to convince Ffoulkes that she could break away to deliver a farewell note from herself and Condorcet to them before rejoining the men at Neuilly.

He wouldn't have it. 'This is going to be tricky enough without putting bloody frills on it,' he'd said.

When everything was ready she lay down on the bed, convinced she wouldn't sleep. In fact, she dozed in fits, waking up in a panic at having missed the dawn—only to find it was still dark. At one point she heard Mme Vernet and Sarrett go to their rooms but there was no sound from Ffoulkes's or Condorcet's.

The first lonely tweet of a blackbird woke her; the sky was still pretending it was nighttime, only a suggestion of gray lay beyond her east-facing window.

She went downstairs and made coffee for them all—Mme Vernet had left the cups ready on a tray—trying to find comfort in familiar movement, the thrum of the kettle. She took the tray upstairs, put it on the hall table, knocked on Mme Vernet's door, then M Sarrett's, took up one of the cups and carried it to Condorcet's room, knocked before entering . . .

He wasn't there. The room was neater than she'd seen it, every book was piled tidily, the bed made, the bergère's cushion plumped up, his misshapen slippers together by the small hearth. Manuscripts, exactly in line, were in a row on the table—the plan for a universal language, his treatise on the equality of women, *A Sure Method of Learning to Count*, an addendum to his work on integral calculus. His pipe lay in its *cendrier* which was clean of its ashes.

The Progress was in the middle, facedown.

She picked up its last page. '. . . *independently of any power that would like to stop it, so long as our globe exists, the tempo may differ but we shall never go back.*'

The word *finis* was written large at the bottom.

Knowing what she'd find, she went downstairs and out into the courtyard. The bar to the gate had been lifted and put carefully to one side where nobody would fall over it. 'He's gone,' she said. 'He's gone.'

She turned round to see Mme Vernet and Sarrett behind her. Both were dressed and for a second it flashed across her mind that they'd been in a plot to keep her safe while Ffoulkes and Condorcet set out together. But Mme Vernet's face was hagridden and Ffoulkes was just emerging from the house.

'He's gone,' she said.

'Not long,' Ffoulkes said, 'I felt his pipe, it's still warm.'

M Sarrett had opened the gate and was looking up and down the empty street.

'He'll be making for the Suards,' he said. 'I can catch him before he gets to the barrier.'

'The Suards?'

'Friends of his,' Mme Vernet said. 'Fontenay-aux-Roses.'

'Stay here, no point in dashing all over the compass,' Ffoulkes said. 'He may have left a note.' He ran back to the house.

Mme Vernet looked at Philippa. There would be no note. His gratitude to them all lay in his going—alone. He wouldn't survive, of course; they all knew that. Not alone. Of all men he was least equipped with the cunning necessary to slink unnoticed through the jungle beyond the gate. That gentle, philosophizing, *valuable* sheep had trotted out into tiger country.

Philippa put her arms round her. 'Perhaps he's going to say good-bye to Sophie. I'll run after him.'

'No,' Mme Vernet said, 'He won't have gone there.' Philippa heard her moan and, turning round, saw that Sarrett had gone.

Everything was shattering, but she *knew* where Nicolas had gone. One last glimpse of his wife and daughter, a note through the lingerie shop letterbox. She could catch him up—he'd be going slowly.

She kissed Mme Vernet's cheek and went out into the Street of the Gravediggers. She caught a glimpse of M Sarrett at the bottom before he disappeared into the shadow of Saint Sulpice. She turned left up the hill, running. When she reached the top, she stopped and peered round the corner.

The sentry outside the Luxembourg was nodding over his musket. She slowed so that her boots made no sound and started running again when she was out of sight. Curfew lifted at dawn but there were still very few people about.

She'd crossed the silent Ile de la Cité before Ffoulkes caught up with her, puffing, just before the Pont au Change. 'Where the hell do you think you're going?'

'He's heading for Saint Honoré.' She pointed across the river. 'I can catch him.'

'No.'

'Just to the end of the bridge,' she pleaded. 'He can't have got much beyond it. He'll be limping, it's amazing he's got this far.'

He looked around. The bridge was deserted. A few bait-sellers were digging for worms in the silt below before the tide came in. 'All right, but no farther.'

She ran ahead, he followed more slowly.

As she got to the other side, two National Guardsmen emerged from behind a plinth that had once held the great equestrian statue of Louis XV.

'Papers.'

She'd left them behind in the attic with her traveling bag.

A pike was leveled at her waist, she felt the length of the other one laid across her back.

'What for?' she said. 'There's no barrier here usually.' But she'd left it too late, she'd paused, and her indignation was marred by a catch in her breathing with which she was suddenly having difficulty.

'There is now,' one of the guardsmen said. 'Better come along.'

They turned her round and began marching her back across the bridge towards the préfecture. She saw Ffoulkes idling at the other end.

Go away, she thought. *Please, God, make him go away.*

As the procession came up, he stood in front of it. 'What's up?'

'Out the way, soldier,' one of the guards told him. 'Nothing to do with you.'

'You silly bitch, you've left your bloody papers behind again,' Ffoulkes said to Philippa. Then to the guard, 'Let her go, mate. She's all right, been bedding down with me.'

'And where's that?'

'Over there.' He'd come up close now. Gently, he pushed the pike point away from her body then jerked a thumb towards the Ile Saint Louis, glimmering in the dawn. His voice went high to assume an aristocratic accent. 'We've taken a room in the bishop's palace, my man.' Then grinned. 'The bishop's gone but the fucking goes on. Come on, mate, let her go. I fought at Valmy.'

And they might have done; the respect for veterans of Valmy, the first glorious victory of the rabble that made up the Republican army, softened their faces into the envying sentimentality of those who hadn't been there. But at that moment an officer on a horse with a plume in his hat came riding up from the region of the Palais de Justice with another guardsman at his stirrup. 'What's going on here?'

Almost apologetically, the first guardsman told Ffoulkes, 'Got to have your papers, citizen.'

He wasn't the fool she was; he'd brought his knapsack with him. He grumbled as he delved into it.

The office leaned down from his horse to snatch the document out of his hand. He looked at it. 'Collet.' He put his other hand inside his frogged jacket and brought out another paper to consult it. 'Collet, Collet.'

And then she knew and he knew. Blanchard had provided his papers, as he'd provided all The League's papers.

Their eyes met. Andrew smiled.

The officer on the horse was a youngster; suddenly, he became younger from amazement as if, looking through a lottery list of prize-winning numbers, he'd found his ticket on it. '*Collet*.' He looked up with disbelief. '*We've got the bloody Englishman.*'

'Run,' Ffoulkes said gently. He threw himself sideways, wrapping his arms round the officer's knee to pull him off his horse. Immediately, he disappeared under a meleé of guardsman.

Philippa later remembered trying to scalp one of the guards by pulling his head backwards by his hair but thought she must have lost sense for a minute afterwards from the shock of what, to judge from the state of her left eye, was a hefty punch in the face.

Her next memory was of her own shadow stumbling ahead of leveled pikes with the sun of a glorious morning at her back, her hands tied, Ffoulkes being dragged along somewhere behind her, and a pedlar turning his head away as he waited for them to pass before setting up his pitch on the bridge.

Chapter Fifteen

H AD it not been out of season with Covent Garden and Drury Lane shut for the summer, those two great theaters might have used their power to persuade the Lord Chamberlain that The Duke's was putting on an illicit play after all and thereby enforced its closure. Both begrudged any success not their own

As it was, *Oroonoko* was the only drama in Town. Better than that, it was a production not to be missed by anyone with pretensions to art. Better even than that, it promoted a good cause; one could watch it with a clear conscience. From the second night onwards, it played to full houses that, had it been bigger, could have been even fuller. It did not matter that the *haute monde* had left London for the leafy provinces. In order to see this play, it came back in road-blocking coachloads.

Gentleman's Magazine wrote: 'Sir Michael Murrough's performance has lit a flame that will not be extinguished in our lifetime.'

The Ladies' Diary thought: 'The play's power to delineate the passions, to move to pity, as well as the high quality of style and diction, must have particular appeal to our fair sex.'

Protests by the Society for the Abolition of Slavery that it was not authorizing the production were ignored. The public assumed it was; play and cause became synonymous. Cowper's *The Negro's Complaint* became *Oroonoko's Complaint* and was printed and sold in the thousands. Hairdressers catered for a craze for 'the Imoinda style.' Fancy dress balls were sprinkled with Oroonokos, Imoindas and Widow Lackitts—these last invariably men. A magistrate reading the Riot Act to a crowd protesting against press gangs was yelled at. 'You're no better than the governor in *Oroonoko*.'

JOHN Beasley was buried in the dusty little cemetery of Saint Dionis near his birthplace in Lime Street. A ferocious atheist, he'd once said he wanted to lie in unconsecrated ground but Makepeace was too distressed to arrange that, even if it had been possible, which she didn't think it was. 'It's better than Chelsea,' she apologized to his spirit. 'You always hated the countryside.'

Anyway, the Reverend Deedes would have balked at one of Makepeace's friends in his local churchyard, let alone a man who had written his own epitaph as:

> '*Here lies the body of John Mark Beasley.*
> *He championed Reason*
> *And died quite easily.*'

The priest at Saint Dionis wasn't happy about that, either. 'Reason' was becoming a dirty word, tarnished with the patina of Revolution. His archdeacon wouldn't like it, he said. However, the sum Makepeace was prepared to pay for the repair of his one-hundred-year-old roof quietened his objections and, presumably, those of his archdeacon.

It was one of the few overcast days of the summer but retaining a clammy heat. The priest, not having known the deceased and suspecting the worst, conducted an unornamented service while eyeing his congregation with suspicion. This was small; but what Beasley's friends lacked in number they made up in devotion. Two undoubted prostitutes wept throughout, so did a printer in multicolored clothing and a tasseled cap. As Mr Lucey said, sobbing, 'The dear boy wouldn't recognize me in black, would he, Jamie?'

There were no relatives; either he had none or they'd disowned him.

There were a couple of shifty-looking, ink-stained representatives from Grub Street, a black man in livery who shouted '*Hallelujah*' a lot, the barmaid from his favorite drinking hole, the Pen and Goose, and a bailiff who turned up for old times' sake, telling Makepeace, 'He were a pleasure to arrest, so he were. Always inquired after the family.'

The grand friends, Goldsmith, Dr Johnson, Reynolds, were all dead and as he'd aged Beasley had grown too cantankerous to make more like them. In any case, Makepeace thought, the independent-minded society to which they'd all belonged had died with them. England's gates were closing against men of free thought; they were unpatriotic.

The odd thing is, she thought, *only England could have produced them*.

Gripping Sanders's arm, she followed the coffin into the graveyard, a small and more friendly place than the church's classical Wren interior. The East End had nestled up to surround it with the back of shops and businesses. From an overlooking ground floor window came the smell of ink and the thump of a printing press that must, she thought, make the man they were burying feel more at home.

As the deceased's oldest friend and, anyway, the giver of the funeral meats now being set out at the Pen and Goose, she was given the right to drop the first clod.

Dust to dust, ashes to ashes. She'd never felt more lonely in her life.

Sanders sprinkled his bit of earth and stepped back to join her. 'Got us into some scrapes, that little bugger.'

'Got us out of them, too,' she said.

'That he did. Never could scare him off, could they?'

It was a more fitting epitaph than Beasley's own, although—and this comforted her—he had indeed died easily. 'Went in his afternoon nap,' Hildy had said.

It was typical of him, Makepeace thought, that the only smooth path he'd ever taken had been death's.

The others departed for the Pen and Goose, and Sanders waited for her at the gate while she said good-bye.

I'm sorry Philippa ain't here for you. She's the only one now that understood and loved you like I did. But she's gone chasing off to France. You'd have approved, I dare say; you never counted the cost, either. I wish she hadn't gone, John. I wish you hadn't, either. There's nobody left.

A large shape loomed up beside her.

'I thought you were at the theater,' she said.

'Ah, well, Aaron's putting 'em through their paces to see they don't get slack. He said you'd absolved him from attending the funeral.'

'Aaron never liked him much.'

'I'm sorry I never knew him.'

'Not many people did. Only enough to kill him with their stinking prisons.' She turned away and they walked towards the gate. 'Will you come to the wake?'

'No, I've been summoned. I've some people to see—they sent a message to the theater.'

Always these mysterious people, she thought. 'Who are they?'

'Me other employers, ye might say.'

Never a straight answer, either.

They went out together into Backchurch Street, Sanders following them at what Makepeace felt was an unnecessarily discreet distance. *Did he suspect? Probably.*

Murrough said, 'You're the keeper of the purse, missus, how long d'ye reckon the play will run?'

'Forever, according to the bookings.' Most productions rarely had a repertory run of more than six nights but since The Duke's company had no repertoire neither was there any reason to limit *Oroonoko*'s availability to a greedy public.

He nodded. 'Now, if I have to go away . . .'

She panicked. 'Where would you go? Why? When would you go?'

'If, I'm saying. *If* I have to go . . .'

'You can't,' she said. 'We . . . we'd lose money.'

'There speaks me little counting house.' He looked around; they were approaching Fenchurch Street. He spotted another churchyard and hurried her into it, sitting her down on a tomb and standing over her. 'I'm sorry to be telling you on this sad day,' he said, 'but I've been sent for and if I have to go it'll be quick with maybe no time to explain. Listen . . .'

'Are you in trouble?'

His little eyes almost disappeared as he smiled. 'No, for once. Or not with the law at any rate, not yet. Listen . . .'

'It's Ireland, isn't it,' she said, dully. 'You're going to do something terrible for Ireland.'

'Will ye *listen*?' He blew out his cheeks and sat down beside her. 'Very well, it's Ireland. And it's France. And the two of them together. My masters set a low score by my acting and think higher of me as a go-between . . .'

'Don't go,' she pleaded, 'I've lost two to France already.'

'Are you listening to me?'

'Yes.'

'Aaron can play Oroonoko.'

'*Aaron?*'

'Ach, he's not a bad actor, not of my caliber of course, but not bad at all. He's well again and he's stamping to do it, which is worse for his health than not doing it at all. And the wonder of *Oroonoko* is you can play him with a limp or one arm or any other deformity slavers inflict in their wickedness. Missus, I want you to retire.'

'What?' She stared at him but for once he was serious.

'Look at yourself. You've suffered enough grief lately to choke a horse. You've worked your little arse thin making a working miracle out of that barn of a theater, which is running itself now. So I'm thinking it's time you took a holiday . . .'

He's going to ask me to go with him.

But he wasn't.

'This Babbs Cove of yours,' he said, 'Aaron tells me its air is balmy, its sands are yellow and the smugglers guard you like a tent-pot of bacon. Go there. Take Jacques with you.'

'Jacques?' She felt she was being swished back and forth under a waterfall of words that became more Irish the more intent they became.

'I'm uneasy for the lad,' he said. 'My informants tell me things don't go well for his father, nor for Danton, neither. It's not that so much, though, it's . . . I don't like the way Blanchard shows an interest in him.'

'He's showing an interest in all of us,' she said, bitterly. Since opening night, Blanchard had been an almost constant presence in the theater. He hadn't merely attended every performance, he came early, slipping in the moment the stage door opened to the staff and cast, sometimes with Félicie, sometimes alone. Turn a corner backstage and he was there. Enter a dressing room and there he was, talking, joking, flattering, asking questions.

The actors accepted him as just another high-born devotee relishing a sniff of greasepaint. But while Félicie was undoubtedly stagestruck, Blanchard's enthusiasm went deeper. Makepeace suspected him of intending to wrest The Duke's away from her now that it had proved a going concern.

'I don't like the man,' she said, 'but . . .'

'I tell you, who he reminds me of,' Murrough said, 'Danny O'Halloran.'

'Who's Danny O'Halloran when he's home?'

'Lovely fella. There was never a wittier man nor one you'd be happier to take home to mother than our Danny. A good member of our branch of the United Irishman, so he was. Attended every meeting, listened to all our revolutionary little plans, even contributed some of his own as I remember—until he sold us all out to the English.' He looked down at her. 'Most of us are still in prison thanks to Mr O'Halloran, and me only getting away with a change of name and your brother's help, God love him.'

On the far side of the churchyard, a man was cutting the grass, scattering butterflies into the air with every swing of his scythe.

Murrough got up and raised Makepeace to her feet. 'Go to Babbs Cove.'

'Why Babbs Cove?' she protested. 'My family's in the north.'

'Some of it's in France,' he said. 'If I can fetch it home, I will. And I imagine Babbs Cove is where we'll make for.' Suddenly, he kissed her. 'Wait for me now, Mrs Hedley, because if I go, I'm coming back.'

He walked her to Fenchurch Street, shook her hand warmly and turned right. Her way was left.

She watched him head for Whitechapel. A lot of Irish in Whitechapel. A lot of Irish everywhere, she thought. Somebody had told her that out of every eleven people you passed in London, one had been born in Ireland.

'And each one of the bastards unreliable,' she said bitterly as Sanders joined her.

'What bastards are those, missus?'

'The Irish.'

'Oh, the Irish. You can't trust 'em.' If one Englishman was worth ten Frenchmen, he was, in Sanders's view, worth a hundred Irish. 'Not but what I'd say that about Sir Mick.'

'I would,' she said.

WHEN she got back to The Duke's after the wake, it was to find the preparations for the evening's performance going ahead much as usual. She heard Murrough's voice echoing down the corridor the moment she'd passed through the stage door and relief stopped her in her tracks for a moment before she became irritated. Still here after those hints of danger and threat of departure. Dramatizing everything like the actor he was. Making himself mysterious. What he called plotting was likely no more than grousing against the government in a Whitechapel alehouse with a lot of other micks.

I can't be bothered with him.

Meeting Sir Boy Blanchard and Félicie on their way out did nothing to improve her mood.

'There you are, missus. We'll be back later. Keep our box for us, will you?'

She might have been the doorman. He was quick to see her displeasure and equally quick to try and dispel it.

'That talented lad of yours . . . Jacques, is it? . . . He's been showing us the mysteries that lie beneath the stage. At least, he's been showing me; Lady Ffoulkes does not care to have her illusions disillusioned, do you Félicie?'

'*C'est de la magie pour moi.*'

'*Et pour moi, tu es comme par magie.*'

The words were beyond her but not the meeting of eyes as they were said. 'And how is Lady Blanchard?' Makepeace asked, innocently. She saw no reason not to remind the two of them that Sir Boy had a wife and Félicie a husband.

'Well,' Blanchard waved his hand, negligently, 'she's well, I thank ee.'

She watched them go out into the street. God forbid that in causing Andrew Ffoulkes's absence she had been the instrument that also upset his marriage.

She put out her hand and grabbed the collar of a figure trying to whisk past her. 'Back.'

Luchet pointed after the couple. 'They have invite me to their club . . .'

'I'm not paying you to go to clubs. Back.'

From the Green Room came the voice of Ninon practicing her scales, there was chatter in the dressing rooms, the dancers on stage were limbering up to a tune from de Barigoule's violin. For once, the sounds of the little world she had created failed to move her.

I'm tired, she thought, and went down to the auditorium to give hell to the lamplighters for having bungled the snuffing of the chandelier after yesterday's interval.

When they got home that night, Hildy took her to one side as the others set about the supper that was always ready for them. 'Jenny wants a private word.'

'Now?' Her daughter was usually in bed by this time.

'However late, she said. Eh, you look thrawn, pet. Eat first.'

But Makepeace went up immediately. Jenny had not attended the theater since the first night and, because Sanders fetched the girl from her Abolition Society work in Clapham in the early evening, the only time mother and daughter had spent together this past week had been on the journeys to Town, when discussion remained general; these last few days Makepeace had spent most of the ride nodding off to sleep.

'Come in, Mama. Please sit down.' It was peremptory. She's nervous, Makepeace thought, she's been rehearsing whatever it is.

'Mama, I am sorry I did not come to Uncle John's funeral. I intended to but circumstances prevented it. However, I am sure he would have approved of the work I am doing for the Society and would understand the need for it to remain uninterrupted at this time. The debate is very soon, you know.'

She is *nervous*. 'He'd understand. What circumstances?'

This wasn't in the script and Jenny brushed it aside. 'Mama, Miss Thornton has invited me to stay with her and her family in Clapham for a while. Hers is a most respectable household and it would be convenient for me not to have to travel back and forth. I should like your permission to accept.'

Makepeace said, 'Of course you can go if you want to. What's the matter, Jen?'

'Nothing.'

'Yes, there is.'

'Nothing, Mama. I shall go tomorrow, then.'

Dammit, was everybody in a conspiracy to perplex her? 'Tell me.'

'I have nothing more to say, Mama. Except . . .' A flush began on Jenny's neck and rose upwards; she was a helpless blusher. '. . . Mr Heilbron has asked if he may call on you soon.'

'Why's everybody asking my permission all of a sudden?' Makepeace sat up; the blush had deepened. 'He's dropping Philippa and switching to you, is that it?'

'Oh, oh, *oh*.' Jenny's fists hammered the air, then, with a self-control her mother hadn't suspected in her, she lowered them to her lap, stood up and went to the door, opening it. 'You are a crude woman, Mama. I bid you good night.'

Makepeace went down to the kitchen in a temper. 'It's that bloody Heilbron,' she said, 'He's taking out a monopoly on my daughters.'

Hildy was putting dishes away. 'It's more nor that.'

'What is it then?'

'She was gannen along the landin' in the dawn. She spied Sir Mick comin' out of your room.'

'Oh, God.'

Hildy nodded. She wiped the table and spread the cloth over the stove chimney to dry. 'I'm for bed. I'll lock up, eh?' On the way out, she paused to stroke Makepeace's cheek. 'Don't you mind, pet. Sanders and me don't.'

Makepeace stood for a while then, suddenly cold, kicked the kitchen chair near the still-warm stove and sat in it. So Hildy and Sanders gave their permission to her carryings-on, did they? Damn their eyes, she didn't need anyone's permission, not Jenny's, not Heilbron's, not anybody's.

I'm fifty years old, in the name of God. I pay my taxes, most of them, what in hell does it matter . . . we're adults, not attached to anyone else— at least, I don't think he is. We ain't doing it in public; I'm not running a bawdy house here. How come it's connubial bliss if a bastard like Reverend Deedes says a few words over it and black sin if he don't? At our age, who cares? Why should I be shamed? Who are we bothering?

They were bothering Jenny, they were bothering moral society and, she supposed, God himself. She could outface society, she could even outface God. But Jenny . . .

Her daughter's disdain had struck to the depths of Makepeace's soul and stirred up the sediment that had been laid down by a New

England upbringing. The insubordinate years since then had not shifted its Puritanism nor washed out the strictures of Goody Busgutt and the hellfire promised to those sexual sinners that righteous old busybody had dragged to the meeting house for condemnation.

I'm bothering me. If it was hypocrisy, and she suspected it was, she was steeped in it, had rolled in it even as they'd made love, transferring much of her guilt to him, blaming him for her own moral slackness.

Yet even if he asked her to marry him, which he wouldn't, probably couldn't, she'd refuse. Marriage to anybody, especially him, was not on her cards; she was too old for another husband. Murrough had been what she wanted—a comrade by day, physical pleasure by night. No dependence on either side.

It had been—a guffaw was forced from her—*fun.*

But it was over.

Sighing, she stood up, put the chair back in its place and went to bed—locking the door to her room before she did so.

HE went four days later. Disappeared. Like a stage trick. As if whisked from sight by one of Jacques's traps. He was in the coach with Makepeace and the others when they went to the theater that day, read a note that awaited him at the stage door, performed, took his curtain calls—and was gone.

It turned out that the only people he said good-bye to were Aaron and Sanders. 'He thanked me very nice,' Sanders said, 'and I was to thank Hildy and everybody as looked after him, very generous he was.'

'How good of him,' Makepeace said.

Aaron said, 'He only had time for a brief word. He said if you've got to leave a party, the best thing was to . . . well, fuck off.'

'Did he.'

'Look at it from his point of view. He was in a hurry. If he'd made his farewells to everybody in the theater he'd have been here all night.'

'Very true.'

Her anger was deadly and she clung on to it so that pain wouldn't take its place. No matter he'd told her it might happen, he could have told her that it had. A passing thank-you-for-having-me would have been nice.

She blocked her mind against the possibility that he had indeed gone to France. He'd become bored with her, he'd found another woman, returned to Ireland, emigrated to America—any of those alternatives were preferable than that he had been sucked into the black vacuum into which Philippa and Ffoulkes had disappeared. With an effort of will, she told herself they were also more likely.

After all, from the first he'd tried to make himself a man of mystery, suggesting he was in danger, pursued. What had happened? Nothing. And that, despite the fact for nearly two weeks he'd been the public's darling. The only pursuit had been by newspapers and gossip pages. Which, she had to admit, he'd avoided except in his persona as Oroonoko with his features concealed by burnt cork.

But no, the man was unreliable, like his race; an overweight will o'the wisp. Doubtless he would materialize somewhere else and inveigle himself into another woman's home and bed. *Well, good luck to her.*

She had enough to do; the theater had gone into mourning for him, cast and staff drooping with despair as if their professional life was over. To make sure it wasn't, she had persuade those who'd booked to see Oroonoko played by Michael Murrough that they would enjoy it as much played by Aaron Burke. Posters had to be pasted over, programs changed, his costume altered, a rehearsal called.

That night Dizzy made an apology and a promise before he began the prologue. Sir Michael Murrough had been called away—there was a groan from the packed house—his role would be taken by the world famous actor Mr Burke; they would not be disappointed.

To Makepeace's surprise they were not. Most of the stalwarts who had come every night only to watch Murrough—and they were quite a few—walked out at once but those for whom the production was new gave its ending the same accolade of a minute's silence before they stood to cheer.

It was the staging Murrough had given the play that made it foolproof, she realized. Aaron was good—his sister was astonished by how expert an actor he had become, though it was skill rather than genius, lending Oroonoko more pathos and desperation than grandeur. But the effects Murrough had devised with Jacques were unaffected by his departure and the cast regained confidence as the audience responded to them. Above all, the quiet, sustained theme of the slave and her child with its last, heartbreaking chord brought down the final curtain on an experience that extended drama into reality.

In the interval, Blanchard had paid her the compliment of inviting her into his box for champagne and sympathy. 'We thought you were done, missus, did we not, Félicie. No Sir Mick, no play, we thought. We should have known you would triumph.'

It was not unpleasant and she allowed herself to be thawed. The question he always asked: 'Any news of . . . ?' suggested comradeship in adversity, an alliance of concern for the missing—until the interrogation became more insistent. 'What *can* Sir Mick be about? Did that bad fellow tell you nothing of his intentions?'

As always Sir Boy's straight, beautiful nose seemed to sniff out what others wished to conceal. She wondered if Murrough had told someone in the cast he intended to go to France and, if so, whether the someone had told Blanchard. The man's interest made her uneasy because it gave validity to her fear, so she refused more champagne and left.

For a while, vexation kept her weariness and anxiety at bay; she was always better angry. Steeling herself to meet Stephen in an upstairs room of Benthall's Coffee House just round the corner from The Duke's, she swept up the stairs in a fury that he had asked her to come to him rather than attend on her.

He disarmed her immediately. 'Knowing how busy you are I would not delay you at Reach House but hoped this place would meet with your convenience.'

'You could have come to the theater,' she snapped, knowing he would never set foot in it.

He merely smiled. 'In any case, I wished to introduce you to my new establishment. At the moment it runs at a loss but I have the backing of the Society for the Suppression of Vice and hopes of persuading the prime minister to reduce the tax on coffee. Did you notice the clientele downstairs?'

She hadn't.

'Artisans,' he said, 'Drinking coffee rather than their usual pint of purl and gin. Shops like these shall be a weapon in our armory against the prevailing evil of drunkenness.'

She was grudging. 'It'll need more than a cup of coffee.' London life had shocked her; her time in the harborage of Chelsea had led her to forget the degradation that existed side by side with the capital's wonders. If anything, it was worse than she remembered; the East End public houses spewed out reeling teetotums of men and women who in turn spewed their drink onto the road and passersby. She'd had to go to the magistrates to report the noise and the nuisance of 'The Bunch of Grapes' next door where a high level of drunkenness was maintained by a local employer who gave part of his weavers' wages to its landlord to pay them in drink. Nothing had been done.

She realized she was being mollified. 'What do you want, Stephen?'

She knew what it was: He wanted to marry Jenny. Or, as he now put it in the course of a long and charming speech: 'To pay my addresses to your younger daughter.'

And although she knew that Philippa would not mind being passed over, indeed might actually rejoice in being freed from a promise she should never have made, Makepeace was so angry on her behalf that she didn't make it easy for him.

'Dear, dear,' she said, nastily, 'How can that be? You're handfasted to my elder daughter.'

'No, missus,' he said gently. 'Philippa has rejected me. You and I both know, and so does Philippa, that going to France was her way of ending the engagement.'

It was true; Makepeace was aware it was true, but she was still aggressive. 'Her way of trying to save a friend and decent man from the guillotine.'

'The Marquis de Condorcet, yes,' he said. 'We discussed him, she and I. I told her I was prepared to see her help him by sending him the necessary papers to leave France but she knew that any deeper involvement could not be tolerated. The man is an atheist.'

'Oh, well, deserves to have his head cut off, then,' Makepeace said.

'Missus, missus.' He refused to be provoked. 'We will not argue over atheism. But, don't you see, Philippa's action has proved she would find me no more suitable as a husband than I would find her as a wife.'

Why did he always have to be so reasonable? Philippa—and it had surprised her mother as much as anyone else—was a chip off the old block; as headstrong as Makepeace had ever been, as freedom-loving. And this man could not endure that in the female, certainly not in a wife. Freedom for slaves, yes. Freedom for women?

Stephen Heilbron, whom the world regarded as a libertarian, hated by slave-owners as a revolutionary, was as rigid in convention as any Puritan. He was not for Philippa, nor she for him.

'Is Jenny going to accept you?' she asked.

'I believe so. She is devoted to my cause and, I like to think, to myself. She has indicated as much.'

Oh, Jenny. Which cause will your life with him be devoted to? The Society for the Abolition of Slavery or his Society for the Suppression of Vice?

Makepeace could hear the bars being cemented into place. Heilbron and his ilk had shut down Philippa's Society for Whatever Rights she'd wanted for women. They would have shut down The Duke's if they could—and, one day, probably would. What came next? A Society for the Suppression of Actresses? The Society for the

Suppression of women like me? The gates were slamming on feminine freedom. Jenny and her generation were being persuaded to
close them on their own imprisonment.

Dear God, she thought, *I've had the best of it.*

'Don't *you* see,' she said, 'that you shouldn't even be asking me
this? We're not trading slaves, Stephen. You don't need me to say yea
or nay, have her, don't have her. If Jenny says she'll wed you, that's
enough. She's old enough to make up her own mind. She can give or
withhold her consent as she likes. For God's sake, man, she is a free
human being.'

'I have your permission, then,' he said.

'Good-bye, Stephen,' she said, and went. There was no point in
staying.

T HAT night, at the theater, they came for Jacques.

It was towards the end of the interval. Makepeace was at the-
front of house, ushering in the half-timers, the people that had come
to fill the upper gallery for the second half of the play.

She was always brusque with them at first, resenting the fact that
they were only paying half the price, but they were invariably poor;
famished-looking students, shop girls, old theater workers who remembered Garrick in his prime. Therefore, just as invariably, she
would end up explaining to them the action of the play so far and
directing the more elderly into any vacant and comfortable seat in
the stalls.

'Oroonoko is an African prince who's been captured along with
his wife by slavers . . .' she was saying to a couple of men when one
of them stopped her.

'Mrs Hedley?'

'Yes?'

'Are you the owner of this establishment?' A neat man—she'd
put him down as a clerk—he made it sound like a bordello.

'I am managing this theater, yes.'

He produced some paper. 'I have here a warrant. You are ordered to deliver to me the body of a certain Jacques de Vaubon, otherwise known as Jack Watt.'

She didn't look at the warrant; she wouldn't have been able to read it for terror. 'Why? What do you want with him?'

'We are informed he's a French spy.'

She gaped at the man. 'He's eleven years old.'

'His age don't matter. Our information is he's son to a notorious French revolutionary.'

'Eleven,' she said. 'He's eleven years old. What are you going to do with him?'

'That's not our business, madam. Or yours. Usually they get sent back to France.'

'No,' she said. 'No, he came here for safety.' *I trust him to you, missus.*

'Not our business,' the man said again. He didn't care one way or the other. 'Our business is executing this warrant. Where is he?'

'He's not here.' *Oh God,* God, she should have denied all knowledge of the boy. Told them he'd gone to Timbuktu, wherever that was. Told them he was dead, which, if he were repatriated to France, he might be. De Vaubon and Danton at war with Robespierre. If they lost, their heads would topple into the basket. The guillotine was killing children quite as young as Jacques.

Images kept pace with fractured thoughts; she was seeing Jacques in a tumbrel with his father, Jacques mounting the steps . . .

And then she saw the eyes of the man with the warrant focused on something across her shoulder, saw him nod as if in response to a direction. She turned round.

Sir Boy Blanchard was standing behind her, a champagne glass in his hand.

She turned back, but the two bailiffs had gone, pushing their way through the crowding half-timers into the body of the theater.

Blanchard was all concern. 'What is it, missus?'

'You,' she said in a long breath. '*You* told them.'

'Told them what?'

But she was running out into the street, down the alley, through the stage door. *He'll be underneath the stage with his traps. Please God, let him be under the stage.* Unless the two magistrate's men were familiar with the geography of a theater, its doors and corridors would bewilder them. *We can make a run for it.*

Sanders. Where was Sanders with the coach? Usually, he came early to fetch them so that he could watch the last scene. *Smuggle Jacques into it and go. Go where?*

'Where's Jacques?' She'd bumped into Bracey.

'Dear Lord, what is it, missus?'

'They've come for Jacques. Bailiffs, magistrate's men. Two of them.' Tears were pumping out of her eyes, she could hardly see. 'They're going to deport him. Bracey, I've got to get him away.'

Polly had come up. 'What's this?'

Makepeace ran on, while behind her Bracey said, 'Something about a couple of quodders come for Jack.'

'*Have* they, the bastards.'

The two men were on the stage now, having clambered under the curtain and were blundering among the flats, knocking one of them over.

Makepeace dodged backstage and lifted the trapdoor. 'Jacques.'

Out in the orchestra pit, the Marquis de Barigoule had brought his baton down to begin the overture to the second half. She hissed louder over the music: '*Jacques.*'

Nothing. A single safety lamp showed a mass of hanging ropes, pulleys and lifts like a torture chamber—but no human being.

She made for the Green Room, then stopped. *The émigrés. Once they heard the hated name de Vaubon, they wouldn't lift a finger to help her save Jacques.*

They'll hand him over. Oh God, this is enemy territory. Where is he?

Where were the bailiffs? She went back to the wings. They were still on stage, staring at a black and commanding Aaron who was saying loudly, 'My dear fellow, I am the leading actor of this production and I do not know the whereabouts of every whippersnapper in its employ, French or not.' He caught Makepeace's eye. 'Fly away with him, I say. And be off with you, too. The curtain is about to rise.'

Of course, that's where he was—in the flies, readying the damn cannonballs for the storm scene. And he'd have heard.

She began praying that neither of the bailiffs would look up; she kept her own eyes rigidly to the horizontal.

Which caught the attention of the better-spoken man. 'Here, you, lady. You come and stand with Nobby. Don't want you warning our subject, do we?'

Makepeace was ushered into the wings on the prompt side and her arm firmly held by the man called Nobby. 'You can't do this,' she said. 'You can't keep me here.'

'Miss, we got a warrant signed by a judge. We can do anything.'

The conversation between the other bailiff and Aaron was still going on. 'I'm not here to stop the play,' the man was protesting. 'We're to apprehend this Vaubon and apprehend him we will. Our information is he's here, so you be a good little actor and get about your business and we'll get about ours. I got a man watching the front and another at the back so he's not getting out. And while you're playacting, I'm searching. That clear?'

Aaron nodded and dragged the man off the stage just in time— the curtain was going up.

Makepeace stood. Just stood. If she was aware of anything, it was only of the grasp on her arm and the voice of de Vaubon. *I trust him to you, missus.*

Somewhere there was guilt—*I brought him here, I should have hidden him*—but it was subservient to a searing grief. He'd be taken from her, as the little slave boy had been taken from his mother. *He's mine, he's my little boy.*

Everything she knew so well, the lights, the music, the rustle of costumes and the smell of greasepaint as one player after another pushed past them to go on stage, thinned to a gray hell where demons capered beyond her comprehension. Only the Countess d'Arbreville and Henri on the other side of the boards, clasping each other, had relevance. *They'll take him away from me.*

To her captor, however, here was an experience he'd never known. He kept nudging her, asking questions she didn't hear and didn't answer. Suddenly, between scenes—she couldn't have said which—she found herself being taken away from the wings and down to the stalls. Two protesting members of the audience in the front row were being ousted from their seats by the display of a warrant. She was sat down.

The bailiff sat next to her. 'It's good, this is,' he said. 'Might as well make oursel's comfy.'

Some sense began to return. *They haven't caught him yet. Somehow he's got away.* Unless, the dampening thought, *unless they* have *caught him and dragged him off already and haven't bothered to tell this dolt next to me.*

She glanced up to Blanchard's box. Félicie, as usual, was transfixed by what was happening on stage, leaning forward, her pretty mouth parted. Blanchard was sitting back, frowning slightly. His eyes flickered and met her own for a second, then looked away.

You did it, she thought. *You told them.* She was as sure of it as of anything in her life. *None of the émigrés, it was you.* But *how* had he known who Jacques was, and *why* had he then betrayed the boy . . . ?

Luchet, she thought. *Luchet told you. No, not you, he told Félicie.* The tutor had laid the information, an I-know-something-important gobbet, at the adored one's feet, and Félicie, of course, had told Blanchard.

But why, then, go to the authorities with such a grubby betrayal? We don't like each other, you and I, but you know how important Jacques is to me and how important I am to Andrew.

Her own words, spoken a long time ago to Philippa, came back to her. 'He's a schemer. I ain't jealous of him, he's jealous of me. He's jealous of everything Andrew has.'

Was it that? As sordidly simple as that? Smashing something in a line of affection that led back to the man Blanchard called his best friend?

Mick knew, she thought. *You're his Danny O'Whatsisname. You're a born betrayer.*

It came to her that tiny changes were occurring in the play on-stage. Familiar lines were being altered, additions made. Widow Lackitt had come on in an unscheduled appearance, gaining a laugh where there shouldn't have been one. Makepeace heard Chrissy say unscripted, as if of one of the slaves, 'Is he not ebonied?' And the answer, 'Black as the Earl of Hell's waistcoat', gaining another laugh.

What are they up to? They're up to something. Then she answered herself: *Bless them, oh God bless them, they're hiding him.*

She had allies. Never on the side of authority, they were upholding liberty as they saw it. This troupe of barnstorming sinners, this ragbag harlequinade of hers was marching to her aid—and Jacques's.

Melting with love and gratitude, she was nevertheless frightened. *Whatever it is, they'll overdo it, they can't help it. Look at them mugging.*

She glanced up to see if Blanchard had noticed; he knew the play as well as she did. His eyes had narrowed, he'd lifted a finger to beckon forward the footman he and Félicie invariably brought with them to stand behind them in the box and run their errands.

The play was ending—it seemed to have lasted a thousand years; Oroonoko and Imoinda were dead.

There was no epilogue; Aaron, who should have read it, was leaving the stage empty except for the separation of the slave mother and child, their hands imploring for each other as they were led off.

The bailiff beside Makepeace was sobbing his heart out.

The usual stunned silence and then the thunderclap of applause.

One curtain call, only one, for Aaron and Mrs Jordan. Only one for the other leading players, despite the roar from the audience.

The whole company came on. Makepeace's bailiff was on his feet, clapping, whistling, stamping; if his prisoner had wanted, she could have slipped away to China without being noticed.

Instead, she was intent on the line of the bowing, curtseying cast, which, she thought, was taking up a fraction more of the stage's width than it had before. Was there one more jewelled, black-corked, beturbaned Indian boy in it than usual? Somewhat shorter than the rest?

She looked up at Blanchard's box. He had seen; he was talking to the footman, pointing. She saw the footman hurry out.

'Want to meet the players?' she asked her bailiff, already dragging him towards the stage. Behind her, a frustrated audience tried to clap the curtain into going up again.

So willing was her captor that, when they reached the Green Room, he pushed Makepeace aside and was lost to her, enveloped into the exuberant, sweating, shouting postmortem that was the inevitable result of another successful night.

Bracey, staggering slightly as if already drunk, pushed her way through the players towards Makepeace. 'We're taking over the Boar's Head for a celebration,' she shouted. 'All of us, in costume.'

Aaron came up and planted a black kiss on his sister's cheek. 'You won't want to come, I expect,' he said, quite as loudly as Bracey. 'You're tired. You'll want to take the coach home *now*. We'll order hackneys later.'

Makepeace looked at him in inquiry.

'Now,' he said.

She nodded.

'Come along then.' With Makepeace on one arm and Bracey on the other, Aaron led the way into the passage and towards the stage door, the whole company following him, still talking and laughing, still in costume, carrying the enchanted bailiff with them.

The other bailiff looked as disgruntled as any man who had spent an hour peering into prop rooms, stumbling over ropes and scenery and generally being hissed at for getting in the way. He held the narrow passage to the stage door, one hand up to stop the oncoming procession while he listened to Blanchard's footman who was whispering in his ear.

'What?' Gabble from over-excited actors tended to inhibit communication.

'He's dressed like a blackie,' the footman said, more loudly, 'turban on his head or was. Smallish chap, about so high.'

'I'll get him.' The bailiff scrutinized Aaron as if suspecting him of having suddenly shot up from 'so high' to six feet tall. He began to walk forward, squeezed past the Widow Lackitt's ludicrous skirt, ignored Makepeace and slowly made his way down the passage, inspecting everyone in it. The stagestruck Nobby was pulled sharply out of the line and told to 'go and help Tom watch the audience come out.'

Blanchard's footman was now talking to someone in the shadows by the door. It was Luchet.

Makepeace went towards him. The tutor, catching sight of her, quailed at her approach. Seeing the look on her face, the footman opened the door and escaped, leaving it ajar to the bad air of the alley and giving Makepeace a glimpse of yet another bailiff, this one with a cudgel in his hand, waiting to stop any eleven-year-old fugitive leaving the theater. Where Jacques was, what plan her company had devised she didn't know. Probably none of them would get away with it, the power of the law would come down on them all but, as God was her witness, she'd deal with the wobbling apology for a human being called Luchet before it did.

She grabbed his coat lapels and stood on tiptoe to put her face near his. 'You betrayed your charge, tutor.'

He didn't try to deny it; he was appalled. 'I did not mean for this to happen . . .'

'I'll write that on your tombstone,' Makepeace said. 'Because, sure as the Devil's in Dockside, if that boy goes to his death your bollocks go with him.'

'Missus, I swear, I did not know she would . . . She ask me who is the boy of mystery. I swear her to secrecy . . .'

'Swore,' Makepeace amended automatically. 'What else did you tell her as she'll have told Blanchard?'

'Nothing, *nothing*.'

She looked behind her. Noise reverberated round the dark little passage. Protest at being kept from celebration was being raised by voices trained to carry, and towards the end of the line, the bailiff was causing the Countess d'Abreville to have hysterics by accusing seven-year-old Henri of being a French revolutionary spy.

Makepeace turned back to Luchet. 'Did you tell her how you and Jacques came into the country? Or where?'

'No, *no*.' This was genuine. 'She did not ask.'

'Are you going to?'

'No.' The man was sulking now. 'She promise she would say nothing but she tell *him*. She betray me.'

'There's a lot of it about.' Satisfied, Makepeace let go of the man's shirt. She'd have liked to hit him, but to create a further kerfuffle seemed unwise and anyway the bailiff was allowing them to go.

He was telling his fellow in the alley to come inside and search the theater now that everyone else was gone. 'I'll see this lot off. Is Tom watching the front?'

'Letting 'em out in groups.'

The usual admirers, male and female, were awaiting the cast at the end of the alley but even in the ensuing melée, the chief bailiff stuck to Makepeace's heels as if instinct told him she could lead him to his prey. Nor could she dodge him because Aaron's arm trapped hers. He walked slowly, both he and Bracey on the other side lowering their heads graciously to the spontaneous applause of the crowd as they passed.

Again, Makepeace had to wonder if Bracey was drunk; instead of her usual graceful walk, the actress was tottering as she went. Seeing Makepeace lean forward to look at her, she gave a broad wink.

They were in the street now, colliding with passersby who stopped to watch the costumed parade in amazement. Some of The Duke's audience was still trapped in the foyer and only being allowed to leave in threes and fours.

Makepeace's coach, an attraction in itself, was waiting outside.

Dizzy had overtaken them and was talking to Sanders. Aaron's feathers nodded towards a one-horse carriage on the other side of the street. 'They intend to follow you home,' he muttered out of the side of his mouth. 'Don't let 'em.'

Sanders had opened the coach door and was letting down its steps. Makepeace felt the bailiff push past her and scramble inside, pulling at the coach's cushions, tapping its roof. Sullenly, he got out again. 'Empty. All right, get in.' He stood by the door to make sure she did.

Aaron helped his sister inside, keeping the door open. 'God-speed,' he said.

She leaned forward to kiss him. 'Keep him safe,' she whispered.

'Same to you,' he said.

Bracey took his place, putting one foot on the steps to raise her face to Makepeace's and kiss it, her great skirts billowing.

Makepeace felt something slither against her ankles. The coach rocked slightly.

Bracey shut the door. The window was down and Makepeace reached out to her with both hands. 'Thank you,' she said; she had difficulty with it. 'And Bracey . . .'

'Yes, missus?'

'Tell the company from me, they were . . . *extra* wonderful tonight.'

Widow Lackitt was grinning. 'We bloody were, weren't we?'

Sanders cracked his whip and the coach jolted forward at a rate that threw Makepeace back against the seat so that there was no chance to wave good-bye to The Duke's and its actors—something for which she was always sorry.

The body on the floor started to get up but she put her foot on its head. 'We ain't out of the woods yet.'

It grumbled. 'I do not like to hide under women's skirts.'

'You be grateful,' Makepeace said. She opened the flap to the box. 'Anyone following us, Sanders?'

'They are, missus. But we got the speed.'

She sighed. This was déjà vu. 'Sanders, why do we always end up on the wrong side of the law?'

'Don't know, missus. But we always do.'

This time, though, she couldn't go back to Reach House. They would know where she lived, and where Jacques lived; Blanchard would have told them. This time—and it struck her hard—she could never go back.

'Where to, missus?'

'Babbs Cove,' she said.

Chapter Sixteen

THE most shocking thing about their trial was how run-of-the-mill it was and how tired the court was. When Ffoulkes's and Philippa's turn came they were merely customers in a long, long queue to be served by men with a tedious job to do before shutting-up time. There was no special interest in the fact that they were English. The Tribunal had tried Englishmen and women before, as it had tried Germans, Dutch, Spaniards, Danes and sentenced them all to death; it killed internationally.

The setting was nice; late-evening sun lit the wonderful ceiling of the Salle de Liberté but its walls echoed back voices sharp with fatigue, and the click of boots as National Guardsman patrolled the line of prisoners at the bar. On the other side of the wooden barrier that separated the body of the court from the public stands there were eight spectators, two of them asleep. The chamber had been absorbing heat all day and had lost none of it. The jury was trying to keep awake but, like the judges, it looked more tired than the prisoners.

Since nearly all crime was now considered a conspiracy against the Republic, the Convention had decreed that all those on conspiracy charges should come to Paris for trial and suspects were being brought to the capital in the thousands from all over France. If prisons and the guillotine were to cope, the process had to be expedited. Elsewhere in the building four other Revolutionary Tribunals were hearing cases—and would do far into the night. To save time, defendants were allowed neither witnesses nor counsel, juries had the choice of two verdicts: guilty or acquittal.

Ideally, the accused were tried in the morning, received their sentence at two o'clock and, if guilty, executed at four. In reality, most had to wait their turn to die, sometimes for weeks.

They were heard in batches. Alongside Ffoulkes and Philippa was a baker, a farmer and his son from the Vendeé, two priests, a shop girl who was pregnant, the *ci-devant* Countess Hervé Faudoas, her daughter, Mme de Galles, and an elderly couple from Saint Omer who were still trying to find out what they were accused of.

Philippa was in a state of detachment through shock; she noticed some things in detail, mostly unimportant, while others passed her by. She might have been watching an inferior play that she had to sit through but on which the final curtain refused to come down. She was aware it was her fault they were there at all and that any moment the guilt of causing Ffoulkes's death as well as her own would obliterate her, but not yet; she couldn't feel anything yet.

She had apologized nevertheless. When he'd achieved some awareness after his battering at the hands of their captors, she'd squinted out of her one good eye in order to dab his bloodied face with her apron and said she was sorry.

Now, here at the bar of the court, she supposed she should apologize again; he didn't seem to have noticed the first time. She touched his hand. 'I'm sorry.'

'So you bloody well should be.' He was odd. Not angry but absent, as if his mind was on other things, as if she didn't deserve his attention. Which, she supposed, she didn't.

She kept expecting God to give her back the minutes at Number Fifteen and again at the bridge so that she could amend them. The Lord must find this massive punishment too great for a moment or two of impetuosity. He would save Ffoulkes, surely.

But the play went on and on and he was showing no sign of intervening in it.

She did thank him for the fact that, by rushing out of Number

Fifteen without her papers, there was nothing to connect her with that address. Nor had Ffoulkes been registered as living there. As long as M Sarrett hadn't been arrested as well, that household could remain as undisturbed as it was before Condorcet entered it.

And where was *he*? She tried to stretch her mind to that wandering innocent but couldn't.

She supposed she really ought to concentrate on the matter in hand.

The president, irritable and tired, was addressing the thirteen members of the jury. 'Interrogation of the prisoners has already taken place, citizens.' His tone suggested they could take the rest of the evening off. With his three assisting judges he sat on the high bench, facing the prisoners from under a broad-brimmed hat with plumes and a tricolor cockade. Before him on the bench lay a bell and two loaded pistols, ready at each hand for any prisoner who became unruly, although it had become apparent that the person he'd most like to shoot was the state prosecutor, Fouquier-Tinville, also beplumed, who sat on a cross bench between jury and accused.

There'd already been prosecution errors. Several of the defendants on the list had been attributed with the wrong sex. Now Fouquier-Tinville got up to announce that he was offering no evidence in the case of the shop girl; she'd been arrested in mistake for her mother who'd been heard to say, 'Fuck Robespierre and the price of bread.'

'It was a confusion by the National Guard, Citizen President. Both the girl and her mother are called Marie.'

'And I daresay both are guilty of disrespect to the Republic,' said the president. 'Let the charge stand. Too much damn paperwork otherwise.' He rang his bell to drown out the prosecutor's protests and the girl's scream.

Fouquier-Tinville sat down, scrabbling among his papers. M Sarrett had said of him that he'd once been a conscientious lawyer. His work now meant he was lucky to get three hours' sleep in twenty-four. The previous week he'd been found standing on the Pont Neuf, staring at the river and muttering: 'Red, red, red.'

One by one the prisoners were led forward to hear the charge against them. The general lassitude smothered indignation, even fear, like a blanket. Waiting for her turn, Philippa knew that, like each of her fellow accused, she would declare herself innocent but not as if there was any point to it, because there wasn't. When he asked each if he or she had anything to say in his or her defense, citizen president tapped his fingers on the table, occasionally yawning.

The *ci-devant* Countess and Madame de Galles didn't even bother; their titles were their condemnation. Both said, quietly, 'Vive le roi.' The priests, too, were guilty by profession, knew it and merely invoked God.

The baker afforded a momentary change of tempo by saying truculently that he expected nothing from 'a load of crooks and idiots like you lot.'

The shop girl was the only one who showed energy; she became hysterical and had to be taken away to the Tribunal hospital.

The Vendeéan farmer began to explain that he and his son had been forced to lodge rebel soldiers in their house or have their crops burned, but he went on too long and citizen president became impatient. 'Yes, yes, it's noted. Next.'

This was Ffoulkes. The charge was conspiracy against the Republic. Any doubt that Blanchard had supplied the information against him was dispelled by its detail. They even gave his name and title in full. 'Andrew Christopher Elphinstone Ffoulkes, so-called Baron of Wulford.'

Around the court one or two heads were raised from interest.

Perhaps they won't kill him, she thought. *From their point of view he's a spy and an aristocrat, but he's an* English *spy and aristocrat. They can use him as a bargaining counter. Isn't that what sides do in war? Exchange a valuable one of yours for a valuable one of ours?*

He didn't look much against the splendor of the chamber and the judges; too shabby, too many cuts on his face. *So valuable*, she thought, *so valuable to me.*

Citizen president was unimpressed; he'd tried aristocrats, spies and Englishmen before; here were merely the three offenses combined. He repeated the formula without emphasis: 'What have you to say in your defense?'

'Nothing, really,' Ffoulkes said. The easy voice seemed to be issuing from somebody else. 'One would just like to point out that the woman there'—a dismissive wave of the hand in Philippa's direction—'the one supposed to have conspired with me is a stranger as far as I'm concerned. Just another female who's mislaid her papers. Saw her being arrested and waded in on impulse. Nothing to do with me. Sorry.'

He was pushed back into line.

Citizen president's eyes had closed, he opened them. 'Next.'

Philippa stepped forward.

'No papers,' Fouquier-Tinville said, on sure ground. 'Gives her name as Bettine Gagnon but believed to be Philippa Dapifer, English, associate of the previous accused.'

Blanchard had been thorough.

'What have you to say in your defense?'

'Nothing.'

The elderly couple from Saint Omer were put forward after her but, like the rest of the court, she'd expended her attention on other things and never did find out what they were accused of.

The jury was directed to an anteroom to consider verdicts and to be quick about it.

'God Almighty, I gave you a chance, blast you,' Ffoulkes hissed. 'Why in hell didn't you take it? It might have worked.'

'Oh, shut up,' she said. 'If I can't die for you, I might as well die with you.'

He became remote again.

I've done it now, she thought. *I've told him I love him.* It seemed a much more momentous utterance than any made in court so far. *Well, he might as well know.*

When the jury didn't appear within fifteen minutes, a National Guardsman was sent to fetch them back.

Every defendant was found guilty—except the two farmers.

'But they're from the Vendée,' citizen president said with ominous patience, 'The Vendeé's in revolt against the Republic.'

The jury foreman was flustered. 'We know, Citizen President, but we decided they were coerced and . . . well, farmers. Paris needs supplies.'

'Look,' said the president, 'they're from the *Vendée*.'

'Ah,' said the foreman. He turned round to peer at his fellow jurymen. 'Guilty, then.' He sat down. He got up again. 'But we did think . . . the defendant who's going to have a baby . . . we did think execution ought to be delayed . . . until she does.'

Citizen president had come to the end of his tether. 'Of course it will, you dolt. Do you think we're in the Dark Ages?'

The prisoners were lined up and led out by guards carrying lanterns. It was a long walk, mostly through a labyrinth of passages. Philippa was two behind Ffoulkes. She heard the *ci-devant* Countess ask him: 'Do you know where one is going, M'sieu?'

'The Conciergerie, Countess. The two palaces are connected.'

'The Conciergerie. Where they held the Queen before they murdered her?'

'Yes, Madame. We'll pass her cell.'

'That is something, then, God give her mercy. To suffer where she suffered.'

How does he know all this? Philippa wondered. She listened to the two chatting as they went along; they had acquaintances in common. She heard Ffoulkes say, like someone discussing the points of an inn, 'If one can pay for it, one can procure a cell to oneself. Otherwise it's the common hall.'

'I have . . . ' The Countess's voice sank to a precautionary whisper.

'I'll see what I can do for you tomorrow,' Ffoulkes promised her. 'Bit late for haggling tonight.'

The Countess, an elderly woman, gave a deep curtsey as they passed the little iron door behind which Marie Antoinette had spent her last hours. Ffoulkes raised her and gently hurried her on; the priests had fallen to their knees and guards were kicking them to their feet.

Past open courts. An exercise yard. Downwards along passages with gilded vaulting. 'But they are taking us into the bowels of the earth,' the old man from Saint Omer complained.

'Bowels certainly got something to do with it,' the baker told him. The smell was becoming thicker as they went, like fog settling on lowest ground.

All at once they were in a great space, the Hall of Arms with its thirty-six blond, branching pillars amongst which Philip the Fair's men-at-arms had waited on their king's orders in the fourteenth century and where hundreds of men and women now passed the time until their execution. It was hot and dark, with a ferocious communal silence, like a lair occupied by sleeping animals.

There was light at its far end where a jailer sat at a table in the entrance to an ogival-roofed corridor. He took their names. 'I ain't separating you women tonight,' he said. 'It's too late, you'll have to bed down here with the men. Get yourselves some straw. Any of you's got chink, I'll see to you tomorrow.'

Bedding straw had been swept into a ceiling-high pile at one end of the corridor and new arrivals from the other tribunals were picking it up in armfuls.

Ffoulkes gathered a great heap for the Countess. Philippa had to gather her own but when she'd have made her bed next to the woman, he picked up enough for himself and nudged her along the corridor into the hall away from the light of the jailer's lantern. 'Here. More private.' She could just see him patting straw into place at the foot of a pillar.

He settled her on the bed he'd made, a cushion of straw between her head and the pillar, then sat down beside her. They talked in whispers.

'We'll get out,' he said. 'I've been in and out of more French clinks than you've had hot dinners. There's always a jailer with a palm to be crossed with silver.'

'Have you *got* any silver?'

'In my boot. Bloody uncomfortable. I'll see about it tomorrow.'

'Will there be a tomorrow for us?' she asked.

'Good God, yes. They'll have announced tomorrow's quota for the tumbrels already, they call out the names the evening before. Plenty of time to work the oracle. Go to sleep.'

He's lying, she thought. Even if it was true that he'd escaped from prisons before, it had been with the connivance of The League and its money, safe house, identity papers. But the lies, his very voice, were the rope she clung onto to stop herself slipping into black fear and drowning in it. Now that she was part of it, the silence wasn't silence at all; it was whimpers, snores and rat-infested rustling. Somewhere, in another part of the building, a baby was crying. A jailer's child? A prisoner's?

The pity of it enveloped her. Women loving men as she loved this one, men loving women, children loving parents, father and mother desperate with love for their child, son, daughter torn from loved parents, brothers, sisters . . . the irreplaceable web people spun to keep each other safe ripped apart. For what?

'Ma's going to be so mad,' she said, just to keep talking and not drowning. 'Do you think she'll know what's happened to us?'

'We'll tell her,' he said. 'Go to sleep.'

'You shouldn't have come after me,' she said. 'I could bear anything if I hadn't got you into this.'

'For God's sake, go to sleep.'

'I can't.'

There was a jerking cry in the darkness; someone waking from a bad dream into actual nightmare, then someone else's voice gentling whoever-it-was until they were quiet again.

'Look,' Ffoulkes said, 'since you insist on flagellating yourself . . . I wasn't going to tell you this, hardly decent considering everything, being your godfather and married and all, but I didn't try and save you out of bloody chivalry . . .'

Somewhere a golden sun rose and melted everything in its path as it crept towards her.

'Fact is, something happened on that bloody bridge when they were marching you across.' He paused. 'You didn't look your best, you know, hair all over the place, black eye . . .'

'That was later,' she said, happily.

'Was it? Well, you weren't Venus rising from the waves and I thought: "Leave it, Ffoulkes, it's her own damn fault. You've got better things to do than get your head chopped off for a scarecrow like that . . ."'

'But you didn't.'

'No, I didn't. That was the moment I realized that if they took you down to hell, I'd follow you. Now in the name of God, let me get some sleep.'

She leaned her head back against the pillar and allowed sunlight to penetrate the marrow of her bones.

'Ffoulkes,' she said.

'What?'

'Do you think they'd provide a cell for two?'

I T was against the rules for male and female prisoners to lodge together but the Conciergerie's rules were crumbling and he arranged it the next morning, he could arrange everything except their freedom. They were to live *à la pistole* by paying twenty-seven *livres* in advance for accommodation for two. He even carried her over the threshold. The cell had two iron beds with mattresses. They only needed one.

She made him blink by undressing the moment he shut the door and she guessed that his wives and other women had shown more modesty. There wasn't time for modesty; they made love immediately and after a rest they made love again. And again.

'How long do you think we've got?' she asked.

'Not long if we go on like this. I won't make roll call.' He rolled off her. 'We'll send out for luncheon, I think. It looks as if I'm going to have to keep up my strength. What would you like to eat, Mrs Fox?'

She thought he was joking. 'A little foie gras, perhaps.' But he'd already got a jailer at his beck and call, and foie gras with toast was what she was presented with an hour later. And a bottle of respectable Burgundy.

'You can get anything brought in if you know the right people,' he said. 'And have enough chink.'

This was apparent; apart from the food, he'd ordered shaving things and new clothes for himself and, for her, a basque, a shift and a muslin gown to go over them.

It is typical of him, she thought, *that we must both look nice for the guillotine.*

The jailer who brought them was a wheezing fat man with the strawberry nose and broken veins of a heavy drinker, name of Albert. 'Anything you want, citizen,' he said as Ffoulkes pressed coins into his hand. 'Anything at all.'

'I have hopes of compromising young Albert in time,' Ffoulkes said after he'd gone. 'Blackmail him into letting us out.'

It was a fiction he indulged in for her; he said there were identity papers they could use stashed in his safe house in Neuilly. He knew, she knew, that Blanchard had supplied the Comité de Securité with details of every *certificat de civisme* he'd ever issued. They'd get out only to be caught and brought back again.

But fiction was all they had, fiction and love. What they didn't have was time.

She watched him shave and got out of bed to put her arms round him, squashing her breasts against his bare back, her eyes just able to look over his shoulder at their reflection in the small looking glass he'd hung from a nail in the wall.

He grinned at her. 'Are you sure this isn't incest?'

'I don't care.'

They'd been given a tiny sliver of life separate from everything they'd known; his marriage, their old relationship, the past, no longer mattered.

It worried him, mainly on her account, that he wasn't being gentlemanly. It didn't worry her; a sentence of death was a rebirth for them both. Almost unconsciously, he'd given her a new name, Mrs Fox. She liked it; it changed her status to that of his mistress.

'I'm an abandoned woman,' she told him.

But even here, he couldn't stop being busy. She had to let him go to make arrangements for the Countess and her daughter. Somewhat resentfully, she wandered out into the Hall of Arms after him. *Hurry, hurry, we've only got today. And it's nearly gone.* It was evening.

The place was fuller than she'd expected, its pillars like great trees in a forest in which the undergrowth was people. Flames from torches streamed up from the holders, lighting the vaulting and giving more life to the gargoyles sculpted on the cornices than the faces of the men and women below. The noise of conversation was nearly deafening.

She stood on the steps and looked around them, dreading to see someone she knew. Was Condorcet here? How could they kill so many?

There was a tug on her sleeve. 'Can I stay by you, citizeness? I don't know anyone else.' It was the shop girl, the one who was pregnant, the one called Marie like her mother. Her full name was Marie Mounier.

They sat together on the steps to talk. Either nobody had explained to her or, in her terror she hadn't understood, that her execution would be delayed until her baby was born. 'Four months, then,' Philippa said, patting the small swell of belly in an otherwise sticklike frame. 'A lot can happen in four months.'

Marie sagged with relief. 'Papa will have time to explain to Citizen Robespierre.'

Her father was on a section committee in the Marais, a good revolutionary, she said. 'Maman supports the Revolution, too, very strongly, but her tongue runs away with her and she said, you know what she said, because she was cross we didn't have enough to eat.' Marie Mounier the Elder, Philippa gathered, had a tongue that did her no favors with her neighbors, one of whom had probably reported her. On the Sunday of the arrest, she'd been out of the house but her daughter had been in.

'She used to be cross because Jean-Philippe won't be able to marry me until he comes home from the war,' Marie the Younger said, 'but now she'll see what a good thing this baby is.'

'Do you want a boy or a girl?'

'A boy, of course. To fight for the Republic.'

Philippa went off to find Ffoulkes. 'If it's the last thing we do, we've got to get that girl out of here before she loses the baby. She's too thin as it is. Could we get a letter to de Vaubon or Danton, somebody who cares, tell them she's here by mistake?'

'I'm afraid not.' He took her hands, frightening her. 'They've just told me. De Vaubon and Danton went to the guillotine this morning. Desmoulins, too.'

She closed her eyes. De Vaubon strode across their lids, swaggering, noisy, full of heart. 'He has a son.'

'They all had children,' Ffoulkes said. 'They died well, apparently. Danton told Sanson to show his head to the crowd when it was off. He said it was worth looking at.'

'Ma will be stricken.'

'I know.' He'd gained a handkerchief from somewhere and wiped her cheeks with it.

'They were here last night, then,' she said. 'I could have talked to him.'

'No. When your name's called you spend the night in special cells downstairs. You wouldn't have been allowed to see him.'

She was suddenly furious. 'Don't you tell me they died well. You can't die well, it's a contradiction in terms.'

'Hang on, Mrs Fox.' He put his arms round her. 'We'll go back to our cell in a minute.'

'Now,' she pleaded. 'Let's go now.'

'In a minute. Hang on to me.'

More prisoners were emerging from the tributary tunnels and staircases leading into the Hall of Arms, jailers herding them from behind.

There was a drumroll.

'Here it comes,' a man next to them said.

Oh God, Philippa thought, *here it comes and I'm not ready.*

People were forming into groups, some on their knees, some clinging to family or those they'd faced trial with. One lot, aristocrats to judge from their ornate clothes and hair, formed a graceful frieze. There was a boy no older than sixteen among them. The old man who stood next to him looked out of place, like a small-town apothecary in his old brown coat and black hose, but the resemblance between him and the boy was strong.

First they were counted; jailers and National Guard pushed through the crowd, lanterns swinging, fingers stabbing, lips shaping numbers, swearing at anybody who moved out of place

Fouquier-Tinville stood on the steps in the light, waiting but paying no attention except to a portable writing desk held by a clerk. He scanned papers, scribbled alterations, signed. When this was over he had to report to the Committee of Public Safety with the list, arrange the necessary number of tumbrels, tell Sanson how many to expect . . . God knew when he'd get to bed.

The clerk found the right piece of paper for him and he read from it without looking up, speaking into the only moment when the prison was totally silent.

'The following will report to the clerk of court's office. For the males: Chateaubriand, Duboeuf, d'Eprémesnil, Huel, Chrétien Malesherbes and Louis Malesherbes, Thouret, Dard father and son, Brun.

'For the women: de Châtelet, Chateaubriand, de Grammont, de Lubormirski, Malesherbes, Valois, Lupin.'

He turned and hurried off.

'All of them,' Ffoulkes said softly. 'Jesus Christ.'

A woman nearby fainted; it turned out her name *hadn't* been read out. Philippa's own knees were weak with relief. They could live another day.

The frieze of aristocrats moved as the old man stepped out of it, took hold of his grandson's hand, patted it and led his womenfolk on the walk to the clerk of the court's office and the cells reserved for those dying tomorrow. The boy was blinking hard in case tears showed. The women glided without expression, except when one of them smiled and held back, waiting for another to catch up.

Ffoulkes stepped out and said something to the old man who paused and inclined his head graciously before walking on.

'Who is he?' she asked.

'Malesherbes.'

She watched the old man go. He'd defended Louis XVI at his trial and Marie Antoinette at hers. Condorcet, who'd loved him, called his brain encyclopedic. 'He is also the greatest gardener in France,' he'd said.

'What did you say to him?' she asked Ffoulkes.

'I don't know. An honor to have known him or something. Went to his chateau once, it was like one vast potting shed. Christ, they're killing the whole family. The whole family.'

She took him back to their cell and closed the door.

I T was like living in a bubble that had alighted to wobble on some protrusion in hell. Inside it was beautiful, iridescent, but with a transparency that showed the horrors outside and a fragility that would be popped any moment by the tip of Fouquier-Tinville's pen.

Daytime was the best; they could wedge the door and make love and play like adolescents—they teased each other a lot. '*Elphinstone*?'

'As bestowed on all eldest Ffoulkes's and I'll thank you not to broadcast it.'

'I won't. You're not bestowing it on our eldest.' The bubble extended into a future in which they ruled a coral island inhabited by happy, obliging natives; they were still arguing over whether its women should have the vote.

He broke the rules. 'I'd have liked children.'

'So would I. It was why I was marrying Stephen.'

'I wondered why it was. Think what that poor devil's been saved.'

His hunger for her was as sharp as hers for him. What light came through the tiny, barred window gave her skin an olive sheen that excited him almost to madness. He made her spend most of the day undressed. 'Not at all what I'm used to,' he'd say, 'I like blond and voluptuous as a rule, not twiggy and small-breasted.'

'It doesn't seem to worry you.'

'Just bein' polite.'

She had no artifice. She couldn't set out to delight him because she didn't know how; she was just delighted *with* him. She had no trouble reaching the climacteric, nor did he, but she wondered if she compared badly with his other women. At one point she tapped him on his back. 'Am I doing this right?'

'Good God,' was all he said, which was satisfaction in itself.

He never mentioned Félicie, nor did she want him to. She knew that if, by a miracle, they returned to their old life, she would have to give him back to his wife and walk away; to be his mistress would be something neither of their consciences could tolerate. As it was, they were stealing nothing.

He never mentioned Blanchard, either.

The nights were bad. There was a death roll call every evening except Saturday's, or Nonidi's—whatever the Revolution called that day of the week now—because Sanson insisted on Sundays off. They'd be dressed waiting for the jailer's rap on the door, he'd take her hand and say, as he always did and *why* she'd never fathomed, 'God Bless the Duke of Argyll,' and they'd march out to the hall to hear whether or not they were going to die next morning.

Not hearing their names read out was a ferocious schadenfreude and then an equally ferocious guilt, as if she'd been saying to those taken away: 'Die *for* us.'

The resultant scenes were awful. On the evening they read out the name of Countess Hervé Faudoas but not her daughter's; Mme de Galles clung to her mother's knees and had to be pulled away. One of the priests, Father Hédé who'd been tried with them, was taken, the other left. The couple from Saint Omer went quietly, hand in hand, still unaware of their crime against the Republic.

They'd go back to their cell and shut the door against the screams and lie down, merely to hold each other.

Gradually, they were drawn into the life beyond their door, Ffoulkes by the helplessness of Mme de Galles, Philippa by concern for the pregnant Marie Mounier for whom Ffoulkes had provided a cell—then, inevitably, for others. They drafted letters of appeal to the Convention and Robespierre for those who couldn't write their own or didn't know how to phrase them.

Ffoulkes bullied the jailers into a fairer distribution of rations. Philippa demanded, and got, a supply of linen to be torn into menstruation towels—something the prison authorities hadn't thought of and other women had been too embarrassed to mention.

For this she was made much of in the Women's Court where the female prisoners did their laundry, a stone-flagged, mossy little place with a fountain set in one wall. Camaraderie was high there and, despite being a foreigner whose country was at war with their own, she was accepted by the common women more warmly than were the female *ci-devants*.

'Well done, English. How did you do it?'

'Pity you had to, though, considering we're all trying to get pregnant.'

It would have horrified the virtuous Robespierre to know that sexual nicety had been abandoned in the Conciergerie. A scrawl on the chimney breast of the Hall of Arms read: 'Fuck Virtue.'

Nearly everybody did—and each other. It wasn't just that pregnancy granted women a reprieve but that few saw any point in going to the guillotine without having tasted what life had left to offer. Prostitutes of both sexes did a roaring trade that earned them money to spend on luxuries, male and female maidens took the opportunity to shed their virginity before they shed their heads, some nuns and priests refused to relinquish their celibacy, others decided not to go to their death wondering.

By day, before the sexes were separated for the night, the Hall thrummed with life in the raw. Saturday nights, when there was assurance of a deathless Sunday, were a Saturnalia. As Ffoulkes said, 'You can't turn a corner without stepping over somebody's bobbing arse.'

'As opposed to the rich bobbing arses in the cells,' Philippa told him. 'This is democracy, this is.'

Extraordinary, she thought, *how we become used to the extraordinary*. She'd even begun to have her hair done—she liked to look nice for him. Her *coiffeur* was a young man known in the prison as 'Lulu.' Ffoulkes loathed him. He was outrageously unpatriotic with flapping silk lapels to his coat and breeches tied at the knee with bows. His hair was heavily powdered and turned up at the back with a comb—'*à la guillotine, cherie*'—with two curls hanging down on either cheek like dog's ears. He tottered about the salon he ran in a corner of the Hall on a pair of women's shoes, which, he said, Mme du Barry had given him before her execution and which were so small that only his toes stuck inside.

He was a commoner but an aristo-lover *par excellence*, a simpering, scented snob who genuflected outside Marie Antoinette's cell every night and considered 'Let them eat cake,' to be the ultimate in wit. He was also one of the kindest people in the prison; he took young Marie Mounier under his wing and, as Ffoulkes's money began to run out, bought fresh milk for her and did her and Philippa's hair for free. 'One must keep busy, dear,' he explained, 'One doesn't want to become *merdeux*.'

To be *merdeux* was the phrase applied to those, and there were quite a few, who sank so deep into apathy that they sat all day in their own ordure.

The ordinary Frenchwomen kept away from him so that his clientele declined as the number of aristocrats dwindled—the number being brought in no longer kept up with those going to their death.

The ones who remained had a game they played in a corridor before lights out. They put a chair on a table, saluted each other in Latin and a beaker of wine: '*Ave Caesar, morituri te salutant*.' One by one they stepped onto a bench and from there to the table where they knelt and rested their head on the chair, stretching their arms out behind them as an imaginary blade fell. The others applauded.

'Aren't they *wonderful*?' Lulu said. 'Do you think they'd let me join in?'

'No.' The pantomime distressed and irritated her. As she told Ffoulkes, 'They're stiffening their resolve not to show fear when the time comes but what's wrong with showing fear?'

'One doesn't.'

'Well, one should. If they howled and screamed, like Lulu says Mme du Barry did, they might move the crowd to pity and this *danse macabre* would stop. But no, we mustn't share human emotion with the mob, must we? We never have and we're damned if we start now.'

'You're getting sansculottish,' Ffoulkes said. 'It's called style, Mrs Fox.'

'It's called exclusivity and it's what caused the bloody trouble in the first place.'

It was the nearest they got to quarrelling. It was hot and she had a new worry; she'd missed a period. For the tiniest part of a second she'd almost screamed with joy, *I'm having his baby*, before reality clawed her back. It would die with her, the tiny heart stopping as hers stopped. The matrons at the Tribunal hospital refused to examine and pronounce on a pregnancy before it had advanced three or four months. Even if she survived until then, she would have to make the choice between declaring the pregnancy and letting Ffoulkes go to the scaffold alone. Dying with him or living without him—but with his child.

Ffoulkes had picked up the paper and was reading it to her, presumably his way of leaving a ticklish issue. 'What do you think of that, Mrs Fox?'

'I'm sorry, I wasn't listening.'

'Are you all right? Aren't you interested in the Convention's latest decree?'

'I was thinking about Mary Wollstonecraft.' *There* was an Englishwoman who'd become pregnant under the Terror. She wondered if Mary had found her survival worth it when she got back to England and the calumny thrown at unmarried mothers. A better terror, perhaps, but still terrible.

'Very sansculottish.'

At least the Republic had abolished that stigma; married or unmarried, mothers were to be given the State's assistance.

It might just be that her period was late; a lot of the women in the Women's Court said they were irregular. Anyway, with a Damocles sword over one's head, there was no point in crossing bridges one wasn't likely to arrive at. Mixed metaphors; it was time to stop thinking. 'Go on reading,' she said.

The latest decree, it appeared, defined enemies of the People as those who'd once worked for the royal government, compromised the war effort, reduced food reserves, who'd spread false rumours or defeatism or sedition, who—as dishonest contractors, vexatious officials, or in any other capacity—had compromised the liberty, unity and safety of the Republic.

'In effect, anybody,' Ffoulkes said, throwing the newspaper to one side.

The Conciergerie was always ahead of the papers, its information from the daily intake of prisoners more reliable. The immediate news was the weather. The summer was becoming the hottest Paris had known, as if God was taking His revenge for having been abolished. The Seine had shrunk from its banks and revealed islands of silt in its course. Women fainted in the food queues, dray-horses collapsed in their traces. The words 'bad harvest' filtered in from outlying farms like a warning that the enemy was at the gates.

In the Hall of Arms the names called out rarely included that of a *ci-devant*—there weren't many left. Now those going to the guillotine were neither aristocrats nor treacherous generals nor dishonest officials, but shopkeepers, clerks, innkeepers, day laborers, clock-makers, agricultural workers—people who worked life's machinery.

The new intakes talked of a dull, deep resentment rising with the heat from the very pavement as people saw a friend, a relative, employer, employee, arrested and taken away.

As with the ground itself, fissures were opening in the Convention, multiplying and cracking so that deputies divided into groups, distrusting each other and the ever-growing power of the Tribunal.

There were madnesses. Someone at the Convention proposed raising the daily output of executions by constructing a gargantuan-wide guillotine that would cut off a hundred heads at a time. Robespierre rejected the suggestion; he said it wouldn't be good for public morale.

Those coming into prison who'd had any contact with Robespierre said he was becoming increasingly isolated, suspicious and, therefore, terrifying. Ffoulkes learned of a deputy who, trying to please his chief, had organized a street party to celebrate the Republic. 'It turns out that Citizen Robespierre does not approve of street parties,' Ffoulkes told Philippa. 'My informant says the deputy has been forced to make an apology that couldn't be deeper if he'd raped Robespierre's sister. Mark my words, Mrs Fox, even frightened deputies, *especially* frightened deputies, won't tolerate this shame much longer. They'll rise against him.'

'Don't say it, don't say it.' As time went on she'd begun to believe that perhaps the authorities were keeping Ffoulkes alive for political motives, a bargaining counter that Pitt would take notice of, but she tried blanking her mind against the thought. Hope was the ultimate cruelty; she saw it being taken away every night.

Lucile, Desmoulins's wife, had been arrested for protesting

against her husband's death and was executed almost immediately, leaving her baby in the care of her mother. A young woman, Cécile Renault, who'd made a half-hearted attempt to assassinate Robespierre, went to the guillotine with fifty others who'd had any connection with her, all dressed in red to denote parricide. Malesherbes's seventy-six-year-old sister went, so did his two secretaries—one of them having been found to have a bust of Henri IV on his mantelpiece. They were taken to the Place de la Révolution in the same tumbrels as former enragés, latter-day Dantonists, farmers who'd hoarded a bushel of grain for themselves.

The joke in the Conciergerie was that the only democracy left in France was the guillotine's.

And Lulu went. Philippa hadn't recognized the name; she didn't know it was him until his voice rang out as Fouquier-Tinville finished reading the list. 'Thank you, my good fellow, thank you. The same tumbrel that the Her Majesty had, if you'd be so good.'

She ran up to hold his hand as they led him away. The simpering mask he wore slipped away, leaving weariness. 'Don't mind,' he told her. 'Dying's easy. Living was *much* more difficult.' He touched her hair. 'Keep that style, dear, it suits you.'

She collapsed and Ffoulkes had to carry her back to their cell.

'I can't bear it, any of it, not any more.'

He rocked her like a baby. 'Yes, you can.'

'It's going on and on. I want it to end.'

'Come on, now, Mrs Fox. This won't do. What would Mary Wollstonecraft say?'

He made her laugh; he always could. Later, in the darkness, he said, 'As hells go, this could have been worse. I found you in it, which was better than not finding you at all. Taken by and large, I wouldn't have missed it.'

'I love you, Ffoulkes. More than life.'

'That's what I mean.'

The next night, when his name was read out among the other

men's, she couldn't believe she'd heard it—not until her own name was included in the women's, at which point she knew her greatest terror had been that he'd be taken and she'd be left.

THERMIDOR 9 (July 27, 1794)
A terrible day, full of noise, marching, running feet and the ringing of tocsins. The political storm that had been gathering so long burst like a giant bubo—and the sky with it, overlaying everything with the shriek of the rain that inhibited vision and confused the ear.

It brought no relief to the Conciergerie. The electricity in the atmosphere penetrated even the deepest cells where men and women, separated from each other, were being prepared for the tumbrels. Prisoners became restless, pacing their cages. Heat was imprisoned with them, as if the layers of water running down the windows upstairs formed a barrier that stopped the outside cooling air from getting in. Night jailers were told to stay on duty in case of an attempted mass breakout.

Rumor blazed in brief flashes, like the lightning. The Convention had turned on Robespierre. Arrested him. No, it hadn't, somebody'd just seen him walking through the Palais de Justice. The Convention was calling on all Paris sections to bring their guards and loyalty to the Tuileries. No, it was the other way round; the sections were in insurrection against the Convention and calling on their guards and loyalty to go to the Hôtel de Ville.

It was both. It was neither. The English had invaded.

In the preparation room, Philippa and the four other listed women were having their hair sawn to ear level. Their chemises were torn to free their neck, hands were tied behind their backs with twine, feet hobbled.

The jailers showed neither sexuality nor harshness; they'd been doing this too long. As each woman was prepared, she was slapped amiably on her rump, like a cow being sent to market. 'Off you go now, girl.'

They were taken out into the passageway where the clerk of the court checked their names against Fouquier-Tinville's list. 'Off you go now,' he said.

They were escorted down the passage to the arcade that led into the Cour de Mai and fresh air.

The eponymous tree in the court's center around which medieval queens had danced on May Day had been cut down to facilitate the passage of the carts as they went in and out, but there was a reminder of countryside in a new intake of prisoners—a batch of Bretons, to judge from the women's caps and aprons—who waited, clutching their bundles, to be taken inside for registration. Haybags hung from hooks ready to refresh today's horses when they came with the tumbrels, and there was a light smell of the manure left by yesterday's teams that the rain hadn't quite swept away.

The storm had left a fine, clear day. The midday sky had been laundered to its cleanest blue and the sun shone, dazzling the prisoners. There was a group of men, handcuffed and hobbled, standing in one corner.

'Hello,' Philippa shouted.

'Good morning,' Ffoulkes shouted back. 'What in hell have they done to your hair?'

His shirt had been dragged down to expose his neck. She shuffled over to him and rubbed her cropped head against his shoulder. 'You're nothing to write home about yourself.'

She was astonished by her contentment. That was one thing about death; it resolved your problems. They'd been allowed to find completion of body and soul in one another; some people lived out their lives without that gift.

He looked down at her, catching the thought. 'Can't complain, I suppose,' he said.

'No.'

After a while, it occurred even to them that procedure was being breached. The tumbrels were late. Faces peered out of the windows of the palace offices, a group of officials stood in the arcade to the Conciergerie entrance talking worriedly.

The jailer who'd brought her out was grumbling to another. 'National bloody Guard,' Philippa heard him say. 'Well, I'm not working extra bloody hours.'

One of the women who'd been prepared with Philippa, a prostitute from her dress—though they all looked like prostitutes with their gowns pushed down to their cleavages—betrayed her sentiments and her nerves by shrieking: 'Long live the bloody King and get on with it.'

Some of the men prisoners began to shout and one of them, a fat and dapper little man, said loudly: 'I demand to see the clerk of the court.'

Ffoulkes caught sight of a familiar figure crossing the court and shouted at it. 'Hey, Albert, what's up?'

'National Guard's late. Can't go ahead without the National Guard.'

Now the carts were arriving, four of them, each with two horses and a driver, but no National Guard. Jailers let down the tailgates. There were twenty-one prisoners—it was a slow execution day. Philippa's ambition in what remained of her life narrowed down to being included in the same tumbrel as her lover. By keeping close and hanging back, they made two of the six in the rear cart.

Fouquier-Tinville had joined the group in the arcade and there was more discussion.

'Something's up,' Ffoulkes said. 'Look.'

From the tumbrel's vantage point, they could see the Seine set like marquetry between its curving banks of silt. People were swarming across the bridges towards them.

'Hey, Albert,' Ffoulkes said. 'Anybody special dying today?'

'There's you,' Philippa said.

He shrugged. 'Flattering, but I don't think so.'

A crowd was forming just outside the gates, others still streaming across the bridges to join it along the Quai de l'Horloge.

The little fat prisoner was complaining loudly. 'I demand to see the clerk of the court, this is most inefficient.'

From a tumbrel nearer the gates a woman shouted that she wanted to pee. A jailer told her to do it where she stood.

The crowd outside was becoming denser by the minute and the jailers inside the court more nervous. Somebody came out with pikes and handed them round, but the faces at the gate weren't so much hostile as . . . Philippa didn't know what it was; curiosity, perhaps, intentness, as if waiting for some promised spectacle.

They have, she thought, *they've come to see Ffoulkes go to his death.*

'Something *is* up,' he said suddenly and turned his back on her. 'Get these bloody knots untied.'

'How?'

'Use your initiative for Christ's sake. And your teeth.'

She turned so that they were back to back and felt the rope round his wrists with her fingers. It was tight. 'Unclench your fists.' When he did, she realized his hands were shaking. 'Don't,' she said, 'Don't hope.'

'Just get the sodding thing off.'

She worked at the knots. Beside her two men, back to back, were trying to release each other as well. The jailers were taking no notice of them, their eyes were on the gates behind her. She heard a kerfuffle. 'What's happening?'

'Two horsemen coming in. Keep working.'

She kept working, craning her neck to catch a sight of the newcomers. Their horses clopped by her towards the group at the arcade and she saw that one of the men was very large. Both wore big slouch hats with red, white and blue plumes. They were accompanied by a troop of armed men on foot; she didn't recognize the uniform. The two men dismounted and joined in the discussion with Fouquier-Tinville.

Ffoulkes was shifting so that he could look at the gates and then the arcade and she kept losing her grip on the cord round his wrists.

She stopped as the two men approached the carts. Fouquier-Tinville came with them. As usual, he had papers in his hands and was splaying them like cards to show to the smaller of the newcomers.

'. . . nor this one, nor this one,' he was saying. 'Citizen Robespierre signed none of them. All of them, *all*, bear the authority of the Tribunal. I don't care what's happened, these are legally authorized and must be obeyed.'

'I don't think you understand your position, citizen. Forty-eight went to the guillotine yesterday who shouldn't have . . . Forty-eight.'

'I was obeying orders.'

'. . . you don't want to add this lot as well. Who are they? Anyone special?'

Fouquier-Tinville sorted through his papers.

Philippa found that their conversation was failing to reach her brain in any sort of order; they might have been speaking Chinese. Instead she watched the big man stroll to the first cart and draw his sword, beckoning its occupants to come to the cart's edge so that he could reach them. *They're going to stab us.*

Instead, the man was cutting the prisoners' ropes. He went along the line doing it. The carts tilted as their occupants rushed to the side nearest the man and turned their backs, bending forward to extend their bound hands behind them—a posture that looked vaguely naughty.

Nobody's stopping him.

'Ah, yes,' Fouquier-Tinville was saying, still consulting paper, 'there are two English. Here we are: "Plotting to overthrow the Republic, enemies of the State."' He was relieved. 'I think you'll agree on those two at least. We must set an example.' He looked up and saw the man cutting the prisoners free. 'No, no. Stop that.'

'We've been setting an example for ten bloody months,' the other man said, 'The people are sick of it.' He pointed to the crowd at the gates. 'Who'd you think they're going to cheer to the guillotine? This lot? Or Robespierre?'

The man with the sword had reached her cart. Obediently, she lined up with Ffoulkes to turn her back and hold her arms out. She felt hardly a pull before her hands were free. *Must be a very sharp sword*, she thought.

Fouquier-Tinville was pestering her liberator. 'You shouldn't do that.'

'Ah well,' the big man said. 'They might as well be comfy.' He looked up at Philippa. 'Miss Dapifer, is it?' He gave a slight bow. 'I'm a friend of your mother's. You might say I'm here on her behalf.'

'Oh,' she said. He spoke French with an Irish accent and his face was as round as it was amiable. She found herself saying, 'And how is Mama?'

'She's well, very well.'

Wiping the sweat from his face, Fouquier-Tinville had turned back to the other man. His head kept nodding as if attached to a spring. 'Citizen, I've only been obeying orders . . .'

'I know,' the man said. 'You can tell them that at your trial.' He was casually dressed, despite his splendid hat, and his cravat was orthodox in its grubbiness but he had authority and his face might have shown humor if Fouquier-Tinville hadn't been trying him to the limit.

He spoke to the clerk of the court, who'd come up. 'We'll have to release the prisoners in batches,' he said. He jerked his head towards Fouquier-Tinville who was poring over papers that were shaking too violently to be read. 'Let them go en masse and they'll lynch him. Get these people down and free them. We're going to need the carts.'

Next she found herself and the others milling around the clerk of the court's office while a harried official scratched their names off a list. The little fat prisoner, almost affronted at the anti-climax of his release, wanted written assurance that he wouldn't be arrested again.

'It's over?' the prostitute kept asking. 'The Terror's over?'

Nobody answered her, nobody knew or, if they did, their brains wouldn't absorb the alteration.

Philippa seemed to be in one place and then another without any physical effort in between. She was back in the Court of May now and caught sight of Ffoulkes. He was angry, furious. He marched up to the man who'd said he was a friend of her mother's and was questioning him, looking slight but aggressive against the man's bulk, like a dog yapping at a lazy bull.

Don't, she thought. Somehow a massive dome that had bricked them in was blowing away as lightly as if it had been constructed from feathers. *Don't*. The wind might change and reconstruct it before they could get out.

The little fat prisoner said, 'I can go then?' Nobody answered him and he began sidling towards the gates. The prostitute slipped through them and into the crowd like an eel returning to water. The chief jailer was trying to shoo the new intake of prisoners out into the Quai de l'Horloge. 'You can go home,' he was saying, 'Go home to Brittainy.' They stared at him and one of them asked, 'How?'

Philippa went up to Ffoulkes and took his arm to try and lead him away. He shook her off. 'Tell me what's *happening*.' He spoke in English. 'I've a right to know.'

The Irishman said, 'Well, no, not at the moment ye haven't. Ah, here's Citizen Deputy Barras. Be polite now.'

Citizen Deputy Barras was the man he'd ridden in with and his authority was growing by the minute; jailers, officials were beginning to jump to his orders; only Fouquier-Tinville, still leaning against the cart and leafing through his papers as if El Dorado might be in them somewhere, was paying no attention.

'What's going on here?' Barras asked.

'I was explaining to this citizen that he was to make himself scarce,' the Irishman said, 'for reasons that you and I have discussed.'

'Hello, Vicomte,' Ffoulkes said.

Deputy Citizen Barras stared at him before turning away. 'Get him out of here.'

The big Irishman took Philippa and Ffoulkes by the arm and scooped them towards the gates. 'Now's not the time.'

They had to wait while jailers sallied out onto the Quai to clear a path through the crowd—not for them but for a procession arriving from the Right Bank. Riflemen were among a large contingent of National Guard trying to march in, none of them able to keep step for the push of people looking to see what they were escorting.

A boy who'd climbed up onto one of the gateposts shouted, 'It *is* him. That's his blue coat.'

The column edged through the gates. In its center men were carrying a stretcher. The figure lying on it was clutching a bandage that wound around his face, like a child with mumps, obscuring most of it and seeping blood. His stained coat had been a pretty blue and his stockings were rumpled round his ankles, showing bare calves of an almost greenish whiteness.

'Christ Almighty,' she heard Ffoulkes say. 'It *is* Robespierre.'

The stretcher bearers laid their burden on the stones and went back to help the rest of their column through the press.

The little fat man edged up to the stretcher and looked down at the figure of Maximilien François Marie Isidore de Robespierre before guards shoved him out of the way. 'So there *is* a God,' he said.

Other men were being escorted in and the crowd chanted their names as they passed.

'*Saint Just.*' A calm, point device man.

'*Couthon.*' In a wheelchair, groaning.

'*Robespierre Le Petit.*' Maximilien's younger brother, Augustin, hopping on his one uninjured leg.

'*Dumas.*' Hatless, still attempting to give orders. He'd been the president of the tribunal that had tried her and Ffoulkes.

Someone shouted, 'Give me back my father, you bastard.'

It was a war cry and the crowd answered it in a roar that was taken up along the quay, then the island, crescendoing across the bridges to Right and Left banks as if all of Paris had been orphaned and wanted the dead returned to it. The guards were having to fight against hands and fists in order to get the rest of the prisoners through, dragging in the human detritus that had once ruled France. Two of them were corpses.

As each was hauled past the gates, he was put straight into a tumbrel. Robespierre was already in one; Philippa saw his bandage trailing over its side. The crowd was trying to get in to reach him. It would tear him to bits.

It was the Irishman who prevented a massacre. He placed him-self in the middle of the gates and shouted, 'Patience, now, patience, citizens. They'll be on their way soon.' An enormous voice, trained to carry, caught the attention of the people trying to get through the gates and silence spread. 'You can accompany them to Madame La Guillotine,' the Irishman said. 'Her most justified feast and, by Jesus Christ Our Lord, let us hope, her last.'

There was a collective sigh, a sound like a huge beast satisfied. 'And now, if you'll excuse me . . .' The Irishman looked round to see that Ffoulkes and Philippa were behind him and used his body like a battering ram to make a path for them out onto the quay.

He led them quickly to a corner of the Pont Neuf overlooking the Left Bank where there was a tiny park off what had once been the Place Dauphine and sat them down on a bench under a chestnut tree. It was a quiet place; the noise from the Quai de l'Horloge came to it reduced to a beat, like far-off machinery.

'May I know your name, sir?' Ffoulkes asked.

'At the moment I'm Citizen *Deus Ex Machina* as far as you're con-cerned. Sir Mick, for short.'

'We appear to have much to thank you for. And now, perhaps you'd tell us what's happened,' Ffoulkes said. He was still angry. She realized he'd been angry all the time, suppressing it only to be brave for her; angry at his humiliation and powerlessness, angry at the ba-nal, bungling, viciousness of it all. She wondered where he found the energy.

At the river's edge an angler was hunched over his line, incurious about all but fish. A woman had set up an easel on the grass and was painting the view, watched by some children. Philippa rested her eyes on them.

'. . . and then, as far as I can gather, he made a mistake,' the Irish-man was saying. 'He went to the Convention and accused unnamed deputies of . . . I don't know what it was—lack of virtue, maybe. Said he'd unmask them on the morrow. Not a bad man, Robe-spierre, a good one actually, so good he was sure he only had to sweep France of its sinners and how happy a little Republic it would be. That's what a monster is, d'ye see, a man who knows he's infallible. Thought he was a political Messiah, so he did. But what he didn't understand and what Jesus, God love um, knew is that we're all sinners. So when he accused unnamed deputies of sin, each man-jack of them thought: "Is it me? Will it be my skeleton he pulls from the cupboard?" And they had to do something about it.'

'Is it over?' Philippa asked, 'Is the Terror over?'

The Irishman leaned forward to look past Ffoulkes at her. 'Ah well . . .'

'What happened then?' Ffoulkes snapped.

'Barras happened.' The Irishman leaned back. 'Citizen Deputy Barras, a man with whom I've had dealings in the past.'

'Vicomte de Barras,' Ffoulkes said. 'We've met before.'

'So I gather, but since he's your passport home, I don't think we'll drag up his title at the moment.'

They're both angry, Philippa thought. *How can everybody stay so angry?*

'Anyway, he's renounced it,' the Irishman said, more gently. 'And he was the one with the bowels to organize against Robespierre, so he was. Took command of the troops, ordered the arrest of our Maximilien and his cohorts. He expected to have to fight, thought there'd be alarums and excursions, calls to arms. There weren't any. Not so much as a whistle against him.'

One of the children with the woman who was painting wandered towards them, a little girl, her head to one side. 'Hello,' she said.

'Hello.' Philippa smiled at her and held out her hand. The child looked at it and ambled back to her mother.

Perhaps I'll have a little girl, Philippa thought. *Or a little boy. One or the other would be nice.*

'. . . not a soul raised a finger. The tocsins rang and went unanswered. *À moi, à moi.* He could call till the cows came home and none but the cows would hear him. Either he shot himself or somebody else shot him, but his jaw's shattered whatever way.'

Sir Mick put a dramatic palm up against his ear; the noise like a machine had changed, become deeper and was accompanied by the tattoo of drums. It seemed to be moving. 'God love him, he'll not be kept in suffering much longer, nor the others. He's on his way. Barras is getting rid of them quick. We should hear the cheer when the blade drops.'

He leaned forward again to look at Philippa. 'And in answer to your question, Miss Dapifer, whether it's the end of the Terror, I don't know. Barras doesn't know. I'm not even sure he and the Convention intended to end it when they set out to arrest Robespierre; they were just hitting back first to save themselves, if you know what I mean. It's what's happened since has amazed them. D'you see, the *people* believe it's the end of the Terror. They want it to be, they're sick of it to their souls. They're greeting Barras and Co like saints from Paradise sprinklin' holy water. And I'm thinking that's an expectation not to be disappointed—or face the consequences.'

He stood up. 'But nobody knows.' He stretched his fingers and waggled his hand. 'I'd not like to bet on the next few days . . . Ah.'

The silence was so sudden it was as if the city had drawn in its breath and was holding it. They could hear birds twittering from the branches overhead. From across the river came a gull's scream, or perhaps it was a man's, then a howl from human throats blasting the sky apart.

The children looked up at the noise and ran towards their mother. She stopped painting and talked to them.

She doesn't know, thought Philippa. *What is she telling them? Just another head, my dears, they always fall about this time of day. She doesn't know it's the head of heads and the last of heads.*

The Irishman was crossing himself. Ffoulkes was saying something.

But I don't feel anything. I should feel hope but I don't; they killed it when they killed Mr Glossop and Lavoisier and de Vaubon and the couple from Saint Omer and Lulu . . . when they killed hope for all of us. It will

never be any different, some other man will come along and want to rule
other men and be prepared to kill to do it. I'm numb.

'. . . which is why I want the two of yous out of Paris and quick,'
the Irishman was saying. 'Barras is keeping his options open, like the
sensible man he is, and you, me dear Baron, are one of those options. If things go wrong, he'll feel the necessity to travel—and fast.
To England maybe. I've persuaded him it won't do any harm to have
a grateful soul like yourself speak for him to Prime Minister Pitt,
saying he was the boyo tried to stop the Terror.'

'I suppose I owe the bastard that much,' Ffoulkes said.

'All things considered, I think you do.' The man became brisk,
feeling in his pockets. 'Now then, here's a purse and some shiny new
papers for yourself and the lady. They should get you through to
Gruchy; you'll be running alongside the news so I don't imagine
you'll encounter too much efficiency at the barriers—the guards'll
be staggering nine ways from Sunday. You've a safe house for
tonight? I thought so.'

He picked up Philippa's hand and carried it to his lips. 'You're to
wait for me at Gruchy. I've some business but it'll be settled in a day
and I'll follow you up. Take care now; I promised the missus I'd
bring ye both home and that's not a woman to break a promise to.'

Philippa held onto his hand. 'Mr Machina,' she said. 'Is there any
word about the Marquis de Condorcet?'

He smiled down at her; he had a good smile. 'Did ye not find
him? No, I've heard nothing. Ach, but with the Terror over—*if* it's
over—he'll be grand.'

They watched him walk away. Before he disappeared, he turned
and waved his hat at them, like an actor taking applause.

'Who is he?' Philippa asked. 'Did he drop from the clouds?'

'I don't know. An Irishman, that's who he is,' Ffoulkes said. 'Told
me he has dealings with the French government. I don't like the Irish
getting secretly together with the Frogs, it always means trouble
for us.'

'Why don't we give them back their damn country then?' she asked, wearily.

'They wouldn't know what to do with it.'

So it goes, she thought. *On and on.* 'We owe him our lives,' she said.

'I suppose so.'

They sat where they were, trying to get the will to move. The angler caught a fish, a little flapping shard of silver, and put it in his creel.

It's going to take him years to get over this, she thought. *I could help him. Please God, don't let Félicie encourage him to hate. Shall I tell him about the baby? I can't. I can't split him in two. He'd never let me go; whether he left Félicie or he didn't, we'd be a sordid couple and he's too honorable a man for that. I'd love him less; he'd love me less.*

She considered the irony; she hadn't been able to tell him because they were going to die; now she couldn't tell him because they were going to live.

I'll have to manage without him. Outcast from society—Reverend Deedes and his friends will see to that. I'll have to go away. Where did the Duchess of Devonshire go to have her illegitimate baby? Oh, yes, France. Well, that's out.

Ma will see me through, she thought. *Bless her, she sent the Irishman to bring us back; she'll be waiting. One thing about Ma, she's never cared for society's rules. Or causes.* Causes kill people. *She's right. It's individuals that matter, seeing the person not the principle. Like Ma does. Like Mme Vernet.*

She felt a minute pulse begin in her veins; she'd thought it had stopped.

There is *hope,* she thought. *'. . . independently of any power that would like to stop it, so long as our globe exists, the tempo may differ but we shall never go back.'*

He's out there somewhere, she thought, *bumbling along, certain of humanity's ultimate good.*

Ffoulkes got up from the bench and walked down to the river's edge, watching the angler.

It'll be worse for him than it is for me; I'll have Ma and the baby. God, I love him so much.

She went to join him.

He stooped and threw a pebble into the water. 'I suppose we've got to go back?'

'There's nowhere else to go. Not for us.'

'No,' he said, 'No coral island for Lord Ffoulkes and Mrs Fox.'

'Shorn lambs,' she said. 'They might have taken you and not me. Now we're both alive and the sun's shining and it's a day of amazements. You followed me into hell and you've carried me out, they can't take that away from us.'

'I did, didn't I? I'm a marvellous fellow. You know what was one of the worst things?'

'What?'

'Letting Blanchard get away with it. Spoiled my sleep, that did.'

She should have known. 'Now you're not to challenge him to a duel. It'd be silly to die the moment you're home. What would happen to the turnips?'

'I'm not going to challenge him to a duel, he's a better swordsman than I am. No . . .' He looked lovingly around at the view. 'That shit-sack owes me money, lots of money. I'm going to bankrupt him and then I'm going to kick his lungs out. No, I'll kick his lungs out first and *then* I'll bankrupt him.' He might have been picking a particularly splendid meal from a menu. 'I'm not vindictive, I may let him out of debtor's clink on his sixty-fifth birthday.'

'I am,' she said. 'Make it his seventieth.'

'Very well.' He tucked her hand under his arm and patted it. 'We'd better go, my love.'

They ambled off together towards the bridge.

'Another good thing,' he said. 'At least those lady natives on our island won't be given the opportunity to vote me off it.'

'Oh, I don't know,' she said. 'They might. One day.'

Chapter Seventeen

S HE did a lot of fishing, not catching many fish, just dangling rod and line over the edge of her rowing boat and allowing the tide to drift her to the mouth of the cove and back again.

She'd wondered if Jacques would miss the theater but he'd begun to work again on the steam engine that would raise water from the well of the Pomeroy Arms without Dell or Tobias having to wind it up. As long as he could mess about with machines, he didn't mind anything much.

When they'd first arrived, the two of them had carried agitation with them; they had been betrayed, they would be pursued, government agents were on their way to arrest Jacques and send him back to France.

Babbs Cove had remained calm. 'What you gettin' in a tizzy for?' Jan Gurney had asked. 'Think any bugger's going to get at un here?' The village had spent generations thwarting government agents in the form of excisemen and no unwelcome visitor could come at it by the clifftop path or the long, long lane from the road or by sea—its three approaches—without warning being given and preparations made.

Nor had any such visitor appeared, which meant that Luchet had kept his mouth shut about the place that had been his port of entry into England.

Jacques himself favored Mme de La Pole as the one who had given him away. That former lady-in-waiting to Marie Antoinette had been particularly imperious in ordering him about and spoken slightingly of his stage effects, thus qualifying herself, as far as he was concerned, as a Messalina.

Makepeace let him believe it. The boy had been shaken by being betrayed at all; it was healthier for him to attribute it to someone with a political motive and unpleasant disposition than to learn so early that villainy could assume a friendly form.

She still didn't understand why Blanchard had done it but was convinced that he had. Murrough had never trusted him, nor had Ninon. And he had hampered Philippa in every way he could. *Spite*, she thought, and had lain awake at nights wondering if, over the years, Andrew had ever mentioned the name of Babbs Cove to his friend. As peaceful day had followed peaceful day and no magistrate's men came for Jacques, she'd been able to assume that he had not.

It had seemed the obvious place to lie up. She and the boy would not only be protected while she decided what to do but, should that necessitate going abroad, they were in a position to sail away immediately.

So far she had made no decision of any kind—other than to let Dell cut her hair. It had grown overlong and troublesome now that she had to dress it herself, so off with it. Dell, for whom Tobias bought the *The Gallery of Fashion* on his weekly trips into Plymouth to fetch supplies and the newspapers, said that short hair was 'in.' Even the gray among the red in the heap of curls on the floor when the operation was finished hadn't bothered Makepeace as it would have done once. She was old, she told herself dully, she was lucky to have hair at all.

The accumulated alarums and excursions and losses of the past weeks had been so severe that now, in the sudden peace, she was afflicted by a sort of acceptant numbness. She felt like a sponge; no thought, just absorbent as if, in the nature of sponges, it was her function to soak up what God sent her without protest.

Apart from sending letters to Aaron, Jenny and Sally back with Sanders—who returned to Reach House so as to be at Aaron's disposal—telling them her whereabouts and situation, she did nothing, initiated nothing, felt very little except lassitude.

At nights she sat in the taproom playing cribbage with Jacques or Jan or Tobias before climbing the Pomeroy's cupboard stairs to bed. She slept late, dressed in the first thing that came to hand, put on the large straw hat that protected her from freckles and the sun and wandered down to the beach for another aimless day, chatting to the children piling seaweed on their sledges to spread on Gurney's fields up the hill, sometimes helping the women collect their lobster pots, but mostly spending it alone in her boat.

Until the afternoon when Tobias rowed out to join her. She saw him pulling across the bay and knew that God hadn't finished with her yet.

As he came alongside, she said, 'It's bad, isn't it?'

Silent, he picked up a newspaper from the thwarts and handed it to her. It was the *London Gazette*, displaying as much excitement as that sober journal could over the news that, in Paris, Danton had gone to the guillotine. Among those who'd gone with them was listed the name of de Vaubon.

'Have you told him?' she asked at last.

'No.'

No, it was her job; her job to fight blackness and pain on her own account in order to inflict them on an eleven-year-old boy. 'I don't know how,' she said.

Jacques was in the inn yard, hammering a piece of metal.

They sat together on the mounting block while she held his hand and told him. 'He was the bravest man I ever knew,' she said. It was true but at that moment it didn't help an exiled motherless boy who would never see his father again.

What did help, a little, was that Babbs Cove went into mourning with them. Its men and women had known Guillame de Vaubon longer than had Makepeace and much longer than had his son; he'd been their smuggling ally on the other side of the Channel. They'd sailed alongside him, outwitted the excise with him, hidden him when he was wounded, nursed him back to strength, danced at his wedding to Diana, toasted the birth of his son.

What's more, they wanted to talk about him. Left alone, Jacques might have endured by shrinking into himself. Instead, every evening, his father came alive again in the Pomeroy Arms as his loving fellow-smugglers resurrected the man with tales of his daring, his seamanship, trickery, how he'd foiled this bloody 'ciseman or that, the fortune he'd earned—and spent among them. Her eyes blurred with tears, occasionally laughing, Makepeace saw her old friend before her again, one foot on a chair, making one of his vainglorious speeches. Jacques cried and laughed with her.

The following days they spent together in her boat, fishing, so that the boy could have some quiet. 'He died for liberty, didn't he?' he'd ask.

'He did,' she'd say. The truth comforted the boy; it didn't comfort her.

At the end of the week, he decided that he ought to get back to his machines. Which was a good sign, she felt, though it left her lonelier than ever.

She quarrelled with Jan when he decided to make another voyage to Gruchy. 'You shan't go,' she shouted at him. France had taken nearly everyone she loved without giving them back, and crossing the Channel in good weather through a Royal Navy's blockade carried a high risk of being caught by one side or the other.

She might as well have argued with the tide; he went anyway and she knew it was as much an attempt to get news of Philippa and Andrew as for the silk and brandy he'd bring back. 'Young Pippy' was a favorite in the village and Jan was still shocked at the perfidy of 'they Thurlestone buggers' in taking her over to France when he had refused for her safety's sake.

For once, her fear was groundless. He and his men were back in three days, their boat laden with contraband. The only news he had of Philippa was stale—she'd arrived at Gruchy, been supplied with an identity and taken the diligence to Paris—all of which they knew already.

The people at Gruchy said that, on arrival, Andrew had also taken the diligence to Paris and had also not returned.

'Don't ee worry, missus,' Jan had said, 'they'll turn up. The Froggies is getting fair sick of that Terror over there. Old Fallon do say as he has to feel his head of a morning for fear they've chopped it off in the night. 'Twill stop soon, I've no doubt, the war'll be over and young Pippy'll come sailin' home large as life and twice as natural.'

'Bless you for going, Jan,' she'd said. 'But Pippy isn't coming back.' She'd absorbed that fact now. She didn't feel anything. Sponges didn't.

It was two days later that Tobias came back from Plymouth with a newspaper folded to an item on its inside page. He handed it to her and she shrank from it. 'No, I can't bear it.'

'You can bear thith,' he said. 'Good or bad, I ain't sure.'

It was a scandal sheet called *About Town* and the article was headed: '*Guilty Flight!*'

Underneath, it ran:

'The Mayfair magistrate has been called to the home of Lord Ffoulkes, a friend of Mr William Pitt and a luminary of London society, to investigate a matter of missing jewels believed to be valued in the region of £3,000. His Lordship has been travelling abroad for some weeks. His return may be rendered dismal by the discovery that not only his jewels but his wife has disappeared. It is this organ's sad responsibility to inform him, on good authority, that Lady Ffoulkes was last seen boarding a vessel bound for Canada in the company of Sir Boy Blanchard, formerly a close acquaintance of her husband. Lady Blanchard is reported to be distraught.'

There was a lot more, but Makepeace's eyes were already stretched in their sockets. 'Blow me,' she said.

'What about that now,' Dell said in disgust. 'Ah, well, the poor lad's well rid of the faithless devils, even for three thousand shiners.'

'Yes,' said Makepeace slowly. 'Yes, he is.' But would Andrew see it like that? He'd loved Blanchard, he'd loved Félicie; the betrayal was profound.

'And Canada now,' Dell said. 'Isn't it all snow and grizzly bears?'

'I hope so,' Makepeace said. 'I certainly do hope so.'

She needed to think about it, so she took to her boat and, because it was a hot day, rowed round to the cave below T'Gallants, the sea portal to the house, hidden from revenue-greedy eyes by a massive tapestry of gorse and brambles hung over its entrance.

The bales of silk and lace her smugglers had just brought back had been hauled up the shaft that led from the cave and stored in one of T'Gallants's many secret cupboards to keep them dry. A comforting number of brandy casks were still piled on the shelf out of the way of the tide.

She tied up the rowing boat and sat on the shelf, absentmindedly nudging hermit crabs into a scuttle and annoying sea urchins by gently poking a finger into the waving fronds of their antennae. It was cool in the cave and its quiet was emphasized by the slight slap of water against the rock edge.

She had no difficulty in imagining Blanchard a betrayer—who knew it better than she did?—but that he'd abandoned everything in order to indulge an adulterous passion confounded her. He was, had been, the man about town *par excellence*. Grand society was, had been, the milieu he swam in. In his case, to throw that away was like a dancer amputating his legs.

And all for the sake of Félicie? Makepeace had no opinion of that young woman's intelligence; she was persuadable. Granted, she was also lovely but it had always seemed to Makepeace that Blanchard's appearances with her on his arm had displayed something like calculation, a-look-at-the-prize-I-could-capture-if-I-pleased rather than the swoon of a man besotted.

Perhaps, by running away with her, Blanchard was depriving Andrew of yet another thing of value—yet at *such* cost to himself. Makepeace didn't know what prices were like in Canada but even jewels worth three thousand pounds wouldn't last that couple forever—not in the style they were used to.

And if I know this, Blanchard knows it. No, there's something else. Our Sir Boy has burnt his boats somewhere along the line and escaping to Canada with Félicie and her jewels is his only option.

Was he overspent, she wondered. Was Canada preferable to a debtor's prison?

Or . . . a tiny worm of hope broke through the dead, protective wall with which Makepeace had surrounded herself . . . had Blanchard reason to believe that Andrew was on his way home? Andrew coming back, indeed, to be told by every servant in his house that Blanchard had been swiving his wife?

Makepeace sat up straight. *It might be that, oh God, it might be that.* Blanchard was part of The League. The League, because of its contacts, received news from France days before it appeared in the press.

It could be, it could be. And if Andrew returned, he might have Philippa with him.

In that moment, the reflection of light on water wobbling over the perimeter of the cave's rocky shelf was more beautiful than she'd ever seen it. She shut her eyes to it; don't think, don't hope. Remain a sponge—it doesn't hurt so much.

And yet, she thought, *I'll have to do something sooner or later. We can't stay here forever, the boy needs more scientific education, university, a life.*

Also, she had to do something for her shamefully neglected third daughter. Sally's letters showed she was happy and settled in Northumberland but arrangements would have to be made. . . .

If Andrew Ffoulkes *were* to come home, she thought, he could persuade his friend Prime Minster Pitt to absolve Jacques of the crime of being his father's son. But—and here numbness enfolded her again—Andrew wasn't coming back any more than Philippa was. It had been foolish to think so.

Where to go then?

Desultorily, Makepeace's mind explored the globe. Europe was no good, France having invaded most of it. Or was Germany still free? Yes, she rather thought it was. She seemed to remember Andra telling her Germany was bulging with fine scientists. She could take Jacques there.

On the other hand, since she had to go with the boy, she didn't fancy spending what remained of her life in a country where she couldn't speak the language. And would Sally like it?

America then. Home. Well, it used to be home until the patriots chased her out. *Bloody revolutionaries get everywhere*, she thought mildly. Perhaps it had improved now it was the United States. Ben Franklin country. Andra had liked Ben Franklin, one of the great en- quiring minds, he'd said. Dead now, like Andra, but perhaps his sci- entific torch had been passed on. . . .

America. She supposed there was a neat inevitability that she should end her days in the country in which they'd begun, the comple- tion of a long and eventful circumambulation which had left her no wiser as to why men chose to kill each other than when she'd set out.

Not yet, though. For a while they'd stay here, in Babbs Cove, where her mind could vacillate, like the light of this cavern, in a limbo of tranquillity.

From which she heard a shot sounding across the bay. The look- out always on guard had fired warning of a visitor.

In one second she was on her feet, the next she was in the boat and rowing like a mad thing. It would be a vessel from France. She'd conjured it up. Andrew . . . Philippa . . .

The great matted curtain over the entrance of the cave ham- pered her exit and she had to scrabble at it before the prow was free and she could get the boat through.

The bay was empty. The visitor, whoever it was, had not come by sea.

Wearily, she thought of bailiffs arrived to arrest Jacques. Well, the lane was always blocked, there would be time for Tobias to drag the boy from his steam engine and hide him until the stranger went away or was certified as friend, not foe—a circumstance of which the village would be notified by yet another round from the sentry's firelock.

She heard it. All's well.

There was a conveyance outside the Pomeroy Arms, though at this distance and from this angle she could not see exactly what it was, except that it gave the impression of being small and shabby. Neither could she see what or whom it had brought to the inn's door. Obviously, whoever it was had satisfactorily proved their credentials.

By the time she'd rowed ashore, the conveyance was gone.

Dell was standing in the forecourt, looking for her, a letter in one hand and an empty beer mug in the other.

'It was an Irishman come in a gig but ye've missed him.'

Her heart raced. 'A big man?'

'No, no, little runt of a fella, and I was to give you this.'

Having resurrected Makepeace's life and then buried it again, she handed over a letter: 'He wouldn't stay but I was to say that the delivery came from a certain Mick Murrough as promised. That's what he called 'em, "delivery as per promised." Funny little fellow he was, a Kerry tinker from his pots and pans and accent but thanked me for the ale polite enough. Anyway, I took them in for didn't they . . .'

But Makepeace had split the seal and was reading. The writing was copperplate and the message not long enough.

> *'I set the tinkers to finding them, for an Irish tinker goes around every back door to mend the pots and listen to the clack, also he can steal the sugar out of a punchbowl. So here they are. I keep my promises, missus.'*

Finding what? Who? What promises?

'. . . and both of them thin as death on wires, poor things . . .' Dell was still rattling on.

Makepeace pushed past her into the inn.

The slave and her child stood in the middle of the taproom floor, his arms wrapped round her legs, her arms circling his head and her huge, terrified eyes glancing left and right for enemies.

Makepeace sank to her knees, sobbing in gratitude.

THEY had to get Dick Tucker, the blacksmith, down from the farm to take the collars off. The woman's was fairly easy, a thick iron thing with a hasp that only needed one hammer blow, though she kept shying when they tried to make her keep still for it. When at last she bent across the sawing horse they used for an anvil, her thin bodice gaped and showed burns on the top of her breasts.

The boy's was more difficult because it was fine silver and fitted his little neck more closely. While it was being filed, he clung to his mother and when Dell wanted to take her away to dress her burns his breathing became panicky and Dell had to let her go.

Jacques tried talking to them in French but their faces remained dull from incomprehension. The only person they didn't shrink from was Tobias. 'Reckon they know my neck had a collar one time, too,' he said.

'Have they said anything? Can you understand them?' Makepeace asked.

He shook his head. 'They ain't from my part of Africa. From the collarth, I'd reckon they were thold apart—look at hith jacket, velvet. I don't like to think where they put her.' He took Makepeace's hand. 'They the oneth from Brithtol, do you think?'

She smiled back at him. 'Perhaps.' She hadn't seen the running woman's face and a terrified child had the ubiquity of all terrified children. Whoever they were, they belonged together and had been reunited, one tiny atonement for the great wrongdoing.

'Thomebody'll be looking for them,' Tobias said.

'They won't bloody get them,' Makepeace said. Sir Mick and his tinkers had plucked these particular brands from the burning and, by Christ, she'd kill to stop them being thrown back into it.

She was alive now, energy practically sparking from her finger ends. There were days when God permitted miracles and this was one of them. She had plans to make; she couldn't think why she'd been so lazy.

'We'll stay on for a bit,' she said. 'The four of us'll move up to T'Gallants, give the place an airing. I'm expecting somebody.'

By this time half the village had come to see the newcomers and was watching them drink the soup that Dell said would hold them until supper. Jan Gurney's wife shook her head over them. 'Poor liddle buggers, thin as a rasher of wind both of 'em.'

'We'll feed 'em up,' Makepeace said. 'Rachel, tell Jan and the lads I'm expecting somebody. He may come by boat. But I suppose I'd better warn the farm as well, in case he arrives by road.'

Rachel was interrogative. 'Ooh-ar?'

'Irishman,' Makepeace said.

'Not more bloody Irish,' Rachel said. 'Us've got enough with Dell.'

''Fraid so. He said he'd meet me here—and he's one as keeps his promises.'

'Wait for me now, Mrs Hedley, because if I go, I'm coming back.'

And though the days slipped by, sweet assurance stayed with her. She reopened T'Gallants House and moved into it with her new family.

Tobias came up to help her, so did Rachel Gurney who was intrigued by this couple without a past. 'What be us going to call 'em?' she wanted to know. 'Eve and Abel, I reckon.'

'We ain't calling them anything,' Makepeace said. 'We're going to wait until they can tell *us* who they are.' For her, their name was Deliverance and always would be.

Their trust was slow in coming but Tobias said it would eventually. 'Little 'un'll learn before she does,' he said.

He was right, he usually was. Jacques managed to persuade the boy to go with him and see his experiments at the inn by making steam engine noises and pointing. The woman watched from the window with Makepeace's restraining hand on her shoulder as the two boys crossed the bridge that lay between T'Gallants and the village. Her fists were clenched.

'He'll be back,' Makepeace told her. 'I promise he's coming back.'

The woman stayed at the window until she saw the boys return-ing, then the tension went out of her. She turned, walked to the kitchen and came back with a broom and began sweeping the hall in the first brisk movements Makepeace had seen her make. She looked up and nodded. Makepeace nodded back.

They were good days. Makepeace saw them draw in from the seat under the great window in the hall, watching the shadow of her house fall over half the village as the sun slid down behind it, look-ing and waiting for a sail as she had looked and waited for so many.

He's late making his entrance, she thought. *Damn actor.*

But she never doubted that he *would* make it; she'd doubted him too much in the past.

I should never have let him go. When he's back, I won't, ever, and the Reverend Deedes can stuff that in his offertory box.

And Jenny? Jenny can marry Stephen Heilbron and be respectable enough for both of us.

Of course, she was asleep—still on the window seat—when the call came and the woman, who could hear a leaf fall, came padding down from upstairs to shake her gently awake.

Makepeace sat up; it was dark and for a moment she didn't know where she was. The woman pointed to the window and said some-thing.

The moon had come up, huge and yellow. Jan Gurney and a cou-ple of his sons were standing on the slipway to the beach.

She opened the window. 'What is it, Jan?'

'Vessel out yonder,' he yelled back. 'Becalmed, we reckon. There's a breeze out to sea but it do incline to fall when ee gets near land . . .'

She didn't want a dissertation on maritime weather. 'What boat is it?'

'Us be wonderin' whether to go out to her or p'raps her'll come in under sweeps or maybe, seein' as she might have passengers, she'll . . .'

It was too far and too dark to see the lineaments of his face but she knew he was grinning. 'You sod,' she shouted. 'What *is* she?'

'Gruchy sloop.'

She was off the seat and running, then running back to put on her slippers because of the shells on the beach, then running to the main door, out of it, running across the bridge.

By the time she got to them she saw that there were other figures, with guns, disappearing into the rocks that edged the beach. It never paid to be trustful in the smuggling business; the sloop from Gruchy might have been boarded by the Revenue on her way across the Channel.

But she knew.

'They're rowing in, Dad,' young Peter Gurney said.

They made her retreat with them up the slipway to the shadow of the wall. 'Just in case, my beauty.'

But she knew. She knew from the grunts that came across the water in time to the creak of rowlocks and the shape of the back against the moonlight as he heaved at the oars.

'He's put on weight again,' she told them.

He had breath enough to sing, though.

> 'Oh missus, oh missus, I'm pantin' to see,
> what apology you're going to make unto me.'

'He's an actor,' she told them.

'Home, lads,' Jan called and men came scrambling down from the rocks, passing her without a word, until she was left alone on the beach.

She walked down to the water's edge and watched him heave the dinghy up on to the sand. 'You took your time,' she said.

'Ah, well, I had revolutions to see to.'

She went up to him and took handfuls of his jacket and buried her nose in his chest. 'I love you,' she said.

'I know. Did ye get the delivery?'

'As per promised,' she said and began to cry.

'Didn't I tell you I was the fella to keep the promises? And haven't I brought back a certain Miss Dapifer and a Lord Ffoulkes with me in that sloop out there? They'll be coming ashore soon.'

He led her up the beach and sat her down on a lobster pot, patting her back. After a while he found another lobster pot but it collapsed beneath his weight, so he found another. He gave it up and sat down on the sand next to her. She put out her hand and he held it.

She watched the moon become bigger and more orange, as if it were taking the heat of the day with it on its descent to the horizon, leaving the air refreshed.

At last she said, 'Are they all right?'

'Fine, fine,' he assured her. 'Except they've fallen in love, poor souls. And so English and so honorable that he's to go back to his wife in the morning and she's returning to a life of abstinence. Robespierre could be proud of them if the bastard wasn't dead.' He sighed. 'They're out there this minute, saying good-bye to each other.'

'Ah.' She sat upright.

'Ah,' she said again. 'Now *there* I believe I can tell them something to their advantage.'

Author's Note

THE Marquis of Condorcet died—apparently by poisoning himself—within four days of leaving Mme Vernet's house, although his wife didn't learn of the death until after the Terror was over in late July. He'd managed to reach the home of two old friends, the Suards, at Fontenay, but they wouldn't let him in—an indication of what the Terror did to relationships. Exhausted and hungry, Condorcet made for an inn. There's a story that he ordered an omelette and, when asked how many eggs he wanted in it, said 'Twelve,' the answer of an ignorant and extravagant aristocrat. I find it difficult to believe; there was severe rationing before he went into hiding and even under the care of Mme Vernet he could not have been unaware of it.

However it was, he aroused the suspicion of the innkeeper, who had him arrested. He was taken to the nearest lock-up and found dead the next morning.

In order to bring in other attitudes to the French Revolution, I've added the fictional characters of Philippa and Ffoulkes to the real, historical people who lived at Number 15 Rue Servandoni (Gravediggers)—a house that still stands. What I haven't made up is the fact that Mme Vernet sheltered Condorcet for nine months of the Terror and that during those months a room in her lodge was occupied by a Jacobin deputy, Marcoz, who didn't give either away.

Robespierre's address to the Convention on Thermidor 8 was the culmination of growing antagonism from several disparate quarters, which, with that last speech, coalesced against him and ordered his arrest. Even then, they couldn't have brought him down without the backing of a people sick of the Terror. The National Guard were reflecting public opinion when they broke into a committee room at the Hôtel de Ville to take him to justice. Whether he shot himself or was shot by somebody else, his jaw was shattered and he suffered horribly for the next fourteen hours until the executioner ripped away his bandage, the guillotine blade dropped and the Terror ended.

Readers Guide
DISCUSSION QUESTIONS

1) As *The Sparks Fly Upward* begins, the two-years-widowed Makepeace Hedley appears to be scandalized by the waltzes danced at Lord Andrew Ffoulkes's ball. Yet, it soon becomes clear that Makepeace's mourning clothes and puritanical protests are a temporary cloak. In what ways does Makepeace conform to her times, and how does she rebel against them?

2) Makepeace's daughter, Philippa Dapifer, wonders at Makepeace's tendency to draw adventures like "a woman who'd been born to trouble as the sparks fly upward." Why is Makepeace consistently entangled in the political upheavals of her day? What qualities does Philippa share with her mother? Why does Philippa believe that she and Makepeace "have to be useful"?

3) Philippa describes the publisher and anarchist John Beasley as "lumpish and grubby and stubborn and not a little pleased" with himself, deciding that most "great martyrs" probably shared the same profile. Is this assessment surprising? How do we usually imagine individuals—whether historical or contemporary figures—who are prepared to die for their beliefs? As various characters in the story stand up for their beliefs, sometimes facing death, do they fit or alter Philippa's initial view of martyrdom?

4) How does poverty influence the choices made by Vladimir the Scratcher and his wife? Of the Marquis de Condorcet's family, Sophie and Eliza, in hiding? Of the French aristocrats in England, including the Chevalier Saint Joly, who is stripped of the Order of Saint Louis by his fellow exiles?

5) As Philippa contemplates the forged passport she has procured for the Marquis de Condorcet, she remembers that "liberty is indi-

visible or it is not liberty," and decides to hand them to Nicolas herself. Why does Philippa resolve to personally smuggle the papers to France? What does she feel is at stake, for herself and for her friend? What does she feel she will gain from the journey?

6)   Why does Makepeace take on the management of the play during her brother Aaron's illness? What draws her to Michael Murrough? What repels her? Given the history of her marriages—to Philip Dapifer, a tar-and-feathered Britishman who rebuked American rebellion; and to Andra Hedley, a hard-nosed entrepreneur who rebuked British aristocracy—why does she find her latest choice of companion so surprising?

7)   When Philippa arrives in France, she notes that everyone, from a young couple in love to a street sweeper, seems to have *"grown used to it"*—the guillotine. Why does this realization sit so heavily with her? What does she mean when she says that the Place de la Greve, that the city of Paris, "would never be the same" again? Why does she say that the revolution has been made "stupid"?

8)   Discuss the play, *Oroonoko*. What does Makepeace expect from the play's debut? How does the performance alter Makepeace's view of Sir Mick and of the company's actors? Why does it seem that seeing *Oroonoko* offers Makepeace and others in the audience a more realistic and moving view of slavery and humanity than they have witnessed before? Why do Reverend Deedes and Stephen Heilbron try to shut *Oroonoko* down, when it is in support of their abolitionist cause? How do different characters choose one cause over another?

9)   Makepeace and Philippa believe that Boy Blanchard's maneuvering is spurred by jealousy—jealousy of the accomplishment, wealth, and status of his friends, and especially of Andrew Ffoulkes. Do you agree? Is Blanchard lying when he hatefully blurts that Philippa is "like to cause the death of my best friend"? Why is Blanchard's double-dealing and betrayal such a blow to Andrew? How